MIXED BLESSINGS

DANIELLE STEEL

MIXED BLESSINGS

Delacorte
Press

LARGE PRINT EDITION

Published by
Delacorte Press
Bantam Doubleday Dell Publishing Group, Inc.
666 Fifth Avenue
New York, New York 10103

Library of Congress Cataloging in Publication Data

Steel, Danielle.
Mixed blessings / Danielle Steel.
p.   cm.
ISBN 0-385-29910-9.
ISBN 0-385-30663-6 (large print).
ISBN 0-385-30664-4 (limited).
I. Title.
PS3569.T33828M59   1992   91-43224
813'.54—dc20   CIP

Manufactured in the United States of America
Published simultaneously in Canada

December 1992

10 9 8 7 6 5 4 3 2 1

BVG

**This Large Print Book carries the
Seal of Approval of N.A.V.H.**

To the miracles in my life:
Beatrix, Trevor, Todd, Nick,
Samantha, Victoria, Vanessa,
Maxx and Zara,
for all the joy and endless
blessings they bring me,

and to the greatest miracle
of all . . . my one and only
love, Popeye,

with all my heart and love,

d.s.

beloved miracle

Tiny miracle of hope,
  extraordinary blessing,
      smallest dream,
how great the love
  to start
        the pitter-pat
  of your clock,
how great the shock
  when you are gone,
      how rare the grief,
        the roar of pain,
and then,
      with luck,
  to be blessed again,
      to have, to hold,
  to give, to share,
      to dare
        the rocks,
          the waves
            again,
  to swim until
    you can no more,

to cry out in the dark
   with longing
      bigger than the sky,
whisper softly,
      bring it near,
   hope the gentler
         spirits hear,
   long wait,
         dark night,
            never dare to breathe,
until tiny fingers
            pluck your sleeve,
   and touch your heart
      with gold,
never too late,
   too dark
      to have a child
         to hold,
miracle of life,
   precious moment
         of them all,
aching whispers,
      anguished call,

until at long last here,
and then to hold you
    in my arms,
ever loved,
    instantly ours,
beloved wonder
oh so dear.

MIXED BLESSINGS

CHAPTER
══1══

The sky was a brilliant blue, and the day was hot and still as Diana Goode stepped out of the limousine with her father. The angles of her face were softer than usual beneath a haze of creamy ivory veil, and the heavy satin dress whooshed softly as the driver helped her out and settled it around her. She beamed at her father, standing outside the church, and then she closed her eyes, trying to remember absolutely every detail of the moment. She had never been this happy in her life. Everything was perfect.

"You look beautiful," her father said softly, with All Saints Episcopal Church in Pasadena rising behind her. Her mother had gone ahead in the other car with her sisters and their husbands and children. Diana was the middle child, classically striving to be better, smarter, more successful. She loved her sisters with a deep, solid affection, and yet she always felt she had to do something more than they did. Not that they had set such impossible standards. Her oldest sister, Gayle, had been set on going to medical school, until she met her husband in her first year of premed, married him that June, and instantly got pregnant. At twenty-nine, she had three adorable little girls of her own now. Gayle was two years older than Diana, and although they were close, there had always been a sense of rivalry between them, and the two women were astoundingly different. Gayle never looked back at a career in medicine once. She was happily married, and satisfied to stay home with her girls, and keep busy with them and her husband. She was the perfect doctor's wife, intelligent, informed, and completely understanding about his hours as an obstetrician. They were planning to have at least one more child, Gayle had confided to her a few weeks before. Jack was desperate for a boy now. Gayle's whole life revolved around her husband, and her children, and their home. For her, the world of careers held absolutely no appeal, unlike her two younger sisters.

In some ways, Diana had more in common with her younger sister, Sam. Samantha was ambitious, competitive, excited about being out in the world, and for the first couple of years she was married, she had desperately tried to juggle both home life and career. But when her second child was born thirteen months after the first, a mere two years after she'd gotten married, she admitted that she just couldn't do it. She quit her job at an art gallery in L.A. and decided to stay home, which was welcome news to her husband. Although for months after she'd quit, Sam felt disappointed not to be working. In the two years they'd been married, Seamus's work had begun to be recognized and admired, and he was slowly becoming one of L.A.'s most successful young contemporary artists.

Sam did free-lance design work from home, but even that was almost impossible to do, with no help and two very young children. She adored being home with Seamus and her babies, and they had a great marriage, and their son and daughter were two little fat cherubs. Everyone who saw them instantly loved them. But still, there were times when she envied Diana's place in the working world, among "grown-ups," as she put it.

But in Diana's eyes, her sisters' lives seemed

so settled. As far as she could see, at twenty-five and twenty-nine, her sisters seemed to have everything they wanted. Sam was happy and at ease in the world of modern art, Gayle was equally so as the wife of a doctor. But Diana had always wanted so much more than they had. She had gone to Stanford, and then did her junior year abroad, in Paris, at the Sorbonne. And she had returned to Paris for yet another year there after graduation. She had found a fabulous little apartment on the rue de Grenelle, on the Left Bank, and for a while she had decided that she really was going to stay there. But after a year and a half working for *Paris-Match,* she got homesick for the States, and her family . . . and most of all, much to her own surprise, for her sisters. Gayle had been having her third baby then, and Sam had been expecting her first, and somehow Diana just felt that she wanted to be with them.

But she felt torn when she got back, and tortured herself for the first few months about whether or not coming back had been the right thing. Maybe she hadn't tried hard enough to stay there.

Paris had been great, but L.A. was interesting, too, and she had landed a great job almost instantly when she returned, as a senior editor at *Today's Home.* The magazine was still new then and the opportunities were exciting. The salary was good, the people were nice, the working conditions were great, and they gave her a fabulous office. Within months she was running shoots, hiring photographers, rewriting some of the stories herself, and flying off to look at extraordinary homes in exotic locations. She even got back to Paris now and then, and London. She shot one issue in the south of France, another in Gstaad. And of course New York, Palm Beach, Houston, Dallas, San Francisco, and other American cities. It was the perfect job for her, and it made her the envy of her friends, and even her sisters. To anyone who didn't realize what hard work it was, it looked extremely glamorous, and so did Diana.

Shortly after she took the job, Diana met Andy at a media party. They talked six hours straight in a little Italian restaurant the night they met, and after that she hardly had time to catch her breath before he asked her to move into his apartment. She waited six months before she did, cautious about giving up her independence. But she was crazy about him, and he knew it. He was wild about her, too, and everything about them was a perfect mesh. They seemed to be ideally suited to each other. He was tall and handsome and blond, had been a tennis star at Yale, was from an old, respected family in New York, and had come to UCLA to go to law school. And as soon as he graduated, he had gone to work in the legal department of a major network. He loved his work, and Diana was fascinated by what he did, and the people he knew there. He was the legal counsel for several important shows and the network was extremely pleased with the way he handled their more complicated contracts.

Diana loved going to business parties with him, meeting some of the stars and talking to other lawyers, big producers, and important agents. It was heady stuff, but Andy took it all in stride. He had a good head on his shoulders, a bright mind, and he was seldom impressed by the glamour of the world he worked in. He liked what he did, and eventually he planned to open his own practice, specializing in entertainment law. But he knew it was still too soon, and appreciated the valuable experience he was getting at the network. He knew exactly where he was going and what he wanted out of life. He had carefully mapped out his career long before, and when Diana walked into his life, he knew within a matter of days that this was the woman he wanted as his wife, and the mother of his children. And they had laughed when they discovered that they both wanted four children. He had been one of four boys, which included a set of identical twins, and Diana wondered if they would have a set of their own. They talked a lot about having kids, and Diana realized that once in a while their sexual carelessness was born of their desire to tempt the fates and get pregnant. Neither of them would have been distraught if Diana had gotten pregnant and forced them into an early marriage. Within months of the day they met, they both talked openly about wedding plans and their long-term intentions.

They lived together in a small but handsome apartment in Beverly Hills. They shared much the same taste, and they had even bought two paintings from Seamus. With their combined incomes, they could afford something really nice. They decorated in stark modern style, and spent all their extra money on art. One day they wanted to start an important collection, but they couldn't afford it now, so they bought what they could and enjoyed it immensely.

But what really pleased Diana about Andy was how well he got on with her parents, and with her sisters and their husbands. As different as Jack and Seamus were, Andy seemed to like both of them, and frequently had lunch with them when he didn't have a business lunch scheduled at the network. And he seemed to be just as much at ease in Seamus's world of art as he was in Jack's world, either discussing medical research or financial investments. Andrew Douglas was an easy, likable guy, and everything about their life together thrilled Diana. They went to Europe together after the first year, and she showed him all her favorite haunts in Paris, and afterward they drove through the valley of the Loire. And then they went to Scotland to visit Nick, Andy's younger brother, who was spending a year there. It was the perfect life, and after they got home, they started making leisurely plans to get married the following summer. They got engaged eighteen months after they met, and set the wedding date eight months later, in June, and decided to go back to Europe for their honeymoon, to the south of France this time, Italy, and Spain. Diana had managed to get three weeks off from the magazine, and Andy had wangled the same amount of time from the network.

They looked for a house in Brentwood, Westwood, and Santa Monica, and even thought about commuting from Malibu when they saw something they really loved there. But in March they found the perfect house, in Pacific Palisades. It had been well loved and well tended by a large family for years, and now the children had grown and gone and the couple who owned it were reluctantly selling. Andy and Diana fell in love with it at first sight. It was big and rambling and warm, there was wood panelling, and there were wonderful trees just outside and a huge garden for the children to play in. There was a lovely master suite on the second floor, and an office for each of them, as well as a handsome guest room. And on the floor above were four huge children's bedrooms.

The closing on the house was in May, and Andy had moved into it just three weeks before the wedding. The night of the rehearsal dinner, which Diana's parents gave at the Bistro in Beverly Hills, there were still boxes everywhere, and Diana had left her bags for their honeymoon in the front hall. She didn't want to spend the night before the wedding with him, and she was spending the night at her parents'. She spent it in her childhood bedroom, and lay for a long time after she woke up, looking at the faded pink-and-blue flowered wallpaper she knew so well. It was funny to think that in a few hours she would be someone else, someone's *wife* . . . what did that mean? Who would she be then? Would it be different than it had been living with him? Would he change? Would she? Suddenly it all seemed more than a little scary. She thought of her sisters then, the men they had married, the children they'd had, and how it had all changed them, subtly at first, and then over the years, they seemed to become sort of a unit with their children and husbands. She was still close to them, but in subtle ways it was just a little different. It was odd to think, too, that a year from now she might have her own child. The idea gave her a small thrill in the pit of her stomach. Making love to Andy was always so extraordinary, but it was even more exciting to think that one of these days it might bear fruit, and they would have a baby. She loved Andy so much, and loved thinking about having his children.

She was still smiling to herself when she got up on her wedding day, thinking about Andy and the life they would share. She went downstairs for a quiet cup of coffee before everyone got up, and her mother came down after that, and half an hour later her sisters and their children arrived to dress there, and help Diana get ready for the wedding. Their husbands had stayed home, both were going to be ushers in the wedding. Gayle's three girls and Sam's one little girl were going to be flower girls, and

Sam's little boy was going to be the ring bearer. He was just two, and he looked so cute in the little white silk suit Diana had picked out for him, she and her sisters had tears in their eyes when they saw him.

Diana's mother rounded the children up shortly after they arrived, and she'd hired a girl to help keep them in order while their mothers dressed. "Typical," Gayle had cracked with a grin and a raised eyebrow. Their mother usually thought of everything, planned for all contingencies, and was so organized as to make everyone groan when she started calling them in June to find out what their plans were for Thanksgiving. But her mother had been a godsend for Diana in putting together the wedding. She had been so busy herself at the magazine, she'd scarcely had time to go to her own fittings, but her mother had handled everything, and Diana knew that, as a result, everything would go smoothly. And so far, it had. Her sisters looked beautiful in their pale-peach silk gowns, and they were carrying the palest peach-color roses. And the little girls looked exquisite, too, in their white dresses with peach-colored sashes, carrying baskets of rose petals in their little gloved hands, as they left for church with their grandmother and mothers. Diana stayed and chatted with her father for the last few, nerve-wracking moments.

"You look just beautiful, sweetheart," he beamed at her. He had always been so proud of her, so decent and kind and supportive. She had no complaints about her parents, there had been no hidden agendas here, no unreasonable demands, no animosities, not even as she was growing up, from what she remembered. Gayle had had a harder time with them, and she and their mother had had their share of violent disagreements. But Gayle was their first, and "I was breaking them in," she always explained later. But Diana had always thought her parents were pretty reasonable, and Samantha agreed with her, most of the time, although at first the senior Goodes had been a little nervous about her marrying an artist. But eventually they had grown to admire and respect him. Seamus was a character unto himself, but it was difficult not to like him.

And they had no reservations at all about Andrew Douglas. He was a lovely man, and they knew Diana would be very happy with him.

"Scared?" her father asked gently, as she paced a little in their living room, waiting the last few moments before going out to the limousine that would take them to her wedding. They still had a little time, and suddenly Diana wished it were all over and done, and they were at the Bel Air that night, or on the plane to Paris the next morning.

"Sort of." She grinned, looking like a kid again. Her long, reddish-brown hair was swept up in a bun beneath her veil, and she looked remarkably sophisticated, and at the same time very young, as she looked at her father. She had always been able to turn to him, to tell him what she felt, to share her griefs and fears with him. But she had no serious fears now, only a few unanswered questions.

"I keep wondering if it'll be different now . . . being married, I mean . . . you know, instead of living together. . . ." She sighed, and smiled again. "It all seems so grown-up, doesn't it?" At twenty-seven she still felt so young, and yet at times so old. But it seemed a good time to be getting married, especially to a man she loved as much as she loved Andrew William Douglas.

"It is grown-up," her father said with a smile, as his lips gently brushed her forehead. He was a tall, distinguished-looking man with white hair and intense blue eyes. He knew her well, and liked the woman she'd become, and the man she was planning to marry. He knew they'd

do well. He had no fears in his heart for Andrew
and Diana. If life was kind to them, they would
go far, and he wished them well for their jour-
ney. "You're ready for it. You know what you're
doing, and he's a good man. You won't go
wrong, sweetheart. And we're always here for
you . . . and for Andy. I hope you both know
that."

"I do." Her eyes filled with tears as she
looked away. She suddenly felt so emotional to
be leaving him, and this house, even though she
no longer lived there. It was harder leaving
him, in some ways, than her mother, who was
busier and more matter-of-fact, and had been
engrossed in straightening Diana's veil and
keeping the children from stepping on her train
before they left for the church. But there were
no distractions now, only love and hope, and an
avalanche of feelings, as she stood in the living
room with her father.

"Come on, young lady," he finally said, his
voice gruff but loving. "We have a wedding to
go to." He grinned at her and offered her his
arm, and he and the driver helped her into the
car with her long train and full veil, and a moment later she was settled in the backseat, carrying her huge bouquet of white roses. The full-
ness of the gown was spread all over the car,

and she was suddenly startled as they drove away to see children waving and pointing at her. "Look! . . . Look! . . . A bride! . . ." It was funny to realize that *she* was the bride, and she felt giddy with excitement as they drove away. Suddenly she could feel her heart pounding, as she readjusted her veil and straightened the lace bodice and huge satin sleeves that had been adjusted endlessly in the fittings. The dress was very Victorian in style, and extremely formal.

They were having three hundred people to the Oakmont Country Club for a reception afterward. Everyone would be there—her old school chums, her parents' friends, distant relatives, people she knew from the magazine, Andy's friends, and a host of people he had invited from the network. His closest friend from work, William Bennington, was going to be in the wedding. And a few of the stars he had worked closely with on their contracts were coming. His parents and all three of his brothers had come too. Nick, who'd been in Scotland, was working in London now, and Greg and Alex, the twins, were at Harvard Business School, but they had all come. The twins were six years younger than Andy, who was thirty-two, and he had always been their hero. They were crazy about Diana, too, and she was looking forward to seeing more of them, to having them come out during vacations from school, or maybe even talking them into moving to California. But unlike Andy, the other Douglas boys preferred the East, and Greg and Alex thought they would probably wind up in New York or Boston, or maybe even in London, like Nick.

"We're not star-struck like our brother," Nick had teased him good-naturedly the night before at the rehearsal dinner. But it was obvious that they admired his success, and his choice of bride. The three boys were clearly very proud of their oldest brother.

Diana could hear the organ music in the church as they stood outside. She took her father's arm, and she felt a little tremor of excitement run through her. She looked up at him with eyes as blue and electric as his own, and as they started up the steps of the church she squeezed his hand.

"Here we go, Daddy," she whispered.

"Everything's going to be just fine," he reassured her, just as he had the night of her first play . . . and the time she'd fallen off her bike and broken her arm when she was nine, and he drove her to the hospital, telling her funny stories and making her laugh, and then holding her tight against him when they set it. "You're a wonderful girl, and you're going to be a great wife," he said to her as they stopped just outside the main door, waiting for a signal from one of the ushers.

"I love you, Daddy," she whispered nervously.

"I love you, too, Diana." He bent and kissed a froth of veil, as the pungent smell of the roses seemed to surround them. It was a moment they both knew they would remember for a lifetime. "God bless you," he whispered as the signal came, and her sisters began walking slowly down the aisle, followed by three of Diana's oldest friends, in the same peach gowns and huge organza hats, and then a cavalcade of adorable children. There was a longish pause as the music became more imperious, and then slowly, slowly, regally and gracefully she came, a young queen going to meet her consort, in the white satin dress with the narrow waist and the beautiful ivory lace inserts. The veil seemed to surround her like a soft haze, and beneath it the well-wishers could see the shining dark hair, the creamy skin, the brilliant blue eyes, the nervous half smile, her lips slightly parted, and then she looked up and saw him, tall and handsome and blond and waiting for her. The promise of a lifetime.

Andrew had tears in his eyes as he looked at her. She looked like a vision as she glided slowly down the aisle carpeted in white satin. And then at last, holding her bouquet in trembling hands, she stood before him.

Andy gently squeezed her hand, and the minister solemnly addressed the congregation, reminding them of why they had come, of their awesome responsibility as family and friends to support the young couple in their vows, for better or worse, in sickness and in health, for richer or poorer, until death did them part. He reminded Andrew and Diana that the road would not always be smooth, that the fates may not always be kind, but that they must be there for each other, in witness to their vows, faithful to each other, and strong in their love for each other and the Lord.

They made their vows to each other in strong clear voices, and by then Diana's hands had completely stopped shaking. She wasn't frightened anymore. She was with Andy. Where she belonged. And she had never, ever been happier in her life. She was beaming when the minister declared them man and wife. The narrow gold band Andy had slipped on her finger gleamed in the sunlight, and as he bent to kiss her, the love in his eyes was so tender that even her mother finally cried. Her father had cried long before that, when he left her at the altar beside the man she loved. He knew that it would never be quite the same for them again . . . she belonged to someone else now.

They walked down the aisle looking radiant and proud, and they were still beaming as they got into the car to go to the club for the reception. And after that, the dancing went on until six o'clock. It seemed to Diana as though everyone she had ever known, and several hundred people she hadn't, had been invited. And by the end of the afternoon, she felt as though she had danced with everyone there, and she and her sisters had had a hysterical time doing the limbo with Andy and his brothers. Both of the twins had had to dance with Sam, since there were four Douglas boys and only three Goode sisters, but Sam seemed to love it. She was only a year younger than the twins, and they were all great friends by the end of the reception. And Diana was touched to see how many of Andy's friends from the network came, even the chairman had come with his wife, although they only stayed for a little while, but it had been nice of them to come at all, and her editor in chief from

Today's Home had come, too, and he had danced several times with Diana, and with her mother.

It was a beautiful afternoon, a perfect day, the beginning of a life she had always dreamed of. Everything had worked out perfectly in her life so far. Andy had come into her life at the right time, they had been happy for the past two and a half years, and she had loved living with him, and now it seemed the perfect time to be married. They were both sure of each other and themselves, and what they wanted out of life. They wanted to be together, to share their lives, and to build a family like each of their own. They had so much to share, so much to give. Diana felt for an instant as though it was almost too perfect, as she stood and looked at him, just before she went to change out of her wedding gown. She hated to take it off, never to wear it again, to turn the reality into a memory. She wanted the moment never to end, as she looked up at her brand-new husband.

"You look incredible," he whispered to her, as he swept her onto the dance floor again for one last waltz before they left the party to begin their life together.

"I wish today would never end," she said,

closing her eyes, and thinking of how wonderful it had been.

"It won't," Andy said quietly, pulling her even closer. "I won't let it. It'll always be like this, Diana. . . . We have to remember that, if things ever get tough between us . . ."

"Is that a warning?" She pulled away a little as she smiled at him. "Are you going to start giving me a hard time now?"

"Very." He grinned, moving closer to her, and his meaning was not lost on her as she chuckled.

"Shame on you." She laughed at him as they continued to waltz around the dance floor.

"Shame on *me*? Who left me alone and went back to her parents' house to be a virgin?"

"One night! Andy!"

"It was not one night . . . it was longer . . . I know it." He pulled her closer to him again, and rested his cheek against her veil, as she gently touched his neck with delicate fingers.

"It was one night. . . ."

"You'll have to make it up to me for weeks, starting"—he glanced at his watch—"in about half an hour." The music slowly came to an end and he looked at her tenderly. "Ready to go?" She nodded, sad to leave their wedding, but it was time, it was after six o'clock, and they were both tired.

Her bridesmaids went upstairs with her while she changed, and Diana slowly took off the beautiful gown and the veil. Her mother carefully hung them up on specially padded hangers, and watched the younger women's excitement with a little smile, from a distance. She loved her girls more than anything. They had brought her such joy, and now she was happy to see them all well settled, and happily married.

Diana put on the ivory silk suit her mother had picked out with her at Chanel. It was bordered in navy blue, with a handbag to match, and it had big pearl buttons. Diana had bought a cream colored hat, too, and she looked wonderfully chic when she went back downstairs to meet her husband, carrying the huge bouquet of white roses.

His eyes lit up as she walked into the room again, and a moment later she had thrown her bouquet, and he had thrown her garter. And amidst a hailstorm of rice and rose petals, they ran to their car, after quick kisses to their siblings and their parents. They promised to call from the trip, and Diana especially thanked her parents for the beautiful wedding. And then they were gone, in a long white limousine, off to the Bel Air Hotel for their wedding night, to stay in a huge suite overlooking the hotel's carefully landscaped gardens.

Andy put an arm around her as the car drove away, and they both sighed in relief and exhaustion.

"Wow! What a day!" he said, as he leaned back against the seat and looked at her in silent appreciation. "You were a gorgeous bride!" It was so odd now to think it was all over.

"You looked pretty good yourself." She smiled at him. "It was such a beautiful wedding."

"You and your mom did a fantastic job. Every time I talked to someone at the network they said it was better than anything they've seen on a movie set." It had been loving and happy and filled with their family and friends, but it also wasn't showy. "Your sisters were a riot too. You guys really get out of hand when you get together, don't you?" He teased her, and she sat up in feigned outrage.

"*We* do! *We* do? I'd say the Douglas boys don't do badly in that department either! You guys were outrageous!"

"Don't be silly." Andy looked demure as he pretended to look out the window, and his new wife pushed him, almost onto the floor, as he chuckled.

"Are you kidding? Excuse me, but do you recall when all four of you did the boogaloo with my mother?"

"I don't remember that." He was all innocence, and they were both laughing.

"You're drunk."

"I must be." He turned around and grabbed her then, and held her close as he kissed her. It was a long time before he came up for air, and when he did, they were both breathless. "God . . . I've been dying to do that all day. I can't wait to get to the hotel and tear your clothes off."

"My new suit?" She looked horrified, and he grinned in anticipation.

"And the new hat that goes with it. I must say, they're very nice though."

"Thank you." They held hands and chatted in the backseat, feeling new in their love again. In a funny way, it was almost like starting at the beginning, except that they were old friends, and everything they did was comfortable and blessed by the love they had for each other.

When they arrived at the hotel, a desk clerk walked them down the path into the main building, and they smiled at each other as they walked past a discreet sign pointing the way to the Mason-Winwood wedding.

"Must be a big day," Andy whispered to her, and she smiled. They glanced at the gardens and the swans, and they were thrilled when they saw their room. It was on the second floor, and it had a huge living room, a small kitchenette, and a fabulous bedroom all done in a delicate French flower print and pink satin. It looked like the perfect place for their wedding night, the living room had a fireplace, and Andy was hoping it would be cool enough that night to light it.

"It's beautiful," she said, as the bellman left, and the door closed behind him.

"So are you." He gently took off her hat and swooped it through the air onto a table. And then he carefully undid her hair and ran his fingers through it, as it fell to her shoulders. "You're the most beautiful woman I've ever seen . . . and you're mine . . . forever and ever and ever . . ." He sounded like a child, telling a fairy tale, but that was what they had promised. And the bride and groom lived happily ever after. . . .

"And you're mine too," she reminded him, but he didn't need reminding, and he had no objection. The elegant new Chanel suit was quickly unbuttoned as they kissed, and the jacket fell to the floor as he lay her on the couch, and a moment later his own clothes were beside it. Their clothes lay tangled on the floor while their bodies lay long and lean and taut as they discovered each other for the first time as man and wife. All their passion, all their promises, seemed to come together in a single moment of abandon, and Diana lay clinging to him as though she would never let him go, not for a moment or a lifetime. Their ecstasy rose, and they shuddered with pleasure, and then lay peacefully in each other's arms long after it was over. It was sunset by then, and long pink and orange fingers of light streaked into the room, as they lay together, thinking of the life they would always share now.

"I've never been so happy in my life," he said softly.

"I hope you always will be," she whispered. "I hope I always make you happy."

"I hope we make each other happy," he added, and then unwound his long limbs from hers and stood up, smiling down at her, and he walked slowly to the window. The black and white swans were gliding smoothly on the pond, and the lawns looked perfectly tended. Young people in brightly colored cocktail dresses were hurrying to an area just beyond their view, as strains of show tunes wafted through the evening air toward them.

"That must be the Mason-Winwood wedding." Diana smiled at him, still lying on the couch, and suddenly hoped that they had just made a baby. They had used no precautions at all this time, they had no reason to anymore. They had agreed not to, and see what happened, as soon as they were married. Both of her sisters had gotten pregnant on their honeymoons, and she suspected that the same might happen to them, which genuinely pleased her.

She stood up after a few minutes and came to stand with him, and just as she did, she saw a young woman in a short white wedding dress run down the path, holding onto a short white veil and a small bouquet, and with her was a girl in a red dress, probably her maid of honor. The bride looked about Diana's age, or thereabouts, an "assisted blonde," attractive enough, in a sensuous way, and the dress had looked elaborate, but not expensive. But something about the way she looked and the nervous way she ran touched their hearts as they watched her. The feelings were all too familiar to them, and they wished her well as she ran to her wedding. . . .

* * *

"Barbie, come on!" Judi, the girl in the red dress, urged, as Barbara stumbled and almost fell in the white satin high heels she had bought at Payless only that morning. "Here . . . take it easy, kid. . . ." Judi extended a hand to steady her, and Barbara stopped to take a deep breath, and stand hidden from the guests, as Judi waved to the best man, mouthing, "Is it time?" He shook his head and held up five fingers, as the maid of honor nodded her understanding. The two women were friends, although they hadn't known each other for all that long a time. Both were actresses who had come to L.A. from Las Vegas the year before, where they had been dancers. To save the meager sums they made, the two girls decided to become roommates.

Judi had had two bit parts since she arrived in L.A., some modeling jobs, and almost got a walk-on in a commercial. Barbie got a part in the chorus of a revival of *Oklahoma!* when it came through town, had tried out for every daytime soap, unsuccessfully, and like Judi, had spent the rest of her time waiting on tables. She got a great job at the Hard Rock Cafe when she first came to town, and got Judi a job there too.

And it was at the Hard Rock that they had both met Charlie.

Judi went out with him first, but they hated each other and had nothing to say, and it was Barbie he kept coming back to talk to. For a while, he ate lunch there almost every day, and then finally he got up the courage to ask her out. It had been easier asking Judi, the first time around—she was so much more casual, so much more matter-of-fact—but he thought Barbie was really special.

He and Barbie dated a few times after that, and by the fourth date, Charlie was head over heels in love with her, and too scared to say it. He even stopped seeing Barbie for a while, but he couldn't stay away. He called Judi and asked her to meet him. He wanted her advice, and he wanted Judi to tell him what Barbie thought of him.

"She's crazy about you, you jerk." It amazed her how any man twenty-nine years old could be so naïve about women. She had never known anyone like him, and neither had Barbie. He wasn't really handsome, but he was "cute," in a boyish way, and so innocent and decent.

"What makes you think she likes me? Did she say anything?" he asked Judi suspiciously, but she laughed again.

"Because I know her better than you do."
Judi knew that Barbie liked his sweetness, his
generosity, and she thought he had taken her to
some pretty nice places. He made a good living
as a rep for a major textile company, he did
pretty well on commissions, he liked taking girls
to nice restaurants, and he lived pretty well for
a single guy. The nicer things in life were important to him. He had grown up dirt poor in
New Jersey, and it meant a lot to him to have a
good life now. He worked hard for it, and he
earned it. "She thinks you're a great guy," Judi
added, wondering if she should have made
more effort with him herself, but he just wasn't
her type. She liked excitement, and Charlie was
too wholesome. He was a nice guy, but she
liked her men racier. She was looking for the
big time, and he bored her. Barbara was a different story though. Judi knew she had grown
up in a small town, won "Miss Everything in
Town" by the time she finished high school, and
then had some kind of blowout with her folks
and ran away to Las Vegas. She'd been thinking
of going to New York for a long time, but it was
just too far from Salt Lake, and Vegas had been
closer. But in spite of the men she'd met there,
and the hard times, there was still something
decent and unspoiled about Barbie, which

made Charlie love her. She liked Charlie too. He reminded her of some of the boys back home, and she found his naïveté refreshing. He was a nice change from the men she'd met in Vegas and L.A., who seemed to expect everything in the world from a girl, from money to sex, and then some. Charlie didn't want anything from her, except to be with her and spoil her, and it was hard not to like that. And he wasn't a bad-looking guy, even if he wasn't exciting. He had red hair and blue eyes, and every inch of him was covered with freckles. He had a boy-next-door quality about him that a lot of women found both endearing and attractive, and it touched Barbie too. Sometimes she thought he might be the solution to a lot of problems.

"Why don't you tell her what you think of her?" Judi encouraged him, and then suddenly three weeks after they started going out, they were engaged. And six months after that, Barbara was standing behind a hedge at the Bel Air Hotel waiting for the signal that would start her wedding.

"You okay?" Judi scrutinized her, as Barbie stood nervously, hopping from one foot to the other, like a frightened racehorse.

"I think I'm going to throw up."

"Don't you dare! It took me two hours to do your hair under that veil . . . I'll kill you!"

"Okay, okay . . . Christ, Judi, I'm too old for this." She was thirty years old, only one year older than Charlie, but sometimes she felt a thousand years older. But when she wore less makeup, and just pulled her hair back in a braid, she looked younger than he did. But she had seen a lot more of life, and she was a lot more jaded. Only Charlie saw the sweetness and purity beneath her flash. Only he was able to reach a part of her she had been sure was gone forever. He invited her to his apartment for his home-cooked meals, they went for long walks, and he talked about wanting to meet her family, but she only shook her head at that, and she never answered his questions. She didn't like talking about them, and she said she was never going back to Salt Lake City to see them, but she never explained it. She had been furious one day when two Mormon missionaries had shown up at the apartment she shared with Judi, trying to get her to come back to the Church and move back to Salt Lake City. She had slammed the door on them, and shouted at them never to come back again. She didn't want any reminders of the life she had left behind in Salt Lake City. All Charlie knew was that she had eight brothers and sisters and about twenty nephews and nieces, but it was obvious to him that something had happened to her there, other than boredom. But she absolutely refused to discuss it.

He was far more open about his own past. He had been abandoned at birth in a train station, his records said, and had grown up in a series of state orphanages in New Jersey. He had been in several foster homes, and twice was considered for adoption, but he was a nervous child, given to allergies and skin problems, and by the time he was five, he had severe asthma. He outgrew most of it eventually, and the asthma had been in control for years, but by the time it was, he was too old for anyone to adopt him. He left the state home at eighteen, took a bus to L.A., and had been there for eleven years. He had put himself through college at night, and his dream now was to go to business school, which would allow him to get a better job and support the family he longed for. For him, finding Barbie was like a dream come true. All he wanted now was to marry her, give her a good home, and fill it with children who looked just like her. He had said that to her once, and she had laughed at him.

"We'd be a lot better off if they looked like

you!" She was a pretty girl, with an amazing figure, but she had never thought much of her looks, or herself, until she met Charlie. He was so kind to her, so protective, so unlike the men she had known, and yet sometimes she still wished he were a little bit more exciting. She had wanted to go out with an actor when she came to L.A., maybe even someone famous. And she had fallen for Charlie instead. And there were still times when she wondered if she should wait for her dream prince, or at least a famous actor. She had taken Charlie shopping to buy new clothes, and tried to introduce him to the latest styles to jazz him up a little bit, but in the end, she had had to agree with him, that on him they just looked silly. He was just a plain-clothes kind of guy. His hair stuck up when he left it too long, so he had to cut it short, and he never got a suntan, he just fried, and after that he blistered.

"I'm not a glamorous type, you understand," he had explained to her seriously one night, over a dinner he had cooked for her. It was his specialty, cannelloni and osso buco and a big tossed green salad. He had actually learned to make it in one of his foster homes, he explained to her, and her heart went out to him when he said it. There were times when she really loved him, and other times when she wasn't quite as sure, and she wondered. Was he right for her? Really, really right? Or was he just generous and nice and convenient? She knew that no harm would come to her with him. But neither would any glamour or excitement.

Nothing was ever clear-cut in her life, the choices were always so damn difficult, the prices to be paid so high, the risks so great . . . except with Charlie. He was offering her everything, everything she had thought she wanted years before . . . or should now. Security, a nice place to live, a nice guy to take care of her, no worries, no headaches, no terror that she couldn't pay the rent this month, no fear that things would go from bad to worse again and she'd have to get another job as a showgirl. What she really wanted was an acting career, and the agents who'd talked to her said she had talent. All she needed now was a break. And she wasn't sure if Charlie would get in the way of that. If she married him, could she still work? Would he object to her career? He said he wouldn't, but he also talked about kids all the time, and that wasn't in the cards for her, not for now, not with him, not yet, and maybe even never. She didn't say that to him, of course, but what if her big break came? What if she got a regular part on a weekly show, or even a big part in an important movie? Then where would she be with her little life? But if the big break didn't come . . . at least she wouldn't be waiting on tables. And maybe it was the wrong way to look at things. She felt guilty about it sometimes, but she had to think about herself. She had learned that lesson a long time ago, right in the bosom of her own family. She had learned a lot of lessons from them, lessons she didn't care to learn again, or even remember.

It was hard not to be swayed by Charlie's constancy, his adoration, his devotion, his just plain decency, and in the end Barbie decided that she really did love him. But now, standing here, it was terrifying all over again. What if she was doing the wrong thing? What if they hated each other in two years, or if it didn't even take that long? "Then what'll I do?" she whispered to Judi.

"It's a little late to worry about that now, isn't it?" Judi said, smoothing down her red lace dress. She had endless legs, and breasts that were exploding out of her cleavage. She had had implants done in Vegas by a doctor she knew there who gave her a great deal on the surgery, and everyone she knew thought they were terrific. Except Barbie, who had thought buying boobs was silly, because her own were big, firm, and real. But hell, Judi told herself, from a distance, who could tell the difference?

Barbie had a sensational figure, with her full bust in sharp contrast to her tiny waist, which was so small that Charlie could put his hands around it and almost touch his fingers. She wasn't tall, but she had shapely legs. She was a striking-looking girl, and even in a burlap bag, she would somehow have managed to look sexy. She just did, no matter what she wore. And now in the short, tight, white satin wedding gown, she was an overwhelming contrast of the innocent and the erotic.

"Do you think my dress is too tight?" She looked nervously at Judi again. She felt as though they'd been waiting forever. She didn't know why they couldn't just have gone to City Hall, but Charlie had insisted he wanted a "real" wedding.

This wedding had meant everything to him, so she'd gone along with it for his sake. She would have been a lot happier spending the weekend in Reno. But Charlie had planned everything, and invited all his friends. They were having sixty guests, and she knew this was the fanciest hotel in L.A.—except maybe the Beverly Hills Hotel, she had told him, but he had

insisted this one was even better. They'd chosen the least expensive menu, and the simplest
plan, but he'd wanted their wedding here, even
if it wiped out most of his savings. "You deserve
it," he'd said to Barbie.

"Your dress is fine," Judi reassured her, and
she honestly thought the other girl looked terrific. Scared, but very pretty. "Everything's
gonna be okay, kid. Just relax." She was beginning to wonder what the delay was, and then
finally Charlie's best man appeared, and the
music began. Charlie had hired a bass, a violin-
ist, and an electric piano for the occasion.

They played "Here Comes the Bride," and
Judi looked toward the little gazebo that had
been set up for the occasion. Charlie had found
a minister somewhere, and he hadn't asked
Barbie too many questions about being a Mormon, so she had finally agreed to let him do the
wedding.

And then Mark, the best man, offered Barbie
his arm, and looked down at her with a fatherly
smile. He was twice Charlie's age, and heavy-
set. He had been Charlie's supervisor at work
for two years, and in some ways, he was almost
like his father. He was still a good-looking man,
although he was overweight, and little rivers of
perspiration were running down the sides of his

face from the neatly combed gray hair at his temples.

He looked very serious as he bent toward Barbie just before they began their walk toward the gazebo.

"Good luck, Barbara . . . Everything's going to be just fine." He patted her hand, and she tried not to let herself think of her father.

"Thanks, Mark." He had agreed to give the bride away, and be best man. He had also given them all their champagne, because his brother-in-law knew a wholesaler with a terrific source in the Napa Valley. He wanted everything to be right for them. He was divorced himself, and had two daughters, one married, and the other in college.

They started off down the aisle, and Barbara tried not to think of what lay ahead, the wedding, or the years of commitment. And then suddenly there he was . . . Charlie . . . looking so sweet and innocent and young, with his blue eyes and red hair and sweet smile. He was wearing a white dinner jacket with a white carnation on the lapel, and he looked like a kid who had borrowed the jacket from his father for the senior prom. It was hard to be afraid of him, or of committing her life to him. And as Mark squeezed her hand encouragingly, she suddenly realized that all her fears were incredibly foolish. No harm would come to her as Charlie's wife. She was doing the right thing, and suddenly she knew it.

"I love you," he whispered as she stood at his side, and as she looked at him, she realized that she really loved him. He was doing something wonderful for her, he was giving her a beautiful new life, and offering to protect her forever. No one had ever done anything like that for her, and she knew, as she looked at him, that he would never fail her. She was suddenly sorry for all the doubts she'd had, all the fears, all the times she had secretly thought she could do better. He was just right for her, a good friend, a good man, a good husband, and she had been a fool to want more. She was thirty years old, and Prince Charming was obviously otherwise engaged somewhere on another planet. Charlie Winwood was enough of a prince for her, she didn't need more than that, didn't want more than he had to offer.

"I love you, Charlie," she whispered to him as he put the ring on her finger, and when he kissed her, he cried, and she held him close to her, wanting to make up to him for all the loneliness in his life and all the sorrow.

"I love you so much, Barb. . . ." There were no words to tell her how much he loved her.

"I promise, I'll be a good wife . . . I really will. . . ."

"I know you will, sweet girl." He smiled at her, and later he toasted her with Mark's champagne, and then led her out on the temporary dance floor. They had set a small dance floor out on the lawn, and there was a buffet near the bar, just beyond the music.

It was a terrific party and everyone had a good time, particularly the bride and groom, both of whom drank handsomely of Mark's champagne, as did all the other guests. And Mark seemed to be having a good time, dancing with Judi. Everyone was in high spirits by the time the band started playing things like "When the Saints Go Marching In" and "Hava Nagila."

Afterward, they played some slow music again, to get everyone calmed down and cooled off. They played "Moon River," and Mark asked the bride to dance, while Charlie danced with Judi.

"You're a beautiful bride, Barb," Mark told her as they danced slowly around the floor. There were a million stars in the sky, and it was warm. It was a magical evening. "You two are going to have a wonderful life," he said with certainty. "And a lot of gorgeous kids to show for it," he announced with assurance.

"How can you be so sure?" she asked, smiling at him. He was a nice man, and a good friend.

"Because I'm so old, and I know so much. And I know how much Charlie wants children." She knew it, too, but she had already told Charlie that she wanted to wait a few years, so she could pursue her career as an actress. He wasn't thrilled with that idea, but they had both agreed to talk about it later. He didn't know it yet, but having kids was the one thing that really scared her. And even Mark talking about it now gave her a queasy feeling in the pit of her stomach.

"May I cut in?" Charlie smoothly interrupted Mark, and handed Judi over to him, as he made off with his bride for the last dances of the evening. They had both had a lot to drink, but Barbie felt as though she were in a dream, and all of the people there seemed so happy. "Did you have a good time?" he asked as he nuzzled her neck, feeling her breasts pressing against him. Every time he touched her it just drove him crazy, and she loved to have a good time. She never said no, she never objected to anything he wanted to do, she was a good sport, and a hell of a sexy woman. He felt like the luckiest guy in the world as he twirled his bride around the dance floor.

"I had a great time." She grinned happily at him. "What about you?"

"Best wedding I ever had." He smiled at her. They were almost the same height, and he looked her in the eye, feeling as though he owned the world.

"That's not saying much." She pretended to pout, and he pulled her even closer.

"You know how happy I am, Barb . . . at least I hope you do. For me, this is the dream of a lifetime." It was the beginning of everything he never had. The love, the warmth, the home, the family, everything he had so desperately wanted.

"I know," she whispered, and her head swam dizzily as he kissed her. All she could think of now was lying on the beach at Waikiki with him. They were leaving for Hawaii in the morning on a great package deal. And they were spending their wedding night in Charlie's apartment. The had talked about spending their wedding night at the Bel Air, but they just couldn't afford it, and she didn't care. She already knew that she would never, ever forget this night or this moment.

*   *   *

In Santa Barbara that night, there was a star-filled sky, too, as twenty-five friends stood silently watching Pilar Graham and Bradford Coleman kiss in the moonlight. There was a long silence and then they turned to look at their friends, with a startled, happy look, and everyone laughed and cheered and applauded. Marina Goletti, the judge who had performed the ceremony, declared them man and wife, and they were instantly surrounded by well-wishers.

"What took you so long?" a friend of Brad's teased.

"We were practicing," Pilar said in a dignified voice, as the white silk Grecian gown molded her long, lithe figure. She swam and exercised every day, and Bradford liked to tell her that she had the body of a young girl. She was a beautiful woman and she was proud of the thick, straight gray hair that hung to her shoulders. It had been almost white since her early twenties, and she had worn it that way for almost twenty years now.

"Thirteen years is a long time to practice!"

One of her law partners, Alice Jackson, whispered to her, "We're glad you finally figured it out and married Brad." She smiled.

"Yeah." Her other partner, Bruce Hemmings, added, "I know, you two just didn't want any scandal now that Brad's been made a judge."

"You got that right." Brad's deep voice rang out just next to her, as he gave Pilar's shoulders a squeeze. "I didn't want anyone accusing her of sleeping with the judge to get special favors."

"As though you'd be that good to me!" Pilar teased right back, as she leaned her body against him. Everything about them suggested the comfortable and intimate and familiar.

And the interesting truth was that they had been archenemies for three years, after Pilar had graduated from law school and moved to Santa Barbara. She'd gotten a job as a public defender and he'd been a prosecutor, and it seemed as though every major criminal case that came up pitted them against each other. She hated his ideas, his politics, his style, his relentless way of hammering at a case until he won, or simply wore down the jury. And more than once, their tempers had flared and they'd had raging battles in the hall outside the court-room. They'd been called to order by the bench more than once, and Pilar had almost spent a night in jail for contempt of court when she'd called Brad a bastard in front of a judge once. But Brad had been so amused by her attack that time that he had compounded matters even more by inviting her to dinner as soon as court was recessed.

"Are you insane? Did you hear what I said?" she had asked him as they made their way out of the courtroom. She was still trembling with anger over his style in trying a rape case.

"You still have to eat. And your client is guilty and you know it." She did know it, and she was uncomfortable, but someone still had to defend him, to the best of his or her ability, and that was her job, whether Brad Coleman liked it or not.

"I'm not going to discuss my client's innocence or guilt with you, Mr. Coleman. That's improper. Is that why you want me to have dinner with you? So you can get me to admit something you'll use against me?" She was furious with him, and she didn't give a damn if he was attractive. He was the Cary Grant of the prosecutor's office. He was in his late forties, had snow-white hair, and all the women in her office talked constantly about how handsome he was, and how sexy. Pilar Graham was not interested in that, not with him. As far as she was concerned, this was strictly business.

"I wouldn't stoop to that," Bradford Coleman said quietly, "and I think you know that. I wish you worked in our office, instead of for the public defender. I'd like to be on the same side of a case with you sometime. We could do one hell of a lot of damage to the opposition."

She had to smile at what he said, and she was flattered by his words, but she didn't go to dinner. She knew he was a widower and he had kids, and she knew he was universally liked. But all she could see when she saw him was her opponent. She never allowed herself to see more than that, until they were once again adversaries in an illustrious case that had been smeared all over the papers. It was a big murder case, and unfortunately, the press had grabbed onto it, and were making as much of it as they could, and it was very ugly. A young girl was involved, accused of murdering her mother's lover. She said the lover had tried to rape her, but there was no evidence of it, and the mother sided against her. The testimony was long and arduous in that trial, the lawyers' tactics brutal, and then halfway through the trial, Bradford Coleman had come to her, quietly, simply, and told her that due to new evidence, he had come to believe that her client wasn't guilty. He asked for a recess, and became the champion of the young girl's cause. It was his skill and his careful investigation that had freed the girl, Pilar always said, not her own work. She had gotten nowhere. And it was then that they had finally had dinner. After three long years. Nothing ever came easily to them, or quickly.

His children had been thirteen and ten by then. Nancy was thirteen, and Todd ten, and from the moment they met Pilar, they resisted the idea that she was going out with their father. Their mother had been dead for five years and they had had Brad exclusively to themselves ever since then. They had no intention of giving him up, even part time, to another woman. At first, the children made life difficult for them, and although Brad and Pilar really were just friends, the children still sensed that something more might develop, and they wanted to stop it. Brad was deeply saddened by their attitude, but Pilar was only sorry for him. Whether it be her or someone else, he needed something more in his life than his work and his children. And the more she came to know him, the more she respected him, the more impressed she was with his mind and his skill and his soul, his unfailing sense of fairness and integrity. He was even more remarkable than people had told her.

And before she knew it, she was head over

heels in love with him and he with her, and they had no idea what to do about his children.

"Never mind your children, what about my work? I can't take cases against you anymore, Brad. It wouldn't be ethical . . . or good for us." Eventually, he agreed with her, and they disqualified themselves when they were slated against each other on a case, and within a year, she went into general private practice and she loved it. He eventually went into private practice as well, and their lives were busy and full, and in the end, even the children got used to their relationship. And little by little, the children grew fond of her, and came to accept her. It had been a long, hard war to win them over to her, but when Nancy was sixteen and Todd thirteen, three years after their romance had begun, Pilar Graham moved in with Bradford Coleman.

They bought a new house in Montecito eventually, and the children grew up. Nancy went off to college, and Todd to boarding school, and by then friends had stopped asking them when they were going to get married. They saw no need for it. They had his children, and Pilar had never wanted any of her own. She felt no need to have a piece of paper to prove anything, Pilar explained when pressed. As far as she was concerned, she was married to Brad in her heart, and that was the only place that mattered.

They went on that way, comfortably, for thirteen years, and when Brad was sixty-one, and Pilar forty-two, he was appointed judge of the Superior Court of Santa Barbara. And suddenly they both realized that it could become awkward for him to be living with a woman to whom he wasn't married. Particularly if the press made an issue of it, which they might. They'd already made several comments.

Pilar looked crestfallen as they discussed it one morning over breakfast. "Do you think I should move out?"

He sat back in his chair, holding the *New York Times* and looking amused as he looked at her. She was as pretty at forty-two as she had been at twenty-six, the first time she was his opponent in the courtroom. "Don't you think that's a little extreme?"

"Well, I don't want to cause trouble for you." She looked very upset as she poured them both another cup of coffee.

"Can't you think of another solution, counselor? I can."

"What?" She looked blank. She really couldn't.

"I'm glad you're not my attorney, Ms. Graham. Has it ever occurred to you that we could get married? Or if you still have an aversion to that idea, I don't know why our living together has to create any real scandal. I'm sure judges are allowed to live with people too. They're only human."

"I don't think it's a good idea for you." He had such a spotless reputation, it seemed foolish to hurt it.

"Then what about marriage?"

She was silent for a long time as she looked out at the sea. "I don't know. I've never really thought about it . . . or not in a long time anyway. Have you?"

"No, because you never wanted to. But I could have." He had always wanted to marry her, but she had always been so determined to stay free, to be two separate entities side by side or intertwined, but not "swallowed up by each other" or "devoured," as she used to put it. And at first, of course, his children might have objected, but no more. Nancy had married the year before and was twenty-six years old by then, and Todd was twenty-three, a grown man, and working in Chicago. "Would it be so terrible to be married now?" he asked with a shy smile, and Pilar hesitated before she answered.

"At our age?" She looked genuinely startled,

as though he had suggested something truly odd, like leaping out of an airplane with a parachute, something she had never even considered.

"Is there an age limit on it now? I had no idea," he teased, and she smiled.

"Okay, okay . . ." She sighed and leaned back in her chair again. "I don't know . . . it just scares me. Everything has been so wonderful for all these years, why change it now? What if it ruins everything?"

"You always say that. But why would it do that? Would you change? Would I?"

"I don't know." She looked at him seriously. "Would you?"

"Why should I, Pilar? I love you. I'd like nothing better than to marry you, and maybe this is just the excuse we needed."

"But why? Other than your appointment to the bench, of course. What's the point? What difference will it make to anyone? And why is it anyone's business?"

"It isn't. It's our business. But I want you to be my wife." He leaned toward her and took her hands in his and then he kissed her. "I love you, Pilar Graham. I will love you till the day I die. I would like you to become my wife, whether I am on the bench or not. What do you think about that?"

"I think you're crazy." She smiled at him, and then kissed him again. "Too much stress at the office. Besides, I like being a little out of the ordinary. I liked having gray hair when I was twenty-five, I never minded not having children when everyone else had one in a backpack and another one in a stroller, I like working for a living, and I don't mind not being married."

"Why not? You should be ashamed to be living in sin like this. Have you no conscience?"

"None whatsoever. They forced me to give it up when I passed the bar."

"I always knew that about you. Well, give it some thought now," he had suggested casually. And that had been just before Christmas. And for the next six months they had discussed it and talked about it, and argued over it, and he had finally sworn that he wouldn't marry her if she begged him. And one evening in May she totally amazed him.

"I've been thinking about it," she said as she made him an espresso after dinner.

"About what?" He didn't know what she was saying.

"About us." He waited for a beat, suddenly worried. She was very independent, and she was capable of anything, any wild decision she had come to on her own and then decided was important. "I think we should get married." She looked matter-of-fact and handed him his coffee, but he was too startled to take it as he stared at her.

"You what? After all those arguments you gave me over Christmas . . . what in God's name made you change your mind?"

"Nothing. I just decided that you might be right, and it might be time." She had thought about it a lot, and it was hard to admit to him that somewhere deep inside of her there was suddenly a yearning . . . to be his . . . to be part of him . . . forever. . . .

"What ever made you think that?"

"I don't know." She looked noncommittal and he grinned.

"You're crazy, you know. Completely crazy. And I love you." He came around the counter and took her in his arms and kissed her. "I love you very, very much, whether you marry me or not. Do you want some more time to think about this?"

"I think you'd better not give me much time." She grinned. "I might change my mind. I think we'd better get it over with quickly." She made it sound difficult and painful.

"I promise I'll make it as easy as I can." He was ecstatic. They picked a date in June and called the children, who were thrilled, too, and they promised to come, whenever it was. They seemed sincerely happy for them. They picked ten couples who meant a great deal to them, and a few unattached friends, her law partners, two of his colleagues, among them Marina Goletti, Pilar's best friend, to perform the ceremony, and of course, Pilar's mother. Both of Brad's parents had been dead for years and Pilar's mother was a widow. She lived and worked in New York, but she had promised to come out for the wedding, "if you go through with it," she said skeptically, which suitably annoyed her daughter.

But true to his word, Brad handled everything, and had his secretary send out the invitations. All Pilar had to do was find a dress, and she, her stepdaughter, Nancy, and Marina Goletti went shopping for it. Pilar was so unglued by the whole idea that the other two almost had to try dresses on for her. But in the end, she found a beautiful Mary McFadden gown of tiny ivory silk pleats, and she looked like a Greek goddess when she put it on. And when the day came, she wore her hair up, with soft tendrils falling near her face, and tiny white flowers woven into it. She looked exquisite, and as she turned to their guests after the ceremony, she looked ecstatic.

"See, it wasn't so bad," Brad whispered to her, as they stood slightly apart, watching their friends have a good time. As always, there was a silent, peaceful bond between them. They had an understanding that had surpassed everything for the past thirteen years; opposition and stress and fear and loneliness and hatred. It was a band of love that brought them together and kept them there, against life's winds, safe in each other's harbor. "Did you do it for me, or for them?" he asked gently.

"It's funny," she said quietly. "I did it for myself, in the end." She hadn't meant to tell him that, but it seemed right now. "All of a sudden I just needed to be married to you, and I knew it."

"That's a nice thing to say." He took a step closer to her and held her close to him. "I needed to be married to you, too, Pilar. I have for a long time. But I didn't want to press you."

"You've always been so good to me about that. It means a lot to me. I guess I just needed time." She smiled sheepishly and he laughed. It was a good thing she had never wanted children. If they had to wait another thirteen years for them, it could have been quite a problem.

"This is the right time," he said gently. "This is when it was meant to be. I love you." As he said it, he looked down at her, puzzled. "Who are you, by the way? Mrs. Coleman? Or Miss Graham?"

"I hadn't thought about that. I'm not sure that at my age I could change it. Forty-two years as Graham is a little hard to wipe out in a single afternoon." She saw something sad but resigned in his eyes then. "But on the other hand . . . maybe in another thirteen years . . . tell you what, why not go for the big time?"

"Coleman?" He looked amazed and touched. It had been an extraordinary day in their household.

"Mrs. Coleman," she said softly. "Pilar Coleman." She smiled at him, looking like a young girl, and he kissed her again and then led her back to their friends in the midst of celebration.

"Congratulations, Pilar," her mother said, as she smiled at her over a glass of champagne, which she held in a graceful hand. Elizabeth Graham was still beautiful at sixty-seven. She had been practicing neurology in New York for nearly forty years, and she had no other children. Pilar's father had been a justice of the New York Court of Appeals, and had been killed at the height of his career in a plane crash, while Pilar was in law school.

"You surprised us all today," her mother said coolly, and Pilar smiled at her. She had matured enough over the years not to take the bait or lose her temper when her mother goaded her, which she seemed to do fairly often.

"Life is full of wonderful surprises." Pilar smiled at Brad, and over his shoulder at Marina. Since the first moment they'd met, when Pilar came to Santa Barbara, Marina Goletti had been like a mother to her, and it meant a lot to Pilar that it had been Marina who performed their wedding. She was one of Brad's colleagues on the bench, but she had been Pilar's friend long, long before that. They had worked together in the public defender's office for six months, and then Marina had become a judge. But by then, she was already a dear friend, and a substitute for the mother Pilar had never been close to.

Pilar's relationship with her mother had always been strained, and it was no secret to anyone that Pilar had almost never seen her parents. They were busy with their careers, and Pilar had found herself sent away to boarding school at the age of seven. She was brought home on holidays and "grilled," as she had described it to Brad, about what she had learned, how fluent was her French, and would she please explain the reason for her most recent math grade. They were strangers to her, although her father had at least made some small effort during their vacations. But even he had very little to say to her, he was far too involved in his work, as was her mother. She had made it clear to Pilar at an early age that what she did with her patients was far more important than any involvement she might have with her only daughter.

"I could never understand why they had children," she had told Brad from the first. "I was never sure if I was a mistake, or just an experiment that hadn't worked out for them. But whatever I was, it was always clear that I was not exactly what they had wanted. My father was relieved when I went into law. I think it was the first time he was actually reassured that they hadn't made a terrible mistake having me in the first place. They didn't even bother to come to my graduations before that. And of course my mother was furious that I wasn't interested in medicine, but I can't say she ever made it very appealing." In effect, Pilar had grown up in schools. She had once jokingly said to one of her law partners that she was institutionalized, just like some of the people she had defended who had grown up in prisons. And for whatever reason, the coolness of her parents' relationship, their indifference to her, and the politics of her own times had made marriage unappealing to her, and having children something she would never even consider. She didn't want anyone to live a life like hers, and she had no idea how to bring a child up herself. She had had no example in her own childhood. In fact, it had amazed her when she first saw Brad with his children. He was so natural with them, so open, so unafraid, they talked about everything, and he was so demonstrative, and so easily able to show emotion. Pilar couldn't even imagine having a relationship like that with anyone, certainly not a child, until little by little, Brad had helped her to open up to what she felt, and share it with those she cared about. In time, she had grown to be completely at ease with his children, and with him. But it still never led her to want children of her own. And seeing her mother now, even on her wedding day, reminded her again of how deeply her parents had failed her.

"You look lovely today, Pilar," her mother

said awkwardly, almost as though she were speaking to an acquaintance, or a stranger. She was completely unable to let anyone in on the deep mystery of her feelings, or whether she even had any to begin with. "It's a shame you and Brad are too old to have children."

Pilar looked at her in complete amazement, unable to believe what she'd just heard. "I can't believe you said that," Pilar said so softly that even Brad didn't hear her. "How dare you make assumptions about our life, or our future?" Her eyes blazed as, from the distance, Marina watched her.

"You know as well as I do that, clinically, you're hardly a reasonable age to start having children." Her mother looked cool and professional as Pilar lost the battle over her emotions.

"Women my age have children every day," Pilar blazed, annoyed at herself for taking the bait again. The last thing in the world she wanted was to have a baby. But on the other hand, her mother had no right to assume that she wouldn't, or worse yet, shouldn't. After the little she'd done for her over the years, the least she could do was offer her privacy, and the right to her own choices and opinions.

"Perhaps in California they do, Pilar. But I see those babies every day, damaged, retarded, children with Down syndrome, some with severe abnormalities and complications. Believe me, you don't want that."

"You're right." She looked her mother right in the eye. "I don't. I never have wanted children . . . thanks to you and Daddy. . . ." And on those words, Pilar disappeared into the small crowd, feeling herself tremble as she looked for Brad. He had drifted away to talk to someone while Pilar seemed to be chatting with her mother.

"You okay?" Marina whispered to her, her own gray hair looking curly and a little frumpy. She was the mother Pilar had never had, the friend she had always longed for. She was wise in many ways, and she had made many similar choices to Pilar's, although for different reasons. The oldest of eleven children, she had raised all ten of her siblings when her mother died, and she herself had never married or had children. "I gave at the office," she always explained, and she had always been sympathetic to Pilar's agonies about her parents. In recent years, the younger woman's pain had dimmed, except on the rare occasions when she saw her mother. "The Doctor," as Pilar called her, only came out to California every two or three years, and the truth was that in between times, Pilar didn't miss her. She called her dutifully, and she was always amazed to find that in the years since her childhood nothing had changed, the calls were still "interrogations."

"Looks like the Doctor was giving you a hard time." Marina eyed her kindly, and Pilar smiled. Just being with Marina always made her feel better about the human race. She was one of those rare people, great souls, who enhance the lives of all those who know them.

"No, she just wanted to be sure that Brad and I understood we're too old to have children," Pilar said with a smile, but her voice sounded surprisingly bitter. It wasn't the lack of children that bothered her, it was the lack of kindness or warmth from her mother.

"Says who?" Judge Goletti looked annoyed on her behalf. "My mother was fifty-two when she had her last one."

"Now, there's something to aspire to." Pilar grinned. "Promise me that won't happen to me, or I'll shoot myself now."

"On your wedding day? Don't be ridiculous." And then, she surprised Pilar by asking a question. "Are you two thinking of having kids?" She knew lots of people older than they were who had had children recently, but she was curious, and she felt that she was close enough to Pilar to ask her. She had been so startled by the idea of Pilar marrying Brad, after being so adamant about staying single all her life, that now all her earlier decisions seemed to be in question.

Pilar laughed openly before she answered. "I don't think you need to worry about that. The last thing on my wish list is kids, in fact, it's so low on my list that I never wrote it down at all, and I don't plan to." She wanted Brad, but the one thing she was sure of was that she didn't want children.

"You don't plan to what?" Brad joined them and slid an arm around his bride's waist with a happy expression.

"I don't plan to retire from the law," Pilar said, looking calm again. His soothing effect made her forget her irritation at her mother.

"Who ever thought you would?" He looked surprised that anyone would even ask the question. Pilar was an excellent attorney, and she was devoted to her career. He couldn't imagine her ever leaving her profession.

"I think she should join us on the bench," Marina Goletti said solemnly, thinking that there was some truth in that, and then she was

distracted by someone and moved away, and Pilar and Brad stood looking into each other's
eyes, alone for a moment, in the swirl of good
friends around them.

"I love you, Mrs. Coleman. I only wish I
could tell you how much."

"You have a lifetime to tell me . . . and I
you . . . I love you, Brad," she whispered.

"You were worth the wait, every minute of it.
And I'd wait another fifty years if I had to."

"Then you'd really make my mother nervous." Pilar laughed, and she looked young and
mischievous as she did.

"Oh? Is your mother worried that I'm too old
for you?" He was, after all, only a few years
younger than she was.

"No . . . she's afraid I am. She thinks we
might go crazy and decide to have half-witted
kids, who would then become her patients."

"How nice of her. Is that what she said to
you?" He looked mildly annoyed, but he wasn't
going to let anything seriously upset him on this
special day he had waited so long for.

"Yes, it is actually. The good doctor thought
she ought to warn me."

"See if we invite her out for our twenty-fifth
anniversary," he said softly as he kissed her.

They danced with each other, and with their

friends. And at midnight, they slipped away quietly to the suite he had reserved at the Biltmore.

"Happy?" he asked, as she leaned against him in the rented limousine.

"Ecstatic." She beamed, and then yawned as she rested her head on his shoulder, and her white-satin-shod feet on the jump seat. "Oh, God . . ." She suddenly frowned as she looked up at him. "I forgot to say good-bye to my mother, and she's leaving in the morning." She was going to L.A. for a medical convention. She'd been very pleased Pilar's wedding date was so convenient for her.

"You're allowed this one time. This is your wedding day. She should have come to kiss you and wish you happiness," Brad said as Pilar shrugged. She really didn't care now. It had taken a long time, but for her the war was over. "I'll wish you happiness instead," Brad said softly and she kissed him again, and knew that she had lived her entire life for this moment. He was everything she had ever wanted, and more, and for just an instant, she was sorry that she hadn't married him sooner.

Her past no longer mattered to her, her parents, or how they had failed her. All that mattered now was Brad, and the life she was going to share with him. And all she could think of as they drove up to the Biltmore that night was their future.

CHAPTER
=== 2 ===

The week after Thanksgiving, Diana was swamped with coordinating shoots for their April issue. They were doing extensive pieces on two homes in Newport Beach, and another in La Jolla. She drove to San Diego herself to oversee the one there, and by the end of the afternoon she was exhausted. The people were difficult, the woman who owned the house hated everything they'd done, and the junior editor she'd assigned to the piece spent most of her time crying on Diana's shoulder.

"Take it easy," Diana told her calmly, feeling on edge herself, and since noon that day she'd had a raging headache. "If she thinks you're upset, she'll get worse. Just treat her like a little girl. She wants to be in the magazine, and you have to help her get there." But shortly after that, the photographer had a fit and threatened to walk out, and by the end of the day, everyone's nerves were raw, most especially Diana's.

She went back to the Valencia Hotel, let herself into her room, and lay on the bed without turning on the light. She was too tired to move, or talk, or eat. She didn't even have the energy to call Andy. She knew she would eventually, but she decided to take a hot bath first, and order some soup from room service. She did that before she ran the tub, and then she went to the bathroom. And when she did, she saw it there. The terrible telltale trace of blood she prayed not to find each month, and always found anyway, despite her prayers, despite their attempts to schedule their lovemaking at the right time to get her pregnant. Despite all of it, it hadn't worked. Again. She wasn't. And for six months, they'd been trying. It was getting discouraging, to Diana if not to Andy.

She closed her eyes when she saw it there, and tears were running down her cheeks when she stepped into the tub a few minutes later. Why was everything so difficult? Why did it have to be that way for her? It had been so easy for both her sisters.

She called Andy at home after her bath. He

had just gotten home from a late meeting at the network.

"Hi, baby, how'd it go today?" He sounded tired, too, and at first she decided not to say anything to him till she got home, but he heard the sorrow in her voice, and wondered what had happened. "Something wrong?"

"No . . . just a long day." She tried to sound normal for him, but her heart ached. It was as though every month someone died, and she went into mourning.

"It sounds like more than that. Trouble with your crew, or the people who own the house?"

"No, no, it was fine. The woman is kind of a pain in the ass, and the photographer threatened to quit twice, but that's par for the course." She smiled sadly.

"So what's up? What are you not saying?"

"Nothing . . . I . . . it's nothing. I just got my period, that's all. It's kind of depressing." Tears welled up in her eyes again as she said it to him, but he sounded undaunted.

"No big deal, kiddo. It just means we get to try again. Hell, it's only been six months. It takes some people a year or two. Just relax. Don't worry so much, and enjoy the ride. I love you, silly girl." He was touched by how devastated she was each month, but he knew nothing was wrong. Besides, they were both under constant stress in their jobs, and that didn't help. Everyone knew that. "Why don't we go away for a couple of days next month, at the right time. You figure it out and tell me."

"I love you, Andrew Douglas." She smiled through her tears as she held the phone. He was such a nice man, and he was so reasonable about her attempts to get pregnant. "I wish I felt as relaxed about it as you do. I keep thinking I should go to a specialist, or at least talk to Jack and see what he thinks."

"Don't be ridiculous." For the first time Andy sounded annoyed, he didn't want her discussing their sex life with her sister's husband. "There's nothing wrong with either of us, for heaven's sake."

"How do you know that?"

"I just do. Now, trust me."

"Okay, okay. I'm sorry . . . I just get so upset . . . every month, I interpret every twinge, every sign . . . every time I'm tired or sneeze or have indigestion, I let myself think I'm pregnant, and then zap . . . suddenly it's over." It was hard to explain to him the disappointment she felt each month, the anguish, the fear, the ache, the emptiness, the terrible longing. They had been together for almost three years, married for six months, and now she wanted his baby. Even the empty third floor in their house suddenly seemed like an accusation. They had bought the house to have kids, and it just hadn't happened.

"Just forget about it for a while, sweetheart. It'll happen, give it time. Now, when are you coming home?"

"Tomorrow night, I hope, if these people don't drive me nuts first." She sighed. Suddenly, the prospect of dealing with all of them the next day depressed her even further. Losing hope again when she got her period deflated everything she did. Each month, it was a terrible loss, an emptiness she couldn't describe to anyone, not even Andy. It seemed absurd, but it was incredible how much she was affected by it each month, and then tried to overcome it, began hoping all over again . . . only to have her hopes dashed again a month later.

"I'll be waiting for you when you get home. Get a good night's sleep tonight and you'll feel better in the morning." It was so simple for him, the pat answers, the encouragement. In an odd way, she wanted him to be worried too. She wanted him to share her fears and her grief, but maybe it was better he didn't. "I love you, Di."

"I love you, too, sweetheart. I really miss you."

"I miss you too. See you tomorrow night." After she hung up, her soup arrived, but she never bothered to eat it. She turned off the lights eventually, and just lay there in the dark, thinking of the baby she wanted so much, and the bright red stain that had ended all hope of that again, for this month. But as she drifted off to sleep that night, she hoped that next month would be different.

Pilar Graham, as she still called herself professionally, sat in her office, staring intensely at a file on her desk, making notes to herself, when her secretary buzzed her on the intercom, and she answered it quickly.

"The Robinsons are here."

"Thanks. Send them in." Pilar stood up, clearly expecting them, as her secretary ushered in a serious-looking couple. The woman was somewhere in her late thirties, with neat mid-length dark hair, the man was tall and spare, not expensively dressed, and slightly older. They'd been referred by another attorney, and she'd been studying their case all morning before she met them.

"Hello, I'm Pilar Graham." She shook their hands, and invited them to sit down, and they both declined tea or coffee. They looked nervous and seemed anxious to get down to business.

"I've been reading your files all morning," Pilar said quietly. She looked serious and mature and intelligent, the kind of person they could have confidence in. But they knew her reputation, too, which was why they had come to see her. She was reputed to be a killer in the courtroom.

"Do you think there's anything you can do?" Emily Robinson looked at Pilar unhappily, and the attorney could see all the anguish lurking there, and she wondered if she could help her.

"I hope I can help, but to be honest, I'm not sure yet. I have to study it more. I want to talk to some colleagues about this case, in confidence, of course. I'm afraid this is the first time I've ever dealt with a surrogate situation. The laws are a little gray in some areas, and they vary incredibly from state to state. It certainly isn't an easy situation, as you know, and I just don't have the answers." Lloyd Robinson had made an arrangement with a seventeen-year-old girl, who lived in the mountains near Riverside,

to have his baby. She had already had two ille-
gitimate children before, and she was more than
willing to have this one. He knew of her
through a school where he'd worked, but no
longer did. Everything had been handled by artificial insemination through a local doctor. He
had paid her five thousand dollars for it, enough
to move to Riverside the following year, live
decently and go to college, which was what she
said she wanted. Without the money he had
paid, she had no hope of that, and she'd be
stuck in the mountains forever.

It had been a foolish thing to do, they knew
now—she was young, unstable, and her parents
had raised hell with the local authorities when
they finally found out. Lloyd had faced criminal
charges, all of which were dropped. But the
court had taken a dim view of his choice of a
mother. For a while there had been a vague
possibility of charges of statutory rape, but
Lloyd had been able to prove that there had
never actually been sexual contact. But in any
case, in the end the girl, Michelle, had refused
to give up the baby. By the time it was born,
she had married a local boy, and he was adamant too. And by the time Pilar was talking to
the Robinsons, Michelle was pregnant again,
with her husband's child. Lloyd Robinson's

child was a year old by then, and the courts hadn't even allowed him visitation. They had explained that, as a "donor," he had no rights. They felt that he had had undue influence on a minor, and they had placed a restraining order on him in lieu of further action. The Robinsons were distraught about it. They acted as though it were a child they knew and loved who had been stolen from them. The baby was a little girl and they kept calling her Jeanne Marie. They had named her after both their mothers, although Michelle called her something entirely different and as Pilar looked at them, she had the feeling that the Robinsons lived in a dream world.

"Wouldn't it have been easier to adopt a child, even in a private adoption?"

"It might have been," Emily said sadly, "but we wanted his child. I'm the one who can't have babies, Miss Graham." She confessed it like a terrible crime, and Pilar felt sorry for her, although she had to admit she found the case fascinating and strange, but what kept coming across to her was their irreversible compulsion to have a baby. "We're too old to adopt legally," Emily explained. "I'm forty-one, and Lloyd is almost fifty. We tried for years, our income wasn't big enough, Lloyd hurt his back and he

was out of work for a long time. Now we're
doing fine. We sold our car, and we both held
down two jobs for a year to save the money to
pay Michelle to have the baby. The rest of what
we made went on legal fees. We don't have
much left," she told Pilar honestly, but Pilar
didn't really care. She was intrigued by the
case. The court had had a social worker's report
on them, and even though they were certainly
unusual, they had no apparent vices and they
both appeared to be decent people, according
to those·who knew them. They just couldn't
have kids and they were desperate to have a
baby. Desperation made people do strange
things, and they had, in Pilar's opinion.

"Would you settle for visitation rights?" Pilar
asked calmly.

Emily sighed and nodded. "We might, if
that's all we could get. But it doesn't seem fair,
Michelle gave up two babies when she was
barely more than a little girl herself, now she's
having another one with the boy she married.
She's going to have that baby, why does she
have to keep Lloyd's?" Emily asked plaintively,
but there was more to it than that, as they all
knew.

"It's her baby too," Pilar said gently.

"Do you think all we'll ever get is the right to

visit?" Lloyd asked finally, and Pilar hesitated before she answered.

"It's possible. Given the court's position now, that might be a step forward. And in time, if Michelle doesn't behave properly toward the child, or if there's a problem with her husband, then you may be able to get custody, but I can't promise you that, and it could take a very long time, maybe years." Pilar was always honest with her clients.

"The last lawyer we saw said he might be able to get Jeanne Marie back to us in six months," Emily said accusingly, and Pilar didn't want to remind her that it wasn't a question of "back to them" since the baby had never been with them in the first place.

"I don't think he was being honest with you, Mrs. Robinson." And neither did they apparently, or they'd still be there with him.

The couple nodded and looked at each other in despair. There was a kind of desperate hunger and loneliness about them that ate at one's heart just to see them.

Pilar and Brad had had friends who were desperate to adopt, and some had even gone to Honduras and Korea and Romania, but none had done anything as foolish as this, or looked quite as forlorn as these people. The Robinsons had taken a chance and lost, and they knew it.

Pilar talked to them for a while, and told them she would be happy to work on it if they wanted her to. She could research precedents throughout the state, and let them know. But they said they'd like her to wait and they'd call her. They wanted to think it over first. But when they left the office, Pilar knew they wouldn't be calling her again. They were looking for someone to promise them the moon, and she just wouldn't do it. After they left, she sat thinking about them for a few minutes. The Robinsons had seemed so lost and so desperate, and so hungry for their unknown baby. They had never even laid eyes on her since her birth, and yet to them she was Jeanne Marie, someone they thought they knew and loved. It seemed odd to Pilar, but she was still sorry she couldn't help them. The case intrigued her and she was staring pensively out the window when her associate, Alice Jackson, poked her head in her office door with a grin, and then an intrigued expression.

"Uh oh, counselor . . . looks like a tough one. I haven't seen you look like that since the P.D.'s office, whenever you got a defendant charged with murder one. Who did this one kill?"

"No one." Pilar smiled at the memory of their days as public defenders. Their other partner, Bruce Hemmings, had worked at the public defender's office too. He and Alice had gotten married years before, and they had two children. Pilar and Alice had always been good friends, although Pilar didn't confide in her as extensively as she did in Marina. But for the past ten years she had been wonderful to work with. "This isn't a murder beef," Pilar said with a pensive smile, beckoning her to come in and sit down. "It's just so damn strange." She briefly explained the case to her as Alice shook her head in wonder.

"Don't even try to make new law on this. I can tell you right now, the best you'll get from any judge is visitation. Don't you remember? Ted Murphy had a case like this last year, the surrogate refused to turn over the child at the last minute. It went all the way to the State Supreme Court, and the father still only got technical joint custody, the mother got physical, and he got visitation."

"I remember it, but these people were so . . ." She hated to say it, but they had been pathetic.

"The only case I've read about where the judge wasn't sympathetic to the surrogate was when she was implanted with a donor egg from the potentially adopting mother. In that case, I can't remember where it was, but I could look it up for you," she said seriously, "the judge ruled that there was no blood relation to the surrogate, that the sperm and the egg were donated by the adopting parents. And she gave the kid to them. But in this case, you don't have those circumstances going for you, and the guy was a real fool to make a deal with a minor."

"I know. But sometimes people do crazy stuff when they're desperate to have kids."

"Tell me about it." Alice sat back in the chair and groaned. "For two years I took hormones that I thought were going to kill me. They made me so damn sick, I felt like I was having chemotherapy instead of hormones to have a baby." Then she smiled up at her associate, looking young as she shrugged her shoulders. "But I got two great kids out of it, so I guess it was worth it." And the Robinsons had gotten nothing. A baby they pretended to call Jeanne Marie, whom they had never seen, and maybe never would.

"Why do people go to those lengths, Ali? Sometimes you can't help but wonder. I know, your boys are great . . . but if you hadn't had kids, would that have been so awful?"

"Yeah"—she said softly—"to me . . . and to Bruce too. We knew we wanted a family." She threw a leg over the arm of the chair as she looked earnestly at her longtime friend. "Most people aren't as brave as you are," Alice said quietly. She had always admired Pilar for her certainty and her convictions.

"I'm not brave. . . . How can you say a thing like that?"

"Yes, you are. You knew you didn't want kids, so you built your life in a way that worked for you, and you never had them. Most people would be too afraid that that wasn't the 'right' thing to do, so they'd have them anyway, and secretly hate them. You have no idea how many mothers I meet at boy scouts, at karate classes, at school, who really don't like their kids and never should have had them."

"My parents were like that. I guess that's what's always made me so sure. I never wanted a child of mine to go through what I did. I always felt like an outsider, an intruder, a terrible imposition on two people who had more important things to do than talk to a little girl, or maybe even love her." It was heavy stuff, but she had talked about it before. It wasn't a startling revelation, but it saddened Alice anyway. And it made her sad, too, to know that Pilar had intentionally deprived herself of children, which Alice felt was one of the few things in life that really mattered.

"You'd never have been that kind of parent, Pilar. Maybe now that you've married Brad, you should rethink your options."

"Oh, please . . . at my age?" Pilar looked amused. Why was everyone so anxious to know if she and Brad were going to have a baby?

"The world of hormones could be yours too," Alice teased as she stood up and looked across the desk at her. They were good friends, and both women knew that they always would be. "Actually, with your luck, you'd probably get pregnant the first time you tried. And don't give me that shit about 'age.' You're only forty-two. I'm not impressed, Grandma Coleman."

"Thanks. But I think I'll spare myself that little headache anyway. Poor Brad . . . he'd be stunned . . . and so would I." She grinned at her law partner and stood up as she glanced at her watch. She had a lunch date with her stepdaughter, and she was going to be late if she didn't hurry.

"Do you want me to do some digging about

surrogates?" Alice was always a good sport about doing research. "I've got some time this afternoon and tomorrow morning."

"Thanks, but I wouldn't spend the time on it. I don't think they'll call back. I'm not even sure they're going to press for visitation. I think they want the whole shot or nothing. I could be wrong, but I think they're going to find someone cheaper than we are who'll promise them the moon, and wind up offering them visitation, if they're lucky."

"Okay. Let me know if they call."

"I will . . . and thanks for the offer." The two women exchanged a smile, and Alice went back to her own office across the hall. She was less busy than Pilar, less intense, less inclined to do litigation. She liked the interesting cases that involved unusual points of law. If she had been a doctor, she would have done research. And she only worked part time now. She stayed home two days a week with her kids, which didn't bother Pilar. They had their own styles, and Bruce did more than his share of work. He liked the civil suits, the corporate cases that went to court. He loved dealing with the institutions, and Pilar loved the people. They were a good team, and on really tough cases they often conferred, and when necessary they hired on

assistants. It was exactly the way Pilar had always wanted to practice law. She felt capable
and independent and free to choose the cases
she wanted to take on, and she liked the people
she practiced law with. She liked Brad's associ-
ates on the bench too. They had an interesting
circle of friends, even though once in a while
she complained that they never saw anyone except judges and lawyers. But the truth was, she
loved it.

Pilar couldn't imagine a life without work, or
the law. As she drove downtown to meet Nancy,
she found herself wondering, as she always did,
how her stepdaughter could stand an idle life,
without working. She hadn't had a job since
she'd gotten married the year before, and Pilar
thought she should. But Brad insisted that his
children had to lead their own lives, and Pilar
did her best not to interfere, or contradict him.
But it wasn't always easy. She had her own
opinions too. Her own list of things she believed in, and work was high on that list. But
apparently not on Nancy's.

When Pilar got to the Paradise, she was ten
minutes late, and Nancy was already waiting for
her, wearing a dark knit dress and boots and a
red coat, her long blond hair brushed back and

held with a velvet ribbon. And as usual, she looked very pretty.

"Hi, darling. You look great!" Pilar swept into her seat, glanced at the menu, ordered as soon as the waiter came, and turned her attention to Nancy. She had the vague feeling that something was bothering her, but she didn't want to pry, and she decided to wait and see what surfaced during lunch. But she was in no way prepared for Nancy's news, which didn't come until dessert, which was a large piece of chocolate decadence with whipped cream and chocolate sauce. Pilar was impressed by her choice when she ordered, and even more so when she saw it. Nancy was certainly in good health and eating well, but at least it didn't show, she was as thin as ever.

"I've got something to tell you." Nancy grinned as she ate great goopy forkfuls of the cake and whipped cream while Pilar watched her.

"I've got something to tell you too. If you eat enough desserts like that, you're going to weigh three hundred pounds by Christmas." She was mildly horrified but amused, too; in some ways Nancy was still such a little girl. And she looked like one as she grinned impishly at Pilar and devoured another huge glob of cake and whipped cream, and then another.

"I'm going to get fat anyway," she said wickedly as Pilar sipped her coffee.

"Oh, yeah? How come? Too many bonbons and TV? I keep telling you, even though your father says I should mind my own business, that you should go to work. Do something . . . even charity work . . . get out of the house . . . get busy . . ."

"I'm having a baby," Nancy interrupted softly, smiling at her stepmother victoriously. It was like a great mystery she had solved, or a secret that only she had, as Pilar watched her in amazement.

"You are?" Pilar hadn't even thought of that. She was such a baby herself that she didn't seem ready for a child of her own, and yet she was twenty-six, the same age Pilar had been when she met Bradford, sixteen years before, almost half a lifetime. "You're pregnant?" Why did that seem so incredible to her? she wondered afterward. But it did. It seemed absurd. And impossible to imagine.

"The baby's due in June. We wanted to be sure everything was okay before I told you. I'm three months pregnant."

"Wow!" Pilar sat back and stared at her. "I'm

speechless." Babies were so much not a part of her life that she never even thought about them, or she hadn't, until that morning. "Are you happy, sweetheart?" Or scared? Or mad? What did one feel? What was it like? She couldn't even imagine it, and had never wanted to. She had never been able to understand that particular craving. If anything, her earnest desire had been *not* to have them.

"I'm very happy, and Tommy's been just terrific." Her husband was twenty-eight years old, and working at IBM. He had a good job, and he would probably be a very good father, but to Pilar and Brad, they always seemed like such children. In some ways, even Todd, her younger brother, always seemed more mature than they did. "It's really wonderful. Except in the beginning I was sick, but now I'm fine," she said simply, polishing off the last of the chocolate decadence as Pilar watched her in fascination.

"Would you like another one?" Pilar said in jest, and Nancy nodded in answer.

"Sure."

"Nancy Coleman, don't you dare! You'll weigh two hundred pounds by the time you have the baby."

"I can hardly wait." The younger woman

grinned, and Pilar laughed as she reached for the check, and then leaned over to kiss her.

"Good for you, sweetheart. I'm happy for you both. Your dad is certainly going to be impressed. This is his first grandchild."

"I know. We thought we'd come by and tell him on the weekend. Don't say anything to him till then, okay?"

"Of course not. I wouldn't spoil the surprise." But it struck her odd that the little girl who had once so vehemently objected to her now told her her most intimate secrets. There was some kind of symmetry in that, or irony at least. They had indeed come full circle.

They left each other outside the restaurant, and Pilar went back to her office after that, grinning to herself. People wanted to know if she and Brad wanted kids, and instead they were having a grandchild. Eventually, she forgot about Nancy's news and concentrated on her work.

It was a long, tiring day, and she was relieved when Brad picked her up and offered to take her out to dinner. She left her car in the garage, and she was grateful not to have to go home and cook. They had a quiet dinner at Louie's Restaurant instead, and he was in an excellent mood as he ordered their dinner.

"What happened to you today?" she inquired with a wry smile, as she sat back in her seat and began to unwind. It had been an odd day for her, filled with hard work, endless demands on the part of her clients, some strange moments, and some unfamiliar feelings. She still couldn't get over Nancy's news, or the prospect of her baby.

"I ended the longest case in recent history today, and I could dance, I'm so relieved." He had had a case in his courtroom that had gone on for two months, and it was tedious and sometimes incredibly boring.

"What happened?"

"The jury acquitted the defendant, and I think they were right."

"He must be a happy man tonight." It brought back memories of her clients when she was a public defender.

"I am a happy man too." Brad smiled at her, looking immensely relieved. "No homework. What about you? Looks like today was a long one."

"It was. Long and strange. I had some people in my office this morning about a surrogate mother/adoption case. The husband foolishly paid a minor to father his child, and ultimately she refused to give up the baby. The state

brought criminal proceedings against him because of her age, eventually dropped them, but
they won't even let him see the child. They
were a strange pair, there was a sad kind of
quiet desperation about them, an unreasoning
attachment to the child, whom they've never
even seen, but call 'Jeanne Marie.' It was so
weird and so depressing. I thought about them
all day, and I really don't think anybody's going
to be able to do much for them. Maybe some
visitation rights eventually, but not much more
than that, unless the birth mother abuses the
child. I don't know . . . it's hard to imagine
what they're feeling. They were so desperate to
have that baby. They tried everything they
could for years to have a child, then tried all the
adoption agencies, and finally this. . . . It's
just a damn shame he went to a minor to
do it."

"He probably would have had problems anyway. You know how those things turn out. Look
at Baby M, and I can cite you a dozen other
cases like it. I don't think surrogates are the
answer."

"For some people, maybe they are."

"Why? Why not just adopt?" He loved talking to her, arguing with her, exploring ideas,
and discussing cases. They were always su-

premely discreet, but discussing their work like that always reminded him of their years as opponents in the courtroom, and what a fine adversary she had been. Sometimes he really missed it.

"Some people can't adopt. They're too poor, too old, whatever. And you can't find babies that easily. Besides, these people really seemed to care that it was *his* baby. The woman almost apologized to me that it was her fault they couldn't have kids." It had been so odd watching her, and so pathetic. Everything about her seemed to reek of sorrow and failure.

"You think you'll hear from them again?"

"No, I don't. I told them what I thought about the case, and I don't think they liked it. I told them it would probably take a long time, and that there was probably very little I could do anyway. I didn't want to give them false hope, which would have been cruel."

"That's my baby, sock it to 'em." He laughed as they finished their first course, and she denied it. But he liked the fact that she was always honest.

"I had to be straight with them," she explained, knowing she didn't really have to explain. He knew her so well. "They wanted that baby so badly. Sometimes that's hard to understand." It was hard to understand a lot of things, even Nancy's obvious and total pleasure about her baby. Pilar could see it, but she couldn't imagine feeling it. And as she had watched her, she had felt like a stranger looking into a brightly lit window. She liked what she saw on the other side, but she hadn't the vaguest idea how to get there, or if she even belonged there. All those feelings of pleasure about a child were totally foreign to her.

"What are you looking so pensive about?" He was watching her and she smiled, as he reached out and took her hand across the table.

"I don't know . . . maybe I'm getting old and philosophical . . . sometimes I think I'm changing, and that scares me a little."

"It must be the shock of getting married," he teased. "It's changed me too. I feel about fifty years younger." He had just turned sixty-two, and he was still the envy of the courthouse. But he grew serious as he looked at her. "What makes you think you're changing?"

"I don't know." She couldn't tell him about Nancy's baby until Nancy told him herself. "I had lunch with a friend. She's pregnant, and she was so excited, she was like a little kid herself."

"First child?" She nodded. "That is exciting," he went on, "but babies always are, even if you have ten of them, there always seems to be room for one more. And even if you're less than thrilled when you find out, it's always exciting when they come. Who was the friend?"

"Oh, someone who worked for us at the office. Maybe it was just that I saw her after those people who'd lost the child to the surrogate. They all seem so sure, so anxious for a child. . . . How do they know they want a baby that much? How do they know they'll even like him when he grows up, or want to be friends with him? My God, Brad, it's a lifetime commitment, with no reprieve. How do people do it?"

"Just nature, I guess. You can't ask too many questions. Maybe it's easier for you that you escaped it." In all the years he'd known her, she had never longed for a child, and he didn't mind, he had his own. They had their work, their lives, his children when they saw them now. They had interests, activities, friends, they traveled to L.A. and New York, and Europe whenever they had time. It would have been more difficult if they had a child, not impossible, but harder to arrange. But he knew that Pilar had no yearnings at all in that direction.

"How do you know I have escaped it?" she asked softly as she looked at him across the table.

"Are you telling me something, Pilar?" he answered, surprised at the look in her eyes. There was something unhappy there, something unfulfilled that he had never seen there before, and then it was gone. It had been there for only the most fleeting moment. And then she looked like herself again, and he decided she was only tired.

"I'm just telling you that I don't understand. I don't understand what they feel and why . . . and why I've never felt it."

"Maybe you will one day," he said gently, but she laughed this time.

"Yeah. When I'm fifty. I think it's a little too late for that even now." She remembered her mother's warning at their wedding.

"Not really, not if you really want it. Now me, however, that's another matter entirely. You'd have to get me a wheelchair and a hearing aid as shower gifts if you ever had a baby."

"Not likely, my love." But a baby wasn't likely either. She didn't want a child, it had just startled her when Nancy had told her she was pregnant. For the first time in her life, she had felt the tiniest gnawing, the smallest emptiness, the briefest of questions, and then she reminded herself of all that she did have, and told herself she was crazy.

CHAPTER
═ 3 ═

Christmas at the Goodes was always an intense affair. Gayle and Jack came every year with their three girls, because Jack's parents had been much older and were both gone now. And Sam and Seamus came almost every year with their two, because Seamus's family was so far away that most years they just couldn't get to Ireland to see them. He was only too happy to stay at home, and spend Christmas Eve and Christmas Day in Pasadena with his in-laws. And the three sisters always had a good time. This year, of course, Diana and Andy were there. And when the three sisters were setting the table on Christmas Eve, Gayle nudged Diana and gave her a look that Diana had always hated. It was the same look Gayle had always given her when she knew Diana had gotten a bad grade, or burned the cookies she was supposed to take to girl scouts. It was a look that said *you failed . . . you blew it, didn't you?* It was something that happened just between them, and Diana tried to pretend she didn't understand, as she carefully folded the napkins.

"Well?" Gayle asked pointedly, as she put the plates on the table. "Come on . . ." She couldn't believe her younger sister was that stupid. She had to know what she meant, but as she pressed her again, Sam started to look worried. She didn't want them to fight on Christmas. "Are you pregnant yet?" Gayle asked pointedly. It was the bad grade again. She had really blown it this time, and Diana's hand shook as she set the last lace napkin on a plate at their Christmas table. They were using the Christmas plates her mother used every year, there was a huge arrangement of red tulips in the middle of the table, and the table looked really lovely.

"No, I'm not pregnant yet, we just haven't had time." Of course not, we've only made love at the right time every month for six months, but she was damned if she would admit it to her sister. "We've both been too busy."

"With what? Your career?" She said it as

though Diana's job were something she should be ashamed of. In Gayle's opinion, *real* women stayed home and took care of their children. "You won't fill that big house of yours like that, you know. You'd better get to it, kid. Time's a wastin'."

Really? Diana thought. Whose? What was their damn hurry, and why did they have to ask her? She had been afraid of that this year. She had even suggested to Andy that they go to the Douglases this time, but he hadn't been able to get away from the network, and they couldn't not come if they were in L.A. Her parents would have been crushed and they wouldn't have understood it.

"It's no big deal," Sam intervened, as she always had, the peacemaker putting oil on troubled waters. "You've got plenty of time. You're both young. You'll probably get pregnant next year."

"Who's pregnant? Not again!" Seamus asked, as he walked through the dining room on the way to the kitchen. "You girls, you get pregnant every time a man looks at you!" He rolled his eyes and shuddered, and they all laughed as he left and then stuck his head around the kitchen door again. "Is the bride pregnant?" he asked. It had just occurred to him, and Diana was quick to shake her head, wishing she had never come. Their questions were a knife in her heart, and for the first time in her life she hated them all, especially her sisters.

"No, I'm not, Seamus. Sorry."

"Well, try again, m'dear . . . and try . . . and try . . . and try. . . . What fun you'll have! Lucky Andy!!" He disappeared again then, and Sam and Gayle laughed, but Diana didn't. She went back into the kitchen herself, without saying a word, and went to help their mother.

And it was after dinner when the subject came up again, but this time it was Diana who asked the questions. She was sitting alone with Jack in the den while the others played charades in the living room, but she had wanted to be alone with her father by the fire. He had gone up to bed finally, and she was quietly rocking in her father's favorite chair when Jack came in and sat down beside her.

"Everything all right with you?" he asked quietly, as he lit his pipe. He had watched her at dinner that night and he didn't think she seemed happy.

"I'm okay." And then she looked up at him with worried eyes, and decided to ask him. "Don't say anything to Gayle, but I wanted—I wondered if I should come and talk to you. . . . How long do you think it's normal to take to get pregnant?" He couldn't help but smile at the question.

"Two weeks . . . five seconds . . . two years . . . it's different for everyone, Diana. You've only been married for six months, you've both got busy, stressful lives. I don't think you should even think about it for a year. Some people say that two years without contraception and no pregnancy means you've got a problem, some think you ought to check it out after one. It takes most couples, with ideal conditions, about a year to get pregnant. If you were older, you might want to start getting worried after six months. But at your age, I'd give it a good year, maybe longer, before I started to worry." She looked immensely relieved and she thanked him before Andy came into the room and joined them. They sat and talked for a long time, about the world economy, the continuing problems in the Middle East, their jobs, the coming year. And for the first time in months, Diana felt relieved and happy. Maybe there was hope after all, she thought to herself as they left, and she thanked her mother, and especially Jack. She hugged him, and he knew what she meant, as he smiled at her.

"Take care," he said quietly, and then they left. The others were spending the night so that the children could have Christmas with their grandparents the next morning. But Diana hadn't wanted to spend the night this year. She had wanted desperately to go home with Andy.

"You okay, sweetheart?" he asked as they drove home on the deserted freeway.

"I'm fine." She smiled. And for the first time in months, she meant it. She snuggled up next to him, and they drove home in peaceful silence. It had been a long day, but a good one. And when they got home, they went to bed, and lay there talking softly about the dreams they shared. Diana felt happy and relaxed, and when they made love that night, for the first time in months, she didn't worry about getting pregnant. It was the wrong time of the month for that anyway, but it was a relief just to make love because they wanted to, without thinking of the date or time, their dreams, or their intentions.

"Oh God, I love you. . . ." Charlie whispered huskily to Barb, as he pulled her down next to him on the couch, and they made love again, with all the little Christmas lights on their tree blinking brightly at them.

"What is it with you?" she teased. "Do Christmas trees make you horny, or what?" It was the third time they'd made love that night, but he could never keep his hands off her. And she always wandered around with no clothes, her fabulous figure enticing him until she drove him crazy.

"I'm just nuts about you," he whispered into her hair as they lay side by side on the couch after they made love. He had already given her her present that night. It was a gold necklace with an amethyst on it. He knew she'd love it, because it was her birthstone. And she had given him a sweater and a tie, a bottle of French champagne, and a special cushion for his back, for his long commute on the freeway. He liked his gifts, though not as much as she liked hers. He had also bought her a black leather skirt, and a very sexy black sweater.

"How about if we drink some of your champagne?" Barbie sat up on one elbow and looked down at him with tired pleasure.

"Uh uh." He pulled her back down next to him. "I'm saving that."

"What for?" She was disappointed. She loved champagne, which was why she had bought it.

"I'm saving it for something important."

"Like what? The way you've been acting to-night, I'd say Christmas was pretty important."

He laughed and shook his head again. "Nope. I mean *important*. Like when you get the Academy Award, or at least a part in a Steven Spielberg picture . . . or your own series . . . or maybe our tenth anniversary . . . or"—he savored the last one—"when we have a baby."

She looked annoyed when she sat up. "Well, I'm glad I'm not holding my breath for those events. It doesn't sound like you're ever going to drink it."

"Sure I am."

"Yeah? When? I hope you're not saving it for a baby." It made her mad when he brought that up. She didn't want to be pressured.

"Why not, Barb?" He wanted one so badly. He wanted so much for them to become a family, and she just didn't get it.

"Because I don't want one. Believe me, I grew up surrounded by kids, and they're a pain in the ass. I can tell you've never seen one." She was much more outspoken with him now, about not wanting kids, than she had been before they were married.

"Yes, I have seen kids. I've been one too." He tried to tease her, but she wasn't amused. Babies did not amuse her.

"Besides, maybe we can't even have one," she said, hoping to scare him off, or at least deter him slightly, for the time being.

"Why not?" He looked shocked. It was the first he'd ever heard of it. She'd never said that before, or not nearly as bluntly. "Is something wrong? Why didn't you tell me?"

"I don't know if there's anything wrong, but I've never been as sloppy about birth control as I am with you, you're always sneaking up on me and not giving me time to take care of things . . . and even after a year and a half of that, I've never gotten pregnant." He wanted to ask her if she had with anyone else, but he didn't want to know, so he said nothing.

"That doesn't mean anything. We're probably not doing it at the right time. You can't just do those things by accident, you know, and expect to get pregnant." But she had before, three times before she left Salt Lake City, and twice in Vegas. She had never been very lucky. Except with Charlie, and more than once she'd wondered. It was either the combination of the two of them, or him, and knowing her own history, she suspected the latter, which didn't bother her at all. She was delighted. But she realized, as she looked at him, that she shouldn't have said anything, at least not on Christmas Eve. He looked deeply worried.

"Have you ever gotten anyone pregnant?" she asked, as she poured them each a glass of wine, and held his out to him. She was still naked, and just seeing her like that brought on an erection. His reactions were certainly healthy.

"Not that anyone's ever told me," he said pensively, sipping at the wine and watching her.

"That doesn't mean anything," she said kindly, sorry she'd brought it up. It seemed unfair to worry him on Christmas. "Girls don't always tell."

"Don't they?" He took another glass of wine, and then another, and after the third glass he got amorous again, but by then he'd had too much to drink, and Barbara led him off to bed, and got in beside him. "I love you," he said to her, as he held her close, feeling her huge breasts pressed against his chest, just the way he loved it. She was so sensuous, and so wonderful and so willing. She was the perfect girl and he knew he loved her.

"I love you too." She smoothed his hair like a child's as he drifted off to sleep, and she held him, wondering why it meant so much to him to have a baby. She knew about the orphanage, and she had had her own problems, too, but the last thing she wanted in life was a family again, or the headache of a baby. "Sleep tight," she whispered as she kissed him, but he was already fast asleep in her arms, dreaming of Christmas morning.

CHAPTER
═══ 4 ═══

In May, Pilar invited Nancy to the house for lunch. Brad was playing golf, and Nancy's husband was out of town for a few days. It was a nice chance for the two women to spend some time together.

Pilar made lunch, while her stepdaughter sat soaking up the sun on the terrace. She was hugely pregnant by then, her due date was only four weeks away, and to Pilar, she looked absolutely enormous. Nancy opened one eye, baking in the sun, as Pilar returned, carrying a tray. And in spite of her size, Nancy jumped up to help her. She was wearing white maternity shorts and a huge pink shirt, and up until only the week before, she and her husband had still been playing tennis.

"Sorry, Pilar, here . . . let me help. . . ." She took the tray from her, and helped set it down on the glass table. Pilar had made a big green salad, and some pasta. "Wow, this looks good." Her appetite had been enormous for the past eight months, but she hadn't gained an undue amount of weight and she still looked very pretty. In fact, Pilar had said to Brad recently, she looked even prettier now that she was pregnant. There was something softer and less angular about her face, something peaceful in her eyes. There was a kind of aura about her now, which intrigued Pilar. She had seen it in other women before, but she had no idea what it felt like. Just looking at Nancy suddenly intrigued her. It frightened her too. But more than that, Pilar was frightened by her own feelings. She seemed suddenly so different. And everything about Nancy fascinated her. She was gentler, less caustic, "mellower," as her husband said. In a funny way, she had grown up in the past eight months, and she seemed less like a spoiled child herself now.

The two women sat down to lunch, and Pilar smiled as she watched her. Nancy looked as though she had a huge beachball concealed under her pink shirt. She could hardly get around it to reach for something on the table.

"How does all that feel?" Pilar asked with a mystified look. It was all so foreign to her. She had had pregnant friends before, but no one really close to her, and she had never paid much attention. Most of her friends had been of the generation that had opted for careers instead of babies. And those who had given in to nature's beckonings had done so late in life, and by then they seemed to drift out of Pilar's immediate circle. "Does it feel weird, or wonderful?" she asked as they ate their salad, and Pilar watched her eyes, as though looking for the secret of life there.

"I don't know." Nancy smiled. "I guess weird sometimes. You get used to it. I forget about it actually. Sometimes I feel like I always was like this. I haven't been able to tie my shoelaces in weeks. Tommy has to do it for me. But I think the weirdest part is knowing that there's a whole person in there, who's going to come out and live with us for the next twenty years. He's going to depend on us, and expect things from us for the rest of his, or her, life. I can't even begin to imagine what that feels like."

"Neither can I," Pilar said pensively, except that she did know in a way, because Nancy and Todd had expected something from her for the past fourteen years. But in some ways, that had always been an option. They weren't hers, and if she and Brad had ever broken up, earlier on anyway, she could have chosen not to see them again, although she certainly would have. But she didn't *have* to, they weren't *hers*. This baby was going to be Nancy's forever. It was going to be a part of her, and a part of Tom, and it was going to be its own person. It was going to be someone important to them for the rest of their lives. The mere thought of that had always terrified Pilar, and now suddenly she found it very touching.

"I think it's wonderful. It's a whole new life, a whole new world, a relationship with someone who's a part of you, who may have a million things in common with you, or nothing at all. It's fascinating, isn't it?" She was completely intrigued by it, although she had to admit that it still seemed like an awesome responsibility to her, and she wouldn't have wanted to go through the birth process to get there. That part of it had never appealed to her at all, and looking at the size of her stepdaughter's girth, she didn't envy her what she would have to go through. Pilar had seen a movie of a delivery once, and all she could think of as she watched was that she was glad she would never have to do anything like that; she was absolutely sure she was never going to have a baby.

"It's funny," Nancy said as she sat back in her chair and looked out at the Pacific Ocean, "most of the time I don't think about the relationship we'll have, or how much like us the baby will be, I just think of how sweet the baby will be, how small, how dependent on us . . . and Tommy is so excited." So was she, it was the most exciting thing that had ever happened to her, and she was nervous about the birth, but all she could really focus on now was the baby. And then she looked at her stepmother, and asked her something she had always wondered about, and never dared say. "How come you and Dad . . . I mean . . . how come you never had children?" As soon as she had said the words, she wanted to take them back again. What if Pilar couldn't?

But Pilar only smiled, and shrugged her shoulders. "I never wanted to. My own childhood was pretty strange, and I've never wanted to put anyone else through that. And we had you and Todd. But I really never wanted kids when I was young. I guess it was just a part missing from my own psychological package. I looked at the women I knew who got married right after school, tied down with two or three kids, in houses and lives they hated. They all looked so trapped to me. They never did anything. It always seemed like a choice to me, and the things I wanted out of life just didn't include children. And after I went to law school, I really never thought of it. I have my career, and then I met your dad, and I've never looked back. The women who had their kids twenty years ago are sitting at home now, with their kids grown and gone, wondering where their lives went. I'm glad that didn't happen to me. I would have hated every minute of it, hated myself, and the man who condemned me to it."

"But it doesn't have to be like that," Nancy said gently. She had gained new maturity, and broader views in the past months; her world, like her belly, had been slowly growing. "I have friends who do both, who have careers and kids. Lots of them, in fact, some of them are doctors, lawyers, psychologists, writers. It doesn't *have* to be a choice, if you don't want it to be."

"Your generation is a lot better at that than mine was. For us, most of the time, it was a choice. You got the big job, the big break, and crawled your way to the top, or you moved to the suburbs and had kids. It was usually as simple as that. Now, people seem to be able to juggle everything, but a lot of that has to do

with how helpful their husbands are, how flexible, and how badly they want it all. You have to
give up a lot of things if you want a family and a
career. Maybe it's just as well I've never had to
make those choices. I think your dad would
have been great at it, though, if we had had
kids. He was terrific with both of you. But I
guess I just never felt the need. I never had that
longing that some women get, that yearning
that won't end till they have children. I've
heard women talk about it, like a disease, but
thank God, I've never felt it." But even just saying those words she felt an odd twinge now.
Like the faintest beginnings of a toothache.

"You're not sorry, Pilar? You don't think you'd
miss it one day, that you'll look back and wish
you'd had them? It's not too late, you know—I
know two women who just had babies who are
older than you are."

"Yeah, who? Sarah is in the Bible, and who's
the other one?" She laughed and Nancy insisted
that she wasn't too old. But something told her
she was, that it was too late for her. She'd made
her choices long ago, and she wasn't unhappy
with them. She had to admit that lately she'd
thought about it once or twice, particularly
since Nancy had gotten pregnant, but she suspected that most of that was just the tremors of

old age, the biological clock ticking away its last moments. She wasn't about to be swayed by it, no matter how touching she thought it all was, or how sweet Nancy's belly looked to her. She was just getting soft in her old age, and that didn't necessarily mean she wanted a baby. She reminded herself of that as she cleared the table.

"No, I don't think I'll be sorry later on. Sure, it would be nice to have a child then, to have someone to talk to and love and be loved by, when I sit in my rocking chair on the porch thirty years from now, but I have you, and I think that's just fine. I don't have regrets about my life. I've done exactly what I wanted to do, in just the way I set out to, and just when I wanted to do it. You can't ask for more than that in life." Or could you? . . . the bitch was that suddenly there were these vague echoes. She had been so sure of herself all her life, so positive of what was right for her, and she was still sure . . . or was she?

"I don't exactly see you sitting in a rocking chair in thirty years. I can't even see my dad doing that then." He would be ninety-two by then. "Maybe you should think about it again." She thought the baby she was going to have was going to be so wonderful that everyone ought to try it.

"I'm too old to think about it now," Pilar said firmly, as though trying to convince herself. "I'm forty-three. I'll be much better suited to being a grandmother when your baby comes." But saying that somehow made her feel sad, and that startled her. Suddenly, she had skipped the middle part. She had been young, and now she was old. She had never had children of her own, and now she was going to be a grandmother. It felt like she had missed the party.

"I don't know why you think you're too old. Forty-three just isn't old anymore. Lots of women have babies at your age," Nancy insisted.

"That's true, but lots of women don't. I think I might be one of them. If nothing else, it's more familiar." She went inside to make coffee then, for herself if not Nancy. They chatted for a while into the afternoon, and then Nancy left. She had some errands to do, and she was having dinner with friends that night. She really seemed to be enjoying her pregnancy, and Pilar had been fascinated to watch her as they talked, she kept rubbing her stomach as though she were talking to it, and once or twice Pilar saw the pink shirt jump, as the baby moved or kicked, and Nancy laughed. She said the baby was very active.

But after Nancy left, Pilar walked aimlessly around the house. She did the dishes from lunch, she sat down at her desk for a while and stared out the window. She had brought some legal files home, but she couldn't keep her mind on them, all she could think of were the things she and Nancy had said that afternoon . . . the questions her stepdaughter had asked her . . . would she be sorry one day? . . . would she regret not having children when she was old? . . . and what about when Bradford died, God forbid, but what if he did and she had nothing left of him, except her memories and another woman's children? But how ridiculous that was, you didn't have babies just to hang on to someone, to have a piece of them when they died. But why did people have children? And why had she never wanted any before, and yet now it was slowly becoming a gnawing question? And why now? Why, after all these years? Was it just jealousy of Nancy, a desire to be young, some crazy idea that had come to her just before menopause? Was this beginning of the end, or the beginning of the beginning? Or was it anything at all? She seemed to have none of the answers.

In the end, after a long battle with herself, Pilar put her legal files away, and called Marina. She felt foolish even as she dialed, but she knew she had to talk to someone. She was just too unsettled after her lunch with Nancy.

"Hello?" Marina had on her official voice, and Pilar smiled as she heard her.

"It's only me. Where were you? You took forever to answer." For a minute, she'd been worried the older woman wasn't home, and it was a relief when she finally heard her voice at the other end.

"Sorry, I was out in the garden, pruning roses."

"Can I interest you in a walk on the beach?"

Marina hesitated, but only for a moment. The truth was that she was enjoying her gardening, but she also knew that Pilar never invited her to walk on the beach, except when she was deeply troubled.

"Something wrong?"

"Not really. I don't know. I think I'm just rearranging the furniture in my head. It's all the same old stuff, but I'm moving it around to different places." It was an odd way to explain what she was feeling, but Pilar just hadn't found the right words yet.

"As long as there's still a place for me to sit

down." Marina smiled, and set her gardening gloves down on the kitchen table. "Want me to come and pick you up?"

"I'd love that." Pilar sighed. Marina was always there for her, always accessible, and warm and kind. Her brothers and sisters still called her in the middle of the night with all their problems, and it was easy to see why. She was so sharp and intelligent, and so incredibly loving. She offered Pilar everything her parents never had, even if it just meant listening sometimes, or working through a difficult decision. Most of the time, Pilar talked to Brad, but now and then something came up that only another woman would understand, although this time she felt sure that Marina would tell her she was crazy.

She was there in less than half an hour, and they drove slowly down toward the ocean, as Marina glanced at her from time to time. Pilar looked all right to her, but it was obvious that she was worried.

"So, what's on your mind?" she asked as she finally stopped the car. "Are we talking about business, or pleasure . . . or the lack of it?" Pilar smiled and shook her head, as they got out of the car. "You and Brad had a fight."

"No, it's nothing like that." Pilar was quick to

reassure her. In fact, things had never been better between them. Getting married had been
the best thing they'd ever done, and more than
ever she wished they had done it sooner. "Actually," she took a deep breath as they started to
walk on the sand, "funnily enough, it's Nancy."

"Again? After all these years?" Marina looked
surprised to hear it. "I thought she'd been behaving herself for the last ten years. I'm disappointed to hear that."

But Pilar laughed as she shook her head
again. "No, it's not that either. She's fine. She's
going to have the baby in a few weeks, and that
seems to be all she can think of."

"It would probably be all you'd think of too if
you had a fifty-pound watermelon strapped to
your belly . . . when you could get it off might
easily become an all-consuming question. It
would to me anyway, I hate carrying anything
heavier than a quarter."

"Oh, shut up." Pilar laughed at her again.
"Don't make me laugh, Mina." It was a name
that her nephews and nieces had called her for
years, and Pilar called her that at special moments. "The crazy thing is that I'm not even
sure what I want to tell you . . . or why I feel
the way I do . . . I'm not even sure what I
feel, if it's real, or an illusion."

"My God, it sounds serious." Marina was half teasing, but she was also watching Pilar's face, and her eyes, and she knew she was deeply troubled and confused. But she also knew that eventually the younger woman would say what she had to. Marina was in no hurry, she could let her take her time to find the words to match her feelings.

Pilar looked at her sheepishly as she tried to put words to the tangle of emotions. "I don't even know where to start. . . . I think it was five months ago, when Nancy told me she was pregnant . . . or maybe it was after that. . . . I don't know. . . . I just don't know anything . . . except I keep wondering if I've made a mistake . . . maybe even a huge mistake. . . ." She looked agonized and Marina looked genuinely surprised by what she'd just said.

"You mean by marrying Brad?"

"No, of course not." Pilar was quick to shake her head. "I mean by being so adamant about never having children. What if I was wrong? What if I regret it one day? What if everyone else is right, and I'm just neurotic because my parents were so rotten to me. . . . What if I could have been a decent mother after all?" She looked anguished as she turned to Marina. And

Marina pointed her to a dune, where they sat down out of the wind, and the older woman put an arm around her shoulders.

"I'm sure you would have been a very good mother, if that's what you wanted to do. But being good at something, or potentially good at something, doesn't justify doing it, unless you want to. I'm sure you would have made a very good fireman, too, but it was hardly a necessary step in your career. Let me remind you that no matter how many people do it, it is still not obligatory to have children. It doesn't make you a bad person, or mean that you're strange, or dangerous, or queer if you choose not to have them. Some people just don't want kids. That's okay. It's fine, if that's what suits you."

"Haven't you ever wondered if you've done the right thing? Haven't you ever been sorry you didn't have children?" She had to know, she was moving into uncharted waters now, and Marina had been there before her.

"Sure," Marina told her honestly. "Once or twice. Every time one of my sisters or brothers or nieces or nephews puts a baby in my arms, there's a tug at my heart, and I think . . . shit, I want one of those! . . . but for me, those feelings are always gone in about ten minutes. I had twenty years of wiping runny noses, changing diapers, cleaning up vomit, doing four or five loads of laundry a day, picking them up at school, taking them to the park, tucking them in at night, helping them make their beds. Christ, I didn't even start college until I was twenty-five, and I didn't get to law school until I was thirty. But at least I made it, and I love all of them, except maybe one or two, but the truth is I love them too. . . . I had some wonderful times with them, some incredibly precious moments. But I didn't want to do that again. I wanted time for me, for study, for work, for friends, for men. I would have gotten married eventually if the right man had come along. And the right guy did, once or twice, but I always had some good reason for not getting tied down at that particular moment. I think the truth is that I was happy being single. I loved my work, I loved the kids. But I'm glad now that I never had any of my own. Sure, it would be great to have a daughter or son who would care what happens to me when I get old, but so what, I have you and ten brothers and sisters and their kids." It was as honest as she could be, and Pilar was grateful to her.

"What if it's not enough one day? What if it's not the same?" Friends and siblings were not the same as one's own children, or were they?

"Then it's my mistake. But I'm not complaining, for the moment." She was sixty-five years old, and going strong. She loved her work on the bench, and she had more friends than anyone Pilar knew. And whenever she could, she seemed to be flying somewhere to see someone, nieces, nephews, sisters, friends. She was a happy, fulfilled woman. And Pilar had felt that she was, too . . . until lately.

"What about you?" Marina turned to look at her, wondering why she seemed so confused and looked so unhappy. "What's eating you, Pilar? Why all these questions about having babies? Are you pregnant? Are you asking me what I think about an abortion?"

"No." Pilar shook her head miserably. "I think I'm asking you what you think about having a baby. And no, I'm not pregnant." She wasn't even sure she wanted to be. But suddenly, for the first time in her life, she had doubts about the path she had chosen.

"I think it would be fine, if that's what you want. What does Brad think?"

"I don't know. I think he'd probably tell me I'm nuts, and he might be right. I was always so sure I didn't want kids. Mostly, because I didn't want to be like my mother."

"You never could be. I hope you at least know

that much by now. You're two entirely different people."

"Thank God."

"Or maybe I should say that one of you is a person, and the other is a little strange." She could never understand the situations Pilar had described to her over the years. All she could do was agree with her young friend that her parents should never have had children. "Is that the only thing that stopped you? Your fear of being like them?"

"It was part of it, but not everything. I just never felt the need for all that. But I never felt the need to be married either, and now I'm sorry I didn't do it sooner."

"That kind of regret is a waste of time. Just enjoy it now, don't spoil it by looking back over your shoulder."

"I don't. But I just don't know what's happening to me . . . I feel as though I'm suddenly changing."

"That's not such a bad thing. It would be a lot worse if you were rigid and immovable. Maybe this is the best thing that could happen to you, Pilar. Maybe you should have a baby."

"But what if I didn't like it? What if I'm just jealous of Nancy, or some insane thing? What if my mother's right, and the baby had three heads, because I'm so old?" There were so many questions to which even Marina didn't have the answers.

"What if there's human life on Venus? You can't know everything, Pilar. All you can do is follow your heart and your mind, and do the best you can. And if you think you want a baby now, then give it some serious thought, and don't worry so damn much about the outcome. For heaven's sake, if everyone worried about it that much, no one would ever have any children."

"But what about you? If you're not unhappy not having children, maybe I wouldn't be either."

"That's ridiculous, and you know it. We're two different people. Our life experiences weren't for even one moment the same. My life has been filled with children for sixty years, you've had none except Brad's kids, and they were pretty big when you came along. Besides, you're married, and I never have been. And I'm perfectly content about that too. It leaves me free to enjoy a variety of people, in whatever way I choose, and that's a lifestyle that suits me. You're happy married to Brad, and maybe one day you would be sorry if you didn't have children."

Pilar sat silently for a long time, staring at the sand, and then she looked up at her friend again, comforted by her words, but she still hadn't found her answers. "Mina, what would you do if you were me?"

"I'd relax, for one thing. That would do you a world of good. And then I'd go home and talk all this out with Brad, but I wouldn't beat it to death. He's not going to have all the answers either. No one will, not even you. To some extent, one has to take a few chances in life. You have to protect yourself as much as you can, but you still have to jump off the diving board sooner or later. And hope you don't bellyflop into oblivion."

"You have a way with words, Your Honor."

"Thank you." The older woman grinned, and then she looked down at Pilar again. "And for what it's worth, if I were you, I'd go ahead and have a baby, and to hell with all that nonsense about being too old. I think that's what you really want to do, and you're too scared to let yourself say it."

"I think you may be right." She usually was. But Pilar had no idea what Brad would say if she told him she wanted a baby. But for the first time in her life, she had an emptiness, an ache, which she had never known before, and it was beginning to make her seriously unhappy.

They walked slowly back to the car after that, and they said little on the way home. It was one of the nice things for Pilar about being with her. She didn't feel she had to make an enormous effort, and she valued what her friend had said. She just needed time to think about it.

"Take it easy, kid. You'll know what you want eventually. Just listen to yourself. You'll know in your gut what you want. You can't go wrong if you follow that."

"Thank you." She gave Marina a warm hug, and waved as she drove away. It was incredible how she was always there for her. And as Pilar walked slowly into her house, she was smiling.

Brad was home when she got back, he was putting away his golf clubs, and he looked suntanned and relaxed and happy to see her.

"Where've you been? I thought Nancy was coming here today." He put an arm around Pilar and kissed her as they walked out to the terrace.

"She was. She came for lunch. I just went down to the beach for a walk with Marina after she left."

"Oh-oh," he said, looking at the wife he knew so well, "that means trouble."

"What do you mean by that?" She laughed, and he pulled her down on his lap, and she sat there happy for the first time in hours. She was crazy about him, and it was equally obvious that he adored her.

"You never go for walks on the beach unless something big is bugging you. The last time you did that you were trying to decide whether or not to take a new partner in, before that it was whether or not to resign from a case you thought involved fraud, and before that I think you were trying to decide whether or not to marry me. That was a good walk." She laughed, but she couldn't say he was wrong. He was right on all counts. "So what was today's walk all about? Did Nancy give you a hard time?" It would have surprised him, though, because all of that was years behind them, and the two women were good friends now. "Or is something big happening at the office?" She had just won an important case in a civil suit in L.A., and he was proud of her, but he also knew how stressful her job was, and how many difficult decisions she had to make on a daily basis. He liked to help her whenever he could, but sometimes even he couldn't help. She had to make her own decisions.

"No, nothing like that, everything's fine. And

Nancy was adorable today." Adorable, and painful. She had opened a part of Pilar's heart that Pilar hadn't even known was there. She had suspected it once or twice in the past year, but she told herself they were just rumblings that didn't matter. Now she wasn't as sure, and she didn't know what to say to Brad. He would think she was crazy. But maybe Marina was right. She had to tell him. "I don't know . . . it's just women's stuff, I wanted to sort some things out, so I went down to the beach with Marina, and she made a lot of sense, as usual."

"What did she say?" he asked gently, still wanting to help her. He had a lot of respect for their friend, but Pilar was his wife, and he wanted to be there for her.

"I feel so silly," she said vaguely.

And as Brad glanced at her, he saw that there were tears in her eyes, which surprised him. He rarely saw her cry. She seldom lost control, but he suddenly realized she was deeply troubled.

"That looks like heavy stuff for a Saturday afternoon. Should I go back to the beach with you?" He almost meant it.

"Maybe." She smiled, and wiped a tear from the corner of her eye as he pulled her closer to him.

"What's bothering you, sweetheart? I wish

you would tell me." He knew it had to be important, if she'd called Marina.

"You won't believe me if I do. It makes me sound so stupid."

"Try me. I hear a lot of crazy things every day, I'm used to it, and I've got big shoulders."

She nestled against him, her long legs stretched over his, her face next to his as she spoke softly. "I don't know . . . I guess seeing Nancy today touched on a nerve I didn't even know I had . . . something I've thought about once or twice in the last year . . . something I've really never thought about before, or cared about, or even knew I needed. But Nancy asked me if I thought I'd ever regret not having children." Pilar started to cry as she said the words, and her husband looked at her in amazement. She had taken him by surprise and he couldn't believe what he was hearing. "I was always so sure I never wanted kids. But I'm not so sure anymore. All of a sudden I find myself thinking about it. What if she's right, and someday I am sorry? What if it's the heartbreak of my life in my old age? What if"—She could hardly bear to say it, but she knew she had to now—"what if something happens to you, and . . . I never have your baby?" She was crying as she said the words and all he could do was shake his head.

She had stunned him. He had been ready for anything but that. Pilar was the last person he would ever have expected to want a baby.

"Are you serious? Are you really worried about these things?" He couldn't believe it.

"I think I am. That's the awful part. What if I suddenly decide I want children?" She looked panic-stricken, and he had to force himself not to smile.

"You may have to call the fire department if you do, to revive me. Pilar, are you really serious about this? Are you thinking about having children *now*?" After all these years? He hadn't even thought about having babies in more than twenty years, and she had always been so clear about what she wanted.

"Do you think I'm way too old?" she asked, looking glum, but he laughed.

"You're not. But I certainly am. I'm sixty-two, I'll be a grandfather in a few weeks' time. Think how ridiculous I'd look." The whole idea just amazed him.

"No, you wouldn't. Lots of men your age have second families these days, some of them are a lot older than you are."

"I'm getting older by the minute," he said, but looking at her, he could see that she was going through some kind of major crisis. "Pilar, how long have you been thinking about this?"

"I'm not sure," she said honestly. "I think maybe it crossed my mind for the first time after we got married. I decided it was some kind of aberration, and then those people came to see me, about the surrogate's child. I kept thinking how strange they were, how desperate they were to have a baby they didn't even know, but the damndest thing was that a part of me understood them. I don't know, maybe I'm just getting old, and a little peculiar. I think it shook me up when Nancy got pregnant. She always seemed like such a kid, and now she seems so content and self-contained. It's as though she's finally found the real meaning in her life. And what if I've missed the point for all these years? What if being a good lawyer and a decent person and a good wife and stepmother isn't enough? What if it's all about having your own children?"

"Oh dear." He sighed long and hard. She was in a real state, and he couldn't tell her she was wrong. But it was late in the day for them to be thinking about having children. "I wish you'd thought of all this a little sooner."

She looked at him seriously then, and her heart was in her eyes as she asked the question,

"If I decide I can't live without my own child, would you be willing to have one?" It cost her everything she had in her soul to ask him that, but she needed to know. She needed to know where he stood, and if it was even an option. And if he said no, she knew she'd have to live with it. She loved him more than any child, but still she was beginning to think that she might want his baby.

"I don't know," he said honestly. "I haven't thought about that in a long time. I'd have to think about it." She smiled at him, relieved that he hadn't said no. There was a chance, and they both needed to do a lot of thinking, about the responsibility, the burden of it, the changes it would make in their lives. But Pilar was almost beginning to think that all of that would be worth it.

"You'd better do your thinking quickly." She grinned, and he looked rueful as he held her.

"Why?"

"I'm getting older by the minute."

"You . . . monster!" he said, kissing her full on the lips, and then longingly, with great tenderness, as they both became aroused, sitting in the sunshine of their terrace. "I knew something dreadful could happen if I forced you to marry me," he growled at her and she laughed at him. "I just wish I'd known all this thirteen years ago. I'd have forced you to marry me then and you could have had at least a dozen children."

"Let's see," she sat up on his lap, looking at him pensively, "if we start now . . . I'm forty-three . . . maybe we could still squeeze in six or seven. . . ."

"Never mind that . . . it'll be a miracle if I survive one . . . but I want you to understand, I haven't agreed to it yet, I want to think about it."

She pretended to look mollified as she stood up and took him by the hand. "I have a great idea for something you can do while you think about it, Brad . . . come on. . . ." He laughed as she led him slowly toward their bedroom. But he was easy prey for her, he always was, just as she was for him. And her heart felt lighter as he kissed her and followed her into their bedroom.

CHAPTER
==5==

Diana sat up on the table after the doctor had examined her. She had gone to her gynecologist for a Pap smear and her yearly check-up.

"Everything looks fine to me," he said with a pleasant smile. He was a youngish man, and her brother-in-law had recommended him to her two years before because it would have been too awkward going to see him. But Jack thought that Arthur Jones was an excellent physician.

"Any complaints? Lumps, bumps, funny pains, unusual bleeding?" he asked once the exam was over, but Diana shook her head, looking unhappy. She had had her period again the week before, so she knew that once again, she hadn't gotten pregnant.

"My only complaint is that we've been trying to get pregnant for eleven months, and so far, nothing's happened."

"Maybe you're trying too hard," he said, echoing what her sisters had said. Everyone who knew said stupid things like "don't think about it," "you're trying too hard," "just forget about it," "stop worrying," but they didn't know the anguish and the grief and the disappointment it caused each month when she discovered they hadn't succeeded. She was twenty-eight years old, she'd been married for almost a year, she had a husband she loved, a job she enjoyed, and now she wanted a baby.

"A year isn't such a long time," the doctor said reassuringly.

"It seems like a long time to me," she said, smiling wistfully.

"What about your husband? Is he worried about it too?" Maybe he knew something about the problem that Diana didn't. Sometimes men were loath to admit to their mates that they'd had problems in the past, or acute venereal diseases, which might make a difference.

"He keeps saying not to worry about it, that it'll happen sooner or later."

"Maybe he's right." Dr. Jones smiled. "What kind of work does he do?" He wondered if there were chemicals involved, or toxins that might inadvertently affect him.

"He's an attorney for a network." She told him which one, and the doctor looked impressed.

"And you work for a magazine, don't you?" She nodded. "Those are both pretty stressful jobs, that could be part of it. But I do want you to understand that eleven months is not an abnormally long time. Most couples get pregnant after a year, but some people take a little longer. What about a vacation one of these days? That might be just what you need."

Diana smiled. "We're leaving for Europe in a week. We planned it just right. Maybe that will do the trick," she said hopefully, and he saw the anxiety on her face, and decided to listen to it.

"I'll tell you what. If you don't find you're pregnant when you get back, we can start checking into things. I can run a few tests, or I can send you to a specialist, whichever you prefer. There's one man I always feel comfortable recommending. He's reasonable and conservative, but he's also very sharp, and extremely thorough. His name is Alexander Johnston, I'm sure your brother-in-law knows him. He's a little older than we are, but he really knows his stuff, and he won't recommend a lot of unnecessary procedures."

"I'd really like to do that," Diana said, feeling hopeful again. Maybe they would get pregnant in Europe, but if they didn't, there was hope. There was someone they could go to.

She thanked the doctor for his encouragement, and went back to work, and that night she tried to tell Andy about it. She mentioned the name of the specialist and told him she'd ask Jack what he thought of him, but Andy surprised her by snapping at her. He was swamped at work, and he'd had a very hard day at the office, and he was getting tired of her pressing him about making love on certain dates, at certain times, and then having hysterics when she got her period and discovered she wasn't pregnant. They were both healthy and young and came from big families, and it was obvious to him that it was going to work eventually, and they'd have plenty of children. But harping at him about it and crying all the time certainly didn't help the situation.

"For chrissake, Di, give me a break. We don't need a goddamn specialist, we just need some time off to relax. Stop pushing!"

"I'm sorry. . . ." Tears filled her eyes as she looked away from him, he didn't understand

how worried she was, or how afraid that something really was wrong. "I just thought . . . I
thought the specialist might help. . . ." She
was crying as she left the room, and he came to
find her a few minutes later.

"Come on, baby . . . I'm sorry. I'm just so
damn tired and stressed out. I've had a shitload
of headaches at work for the past few weeks.
We'll have a baby, don't worry about it." But
her persistence annoyed him sometimes. She
was so determined to have a child. Sometimes
he felt as though it was the only real goal she'd
ever had, or maybe she was just competing with
her sisters.

"The doctor thought that maybe on vacation . . ." She looked at him apologetically, not
wanting to annoy him. And Andy sighed at her
and took her in his arms.

"The doctor's right. A vacation is just what
we need. Now, promise me you won't worry
about this for a while. I'll bet he also told you
that nothing that's happened so far is abnormal."

She smiled sheepishly at her husband and
nodded. "Yes, he did."

"All right then," he said firmly, and then
kissed her.

And when they went to bed that night, Diana

seemed a little calmer on the subject. Maybe everyone was right. Maybe she was foolish to worry.

She leaned over to kiss Andy good night, but he was already fast asleep, and snoring softly. She looked at him for a long moment, and then lay back on her pillow. It was odd how wanting a baby this much sometimes made her feel so lonely. It was as though no one ever understood how sharp the yearning was, how great the need, not even Andy.

The trip to Europe went splendidly. They went to Paris and the south of France, and then they flew to London to see Andy's brother. And as closely as Diana could figure it, if she'd gotten pregnant, it would have been at the Hotel de Paris in Monte Carlo. The skies had been blue, the hotel was divine, and Andy said he couldn't think of a better place to make a baby.

They enjoyed seeing Nick in London, too, and the rest of the trip was easy and fun, and just what the young couple needed. Neither of them had realized how tense and exhausted they were until they got away from the pressures of L.A. and rediscovered how wonderful it was spending time with each other and relaxing. They went to restaurants and museums and churches, lay on beaches, and even spent a weekend fishing in Scotland with Nick and his girlfriend. When they got back to L.A. in June, they both felt like new people.

Andy went off to his first day of work with a smile, and Diana cheated and took an extra day off to unpack their things and recover from the trip and get her hair done. It was Friday anyway, and she figured that if the magazine had lived without her for this long, they could manage until Monday morning. She wasn't anxious to get back into the hysterics of publishing and she tried to talk Andy into staying home with her, too, but he really felt he had to get back, although he was sorry to do it. But they were both looking forward to the weekend.

Andy played tennis on Saturday morning with Bill Bennington, and it was nice to relax and talk about the trip. They had gone to law school together at UCLA, and Andy had gotten him his job at the network. They were good friends, and sometimes he was someone comforting to talk to. Bill had even been in his wedding.

"How was Nick?" Bill asked as they stopped for something cold to drink after the game.

"Great. He's going out with a cute girl. We spent a weekend with them, fishing in Scotland." Bill had a younger brother, too, the same age as the twins. They had a lot in common. "We really liked her." She was English, very pretty, and a lot of fun, and Diana thought that Nick was more serious about her than he admitted to his brother.

"I'm going out with a cute girl too," Bill suddenly admitted sheepishly, as he set his drink down.

"Are you telling me something, Bennington?" —Andy eyed him with amusement and interest—"or is this just regular news?" He always took out good-looking girls. He had a penchant for models and starlets. He was a good-looking guy too. But most of the time he seemed to be into numbers rather than any one serious attachment.

"I'm not sure yet. She's pretty terrific though. I want you to meet her."

"What does she do, or is that redundant?" Andy grinned, amused by the boyish look of excitement on his friend's face.

"You're not going to believe this—she's an attorney for a rival network. She just got out of law school. She's really an unusual girl."

"Uh oh." Andy couldn't resist teasing him, but he was pleased for his friend. Bill Bennington was one of his closest friends and favorite people. "Sounds like this could be serious."

"You never know." Bennington smiled mysteriously, and the two men walked across the parking lot of the club where they played tennis. They met every Saturday, as long as they didn't have other plans, and one or two evenings a week, if they weren't tied up at the office. And Bill thought Andy had looked very tense before his trip. He was glad to see him looking so much more relaxed now. "How's my favorite magazine editor, by the way? Still working her tail off?"

"Up until we left. Actually, she took the day off yesterday, which is a good sign. I think she's come back relaxed and with a better outlook on a lot of things. She was pretty uptight before we left."

"So were you. You were even beginning to make me nervous. I wasn't sure if something was wrong at work, or you were just worried about other things, but you didn't look like a happy camper when you left."

"I don't know." He wasn't sure how much he should tell him about Diana's concerns about getting pregnant. "I guess I was just tired. Diana was pretty nervous before we left, and I guess I caught the bug from her."

"Nothing serious, I hope."

"No . . . not really . . . she's getting pretty anxious to have a kid, but I think she's premature in getting worried."

"You guys have barely been married a year, haven't you? How long's it been?" He seemed surprised that they were already thinking about having a baby.

"We've been married a year today." Andy smiled at him. "It seems hard to believe, doesn't it?"

"God, I can't believe that. Well, don't start having kids too soon. You won't want to play tennis with me anymore. You'll have to run home and help Di change diapers."

"Now there's an image . . . maybe I'll just tell her to forget it for another year."

"Why don't you do that? And then maybe we can be pushing swings together in a couple of years."

"What a thought." Andy looked at his friend with a grin as they stood next to Bill's silver Porsche. "It's hard to imagine all that, isn't it? I can still remember my father carrying the twins around, one on each shoulder. Somehow I don't feel ready for that yet. But Diana is. She's really anxious to get started." He didn't want to admit that they'd been hard at it for a year, and nothing had happened.

"Well, don't be in too much of a hurry, big guy, kids are forever."

"I'll tell Diana you said that."

He waved as Bill drove off, and wondered how long the new girlfriend would last, as he drove home to Diana. She was in great spirits when he got home, and he found her puttering in the garden. She looked up with a grin as he approached, looking handsome and lean in his white tennis shorts, and he stooped to kiss her.

"Happy Anniversary, Mrs. Douglas." There was a Tiffany box concealed in the pocket of his white shorts, and he pulled it out and handed it to her.

"You spoil me." She sat back on her heels and quickly opened the blue, wrapped box, and inside was a beautiful gold ring with a small sapphire in it. It was a handsome ring, and the kind of thing he knew she would wear constantly. She looked up at him, thrilled, as she kissed him.

"I love it!"

"I'm glad." He looked pleased. "I think first anniversary is something like plastic, or paper, or clay, something really great like that. . . . I figured you wouldn't mind if I skipped ahead a few years."

"I'll forgive you this once . . . but next year I want the real thing, like aluminum or copper." She smiled at him, looking suntanned and relaxed in their garden.

"Baby, you got it!" He swept her to her feet, and they went inside and she gave him his present. She had bought a beautiful set of leather luggage for him. He had been admiring it all year and he was stunned when he unwrapped it. They were generous with each other, on holidays and throughout the year. He loved buying her little things for no special reason, and coming home with an armload of flowers for her. And she did much the same for him. They were both well paid, and they could afford to spoil each other a little.

In fact, Andy had made reservations for them at l'Orangerie for that night, which was extravagant, but he knew it would remind them of Europe. They had eaten at some fabulous restaurants and gone to some wonderful places while they were away, and he thought it would be fun to splurge on their anniversary.

Diana wore a new dress that night when they went out. It was white silk, and very low cut, and she had bought it in London and saved it for this very special occasion.

"Somehow I thought I should wear white again," she teased when he saw her in it for the first time that night.

"I hope that doesn't mean you still think you're a virgin."

"Hardly." She grinned. And they left early to drop in at Seamus's latest opening at the Adamson-Duvannes Galleries. Diana had promised her sister that they'd stop by on the way to dinner. They both looked beautiful and tan as they got into Andy's car, and he leaned over to kiss her.

"You look absolutely gorgeous!" he raved appreciatively, and she grinned.

"So do you." She still had the glow she had acquired on their trip, and without saying anything to her, Andy found himself wondering if she was actually pregnant.

She was wearing her new ring, and on the way to the gallery, Andy teased her about taking another trip so he could use his new luggage. It had been an easy day, and they had spent the afternoon in bed, making love, before they dressed for dinner. So far, it had been the perfect anniversary, and driving to Adamson-

Duvannes, Andy filled her in on Bill's new girlfriend.

"An attorney?" Diana looked amazed, and
then she smiled, thinking of their friend. "Well,
that won't last more than ten minutes."

"I'm not so sure." Andy shook his head,
thinking about what Bill had told him. "He
seems pretty smitten."

"He always is, until the next one comes
through the door. He has the same attention
span as my three-year-old nephew."

"Now, come on, Di, be fair, Bill's a great
guy." But he couldn't deny that there was a certain amount of truth to what she was saying.
And she laughed as she forced Andy to admit it.

"I never said he wasn't. I just said he can't
stick with anything or anyone for more than five
minutes."

"Maybe this time will be different," Andy
said, as he pulled into a parking space on San
Vicente Boulevard, just beyond the gallery. He
helped Diana out of the car, and followed her to
the gallery, where Seamus was engaged in ar-
dent conversation with an Asian man all dressed
in black just inside the doorway.

"My God . . . look at you . . . it's a movie
star, fresh from Europe!" He raved about his
sister-in-law, and introduced them both to a

well-known Japanese artist. "We were discussing the potential impact of art on an already
comatose, decadent culture. Our conclusions
were not exactly cheering." Seamus mused,
looking impish, and as usual, full of the devil.
He loved to play, with people, with words, with
paints, with ideas, with anything he could get
his mind or hands on. "Have you seen Sam?" he
asked Diana, as he dragged Andy toward the
bar, and pointed her in her sister's direction.
She was standing in the midst of a group of
women, in front of a huge painting on the far
wall, and both her children were clinging to her
legs, and swatting each other, although she
seemed not to notice as she chatted with the
women.

"Hi," Diana said quietly as she walked up to
her.

"Well, look at you," Sam said admiringly. She
had always thought that Diana was the prettiest
of the three sisters. The best looking and the
most capable . . . probably the smartest. She
seemed to have it all, as far as Sam was concerned. Although Diana would never have
agreed with her, if Sam said it to her. And if she
had, she would have traded it all anyway for her
sister's two children. "You look fabulous. How
was Europe?"

"Really fun. We had a terrific time." Sam introduced Diana to her friends, and eventually they all drifted off to find the men or women they had come with. And then Sam looked earnestly up at Diana and lowered her voice, as she asked the question.

"So . . . did you get pregnant on the trip?" She looked so earnest and so concerned, but for a moment, just looking at her, Diana hated her for asking.

"Is that all you think about? Isn't there *ever* any other subject? Every time I see Gayle she asks me the same thing. Christ, don't you two *ever* think of anything else?" The worst part was that she herself couldn't think of anything else either. It was as though, in her family, you weren't validated unless you were pregnant, or had children. Well, she had done her best, goddammit, and so far it just wasn't working.

"I'm sorry. I just wondered. I haven't seen you in a while, and I thought—"

"Yeah, I know . . ." Diana sounded depressed as she answered. They meant well, but they got to her every time. Their questions were like a constant accusation. Wasn't she trying hard enough? What was wrong with them? Were either of them abnormal? Diana wondered about those things, too, and she didn't have the answers, for herself or her sisters, or their parents.

"I assume that means no," Sam said softly, trying it again, and Diana looked daggers at her.

"It means give me a break, Sam, and it also means I don't know yet. Are you satisfied? Do you want me to call you the minute I get my period, or should I fax you? Or maybe just a nice billboard on Sunset would do it, so Mom wouldn't have to call her friends and tell them, so far, nothing doing with poor Diana." She was almost in tears as she spat out the words and Sam felt sorry for her. It had been so easy for all of them, but it just didn't seem to be for Andy and Diana.

"Don't be so sensitive, Di. We just want to know what's happening with you, that's all. We love you."

"Thank you. Nothing's happening. Is that clear enough for you?" Or at least she didn't know yet. But her encounter with her sister had left her on edge, as Seamus and Andy joined them. Seamus had their little boy riding high on his shoulders.

"The new paintings are great," Andy said enthusiastically, noticing instantly the strain on Diana's face, and they left shortly after. She was quiet as they drove to the restaurant, and he didn't say anything. As usual, her sister's questions had profoundly unnerved her.

"Something wrong?" Andy asked finally. She was so much moodier than she used to be, but she had been a lot better in Europe. "Did your sister say something to upset you?"

"Just the usual," she snapped at him. "She asked whether or not I'm pregnant."

He glanced over at her, and answered softly. "Just tell her to mind her own business." He leaned over to kiss her, and Diana smiled in spite of herself. He was so sweet to her, and she felt foolish for letting her sister upset her.

"I hate it when they ask. Why don't they just wait and see?"

"Probably because they love you, and they mean well. Besides, maybe you are anyway. I don't know, that last time in Monte Carlo seemed pretty incredible to me, what did you think?" She smiled as he reminded her, and she leaned over and kissed his neck while he drove.

"I think you're incredible. Happy Anniversary, Mr. Douglas." It was hard to believe that it had been a whole year since they'd gotten married. She loved being married to him, and it had been a busy year for them. Her only regret was that she hadn't gotten pregnant. But there were other things that mattered in their lives, too, their work, their friends, their families, it wasn't as if the only thing they cared about was having a baby. But there was no denying that it was important to them, and especially to Diana.

"Do you think I'm stupid to care so much . . . about having a baby, I mean?" she asked Andy softly as they drove to l'Orangerie.

"No, I just don't want you to get too fixated on it. I don't think that helps anything."

"It's easy to do though. Sometimes I think my whole life revolves around my cycle."

"Don't let it. Try to forget it as much as you can. I keep telling you that"—he smiled as he relinquished the car to the valet—"but you just don't listen." He kissed her again, and held her for a long moment. "Just don't forget who the really important people are . . . you . . . and me. . . . The rest will fall into place when it's meant to."

"I wish I could be as nonchalant about it as you are," she said enviously. He was so sensible and calm.

"I'll bet if you can make yourself relax about it, you'll get pregnant like that." He snapped his fingers, and she laughed and looked at him as she took his arm.

"I'll try it."

They walked into the restaurant, and a few

heads turned, admiring the handsome young couple. They were shown to a quiet corner table, and talked easily as he ordered wine, and they looked over the menu for their dinner. She was feeling better again after her brush with Sam. And by the time Andy ordered for both of them, they were in good spirits.

They had caviar with scrambled eggs served in eggshells with chives for their first course, and then lobster and champagne, and it was only after dessert that Diana excused herself to go to the ladies' room to freshen her makeup. She looked beautiful in her English dress, and her hair shone as she combed it. And after she put her lipstick on in the ladies' room, she went to the bathroom before going back to the table, and there she found the telltale sign, a bright red rush of blood that told her their lovemaking in Monte Carlo had been fruitless. She couldn't even catch her breath for a moment as she sat there, and the tiny cubicle reeled around her. She forced herself to be calm again, to deal with it, but when she went to the sink to wash her hands, she felt grief-stricken and empty.

She was determined not to let Andy know, but he saw something in her eyes as she walked back to him, and without even asking he knew. He knew her timing now, and he had known weeks before that this weekend would tell them whether or not their mission had been successful in Europe. He knew now, just looking at her, that it wasn't.

"Bad surprise?" he asked cautiously as she sat down. He knew her so well now, and she was touched by it, but she was too distressed to be aware of his feelings. It was depressing for him, too, and little by little, she was making him feel like a failure.

"Yeah, bad surprise," she answered, and looked away. As far as she was concerned, the whole trip had been a waste. At the moment, she thought her whole life was.

"It doesn't mean anything, sweetheart. We can try again." And again . . . and again . . . and again . . . and always for nothing. Why? Why even try anymore? Who said she was foolish to worry?

"I want to go to the specialist," she said gloomily as the waiter served their coffee. Their evening was ruined now, or at least as far as she was concerned. Her whole goal in life had become their baby. Nothing mattered anymore in comparison to that, not her job, or her friends, or sometimes even her husband. Despite her claims that the baby wasn't the whole picture to her, it was, and they both knew it.

"Why don't we talk about it some other time?" Andy said calmly. "There's no rush. We're not desperate. It's only been a year. Some people think you shouldn't go to a specialist until after two years." He tried to reassure her, but she was on the verge of tears, and extremely nervous.

"I don't want to wait that long," she said tensely, feeling cramps, and hating what they meant. She hated everything about it.

"Fine. Then we'll go in a couple of months. We don't have to rush into it, and you should check the guy out before you see him."

"I did. Jack says he's one of the best in the country."

"Great. So you're telling Jack our troubles again. What did you say to him? That I can't get it up, or I had mumps as a kid, or it's just not working?" He was angry at her for making such a big deal of it, and putting him on the spot, and making him feel like it was all his fault. Not to mention what she was doing to their anniversary, and their evening.

"I just told him I was concerned, and my gynecologist had given me that name. He didn't ask any questions. Don't be so touchy." She tried to soothe him, but he was angry now, and disappointed. And secretly, he felt as though he had failed her.

"Why shouldn't I be touchy, for chrissake? Every month you act like you're going to die when you get the curse, and you look at me with those sad eyes as though to say that it's all my fault and why the hell can't I shoot you a good one. Well, to tell you the truth, I don't know why. Maybe it is my fault, maybe it's not, maybe it's goddam nothing except you driving us both nuts about it. But if it's going to help, go to the specialist, do whatever the hell you want, and if I have to, I'll come with you."

"What do you mean, 'if you *have* to'?" She was hurt by what he'd said, and it was obvious to both of them that their evening was ruined. "This isn't just my problem. It's happening to both of us."

"Yes, it is, thanks to you. But you know, there's a chance that it just doesn't have to. Maybe you're just manufacturing all this stress because you're so goddam hysterical and neurotic about having a baby. And you know what? I don't give a damn if your sisters got pregnant at the altar. We haven't, and so fucking what? Now, why don't you just let it be for a while, and see if we can have some kind of a life, like two normal human beings."

She was crying when they left the restaurant, and they didn't speak to each other all the way home. Diana locked herself in the bathroom for a long time, and she sat there and sobbed over the baby she hadn't conceived and the anniversary that had been ruined. And she wondered if what he had said was true. Was she completely neurotic about this? Was she wrong? Was it all about competing with Gayle and Sam? Or was it real? And why was it that no matter how hard she tried, she was never quite as good as they were?

Andy was waiting up in bed for her when she finally emerged, wearing a new pink satin nightgown he had bought her in Paris.

"I'm sorry," he said softly as she approached the bed. "I guess I was disappointed too. I shouldn't have said all those things." He put his arms around her and pulled her close to him, and he could see that she had been crying. "It doesn't matter, baby. It doesn't matter if we never have kids. You're the one I love. You're the one who's important." She wanted to tell him that she felt that way, too, but the truth was that part of her didn't. She loved him, but she wanted their baby, too, and she knew that until that need was fulfilled, there would always be something missing from their marriage. "I love you, Di," he whispered to her as he pulled her down next to him on the bed and quietly held her.

"I love you, too . . . I keep feeling as though I've failed you."

"That's bullshit," he said, and she smiled. "You haven't failed anyone. And you'll probably end up with twins after all this and make your sisters wild with envy."

"I love you." She was smiling again, and her heart felt lighter. She was sorry she had ruined their evening.

"Happy anniversary, sweetheart."

"Happy anniversary," she whispered. He turned off the light and held her for a long time, thinking about their future, and wondering what would happen to her if they never had a baby.

Bradford and Pilar spent their anniversary night at home. They had been planning to go out to El Encanto, but Tommy called them just before they left and told them that Nancy was in labor. They spoke to her for a few minutes, too, and Pilar told her that they would wait at home until they heard the news. But Brad looked disappointed when they hung up.

"Why'd you tell her that? It could take hours. The baby might not be here till tomorrow morning."

"Come on, sweetheart. We can go out tomorrow night. It's our first grandchild, and we should be here, if they need us."

"One thing you do not need when your first child is born is your father."

"I just think we should be here. What if something goes wrong?"

"All right, all right . . . we'll stay home." He loosened his tie and looked at her ruefully, grateful that she was always so attentive to his children, and had been for so many years. They were very lucky to have her, and he was glad that they finally knew it.

Pilar walked into the kitchen to cook dinner for him, and they ate pasta and drank wine while sitting in the moonlight on the terrace.

"Actually," he said, smiling at her, "maybe this is better than El Encanto. It's certainly more romantic. Have I told you lately how much I love you?" He looked handsome and young in the moonlight as he said it, and she looked beautiful in a soft blue silk dress the same color as her eyes.

"Not in the last two hours. I was beginning to worry."

They stayed out on the terrace after she cleared their plates away, and he talked about how nervous he had been when Nancy was born. He had been thirty-five, which wasn't young for a first baby in those days, but he'd been terrified and felt like a kid while he paced the waiting room, waiting for their baby. He said he'd been an old hand at it when Todd was born, and he'd handed out cigars to everyone in town, he was so proud. He confessed to her then that he'd bought some cigars a few days before and he was going to do the same thing when Nancy had her baby.

Pilar felt happy for them as she thought about it, she knew how excited they were, and she hoped things were going well. And they were both surprised when the phone rang just after ten-thirty. They were still sitting on the terrace, and Pilar ran to answer it. It was Tommy, and then Nancy, sounding happy and excited. They'd had a little boy, weighing in at just over nine pounds.

"And it only took three and a half hours from beginning to end," Tommy announced proudly, as though Nancy had performed a feat no one else had.

"Who does he look like? Me, I hope," Pilar teased, and they laughed.

"Actually," Nancy said, sounding immensely pleased, "he looks just like Daddy."

"Thank God." Brad's voice came across the line, he had just picked up the extension in the bedroom. "He must be a handsome guy."

"He is," Tommy added proudly.

Brad asked if everything was all right, and they told him it had been perfect. Nancy had had no anesthetic at all, she had had the baby naturally, and Tommy had helped her. And after a few minutes they all hung up the phone, and Brad walked Pilar slowly back out to the terrace, smiling proudly. He had a grandson.

"Things sure have changed," he murmured as they sat down. "If anyone had asked me to be there when my children were born, I probably would have fainted."

"Me too." Pilar smiled. "That part never did hold much appeal. But they sounded so happy, didn't they? Like kids, all excited and proud and pleased." She felt tears fill her eyes as she said it. It was a feeling she had never known, and probably never would now. And then she looked up at him and smiled. "Funny. You don't look like a grandfather," she teased.

"That's good news. Would you like a cigar?"

"I think I'll pass." But she knew what she

would like, as she sat looking out into the darkness that was the ocean.

"What were you thinking just then?" He had seen the look in her eyes, and it touched him deeply. There was something lonely and raw deep within her that he never saw. But it was there now, an undeniable avalanche of feelings. The feelings were so deep that even with him she didn't dare bring them to the surface.

"I wasn't thinking about anything," she lied.

"That's not true. You were thinking something very important. You never look like that, Pilar. Tell me what you were thinking. . . ." She had looked like that the night she agreed to marry him, and only once or twice in the years before that. He took her hands in his, and moved closer to her. "Pilar . . . what is it?" He was startled to see when she turned to him that she was crying. There were long rivers of silent tears on her cheeks and an age-old look in her eyes that made him want to reach out and hold her, to keep her protected from the sorrow that overwhelmed her.

"I was just thinking . . . it's silly of me . . . they're young, and they deserve all this . . . I was just thinking of what a fool I've been." He could barely hear her voice in the soft darkness. "I was just thinking how much I'd love to have your baby. . . ." Her voice drifted off and he didn't say anything for a long time, he just held her hands and watched her.

"You mean that, don't you?" he asked softly. He wished with all his heart that she had come to it earlier, for both their sakes, but it was impossible to ignore the naked longing in her eyes, or the way she had said it.

"Yes, I do mean it," she said, and it reminded him of when she had accepted his proposal of marriage, after so many years of insisting that she wanted to stay single. And now, after all these years, and the absolute conviction that she never wanted children, now at the eleventh hour . . . she wanted to have his baby.

He put his arms around her then and held her close to him. He hated knowing that somewhere deep inside her she felt so empty. "I don't like your not having what you want . . . especially when it's important. . ." he said sadly. "But on the other hand, I'm awfully old to start having children again. I may not even live to see them grow up," he said seriously, and she smiled. She understood. She wasn't trying to force him.

"I need you here till I grow up, and that could take a lot longer," she said, wiping her tears away.

He laughed gently. "You could be right." He sat back and looked at her then, and smoothed the tears from her cheeks with loving hands. "So what are we doing about this baby?" He asked with a look of amusement.

"Which baby? Nancy's?"

"No. Yours. Mine . . . ours . . . the one you seem to want so badly."

"Are we doing anything about that?" She looked at him in amazement. She hadn't even wanted to tell him what she felt, because she didn't want him to feel pushed, but he had pressed her and she had told him.

"Is this really something you want very, very badly?" he asked seriously, and she nodded with an overwhelming look of love in her eyes. "Then we'll try it. I can't make you any promises at my age. For all I know, none of the machinery works anymore anyway, at least as far as making babies. But we can certainly try . . . it might be fun. . . ." He grinned wickedly at her and she threw her arms around his neck. He had totally taken her by surprise with his reaction, but not as much as she had surprised herself or him. If anyone had ever told her she would one day want a child, she would have laughed till she cried. And now, finally, she wanted a baby so badly that she was crying.

"You're sure?" She looked at her husband tenderly. "You don't have to do this."

"Yes, I do . . . I wanted to have children with you a long time ago, you know. You just like making me wait for things, don't you?"

"Thank you for waiting," she whispered softly, hoping that it wasn't too late for either of them. That was possible, and there was no way to know. They'd just have to try, and see what happened.

Charlie had bought champagne and a beautiful little ring for Barbie for their anniversary. He wasn't sure why, but he had the distinct impression she'd forgotten what the date was. He didn't want to say anything, because he wanted to surprise her himself. He was planning to cook dinner for her, shower her with champagne, and give her the ring, which was heart shaped and had a tiny ruby in the center. He had bought it at Zale's, and he thought she'd really love it. She loved jewelry and clothes and pretty things, and Charlie loved buying her little surprises. He loved buying everything he could for her, she was so beautiful, and he loved her so much, and as far as he was concerned, she deserved it.

She had told him that she had an audition for
a detergent commercial the morning of their anniversary, and she was going shopping with Judi
and her roommate that afternoon when she was
finished. They were going shopping at the
Broadway Plaza, and she said she'd be home in
time for dinner. Charlie hadn't wanted to make
an issue of it, because he didn't want to spoil
the surprise he had planned for her. But by six-
thirty he was beginning to panic. She was usually pretty reliable, but when she went out with
Judi and the girls, sometimes they had a few
drinks, and she forgot the time. He hoped she'd
be home before much longer. And the audition
had probably been stressful for her, it was a
national, and she wanted to be an actress so
badly.

Barbie had only gotten half a dozen parts in
the past year, and none of them amounted to
much, except one where she got to dance and
sing, dressed up as a California raisin. But so far
her big break hadn't come, and her Hollywood
career hadn't happened. She did a little free-
lance modelling whenever she could, mostly
bathing suits, and Charlie was proud of her. He
didn't mind her acting or working as a model,
but he didn't want her waiting on tables anymore, or even working in a store, like Judi did.

For the past six months, she'd been working in the cosmetics department of Neiman-Marcus, and she kept trying to get Barbie to come to work there, too, but Charlie didn't want that for her. They made enough with his commissions to get by most of the time. Now and then, things got a little tight, but when they did, he cooked macaroni and cheese, and they stayed home and watched TV, and then eventually another commission would roll in, and he'd come home with a big bunch of flowers for Barbie. He was always good to her, and sometimes his kindness made her feel guilty.

She tried to explain it to Judi sometimes. It felt wrong sitting around at home, doing her nails, calling her agent, going downtown to meet Judi for lunch, when she knew Charlie was working so hard to support her. But Judi thought it was just fine, and told her how lucky she was, and Barbie had to admit she enjoyed it. After years of work, as a showgirl, as a waitress, even pumping gas once in Vegas between jobs, now she felt like a real lady of leisure. And she was good to him, too, or at least she tried to be, but it still seemed weird to her to be married. It seemed strange to answer to someone for where she went or what she did, to be hooked up with one man, to stay home all the time, instead of going out to party. Sometimes she still missed the old days, especially when she went out with Judi and the girls, and heard what they were up to. But then she'd come home to Charlie, and he was so sweet and decent to her, it was impossible not to love him. She just wished he could be a little more exciting, but the plain truth was, he wasn't. But he was steady, and she could count on him. No matter what, Barbie knew he would always be there for her. And sometimes even that frightened her, it was as though she could never escape him. And then she would ask herself why she would want to.

By seven o'clock, Charlie had dinner ready, and the table was set, and then he went to take a shower and get ready for Barbie. He put on his blue suit, and took his gift for her out of the drawer where he had hidden it. The champagne was in the fridge, already chilled. And by seven-thirty he was completely ready. He turned on the TV, and by eight o'clock, his roast had started to fray around the edges. And at nine o'clock, he was completely frantic. Something had obviously happened to her. She'd probably had an accident, he told himself, he knew what a lousy driver Judi was, she got into accidents constantly. He called her, and there was no one home, and then he called again at nine-thirty.

The phone machine was on, so all he could do was leave another message. But at ten o'clock, when he called, Judi picked up the phone, and she sounded a little startled when she heard it was Charlie.

"Where's Barb?" he said, the minute he heard her voice. "Is she all right?"

"She's fine, Charlie, she left a little while ago. She should be home any minute. What's all the excitement about?" Judi sounded annoyed and Charlie sounded desperately worried.

"How's she getting home?" Why didn't Judi drive her?

"She took a cab. She may not be home for a while, but she'll get there eventually, Charlie. Keep your shirt on. You're keeping her on a pretty short leash these days, aren't you?"

"It's our anniversary," he said sadly.

"Oh." There was a long silence at the other end. "I'm sorry." They had gone out, and had a few drinks just as he had guessed, and she had forgotten the time, until well after nine-thirty.

"Thanks." He hung up, and went to turn off the oven. Why had she gone out with Judi and the girls again? Why tonight, on their anniversary? And why hadn't he told her? All he wanted to do was surprise her with some champagne and a homemade dinner. It would have been easier to tell her what he was planning. He knew how vague she was, how she liked to float around and visit friends. It had been really stupid to try to surprise her.

He heard her key in the door at ten forty-five, he was watching the news, and he jumped up when she walked in. She was wearing a tight black dress and high heels, and she looked incredibly sexy.

"Where were you?" he said anxiously.

"I told you. I went shopping with Judi."

"That was eleven hours ago. Why didn't you call me? I'd have picked you up."

"I didn't want to bother you, sweetheart." She gave him a peck on the cheek and then noticed the table. She looked startled, and then suddenly deeply guilty. "What is this? What did you do?"

"It's our anniversary tonight," he said softly. "I cooked dinner for you. I guess it was dumb to try to surprise you."

"Oh, Charlie . . ." Tears filled her eyes as she looked at him. She felt like a real louse, particularly when he poured the champagne and brought out the remains of the roast beef and Yorkshire pudding.

"It's a little well-done." He grinned sheepishly, and she laughed as she kissed him.

"You're the best," she said, and she actually meant it. "I'm sorry, baby. I just didn't remember. That was really stupid of me."

"It's okay. I'll know for next year. I'll make a date with you, and we'll go to a restaurant. Someplace really fancy like Chasen's."

"This looks pretty fancy to me." Most of his dinner was burned, but the champagne tasted great to her. She'd already had more than a few drinks, but she never minded a few more. And a little while later, they were on the couch making love, her black dress and his blue suit lying in a heap on the floor, and Charlie didn't give a damn about his burned dinner.

"Wow!" he said happily when they finally came up for air. "Wow . . . wow! *Wow!*" She laughed at him, and they made love again, and it was three o'clock in the morning when they finally headed for their bedroom. They didn't wake up the next day till noon, and when they did, Barbie had a terrible headache. She could hardly see when he opened the shades, and then he remembered the gift he'd meant to give her the night before, the little box from Zale's. He went to get it and handed it to her as she lay in bed, complaining about her headache.

"I don't know why I like champagne so

much. It makes me feel like I have jackhammers in my head the next morning."

"It's the bubbles. Or at least that's what someone told me." He never really drank enough to bother him, but there were times when she did. She could never resist when she got her hands on a bottle of bubbly.

"What is this?" She was slowly tearing the paper off the little box and squinting at him, as she lay on their bed in all her naked glory. She was a remarkable-looking girl, and he could never keep his eyes or his hands off her body.

"It's an anniversary gift, but if you take much longer opening it, I may have to interrupt you." It was almost painful looking at her, just seeing her like that always made him want her. In the past year she had become a serious addiction. And then finally, she opened the box and found the ring, squealed with delight, and said she loved it. He did so much for her. No one in her entire life had ever been as kind to her, yet there were still times when, because of her past, it was hard for her to open up and trust him. But when he was this sweet to her, she always felt guilty about it.

"I'm sorry about last night," she said huskily, and then she slowly rolled over toward him, and he forgot everything except her legs and her hips and her thighs, and the incredible breasts that never ceased to amaze him.

They didn't get out of bed again until two in the afternoon, and then they went to take a shower together, and they made love again. Charlie was in great form and much better spirits.

"Actually, in spite of a slow start, I'd say this was a great anniversary." He grinned as they finally dressed for dinner. They were going out to meet friends, and maybe go to a movie.

"I think so too," she said, smiling at her ring, and then she kissed him. But as she looked at him, she could see that he was hesitating about something. He had the look he got when there was something he wanted to ask her, but was afraid to upset her. "What's up? . . . never mind. . . . I know . . . wrong question."

He laughed, and was surprised at how well she knew him.

"What's bothering you? You look like you want to ask me something." She slipped into a short, tight black-leather skirt as she spoke, and high heels, and reached into her closet for a sweater. She had her blond hair piled high on her head, and she looked like a rounder, more sensual Olivia Newton-John, as Charlie sat admiring her while she was dressing. He was a

nice-looking young man, but he looked completely out of his league when he was with
Barbie.

"What makes you think I want to ask you
something?" he said hesitantly. Sometimes ex-
pressing his feelings to her made him feel awkward.

"Well, come on." There was nothing shy
about her as she stood in front of him with the
black sweater stretched tight across her bosom.
He'd been planning to ask her the night before,
after the champagne and the ring, and maybe
before they made love, or even after. But the
events of the evening had gotten slightly out of
order. They'd made love all night and never
even bothered to have dinner.

"Come on, what is it?" she asked impatiently,
and he started looking nervous. He didn't want
to ask at the wrong time, or maybe she'd get
angry. She knew it was something she didn't
like to talk about, but it meant so much to him.
He knew he had to.

"I'm not sure this is the right time." He hesitated, afraid to blow it.

"My mother always said, 'Don't throw one
shoe,' so what's on your mind, Charlie?"

He sat down on the bed, trying to find the
right words. It was so important to him, he

didn't want to get her back up. And he knew she had her own opinions on the subject. But he had strong feelings about it, too, and at least he wanted to try to discuss it with her.

"I'm not sure how to say this . . . or how to tell you how much it means to me, Barb . . . but . . . I really want to have a baby."

"What?" She turned around and looked at him. She looked like an angry cat in her black angora sweater. And she stood looking at him with obvious displeasure. "You know I don't want kids, Charlie. Not now. Jeez, I just almost got a commercial this week. If I get pregnant, my whole career could wind up out the window, and I could wind up selling lipsticks at Neiman-Marcus like Judi."

He didn't remind her that her "whole career" consisted of a few walks-ons, a lot of auditions for commercials she didn't get, the car show, and the back line of the chorus in *Oklahoma!*, not to mention a very unpleasant year in Las Vegas. Her only real success had been doing ramp work, in bikinis.

"I know," he said understandingly. "But you could put your career on hold for a while. And I'm not saying we have to do it right away. But I want you to know how important it is to me. I want a family, Barb. I want kids. I want to give someone what I never had, a mother, a father, a home, a life. We could make a real difference in our children's lives. I really want to do that. We've been married a year now and I thought it was time to say it."

"So join the Peace Corps if you want to play with kids. I'm not ready for that. I'm almost thirty-two years old, and if I don't go for the gold now, it'll be gone when I get there."

"I'm thirty, Barbie. Thirty. And I want a family." His eyes pleaded with her, and she looked suddenly very nervous.

"A family?" she asked, raising one eyebrow as she leaned against the wall in her tight black-leather skirt, looking incredibly sexy. "How many kids is that? Ten? I've been in one of those. It stinks. Believe me, I can tell you." More than he knew, more than he'd ever know, or she would tell him.

"It doesn't have to be that way. Maybe your family was like that. But ours wouldn't be, baby." He had tears in his eyes when he spoke to her. "I need that in my life . . . it's not going to be right for me until we have that. Can't we at least try now?" They'd talked about it before, and it was something they had never really come to grips with before they were married. Charlie had always been outspoken about wanting kids, and Barbie had vacillated between being honest with him when she said she didn't want any at all, and trying to keep him happy by saying "maybe later." But later seemed to be coming at them faster than Barbie wanted.

She looked unhappy and stared out the window before looking back at him. There were memories that she didn't want to share with him, but she had no desire to be part of a family again, or fill her life with children. She knew she'd never want that. She'd tried to tell him that when they first met, but Charlie just didn't want to hear her and she knew he still didn't believe her when she said she didn't want children. "Why now? It's only been a year. Everything's fine like this, why screw it up?"

"It won't screw it up, it'll make it better. Please, Barb . . . just think it over." He was begging her, and she could hear it in his voice, but all that did was make her hate him. He was pushing her, and it wasn't fair to her. Particularly not on that subject.

"Maybe it wouldn't work anyway," she tried to discourage him any way she could. "Sometimes I wonder if there's something weird about us. Half the time we don't use birth control. I've never been so sloppy in my life, as I am with you, Charlie, and nothing ever happens." She looked at him knowingly, and then she smiled. "Maybe we're not meant to have kids." She kissed him and tried to arouse him, which was never difficult. "I'll be your baby, Charlie," she said in a voice that ripped his socks off.

"That's not the same thing." He smiled, successfully distracted. "Nice though . . . very nice in the meantime." But as far as Barbie was concerned, there was no "meantime." And as he kissed her, he wondered if he could trick her into being even more careless. Maybe even at just the right time of month. Maybe that made more sense than trying to convince her, and he knew that the minute she had a baby, she'd love it. And as he thought that, he decided to pay more attention to her cycle. Maybe if he knew when just the right time was, he could bring home a bottle of champagne, and bingo . . . they'd have their baby. The idea cheered him no end, as they finished dressing and went out. And not knowing how intent he was on his plan, Barbie was in excellent spirits, and figured maybe he'd decided to be reasonable and forget his ideas about a family for a while. She had never actually told him she wouldn't have kids, but she had never told him she would either. And one thing was sure, as far as she was concerned, no matter how badly he wanted a baby, she was not going to have one.

CHAPTER
6

Nancy and Tommy brought the baby to Brad and Pilar's on the Fourth of July, and it was extraordinary to realize how he had changed them all. Nancy and Tommy seemed suddenly terribly grown-up and responsible, and Brad was cooing over his grandson and holding him every minute. He couldn't imagine how they had ever lived without him. Pilar loved holding the baby, too, and it amazed her to think that she might have her own one day. It was an incredible feeling.

Adam was fat and round, and happy to sleep in anyone's arms, his eyes were huge and blue when he was awake, and just holding him felt delicious.

"He looks good on you," Brad said softly

when he walked by Pilar late in the afternoon as she held the baby. "Maybe he'll have a new aunt or uncle soon," he teased and she smiled. They had worked at it the week after their anniversary, and she was waiting to see what would happen that weekend.

But she was startled that night, after the young people went home, when she discovered that she wasn't pregnant. She came out of the bathroom looking surprised and devastated. She was used to accomplishing what she wanted the first time.

"Sweetheart, what's wrong?" Brad saw her and he thought she was sick. She looked like a ghost, but she sat down on the bed next to him, and he could see that she'd been crying.

"I'm not pregnant."

"Oh, for heaven's sake." He smiled gently. "I thought something terrible had happened."

"Isn't that bad enough?" She seemed so stunned. It was rare for success to elude her. But Brad knew better.

"After fourteen years? Just because you tried once, doesn't mean you're going to get what you want the first time around, you know. You may have to put a little more effort into it than that." He leaned over and kissed her, and she smiled, but she was still looking forlorn. "Just think of the fun we'll have trying."

"What if it doesn't work?" she asked, frightened now. This wasn't as easy as it seemed. Brad looked at her intently, wondering how she'd take it if it didn't work, ever.

"If it doesn't work, Pilar, then we'll have to live with that. But we'll give it our best effort. We can't do more than that," he said quietly.

"At my age, I should probably go to a specialist right from the start," she said worriedly.

"At your age, women have babies all the time, without specialists, or any heroic efforts. Just relax. You can't control the entire world. Just because you decided you wanted a baby three weeks ago, doesn't mean you can just make it happen overnight. Give it a chance. Relax . . ." He pulled her next to him on the bed, and he held her, and after a while she relaxed, and they talked quietly for a while about their plans and the baby they hoped to have. *If* they had one.

Brad thought it was way too soon even to think about a specialist, and he told her so that night, but he also agreed, when she pressed him about it, that if it turned out they needed one, he was willing to go with her.

"But not yet," he reminded her as he turned off the light. "I really think that what we need," he said softly as he moved closer to her beneath the sheets, "is a lot more practice."

For Diana, the Goodes' Fourth of July picnic had been a nightmare. She had just discovered that she wasn't pregnant again two days before, and her sisters hounded her mercilessly about why it wasn't happening, and did she think Andy had a problem.

"Of course not," she defended him, feeling as though she were being run over by steamrollers until she couldn't even breathe as they moved closer. "It just takes time."

"It didn't take us time, and you're our sister," Gayle announced. "Maybe he has a low sperm count," she said suspiciously, relieved to blame him. She had already said as much to her husband.

"Why don't you ask him?" Diana snapped at her, and Gayle looked hurt by her reaction.

"I was just trying to be helpful. Maybe you should tell him to go see someone." Diana didn't tell her older sister that she had an appointment herself with a specialist the next day. As Andy said, it was none of their business.

But it was her sister Sam who really took the wind out of her, and delivered the ultimate blow with her unexpected announcement. She told them all over lunch, and Diana thought she was going to throw up as soon as she heard it.

"Okay, guys . . ." she started to say, and then she looked sheepishly at her husband, and he grinned. "Should I tell them?"

"Nah." He laughed. "Tell them in six months. Keep them guessing till then." Everyone loved his brogue and his easy style. He had been well liked in the family ever since he'd married Samantha.

"Come on," Gayle complained, "tell us."

"Okay." Sam grinned happily. "I'm pregnant. The baby's due on Valentine's Day."

"How wonderful!" their mother exclaimed, and their father looked pleased too. He'd been chatting with Andy, and looked up to congratulate his daughter and son-in-law. That would make six grandchildren, three each for his oldest and youngest daughters, and none for Diana.

"That's great," Diana said woodenly, as she kissed Sam, who whispered the ultimate dig, without even trying.

"I thought you'd beat me to it, but I guess not!" For the first time in her life, it made Diana want to slap her. She hated her as she listened to her laugh and brag, as everyone teased and congratulated and made a fuss over her. But the worst of it was that when all was said and done, in the end, Sam would have the baby, and not Diana.

She didn't say a word to Andy on the way home, and when they got back to their house, he finally exploded.

"Look dammit, it's not my fault, don't take it out on me!" He knew exactly what was bothering her, had known it from the moment Sam had made her announcement. And her eyes seemed to be full of silent accusations.

"How do you know it's not your fault? Maybe it *is*!" And then she regretted it the moment the words were out. She sat down on the couch with a look of despair, and he looked shattered. "Look, I'm sorry . . . I don't know what I'm saying. They just upset me so much. They don't mean to, but they say all the wrong things, and Sam just blew me away when she said she was pregnant."

"I know, baby." He sat down next to her. "I know. We're doing everything we can." He knew she was going to see the doctor the next day. "They'll probably tell us that we're fine. Just relax." She had come to hate that word more than any other.

"Yeah . . . sure . . ." she said, and went to

take a shower. But all she could think of were her sisters. *"I'm pregnant."* . . . *"Maybe he has a low sperm count."* . . . *"I thought you'd be pregnant first, but I beat you to it."* . . . *I'm pregnant . . . I'm pregnant . . . low sperm count.* . . . She stood crying in the shower for half an hour, and after that, she went to bed without saying a word to Andy.

The next morning dawned brilliant and sunny. It was almost an affront for the weather to be so nice when she felt so lousy. She had taken the day off from work. Lately her job had been getting to her, the pressure, the deadlines, the politics, the people. It had been fun before, but now even that seemed bitter without a baby.

Even her one close friend at work had noticed that Diana had lost some of her sparkle. Eloise Stein was the food editor at the magazine, and she had finally dared to bring it up the week before, over a quick lunch at Eloise's desk, where they were tasting the results of some unusual French recipes Eloise had unearthed in Paris.

"Something bothering you these days?" Eloise had asked her pointedly. She was intelligent, and beautiful, and very perceptive. She had gone to Yale, and then did graduate work at

Harvard. She was originally from L.A., and
eventually she had come home to roost, as she
put it. She was twenty-eight, and she was living
in a little apartment adjacent to her parents'
house in Bel Air. But considering how much
she had going for her, she was surprisingly unspoiled, a beautiful girl, and she had been a
good friend to Diana since she'd come to the
magazine a few months before, and she was fun
to be with. Diana and Andy had tried to fix her
up with Bill Bennington once, but she had terrified him, too capable, too grown-up, although
he had put it down to too skinny and too tall.
She looked like a model.

"No, I'm okay." Diana had brushed off her
question, and complimented her on the goodies
they were eating, among them rillettes, and a
recipe for tripe that reminded Diana of her days
in Paris. "It's hard to believe you ever eat," Diana said, looking at her. She was thin, with big
blue eyes, and long, straight blond hair.

"I was anorectic in college," Eloise explained. "Or at least I tried to be. I think basi-
cally I liked food too much to stick with an-
orexia for very long, and my grandmother in
Florida kept sending me cookies." Then she
looked up at Diana again, not one to be put off,
which was why she was doing so well at the

magazine. "You didn't really answer my question."

"About what?" Diana looked vague, but she knew exactly what she was asking. And she liked this girl, but she wasn't sure she wanted to take anyone into her confidence about her problems. The only one who knew how distraught she was, was Andy.

"Something's bothering you. I don't mean to pry, but you're starting to get that look of people who walk into walls while assuring you they're fine."

"Is it that bad?" Diana looked horrified, and then suddenly laughed at the description.

"Not really, but I've noticed it. Should I mind my own business, or do you need a buddy?"

"Actually . . . no . . . I . . ." She had started to tell her that she was fine, and then suddenly found herself crying. All she could do was shake her head as the tears poured down her cheeks, and she sobbed uncontrollably, and the tall blond girl ran a gentle hand across her shoulders, and kept handing her paper towels to blow her nose in. It was a long time before Diana could stop crying. "I'm so sorry . . . I didn't mean to. . . ." She looked up with a red nose, and red eyes that were still watering, but she felt better. It had been a relief to let her hair down. "I don't know what happened."

"Yes, you do, you needed that desperately." Eloise gave her a warm hug, and poured her a strong cup of coffee.

"I guess you're right." Diana took a deep breath and faced her. "I'm having problems . . . at home, I suppose one could say. Nothing terminal, just some things I need to adjust to."

"With your husband?" Eloise asked, looking sorry for her. She liked Diana a lot, and she also liked Andy. She was sorry to hear they were having trouble. They had looked so happy the last time they'd all been out to dinner.

"No, I can't really blame this on him. I think it's more my fault. I've been putting a lot of pressure on him . . . we've been trying to have a baby for over a year, and it just hasn't happened. And I know how stupid it must sound, but every month it's like a death in the family, a terrible disaster I have to face again, and I just dread it. All month I hope that this time it worked, and when I find out it didn't again, it just breaks my heart. Isn't that stupid?" She started crying again, and blew her nose in another paper towel.

"It's not stupid," Eloise reassured her. "I've never wanted to have a child, but it's probably pretty normal. Also, for people like us, who're used to running things, and being in control, it's probably pretty frightening when things don't go the way we want to. You know, that devil word 'control,' there's probably a little of that in the grief too: the total loss of power, over not being able to influence whether or not you have a baby."

"Maybe. But it's more than that . . . it's hard to explain . . . it's just this incredible emptiness . . . this terrible yearning. It just makes me want to die sometimes. I can't talk to anyone, not even Andy. I just die inside, and everything else freezes up until I'm in a shell. It's the loneliest feeling I know. I don't even know how to describe it."

"It sounds awful," Eloise said sympathetically, and it explained perfectly what she had seen at the office. Diana had begun to shut everyone out, and lock herself in, and there was almost no reaching her anymore. It would be no surprise if it were affecting her marriage. "Have you seen a specialist?" She wanted to ask her if she'd seen a therapist, too, but she didn't dare, and she was touched that Diana had confided in her as much as she had. She felt honored.

"I'm seeing one next week actually. Someone named Alexander Johnston." She didn't know why she even bothered to say the name, but since she was confiding in Eloise, it seemed reasonable to tell her about him, and Diana was surprised when she saw her smile, as she poured another cup of coffee.

"Have you heard the name?"

"A few times. He's my father's partner. My father's a reproductive endocrinologist. If things really get bad, they might push you off on him, or if you do IVF, in vitro fertilization, then Daddy might do it. He doesn't take a lot of new patients anymore, except if they're referred by Alex, or one of his other partners. You're in good hands with Alex Johnston." Diana felt relieved, and she looked at her in amazement. It was a smaller world than she thought, even in that field. "Do you want me to say something to him, about knowing you?" Eloise asked cautiously, not sure how Diana would feel about it.

"I'd rather not. I think I'd rather just keep this business, but I'm glad to know that I picked the right office."

"The best. They'll work it out. The statistics are pretty impressive these days. I grew up on that stuff. I'm not sure I ever thought people just 'did it' and got pregnant. I think I always assumed that my father had to be there to help them." It was an intriguing idea, and Diana laughed at the image Eloise painted.

Eloise had finally asked her, while they were eating incredibly good apple tarts with crème fraîche, why she didn't take some time off to work it all out. It might be easier on her, and maybe even on Andy, but Diana said she didn't think she could, and in the end, she admitted that she didn't want to.

"I can't just walk out on work. Besides, what would I do with myself? Both my sisters did that, and they're at home now with their kids. But you know, I'm not sure I could just stay home, not now anyway. Maybe if I had a baby. Right now it gives me something to think about while I count the days, and wait to take my temperature every morning."

"I'm not sure I could stand all that. How do you do it?"

"I want a baby very badly. I suspect you do a lot of things, if you have to." From listening to her father talk about procedures he performed, Eloise knew that even better than Diana.

Diana was thinking of her as she drove to the Wilshire Carthay Building, wondering if she would catch a glimpse of Eloise's father. It still seemed amazing to her that by sheer chance she had made an appointment with her father's partner. And everyone she'd talked to said that Alex Johnston was very good, but as Diana rode up in the elevator, she was suddenly desperately nervous and very frightened.

The waiting room was quiet, but elegant, done all in cream and oatmeal colors, with expensive modern art on the walls, and a huge palm tree in the corner. Diana was told to take a seat, and a few minutes later she was ushered into the inner sanctum. There was a long hallway, with more art, and skylights high overhead, and at the end of the hall the nurse led her into a room that was panelled in bleached wood, with a beautiful rug on the floor, and a handsome sculpture of a woman and a child stood in the corner. And oddly enough, even seeing a piece of art depicting a mother and child caused her pain now.

She thanked the nurse and sat down, trying to stay calm and think of Andy. She was terrified of what they were going to do to her, or what they would find, but a moment later she was pleasantly surprised when she met the doctor. He was a tall, sandy-haired man, with long graceful hands and intelligent blue eyes, and in some ways, he reminded her of her father.

"Hello." He smiled at her warmly, and shook

her hand. "I'm Alex Johnston. It's nice to see you." And he actually sounded as though he meant it. He chatted with her for a few minutes about what she did, and where she was from, and how long she'd been married, and then he pulled an empty chart closer to him on the desk and took out a pen as he glanced at Diana warmly. "Why don't we make a few notes here, and get down to business. What brings you here, Mrs. Douglas?"

"I . . . we . . . we've been trying to get pregnant for a little over a year, thirteen months to be exact, and so far nothing's happened." She admitted to him, too, that they had also been somewhat careless about birth control before their marriage, and she had never gotten pregnant then either.

"Have you ever been pregnant? Any live or still births? . . . or abortions?"

"None," she said solemnly. Without even knowing him, she already had enormous respect for him, and complete faith that he was going to be able to solve their problem.

"Have you ever been 'careless' about birth control before this?" he asked, watching her closely.

"No. I've always been careful about birth control."

"What methods have you used?" The questions went on and on about her methods of birth control. He particularly wanted to know if she'd ever had an IUD, which she had while she was in college, or if she'd been on the pill, and for how long. He wanted to know about venereal diseases—which she'd never had—cysts, tumors, pains, hemorrhages, accidents, severe infections of any kind, surgeries, or any history of cancer, or family diseases like diabetes. He wanted to know everything about her. And at the end of her long recital of all the things she didn't have, he reassured her that a year was not a long time to achieve pregnancy, although understandably it might seem long to her and her husband. But there was no reason to panic. He even said that if she wanted to, at her age, he could comfortably recommend letting them try on their own for another six months, or even a year, before doing any serious investigation, although he said that he personally preferred doing tests after one year without conception.

"Why don't we check out a few things now, a few simple steps. I can do a preliminary examination, to make sure you don't have a minor infection that might be upsetting the balance." He smiled at her, and she agreed that she would rather proceed now, rather than wait any

longer. She knew that she couldn't stand another six months of hope and heartbreak. She
wanted to know why nothing was happening.
She just couldn't believe there wasn't a simple
explanation, and she'd rather find it out now
than a year later, so they could fix it and get on
with it, and she explained all that to Dr. Johnston.

"There's also the distinct possibility"—he
smiled at her—"that there's nothing to fix at all,
and you're perfectly healthy and you just need
to be patient. Or, if there's any basis for concern, we can begin examining your husband."
She and Andy had agreed that they would start
with her, and then see what the doctor said
about seeing Andy.

"I hope you don't find anything," she said
quietly and he said he hoped so too, and mentioned vaguely that so far only the fact that
she'd once had an IUD concerned him. He
stood up then and directed her to a room across
the hall, where she could change and he would
perform his examination. Today would be very
little more than a pelvic. He had just explained
to her that the bulk of his tests would have to be
in approximately two weeks, right around the
time of ovulation. They would check her cervical mucus then to see if it was "inviting"

enough to the sperm, or if it was hostile. And if it was hostile, there were further tests they would do, like a cross-match. But at the time of ovulation, they would do an ultrasound, to see how her follicle was maturing before ovulation, and a postcoital test, which was only a slide test to check her mucus, and Andy's sperm for motility and number.

But today all he was going to do was the pelvic, to check for growths, cysts, infection, or deformities, and then they would draw blood to check for HIV, low-grade infections, and to check her immunity to rubella. He also wanted a complete blood count, and he would be doing cervical cultures after the pelvic, to check even further for infections. Sometimes a simple infection was the key to the whole problem.

It seemed as though they had a lot planned, although the only tests they were doing that day were simple ones, but at least she finally felt as though they were doing something to find out what was going on in her body. She smiled to herself as she remembered what Andy had said to her the night before. He had told her about a problem he'd had with his nose when he was a child. It had gotten terribly stopped up, until he could barely breathe, and his mother had taken him to a specialist, to check his adenoids and tonsils.

"And you know what it turned out to be?" he asked solemnly, as he lay in bed with an arm around her.

"I don't know . . . a sinus infection?"

"Much simpler than that. Raisins. I'd shoved a whole bunch up my nose a few days before, and they just kind of sat there all warm and cozy, and grew, and I was afraid to say anything to my mother. So when you see the doctor tomorrow, sweetheart . . . don't forget to tell him to check for raisins." She smiled again as she thought of the story, while the doctor examined her, and it reminded her again of how much she loved Andy.

But Dr. Johnston did not find any raisins. Nor did he find any deformities, or tumors, or cysts, or any sign of infection. Everything checked out perfectly, and Diana was relieved, as a technician came in to do the blood work.

And once she was dressed, the doctor explained that he wanted her back in ten days to do the tests he had already discussed with her, and that they would tell them exactly when to time their lovemaking this month, at the fertile time, and he wanted her to use an ovulation kit the following week to check her urine for a surge of luteinizing hormone, or LH, which would occur just before ovulation. It sounded very complicated, but actually, it wasn't. It was just new. And he wanted her to continue taking her temperature, which she had done anyway for the past six months, and even that drove Andy crazy. He said it was like living with a hypochondriac, with a thermometer shoved in her mouth every morning. But as always, he was a good sport about it, if she thought it would help them get pregnant.

Before she left, the doctor also suggested to Diana that she and Andy slow down a little bit, if they could, take some time off from work, spend time doing the things they liked to do, even if it meant sacrificing time with friends or work-related projects.

"Stress can play an important part in infertility too. Try to wind down as much as you can, both of you. Get lots of fresh air, eat well, sleep." It was all easier said than done in the modern world, and he knew it, but he also thought it was worth saying. He had said again that more than likely there was nothing wrong with either of them, and all they needed was a little more time and things would happen naturally. But if there was a problem, he assured her, they would find it. But as she left his office, feeling hopeful and excited and nervous, she remembered something else he had said, that roughly fifty percent of the couples treated for infertility gave birth to healthy babies, but there were others, healthy themselves, with absolutely nothing wrong with them, who never got pregnant. It was something she would have to face, if it ever came to that for them, but she didn't know how she would do it. Just being there, talking to the doctor about the various possibilities, the tests she might have to face, made her realize for the first time just how much she was willing to do to have a baby. She would do anything, short of stealing one.

She was exhausted as she drove home, and for a minute she was tempted to go to the office, but she had taken the day off anyway, and it was after one o'clock, and she remembered what the doctor had said about not pushing herself. So she decided to go shopping instead, and as she walked through Saks, she felt deliciously guilty. She called Andy from the store, but he was out to lunch, and eventually she went home, and decided to make him a really fancy dinner.

He called her at three o'clock, and he could hear the lighter tone in her voice when she answered. At least they hadn't found anything terribly wrong with her yet. And maybe it was his fault. Actually, for the past month or two he'd been beginning to think so.

"So?" he said, sounding warm and sexy over the phone, "Did they find them?"

"Find what?" She sounded puzzled.

"The raisins. Didn't you tell him?"

"You silly . . ." She told him all about the questions they'd asked, the exam they'd done, and the tests that lay ahead, none of which sounded really awful. She'd been really afraid that the treatment would be ghastly, but so far none of it sounded too daunting.

"So you go back in two weeks?"

"Ten days, and meanwhile I still take my temperature every morning, and start checking my urine with the kit next week."

"Sounds complicated to me," he said, wondering what the future held for them, and especially for him. Maybe the tests would be worse for him when they got to them. He still thought the whole thing was unnecessary and more than a little scary. But he was willing to go along with it, for her sake.

"By the way," he said, after she'd explained it all to him, and told him everything she could about Dr. Johnston, down to the shoes he wore, and the list of diplomas on his office wall, "you're not going to believe this."

"You got a raise," she said hopefully; he worked like a slave for the network.

"No, but it's coming, according to sources close to the top. But this is pretty good too. Try again."

"The head of the network got arrested for exposing himself in the cafeteria," she said, closing her eyes and thinking creatively.

"Very nice . . . I wonder if there's anything to that? . . . No, I'll tell you myself, since you'll never guess, and I have to be in a meeting in two minutes. Bill Bennington is marrying his little lawyer friend on Labor Day, at her parents' summer house at Lake Tahoe. Can you believe that? I almost choked when he told me. I was eating a corned beef sandwich with him downstairs, and I thought he was kidding, till I saw his face. Can you believe it?"

"Actually, you know, maybe I can. In a funny way, I think he's ready."

"I hope so. He'd better be anyway. The wedding's only about seven weeks away. They're going fishing in Alaska on their honeymoon."

"*Yerghk!* You'd better talk to him."

"I'd better get my ass to my meeting. See you later, sweetheart. I'll be home around seven." And as always, he was true to his word, and she had a terrific dinner waiting for him. She had used one of Eloise's French recipes, and played around with it a little bit. She made leg of lamb with a light garlic sauce, string beans, and wild mushrooms. And for dessert an apricot soufflé that was perfection.

"Wow! What did I do to deserve all this?" he asked happily, as they finished dessert and she poured him a cup of coffee. She was feeling better than she had in a long time, and he could see it.

"I just thought it would be fun to have a nice dinner, since I was a lady of leisure today."

"Maybe you should stay home more often." She liked doing that, but she liked working too. Unlike her sisters, she had conflicts about that, and knew she might still have, even if they had a baby. But she didn't have to face that yet, all she had to do was "relax and slow down," according to the doctor. She told Andy about that, too, and he liked the idea, and immediately suggested they go to Santa Barbara for the weekend.

"I'd love it." He'd also made a date with Bill Bennington and his bride-to-be that week. Suddenly life felt like more fun, and she wasn't sure why, except that she felt sure that the doctor was going to find a way to help them have their baby, and that cheered her.

They had a good time that week, and they
were crazy about Bill's fiancée, Denise Smith.
She was everything he said she would be, and
she invited them to her place for dinner the
following week, but Andy was surprised when
Diana put her off with vague excuses. But later
on she told him that she would be ovulating
then, she had to go to Dr. Johnston for tests,
and they had to make love on schedule. She
didn't want to add to all that the strain of a
social schedule.

"Maybe it would be a relief instead of a
strain," Andy said testily, but Diana still didn't
want to go, and they made plans with Denise
and Bill for the following week instead, although Andy was still annoyed about it. But Diana was busy pursuing their baby.

She continued to take her temperature reli-
giously every morning before she got up, and
she began using the LH kit as she'd been told
to, and the test turned blue on exactly the day
the doctor said it would, and that afternoon she
went to his office for him to check the mucus in
her cervix. He said it looked fine to him, "Very
nice and friendly," as he put it, and Diana
laughed nervously. He suggested that Andy and
Diana make love the following morning, and
Diana was to come in as soon as possible after-

wards for the postcoital test that would show how Andy's sperm were behaving.

She went back to work late that afternoon, and had coffee with Eloise, and that night she brought Andy up to date on the latest developments, and told him they'd have to make love the next morning.

"What an ordeal," he said jokingly, but as it turned out, it was. He'd had indigestion the night before, and he really didn't feel well when he woke up. He thought he was getting the flu, and he didn't think "things were going to work out," as he put it.

"But you have to," Diana said tensely as they lay in bed, and she tried to help him. "This is the day I ovulate, and I have to have the postcoital test today. I took my temperature and it's way down, which means I'm probably ovulating today. . . . Andy . . . you have to." She looked at him accusingly, and he wanted to tell her to go to hell, but he didn't.

"Great. Thanks for the important message from my sponsor." He rolled over in bed then and masturbated for a while, and finally brought some life into things and then rolled over and made love to his wife, but there was nothing romantic about any of it. It wasn't even pleasant. And then, without another word to her, he got out of bed and went to take a shower. It wasn't much fun this way, feeling pressed about what day and what time you made love, or even how. And they were both tense and quiet with each other over breakfast.

"I'm sorry," Diana said softly.

"Don't be," he said from the other side of the paper. "I just don't feel great today, that's all. Forget it." He hated making love to her like that, on command, and he was still nervous about what they were going to do to him, or what they would discover.

But the postcoital test, as it turned out, showed that his sperm appeared to be normal. They were swimming around happily, and he seemed to have a pretty dense sperm population, and high motility, all of which was excellent, according to the doctor.

Dr. Johnston also wanted to do an ultrasound on her, to clarify a number of important points that were crucial to her evaluation. He needed to know about the thickness of her uterine lining, the size of her follicle, and if her body was responding to her own production of hormones. And he assured her that the scan wouldn't be very unpleasant, and it wasn't. And she was relieved that so far everything appeared to be normal.

And when she returned again two days later for yet another ultrasound scan, to see if the follicle had ruptured and released the egg, he was able to tell her that it had, and they were another step further.

Bill and Denise invited them out to dinner again the next day, but Diana was so exhausted from the strain of worrying about all of it, and getting to the doctor three times that week for tests and scans, that she just didn't feel like going out, and in the end, she urged Andy to go out without her. She just wanted to go to bed and relax, and she was praying that this month she might have gotten pregnant. Nothing seemed to matter anymore except that. Even her job was less important to her now. But at least now she could talk to Eloise. But even her friends and family seemed less important to her as they forged ahead with the doctor. Their whole life seemed to have a single purpose to it now, even more than before. Sometimes she felt as though she were losing sight of Andy.

On Monday she went back to the doctor again, and had blood drawn to check her progesterone levels during the mid-luteal phase, seven days after ovulation. Her temperature had gone up immediately after the LH surge, which was normal, and indicated that she had ovulated. And now all they could do was wait, and see if she was pregnant.

It seemed an interminable ten days while they waited, and she could hardly keep her mind on anything. It also seemed crazy to think that things were going to be different this month. They hadn't given her any medication, all they were doing was gathering information. But her hopes were high anyway, and she began to feel nauseated two days before she was due to get her period, and her hopes skyrocketed on the morning it was due and she didn't have it.

She called Dr. Johnston from the office that day, and he told her to wait a day or two, her body wasn't a machine, and there were variations in the norm. And that night, she got her period, and lay in bed and sobbed after she discovered it. She was crushed and now she wondered what tests they would have in store for her. The whole thing was becoming more and more depressing.

And when she called the doctor the next day, he suggested that Andy make an appointment to come in. So far, all of her tests had been normal.

"Great. What does that mean?" Andy asked testily when she told him that night that he

needed to call Dr. Johnston for an appointment.
"That he thinks it's my fault?"

"What does it matter whose fault it is as long
as we find out everything's okay? I don't care if
it's your fault or mine, maybe it's no one's fault,
maybe nothing's wrong. Maybe everyone was
right to begin with, and all we need is time.
Don't be so uptight," she told him gently, but
he was even more annoyed when he called for
the appointment and they told him to bring a
vial of fresh semen with him. And he had been
told not to have intercourse for three days before taking the sample.

"Great." He complained to Diana that night.
"What am I supposed to do? Jack off at the office, and then run to the doctor? My secretaries
will love it."

"Do you think I loved running in there three
different times for an ultrasound scan? Stop
making this worse than it is." But it was bad
enough, and they both knew it.

"Okay, okay." He didn't say any more about
it, but things were tense between them, and
Andy was vile with her the morning he went to
Dr. Johnston for tests, and he was openly hostile to the doctor as he sat down in his office.
No, he had never had gonorrhea, syphilis, chla-
mydia, herpes, or any of the diseases the doctor

mentioned. He had not had infections, tumors, problems with his erections, impotence, or any major diseases in his lifetime.

The doctor was well aware of his hostility, but he was used to it with other patients. It was upsetting for anyone being there, and he was challenging Andy's manhood.

He explained that he was going to take blood from him today, in order to check his hormone levels, and with the semen he had brought with him they were going to do both analyses and cultures. A sperm count would be done, as well as a full hormone profile, and it was also possible that he would have to come in to have blood drawn again, because male hormone levels varied greatly, even depending on the time of day, or the man's health at the moment.

And after the blood work was done, the doctor checked him for varicoceles, which were varicose veins in his testes that could interfere with fertility and be a serious problem.

And just as Diana had been, by the time Andy was finished, he was exhausted. None of it had been particularly gruelling, but just the emotional strain of it had been deeply upsetting.

And when the tests came back, Andy was relieved to discover that they were normal. His sperm count was just over two hundred million sperm, which the doctor said was extremely healthy, and the sperm concentration was a hundred and eighty million sperm per milliliter. And all his hormone tests were normal.

"Now what?" Andy said quietly, but feeling greatly relieved, when Dr. Johnston called him himself three days later with the test results. In some ways, he was enormously pleased to know that there was nothing wrong with him, but suddenly he was beginning to worry about Diana.

"Does this mean we're both okay, and it'll just take time?" If that was the case, it had been worth the stress, just to get the information. But Johnston wasn't ready to let them off the hook yet, now that they had started.

"It could certainly. But I'd like to go a few steps further with Diana. I'm still concerned about the IUD she had several years ago, and I'd like to do a hysterosalpingogram on her this month before she ovulates. It's a study of the upper reproductive tract, by flushing it with radiopaque dye, and taking an X ray." He made it sound extremely ordinary, but Andy was suspicious.

"Is it painful?"

"Sometimes," he said candidly, "not always.

It's uncomfortable." That was Andy's least favorite word when used by medical technicians. "Uncomfortable" usually meant you were not quite writhing on the floor, but almost. "We can give her some pain killers at the hospital. She'll have to take doxycycline for a few days before, just to make sure there's no infection, and she'll stay on it afterward. Not everyone prescribes antibiotics for this procedure, but I prefer it, to be on the safe side. In a lot of cases, the test itself flushes out the tubes, and people get pregnant within six months after they've had it."

"Sounds like it might be worth a try," Andy said cautiously.

"I think so," Dr. Johnston said quietly. "I'll call her."

But when he did, Diana wasn't as sure. She had heard nasty things about that test from women in her office. They said it was painful, and one of them had been allergic to the dye solution they'd used and had a frightening reaction. She asked Eloise what she knew of it, which wasn't much. But it was obvious that, no matter how smoothly it went, the hysterosalpingogram was no picnic. But it also offered important information that they wanted. A dye would be flushed into her and they would see it move through her tubes on a TV screen. It would show any deformities in her uterus, tumors that might have escaped the scan, and blockage of her tubes, which Dr. Johnston now had a faint suspicion might be the problem. He told Diana that if they did the hysterosalpingogram and it was normal, there would be no need to proceed any further. She could assume that eventually she'd probably conceive and she and Andy could stop worrying about their reproductive organs. If, however, the HSG showed anything unusual, they could do a laparoscopy later that month, and they would have all their final answers. He didn't believe in torturing patients for months with unnecessary tests or long-drawn-out answers. Since her ovulations had proven to be normal and her mucus and his sperm were both normal and compatible, the only thing he wanted to see now was that her tubes were indeed clear, and then the testing would be over.

"What do you think?" Dr. Johnston asked Diana on the phone. "Do you want to do the HSG this month and get it over with, or wait and try again? We can wait of course." But the truth was he didn't recommend waiting. He didn't believe in breaking one's heart repeatedly, trying again and again when there was no hope, or an unresolved problem.

"I need to think about it tonight," she said nervously. "I'll call you back tomorrow."

"Fine."

She felt as though she never got away from him anymore. For the past month, they had scarcely seen their friends, she couldn't concentrate on her work, didn't want to see her family. And even Andy had stopped calling his brothers. All they did instead was take temperatures, make out charts, get tests, and run to doctors. Dr. Johnston had warned them it would be like that, and he had also mentioned that a therapist could be very helpful. But they had no time for that either. They were too busy working, and doing their tests, and trying to support each other through what was beginning to feel like a constant crisis.

"What do you think, sweetheart?" Andy asked her gently that night. "Do you want to do the bingogram, or whatever they call it?" She smiled at him, she still wanted to know why they hadn't gotten pregnant. And yet, this test really frightened her.

"Will you go with me?" she asked anxiously, and he nodded.

"Sure, if they'll let me."

"Dr. Johnston said he would. He wants to do it on Friday."

"That's a good day for me," Andy said rapidly. "I don't have any big meetings."

"Great. Then why don't you have it done," she said testily, and he backed off and went to make them both a cup of coffee. And when he came back, she looked up at him unhappily. She had made up her mind. It was worth it, just for the information.

"Okay. I'll do it."

"You're a brave girl, Di." He wasn't sure how he would have felt in her place. So far, his share of the tests had been very easy.

On Friday morning, they met the doctor at the hospital, and he explained the procedure to them in a small examining room, and he gave her two pain pills. A nurse applied an iodine solution to the area, another nurse administered atropine and glucagon to relax her muscles, and a moment later the dye was carefully inserted. Diana could see the pictures herself on the monitor, although they meant nothing to her. And fifteen minutes later, it was over. Her knees were shaking, and she had cramps, but she was relieved that it was finished, as was Andy, who thought she'd been incredibly brave. He had almost wished he could do it for her. And more than once, he had wondered if it was all worth it. He was beginning to doubt it. Why in God's name did they need a baby?

"You okay?" he asked Diana worriedly as she winced and sat up. But she nodded. She had survived and all she wanted to know now was what Dr. Johnston had seen there. He was conferring with two technicians standing by, and he and the radiologist were carefully studying one of the pictures. There was an area free of the dye that seemed to be holding their attention.

"What's happening?" Andy asked softly.

"Well, we've got something interesting here." Johnston turned to both of them. "We'll see. We'll talk about it later." Andy and a nurse helped Diana clean up, while Johnston and his associate consulted the screen several times again, and eventually Diana sat down quietly with her clothes on. She still looked a little gray, but she looked calm as Johnston turned to face them.

"How do you feel?" he asked gently, and she shrugged.

"Like someone ran over me with a bulldozer," she said honestly, and Andy put his arms around her and held her.

"I think doing the test was well worth it," Johnston said quietly. "We may have found our culprit. Your right tube looks like it's blocked, Diana. And your left one looks a little hazy too. I'd really like to schedule you for a laparoscopy next week so we can see what this is all about. We may have found our answer."

"And if they're blocked?" Diana looked very frightened. "Can you open them?"

"Possibly. I don't know yet. I'll know a lot more after the laparoscopy."

"Shit," she said, and stared at them, and then at Andy. She hadn't been prepared for bad news. And even knowing that there was indeed a problem wasn't the relief she had thought it would be.

She scheduled the laparoscopy with him the following week. It was a surgical procedure that involved a small incision near her belly button through which they would insert a telescope that would allow them to see her tubes, her uterus, the entire area, and any possible ob-structions. And this time, he promised there would be no pain. It would be done under gen-eral anesthesia.

"And then? Afterward?" she asked, wanting to know it all now.

"We'll know where we stand, Diana. But the HSG told me that we've been right to be ag-gressively persistent." She didn't know whether to be grateful to him or hate him, but they thanked him and left the hospital half an hour later. And instead of relief after getting through a difficult test, now she had surgery to look forward to the following week. It was almost too much to think of. And she felt ten thousand years old as she walked into their house and picked up the phone mechanically when she heard it ringing.

It was her sister, Sam, wanting to know how she was. She was the last person on earth Diana wanted to talk to.

"Hi, Sam. I'm fine. How are you?"

"Fat," her sister complained. She always got enormous during pregnancy, and she was now three and a half months pregnant. "You sound awful. Is something wrong?"

"I've got the flu. I'd better go."

"Okay, love, take care. I'll call you in a few days." Don't, Diana whispered to herself as she hung up the phone . . . don't call me again . . . ever . . . don't tell me how fat you are . . . how pregnant you are . . . about your children or your baby. . . .

"Who was that?" Andy walked in just behind her.

"Sam," she said tonelessly.

"Oh." He understood immediately. "You

shouldn't talk to her. Don't answer the phone anymore. I'll tell her you're out." But Andy's brother, Greg, was no better when he called them that night and asked when they were going to have a baby.

"When you grow up," Andy joked with him, but the remark hurt even him. And it would have killed Diana.

"Don't count on that," his brother said.

"I figured."

He also wanted to come and visit for Labor Day, and Andy didn't think he should. He didn't know how she'd feel after the laparoscopy the next week, and Labor Day was just around the corner. Maybe she'd be really depressed by then . . . or having surgery . . . or maybe even pregnant. It was impossible to make plans anymore, or even lead a normal life. Sometimes Andy wondered how other people stood it, or even afforded it. So far, the tests had been incredibly expensive. And the laparoscopy was going to be even more so.

Greg said he understood and he'd come out another time. Andy had told him he was just too busy at work to have houseguests, which made him sound unfriendly. But it was better than telling him what a mess their life was at the moment.

"It's turning our life to shit, isn't it?" Diana said sadly as they ate dinner in their kitchen that night. The house seemed too large for them now. There were too many rooms they didn't use, a whole floor of bedrooms they might never have any use for.

"We can't let that happen, sweetheart," Andy insisted valiantly. "And the doctor's right, by the end of August, we'll know everything, and then we can take it from there. If something's wrong, they can probably fix it in no time."

"And if they can't?"

"We have to live with it, don't we? There are a lot of possibilities." He'd been reading a lot lately about in vitro fertilization.

"I won't let you just 'live with it,' " she said, as her eyes filled with tears. "I'd rather divorce you and let you marry someone who can have children."

"Don't be stupid." Just hearing her say that to him, and knowing how she felt, upset him deeply. "We can adopt, if nothing else."

"Why should you? You don't need to do that. You're not the problem. I am."

"Maybe no one is. Maybe he's wrong. Maybe the blockage he saw is something you ate for lunch, for chrissake. Okay? Why don't you just wait till we find out." He raised his voice at her, and then shook his head. She was right. It was turning their life to shit. And the strain was telling on both of them.

"Yeah," she said sadly, "maybe it's raisins." But Andy didn't smile at her this time, he just couldn't.

CHAPTER

7

The days before the laparoscopy seemed to drag, and then suddenly it was Friday. Diana hadn't had anything to eat or drink since the night before, and Andy drove her to the hospital early that morning.

They gave her a shot almost as soon as she got in this time, and they wheeled her away as she gazed sleepily at Andy and waved. And when they brought her back to him at noon, she was still very groggy. But Alex Johnston had already been to see him by then, and Andy knew all the bad news, before she did. Andy said nothing to her when she came to, and Dr. Johnston came back to see them that afternoon and tell them the entire story.

"How did it look?" she asked nervously as

she sat up, when he came into the room. For a fraction of a second, he didn't answer. He glanced at Andy, and then sat down and looked at her. He didn't have good news for her, and as she looked at him, she knew it. "It's not good, is it?"

"No, it isn't," he said quietly. "Both tubes are badly scarred, one appears to be fully blocked, and the other is badly damaged. There are severe adhesions on both ovaries. I'm afraid that an egg would never make it through the tubes. We didn't get good news today, Diana." She stared at him in disbelief, unable to believe what he was saying. It couldn't be as bad as he said, or could it?

"Can you fix it?" she said hoarsely.

He shook his head. "There's absolutely nothing we can do. The one tube looked like it had some possibilities, but you've got severe adhesions on both ovaries and the bowel. The damage is so great, I just don't see how we could fix it. It's not entirely impossible that an egg could get through, but it's extremely unlikely. Stranger things have happened. But I'd say you've got about a one in ten thousand chance of ever getting pregnant. And the adhesions on the ovaries are so great that an attempt at egg retrieval could damage the bowel. That pretty much rules out in vitro fertilization. I think if we did anything, we'd have to go with an ovum transplant, using another woman's egg fertilized by Andy's sperm and put back in your womb, but there's no guarantee of that succeeding either. It looks as though your whole reproductive system was traumatized by a severe infection, probably from your IUD, a 'silent' infection, as we call them, with no symptoms, no warning.

"I think if you got pregnant at all, it would be a complete fluke, and we don't see a lot of those in this business. There's really not much we can do, except a donor ovum, or adoption."

There were tears streaming down her face and Andy was crying too. He reached out and held her hand as tightly as he could. But there was no way he could take away the pain of what she was feeling, or the truth of what they'd found. All he could do was wish that things had been different.

"How did this happen to me? Why didn't I know? Why didn't I feel it?" A whole part of her had died and she hadn't known it until now. It seemed impossible that something so cruel had happened.

"That's the nature of a silent infection," Dr. Johnston explained, "and an IUD is most often the culprit. Unfortunately, it's not uncommon. No pain, no sign, no discharge, no fever, but an infection so severe that it destroys the tubes, and in this case even the ovaries with adhesions. I can't tell you how many young women we see like that. I'm just sorry it happened to you. It's not fair, but you do have other options." He wanted to give her hope, but he was only bringing despair. The dream of having her own baby was over.

"I don't want another woman's egg. I'd rather not have children."

"You say that now, but you might want to think about it later."

"No, I won't, and I don't want to adopt," she screamed. "I want my own baby!" Why had her sisters been able to conceive so easily? Why was it possible for everyone else and not for her, and why had she used the damn IUD? She wanted to lash out at someone and there was no one to blame, no one to rail at, no way to make the pain stop and make it better. Andy took her in his arms as she sobbed, and eventually the doctor left them to each other. There was nothing more he could do now.

"I'm sorry, sweetheart. I'm so sorry," he said over and over again, as he held her. And a little while later they went home, her tummy sore, her womb not only empty but barren.

"I can't believe it," she said to Andy as she walked in the front door. And then she looked around her with horror. She even hated this house now. "I want to sell this house," she said, and then walked into their bedroom. "Those rooms upstairs are like an accusation. 'You're sterile!' they scream. 'You'll never have a baby.'" She wanted to die as she thought of what the doctor had told her.

"Why don't we think about what he said, about other options," Andy said calmly. He was trying not to upset her more, but he was upset too. It had been a ghastly day for them, and now they had to look ahead to what they were going to do with an entire lifetime. Nothing had gone according to plan, and the prospect of changing their plans wasn't easy or pleasant. "That thing with the donor egg might be terrific."

"It isn't *terrific*!" She screamed at him, acting like someone he had never met before. "There is nothing *terrific* about that disgusting process. *Terrific* is having your own baby, and I *can't*. Didn't you hear him?" She was sobbing hysterically, and he didn't know what to do to calm her. It was depressing for him, too, but it was worse for her because the fatal flaw they had found was in her body.

"Why don't we talk about this some other time," he said, gently turning down their bed so she could get in. He knew she had to be in pain from the incision.

"I don't ever want to talk about it again. And if you want to divorce me, that's fine," she said, still sobbing as she climbed into their bed, looking devastated.

He smiled sadly at her. She was a mess, but she had every right to be, and he loved her more than ever. "I don't want to divorce you, Di. I love you. Why don't you just get some sleep? We'll both be a little more clearheaded about this tomorrow."

"What difference will that make?" She growled miserably as she lay down. "There is no tomorrow anymore. No next week, no blue tests, or temperatures. There's nothing." They had taken away hope, but with it, they had taken constant disappointment. Maybe that wasn't such a bad thing, he told himself as he pulled the shades and left the room, hoping that she would sleep finally. But all she did was cry all through the weekend. And on Monday she went to work looking like someone had died.

And the only smart thing she did was refuse to take any calls from her sisters.

She looked like a zombie for the next week, and in spite of all his efforts, Andy could do nothing to console her. Eloise at the office even tried to take her to lunch, but Diana put her off. She didn't want to see or talk to anyone—not even Andy.

Before Labor Day he tried to talk her into going to Bill and Denise's wedding, at Lake Tahoe, but she flatly refused to go, and after fighting about it for a week, he went without her. She didn't seem to mind, and he didn't have a great time, but it felt good to get away from her fury, and the constant dull ache of their problems. It was a constant agony, and he had no idea how to convince her that their life wasn't over. "Neither you nor I have died," he said finally, "nor do we have terminal diseases. The only thing that's different is that we know we're not going to have a baby. But I refuse to give up my marriage for that. Sure I want kids. And maybe one day we'll adopt some. But right now, there's you and me. And we are going to destroy each other if we don't pull ourselves together." He was determined to put normalcy back into their life, but Diana couldn't even remember where to find it.

She argued constantly with him and she raged about everything, or some days she didn't speak to all. The only time she seemed sane at all was when she went to work, but by the time she came home again, she was always half crazy, and sometimes he wondered if she was trying to kill their marriage. She wasn't sure of anything anymore, of him, herself, their friends, her work, and least of all their future.

On Labor Day Saturday, Charlie's old friend Mark took him out to dinner. His current girl-friend was away for a few days to visit her parents in the East, and the day before, at work, he had discovered that Charlie was alone, too, for the weekend.

They went bowling that afternoon, and then they went out and had a few beers and watched the ballgame at Mark's favorite bar. It was the kind of afternoon they both loved, and rarely had time for. They both worked hard, and most weekends Charlie did what Barbie wanted to do, which usually meant shopping, or stopping by to see friends. And the one thing she really hated doing with him was bowling.

"So what's new, kid?" Mark asked congenially, as the Mets hit a home run. He loved

spending time with Charlie, and Mark was genuinely concerned about the younger man's well-
being. He had never had a son of his own, just
two girls, and sometimes he thought he felt
about Charlie the way he might have felt about
a son, if he'd had one. "Where'd Barbie go?
Back to Salt Lake City to see her folks?" He
knew that was where she was from, but not that
she would have died before going to visit her
family again. Charlie never gave away any of
her secrets.

"She went to Vegas with a friend," Charlie
said matter-of-factly, and smiled at his friend.
He loved Mark, too; he had been incredibly
good to him at work, and for three years now
they had been fast friends and good buddies.

"Are you kidding?" Mark looked shocked.
"What kind of friend?"

"Her old roommate, Judi. They went back to
see some old pals. They used to live there."

"You let her go alone?"

"I told you . . . she went with Judi." Charlie looked amused at his concern.

"You're crazy. Judi is gonna be off in ten seconds with some guy, and what do you think is
going to happen to Barbie?"

"She's a big girl. She can manage on her own.
And if she has a problem, she'll call me." He felt

totally confident that she'd be fine, and she'd been so excited about going. She hadn't been back in almost two years, and the seaminess of it had faded from her mind. All she remembered now was the razzle-dazzle and the excitement.

"How come you didn't go?" Mark asked as they ordered a pepperoni pizza.

"Ahh . . . that's not my scene." Charlie shrugged. "I hate that stuff. All that noise and craziness, I don't like to gamble, I can get drunk here at home if that's what I want to do"—which it seldom was—"What do I need to go to Vegas? She'll have more fun there with her girlfriends, than with me dragging along, while they giggle and squeal and talk about boyfriends and makeup."

"She hasn't gotten that stuff out of her system yet, has she?" Mark looked seriously concerned, and Charlie smiled, touched by his friend's involvement.

"What stuff? Boyfriends and makeup?" Charlie teased. He totally trusted Barbie. "She's fine. She just likes a taste of glamour now and then, it makes her feel like she's still an actress. She hasn't had much work this year, and our life is pretty quiet." He liked it, but he knew she missed the excitement of her old life sometimes, even though she always said she was glad to have escaped it with Charlie.

"What's wrong with quiet?" Mark growled, and the younger man laughed.

"You sound like my father . . . if I'd had one." Charlie loved the fact that Mark cared that much. No one ever had before, except, of course, Barbie.

"You shouldn't have let her go to Vegas. Married women don't do shit like that. They're supposed to stay home with their husbands. What do you know? You never had a mother as a kid. But if my wife had done that, I'd have divorced her on the spot."

"You did anyway," Charlie teased, and Mark grinned sheepishly.

"That was different. I divorced her because she was having an affair with someone else." His best friend at the time, Charlie knew. And she had taken his two girls and moved from New Jersey to L.A., which was how he had come to California. He had come to be closer to his daughters.

"Don't worry so much. We're fine. She needed a little fun, that's all. I understand it."

"You're too good-natured. Let me tell you!" He wagged a finger at him as the pizza arrived. "That's how I was, and I learned . . . now I'm tough!" He pretended to look stern, and they both knew he was a pushover for women. They could have anything they wanted from him, as long as they didn't play around with guys. That was one thing he wouldn't put up with. But he was being sincere with Charlie too. He would never have let any of his girlfriends leave him for a weekend and go to Las Vegas.

"So what's new with you?" Charlie asked, while they continued to eat the enormous pizza. "How are Marjorie and Helen?" They were his daughters. One was married, and the other was still in college, and they were the pride of his life. He was crazy about them both, and anyone who didn't think they were sensational didn't last five seconds in his life, particularly women.

"They're fine. Did I tell you Marjorie is expecting in March? I can't believe it . . . my first grandchild. They already know it's a boy. Things sure have changed since my day." And then he frowned, wondering when Charlie was going to take a step in that direction. Maybe that was just what Barbie needed, to keep her home from weekends in Vegas. "What about you? No little ones on the way? It's about that time, don't you think? You've been married, what now? . . . fourteen, fifteen months? That would settle the little lady down in a hurry."

"That's what she's afraid of," Charlie said sadly, but the issue wasn't just what she wanted, but what wasn't happening. According to the books he'd read on the subject, and there had been quite a few lately, they were making love at exactly the right time every month to produce a baby. But after four months of intense attention to his plan, absolutely nothing had happened. And Charlie was beginning to get worried.

"She doesn't want kids?"

"That's what she says now," Charlie said, undaunted by her words, and trying to convey as much to Mark. "But she'll change her mind eventually. Nobody can resist kids. She's just afraid it'll screw up her career if she gets pregnant, that if her big chance comes, she won't be able to take it."

"Maybe it'll never come. You can't sacrifice kids for that," Mark said firmly. He wasn't at all sympathetic to Barbie's whims. He thought she was spoiled rotten, and he didn't like seeing Charlie do it. "You ought to get her pregnant, no matter what she wants," Mark said, sitting back in the booth with a satisfied look, and Charlie sighed.

"Things aren't always that simple."

"She on the pill?"

"No. I don't think so anyway." He hadn't even thought of that, but he didn't think she was devious. She just didn't want a kid right now, and she used her diaphragm, whenever she wasn't too lazy to get out of bed, which, fortunately for Charlie, wasn't often. They were very sloppy about birth control, so much so that Charlie was growing increasingly concerned about their lack of results. And she had said as much herself months before when she said she was surprised, as careless as they were, that she never got pregnant. "I don't know"—he looked sheepishly at his friend—"it just hasn't worked so far." He sounded discouraged, and Mark looked sympathetic and worried. He knew how badly Charlie wanted a kid, and he thought it would be the best thing for him, not to mention keeping Barbie down on the farm, which was just what she needed.

"Maybe you're not doing it at the right time. You can't just do it any old time, you know. There's a whole science to this. You should ask your doctor." He wasn't too up on it himself, his first daughter had been conceived in the back of his car when he was nineteen and not yet married to her mother. And their second one was born ten months after the first one. After that she'd had her tubes tied, and his current girlfriend took the pill. But he knew perfectly well that there were right and wrong times to do it, and he wasn't sure if Charlie knew that.

"We've been doing it right on schedule, according to the books I've been reading."

"Maybe you should just relax then," he said conspiratorially. "You're healthy and young, it'll happen sooner or later."

"Maybe." But it was beginning to depress him that it hadn't happened yet, and he was getting worried.

"You think something might be wrong?"

"I don't know." The worry in Charlie's eyes touched Mark, and he patted his shoulder and ordered them both another round of beers. It was a nice, friendly evening.

"You have mumps as a kid, or VD a lot when you were screwing around?"

"No." Charlie smiled at the earnest questions. "None of that."

And then Mark frowned, looking at his young friend with concern. "You know my sister and her husband had a lot of trouble having kids. They were married seven years and nothing happened. They live in San Diego. And he went to a great doctor up here. My sister had to take hormone pills or shots or something, and I'm not sure what they did to my brother-in-law, except that I know he had to wear Jockey shorts with ice cubes in 'em for a while. Sounds great, doesn't it? But bam, bam, bam, they had three kids just like that. Two boys and a girl. I'll get his name for you the next time I talk to her. He was some fancy guy in Beverly Hills, it cost them a fortune, but it was worth it. The kids are terrific."

Charlie was still smiling at the image of Mark's brother-in-law wearing Jockey shorts filled with ice cubes, when their beers arrived, and they both laughed. Life was sweet sometimes, just being with a friend, and spending an easy evening. He loved being with his wife, but he couldn't talk to her about the things he cared about, and everything she was interested in was so completely different. He and Mark had a lot in common, and Charlie really valued his friendship.

"I'm not sure if I'm dying to put ice cubes in my shorts, you know."

"Listen, if it works, what the hell . . . right?"

"It's too bad I'm not married to you," Charlie teased. "I like the way you feel about kids." He smiled at his friend.

"They're the greatest. I'll get you the name of

the doctor," he said insistently, determined to help, as always.

"I'm not even sure something's wrong, maybe we haven't tried for long enough. I've only been really serious about it since June. They say it can take a year for even a normal couple to get pregnant."

"I wish I had been that lucky, just once." Mark rolled his eyes and they both laughed. "Anyway, what harm can it do to check it out? Then the guy tells you you're in great shape, you feel like a stud, you come home and throw her on the floor and take her, and bingo, she gets pregnant. That's all the doctor does . . . it's a little morale booster for the troops at home, right?"

"You crazy guy . . ." Charlie was more touched by his concern than he knew how to tell him.

"Me, crazy? Am I the guy who let his wife go to Las Vegas? I think you're the crazy one here."

"Yeah. Maybe so." Charlie smiled, but he felt better than he had in a long time, and the Mets were winning as they finished their beers. It was ten o'clock before Mark drove him home, and after he dropped Charlie off, Charlie walked slowly up to their apartment, wondering if he should see the doctor. It seemed a little extreme to go to a specialist so soon, and there was probably nothing wrong with him at all, but in another way, it might be reassuring. It was odd to think of it though, considering the fact that Barbie didn't realize he was making a concentrated effort to get her pregnant. She had no inkling at all. In fact, he was the last thing on her mind that night, as she partied with her old friends, and ran into some guys she hadn't seen in years, in Vegas.

On Labor Day weekend, Pilar discovered for the third time in three months that she wasn't pregnant. She was depressed this time, but philosophical. She and Brad had already agreed that if it didn't work this time, she was going to see a doctor. She had been making discreet inquiries for a while, and Marina had told her about a reproductive specialist in Beverly Hills, and if she was as good as Marina's source said, it was worth the drive to see her. L.A. was only two hours away, and the doctors she'd called to check on her all said she was fantastic, and well worth it.

On the day after Labor Day Pilar made an appointment for the following week. Normally she would have had to wait months, but Marina's friend intervened, and asked if she would see her quickly, and she agreed. And Brad had also agreed to go with her.

He wasn't entirely sure that he liked the idea that Marina had found them a woman doctor, but Pilar felt strongly about it, and he thought it was important for her to feel at ease with the physician they went to.

"What are they going to do to me?" he asked nervously on the drive down. He had had to recess the case he was on for the afternoon, which was something he did very rarely.

"I think they'll probably cut it off, check it out, and sew it back on. No big deal. They won't start the big stuff till next time."

"A big help you are," he growled and she laughed, grateful that he had come along. She was nervous about the visit, too, and she didn't know what to expect. But the moment they met Dr. Helen Ward, a small, neat-looking woman with bright blue eyes and salt-and-pepper hair, they knew they had come to the right office. She was intelligent and calm, totally focused on what they wanted from her, and clear in the information she gave them. At first, Brad thought she was a little too cold and too clinical, but as they talked for a while she seemed to warm up to them, and she had a nice sense of humor. She practiced medicine the way Pilar practiced law, with compassion and intelligence, but also with immense skill and professional precision. And it reassured both of them to see that she had gone to medical school at Harvard, and she was in her mid-fifties, which pleased both Brad and Pilar. She had been particularly clear that she didn't want a young, fiery, experimental doctor. She wanted someone serious and calm, who would choose the more conservative routes, while still doing everything she could to help them.

After an initial chat, she began their charts, and asked them each intense questions about their health, and past and present medical problems. Brad was pleased to see how comfortable Pilar was with her, especially when she told her about the abortion she'd had when she was nineteen. She didn't like talking about it, but she had told Brad about it late one night, after a lot of wine, but she also told him that to this day she still felt guilty. She had had every good reason not to have the baby, she had been a freshman in college, with no way of supporting a child, and the baby's father, her first affair, absolutely refused to help her. Her parents would have disowned her, or worse, or so she thought.

And she had been just terrified, and desperate enough to have an illegal abortion in Spanish Harlem. And now, more than once, she had found herself wondering if that abortion was part of the reason she wasn't getting pregnant. But Dr. Ward assured her that that wasn't likely.

"Most women who have even several abortions go on to have healthy children, and there's nothing to prove that women who have had abortions have a harder time getting pregnant. If you'd had a serious infection afterward, that would be another story, but from what you've described, it sounds pretty normal." All of which reassured Pilar immensely.

They talked about Brad's children, their birth control for the past fourteen years, and after she took their histories, she did an exam on Pilar, and found no noticeable problems. As always, with infertility, she was particularly wary of infections.

"Is there any particular reason why you both wanted to come here? There's nothing in either of your histories that suggests any kind of complications, and three months of trying to conceive is really very early to be getting worried," she said encouragingly with a warm smile and, more than ever, Pilar decided she liked her.

"That's fine if you're sixteen, Doctor Ward. I'm forty-three. I don't feel like I have a lot of time to play around with."

"That's true, and we could check a few things, your FSH and progesterone levels, which could affect your ability to get pregnant, thyroid and prolactin, for the same reasons. We like to see your progesterone levels above a certain point to ensure conception. We can check your temperature every morning, and keep a basal body temperature, or BBT, chart. And we might give you a little boost with some chlomiphene, just to see if that helps. Chlomiphene isn't always useful in women over forty, but it might be worth a try if you're willing. It's a hormone that will fool your body into producing unusually high levels of progesterone, to help you get pregnant."

"Will it make me grow hair on my chin?" she asked bluntly, and the doctor laughed.

"Not that I've ever seen. It may make you a little tense though, a feeling of stress for the five days that you take it, and shortly thereafter. It causes some people minor problems with their vision, mild headaches sometimes, and it can cause nausea, mood swings, even ovarian cysts, but usually there's nothing major."

"I think I'd like to try it," Pilar said confidently. "What about anything stronger? Hormone shots?"

"I don't see any reason for that yet. We don't want to get overenthusiastic about interfering with nature."

She didn't want to go overboard on a woman with no obvious problems. Dr. Ward suspected that, if Pilar could have, she'd have asked for more drastic measures, like in vitro fertilization, where they would provoke her ovaries to produce several eggs with the use of hormones, then take several of the eggs from her ovaries, fertilize them in a petri dish with her husband's sperm, and then put them in her uterus and hope she stayed pregnant. It proved very successful sometimes with the fertilization of the egg, if both sperm and eggs were healthy, but it did not guarantee that the patient would be able to stay pregnant. But at Pilar's age, there was no question of in vitro fertilization. Most centers refused to do it on women over forty. And IVF was not an easy process. It required heavy doses of hormones, careful removal of the eggs by experienced hands, and the procedure only had a ten to twenty percent success rate. But for the lucky few who succeeded with it, it was a godsend.

Dr. Ward did a few simple blood tests on Pilar, gave her a prescription for chlomiphene, asked her to start taking her temperature every morning before she got out of bed, showed her how to keep the BBT chart, and then she gave her a kit that would detect the LH surge before ovulation.

"I feel like I just joined the Marines," Pilar said to Brad as they left, carrying their kit and all Dr. Ward's instructions about when to make love, and when not, and how often.

"I hope not. I liked her. What did you think?" Brad had been impressed by her intelligent views, and conservative positions. She refused to be pushed into doing too much just because Pilar was well-read and knew something about some of the more sophisticated options.

"I liked her too." Pilar was disappointed, though, that she didn't have any miracles up her sleeve. She seemed to favor a very conservative approach, but that was what they had wanted. And their options were limited anyway, because of Pilar's age. She was too old for in vitro fertilization, even if they needed it, and maybe even for chlomiphene, although she was going to take it.

Dr. Ward had suggested intrauterine insemination. She felt it might give them a better chance at conceiving, if Pilar didn't manage it on her own with the chlomiphene.

"It all seems so complicated for something that should be so simple," Brad said, still surprised by all the elaborate tests and medicines and mechanics for the infertile.

"Nothing's simple at my age," Pilar complained, "even putting my makeup on is a lot more work than it used to be." She grinned and he leaned over to kiss her.

"You sure you want to do all these things? That medication doesn't sound like much fun. You have enough pressure at work without taking pills to make you feel more stressed."

"Yeah, I thought of that. But I want to give us the best chance we can get. I'd like to try this." Now that she had made up her mind, she wanted to do everything she could to have a baby.

"Okay. You're the boss," Brad said warmly.

"No, I'm not. But I do love you." They kissed and drove back to Santa Barbara after having dinner in L.A. at the Bistro. It was a pleasant evening for them, a nice chance to get away. And when they got home, Pilar put out all her new treasures in her bathroom, the LH kit, the thermometer, the chart. And they had stopped to fill the prescription on the way home. She didn't have to start it for another three weeks, and only if she didn't get pregnant during this cycle. Meanwhile, she had to start taking her temperature, and using the kit the next day, and the following week she was going to try to get pregnant.

"It looks like an arsenal of hope, doesn't it?" Pilar smiled at Brad as they brushed their teeth, and she waved at all the paraphernalia on her dressing table.

"That's all right, if that's what we have to do. No one said it had to be easy, or simple. All that matters is the result, in the end." And then he sobered a little, as he leaned over to kiss her. "And if the result happens to be that you and I are alone, and all this doesn't work, then that's all right, too, and I want you to know that. I want you to think about that, Pilar, and try to make your peace with it too. It will be wonderful if it works, but if it doesn't, we still have each other, and a life full of people we love and who care about us. We don't *have* to have this baby."

"No, but I'd like it," she said sadly, as she looked at him, and he put an arm around her shoulders.

"So would I. But I won't risk what we have for it. And I don't want you to either." He knew from others that the process could become so obsessive it could destroy a marriage, and that was the last thing he wanted after waiting so long to marry her. What they had was just too precious.

She was still thinking about what he'd said as she sat staring into space at her desk the next morning. She had dutifully taken her temperature the moment she woke up, and before getting up to go to the bathroom, and charted it neatly on the graph that came with the thermometer. She had done the LH kit right before she went to work. That took a little more time, juggling a urine cup and half a dozen tiny little vials of chemicals in her bathroom. But the results showed that her LH surge hadn't occurred yet, which meant she wasn't ready to ovulate. Brad was right. It did seem complicated for something that should be simple.

"What are you looking so unhappy about?" Alice Jackson asked as she walked by Pilar's office.

"Oh . . . nothing . . . just thinking . . ." She sat up, and tried to forget what she'd been mulling over, but it wasn't easy. All she seemed to think about these days was getting pregnant.

"It doesn't look like a happy thought." Alice stopped for a moment with her arms full of files.

She was researching a difficult case for her husband.

"It is a happy thought, just not an easy one," Pilar said softly. "How's your case coming?"

"We're almost ready for trial, thank God. I'm not sure I could go through another six months of this." But they both knew she would if she had to. She loved working with Bruce, and doing research for him. Sometimes it made Pilar wonder what it would have been like to work with Brad. But she couldn't imagine it, much as she valued his advice. They were both too definite in their styles, too strong in their opinions. They were great as husband and wife, but she suspected they would have been considerably less so as partners. She was more of a bleeding heart than Brad, and she liked taking on difficult, near impossible cases, and then winning them, preferably for the underdog. There was still a lot of public defender in her. Brad, on the other hand, had never stopped being a D.A., or so she said, when they argued about the law. But most of the time, the arguments were pretty friendly.

The telephone rang before she could continue her conversation with Alice Jackson about her case, and then her intercom buzzed, and their receptionist told her it was her mother.

"Oh, God," she said, and she hesitated, wondering if she should even take the call. Alice saluted her and moved on, with her arms full of briefs for Bruce. "Okay, I'll take it," she said into the intercom, and then pressed the button on the line that was lit. It was noon in New York, and Pilar knew that her mother had been working for five hours by then at the hospital, she'd be ready for a quick lunch, and then another five or six hours of patients. She was tireless, and she set a gruelling pace, still at her age. Brad had said more than once that it was an encouraging omen for Pilar, and she always rather less charitably suggested that her mother was too driven to slow down, and too mean to quit; it had nothing to do with omens.

"Hi, Mom," she said casually, wondering why she'd called. She usually waited for Pilar to call her, even if it took a month or more. Pilar wondered if she was coming out for another convention. "How are you?"

"Fine. There's a heat wave in New York today. It's incredibly hot. Thank heavens our office air conditioning is still on. How are you and Brad?"

"Buried in work, as usual." *And trying to have a baby.* The vision of her mother's face if she knew actually made her smile, as she continued the conversation. "We've both been pretty busy. Brad's been on a long case, and half of California seems to have come through my office this month."

"At your age, you should strive for the bench, like your father and Brad. You don't need to be handling cases for all of California's liberal riffraff." *Thank you, Mother.* The call was typical of most of their exchanges. Questions, reproaches, mild accusations, tangible disapproval. "You know, your father was on the bench when he was quite a bit younger than you are. And he was appointed to the Court of Appeals at your age—it was quite an honor."

"Yes, I know it was, Mother. But I like what I do. And I'm not sure this family is ready for two judges. Besides, most of my clients are not 'liberal riffraff.' " But she was annoyed at herself even for trying to defend herself, her mother always provoked her to do that.

"From what I understand, you're still defending the same people you were defending in the public defender's office."

"No, fortunately, most of these have more money. So how about you? Busy in the office?"

"Very. I've appeared in court myself twice recently, testifying in cases that involved neurological injuries. It was very interesting. And of course, we won both cases." Humility was not one of Elizabeth Graham's strong suits and never had been, but at least she was predictable, which made her easier to deal with.

"Of course," Pilar said vaguely. "I'm sorry . . . I've really got to get to work. I'll call you soon . . . take care." She hurried her off the phone with the same feeling of defeat she always had when she talked to her mother. She never won, her mother never approved, Pilar never got what she wanted. But the sheer stupidity of it was that she had known for years that she wouldn't. Therapy had taught her that long since. Her mother was who she was, and she was not going to change. It was Pilar who had to change her expectations. And for the most part, she had, but there were still moments, like when she called, that Pilar expected her to be someone different. She was never going to be the cozy, sympathetic, warm-hearted loving mother Pilar had always wanted. And her father had been much the same. But she had Brad for that now, for all the loving and support and kindness she had craved for so long and never had, and when she needed the illusion of a mother near at hand, she had Marina for that, and so far neither of them had ever failed her.

She called Marina that afternoon, during a

recess in court, to thank her for the referral to Helen Ward, and Marina was pleased that she had liked her.

"What did she say? Was she encouraging?"

"Pretty much. At least she didn't say what my mother did, that I'm way too old and we'll have deformed children. She said it might take some time and a little effort."

"I'm sure Brad will be happy to oblige," the older woman teased, in sharp contrast to the retort Pilar would have gotten from her mother.

"He suggested as much himself." Pilar laughed. "And she gave me some pills, but they may or may not work. The bottom line on all this is that there's hope, but I ain't no spring chicken."

"Who is? Just remember my mother . . . last baby at fifty-two . . ."

"Stop that. Every time you remind me of that, you scare me. Promise me I'll at least be under fifty."

"I will promise you no such thing." Marina laughed good-naturedly. "And if the good Lord means for you to get pregnant at ninety, you will. Just read the *Enquirer*, for heaven's sake."

"You're a big help. This is not a freak show, Judge Goletti, this is my life . . . or is it? My mother called today, that's always fun."

"What little bits of good cheer did she share with you today?"

"Nothing much. A heat wave in New York, and a reminder that my father was my age when he was appointed to the Court of Appeals."

"Oh, you dismal failure. I had no idea. . . . How nice of her to remind you."

"I thought so too. She thinks I ought to try for your job, by the way."

"So do I. But that's another conversation, and right now I have to get back out there, and be a judge. I've got a felony drunk-driving case this afternoon that I could live very happily without. The defendant walked out of his completely demolished car unscathed, having just killed a thirty-year-old pregnant woman and her three children. Fortunately, there's a jury, and they'll have to make the decision."

"Sounds like a rough one," Pilar said sympathetically. She loved their exchanges, their conversations, their friendship. She was never disappointed in Marina.

"It will be a rough one. Take care. I'll talk to you soon. Maybe we can have lunch, if you're not too busy."

"I'll call you."

"Thanks. Bye." They hung up, and they both went back to work.

They never had time to have lunch that week, or the following one. They were just too busy, and so was Pilar until Brad suggested they go away for a few days, to a very romantic little hotel he knew in the Carmel Valley. As he referred to it now, it was "blue week." Her LH, or luteinizing hormones, were about to surge, and she was going to ovulate within the next day or two. And Brad thought it might be nicer to go away to deal with the event, rather than stay home and field crises on the bench, and in her office.

But by the time they got to the hotel, they had both had such a difficult few days at work, that they were both exhausted. And it was a relief to be alone in luxurious surroundings, just to be together and talk and think, without the interruption of telephones, or an avalanche of briefs and memos.

And in spite of the hectic days that had preceded their trip, they had a good time cruising the antique shops in Carmel. He even bought her a small, very pretty painting. It was of a mother and child on a beach at dusk; it had an impressionist flavor, and she loved it. She knew if she got pregnant now, that painting would always have special meaning for her.

They went back to Santa Barbara after two

days, happy and relaxed, and convinced that they'd done it this time. She was almost sure of it, she told Brad. Until she got her period again the following month, and had to start taking the chlomiphene. And it did exactly what the doctor had said it would. It made her feel wound up as tight as a watch spring. She was ready to jump at everything Brad said, and she wanted to strangle her secretary at least six times daily. She had to control herself not to lash out verbally at her clients. And she almost lost control of herself arguing with a judge in the courtroom. Just controlling her temper was suddenly a full-time job. And she had a constant sense of exhaustion from the medication.

"This is fun, isn't it?" she said to Brad. "You must really love it." She had been hideous to him for two weeks and she could barely stand herself, let alone understand how he could stand her. It was a lot worse than she'd thought it would be, but it was worth it if she had a baby.

"It's worth it if it helps," he reassured her. But the trouble was that, once again, it didn't. They had been trying for five months by then, and the following month Dr. Ward had scheduled them for artificial insemination, the week before Thanksgiving.

They had discussed it with her at great length, before deciding to try it, and she had assured them she thought it might make a difference. What she wanted to do was increase Pilar's dose of chlomiphene that month to twice the dose she'd been taking—which wasn't great news to Pilar—do an ultrasound just before ovulation to check the development of her follicle, give her a shot of another hormone, human chorionic gonadotrophin, or HCG, the night before she ovulated, and then perform an intrauterine insemination, delivering the sperm directly into the uterus, making the meeting of sperm and egg that much easier, and perhaps that much better.

Pilar wasn't crazy about taking the drugs. She was already unbearably tense on the amount she was taking, but Helen Ward assured her it was worth a try, and they made a reservation at the Bel Air for two days, on what they believed were the right dates, based on what they could expect from the drugs, and what they had learned from her temperatures. And Dr. Ward warned them not to make love for three days before, so as not to deplete Brad's sperm count.

"I feel like a race horse in training," he teased as they drove to L.A. And by then Pilar felt almost human again. She had taken the last dose of chlomiphene five days before, and she was just beginning to feel like herself again, a small gift for which she was now extremely grateful. Just having a day when she didn't feel as though her head were going to blow off, and she didn't have a fight with Brad, had suddenly become very important.

They went straight to the doctor's office when they reached L.A., and the doctor did a transvaginal ultrasound to examine her ovaries, and she was pleased with what she found. She gave Pilar the HCG shot immediately after that, and asked them to come back at noon the next day, which left them a whole afternoon and night free to do anything they wanted, except make love. And they were both surprised to find that they felt excited and anxious.

"Maybe by tomorrow I'll be pregnant," she whispered, and that afternoon he bought her a beautiful antique diamond pin, in the form of a small heart, at David Orgell on Rodeo Drive, and then they went down the street to shop at Fred Hayman. It was an extravagant afternoon, but they were both on a high, and terrified that it might turn into a down before they knew it.

They had drinks at the Beverly Hills Hotel, and dinner at Spago and then went back to the Bel Air, and walked quietly through the gardens, watching the swans, before they went to bed. And they both lay there awake for a long time, thinking about tomorrow.

The next morning, they were both nervous when they left the hotel, and Pilar was shaking as they got in the elevator of Helen Ward's building.

"Isn't this stupid?" she whispered to Brad. "I feel like a kid about to lose her virginity," she said, and he smiled. He was edgy too. He didn't like the idea of having to produce the semen in the doctor's office. The doctor had assured them that Brad could take as long as he wanted to, and Pilar was welcome to help. But the whole idea seemed incredibly embarrassing, and they were both dreading it. But they were both surprised by how smoothly it went once they reached her office.

They were ushered in through a separate door, into a private room that looked more like a well-appointed hotel room. There was a bed, a television with erotic videotapes, a stack of magazines to arouse their "guests," and assorted erotic implements and vibrators designed to make the task easier than it might otherwise have been. And on the table there was a small vial for the purpose of collection.

Nothing was said about when to come out, or

how much time they had, and before leaving them, the nurse asked them if they would like coffee, tea, or soft drinks. And then suddenly Pilar started to laugh as she looked at him. He looked so serious and well dressed, but she couldn't help herself, suddenly the whole thing seemed ridiculously funny.

"It's like checking into an adult motel, isn't it?" She giggled and he started to laugh too.

"How would you know?"

"I've read about them in magazines." She laughed again, and he pulled her down next to him on the bed with a rueful smile.

"How did I ever let you get me into this?" he said as he looked at her.

"I'm not sure. I was wondering the same thing on the way here. And you know what?" She looked at him seriously. "If you don't want to do this, it's okay with me. You've been wonderful about all of it, and maybe I am going too far . . . I didn't mean to . . . I don't ever want to make you uncomfortable. . . ." She was feeling guilty about putting him through it. It wasn't his fault she was so old. His sperm was fine, it was her body that was giving out. And if she had let him think of children earlier, they would never have had to go through this.

"Do you still want a baby, Pilar?" he asked

her gently as they lay on the bed talking, and she nodded sadly. "Okay, then stop worrying, and let's have a good time." He got up and put an outrageous film on the TV, and it embarrassed her, but she thought it was funny, too, and then she helped him take his clothes off. She took her clothes off, too, and began teasing him while he watched the screen, and he was very quickly aroused, and so was she, and she was almost sorry to have to waste it. He was throbbing with desire to enter her, and she held the cup as close to her as she could, as she rubbed and teased and titillated and kissed, until they achieved the desired results, and he lay spent in her arms. It had been different for both of them, but it hadn't been entirely unpleasant.

They took a quick shower, and dressed, and rang for the nurse, holding out the cup to her when she arrived. And she asked Pilar to come with her.

"May I come too?" Brad asked hesitantly. There seemed to be nothing about this process that they hadn't shared so far, and he wanted to be there for her, too, if there was going to be any unpleasant part of the treatment.

The nurse told him he could join them, and Pilar took off her clothes again and put on the gown, and lay down on the insemination table nervously. And a moment later, Dr. Ward came in and transferred the freshly washed sperm into a hypodermic. A small tube was then fed into Pilar's uterus, and the sperm from the hypodermic was carefully injected, and within minutes it was over, the tube was removed, and Dr. Ward asked her to lie there for half an hour before leaving. The doctor left them alone, and she and Brad chatted quietly, and he teased her that he had thought they were going to use a turkey baster.

"I feel like the turkey lying here," she said. The whole process had been surprisingly simple, but it seemed so exhausting. It was emotionally draining to try so hard, and strive so hard for what you wanted.

"I bet this will work," he said hopefully, and then he laughed thinking of the movie they'd watched in the other room. "We'll have to get some of those," he teased, and she laughed. She was a good sport about all this, but so was he. And it wasn't easy for either of them. But sometimes good things weren't.

"We're all set." The doctor stopped in to see them again before they left, and reminded her that all her hormone tests had been normal, and her progesterone levels had been very high ever since she'd started taking the chlomiphene. But she also warned them that it could take from six to ten times before it "took." "You're going to be seeing a lot of me, more than your friends or your family," she had warned, but the Colemans said they wouldn't mind it.

She wished them a happy Thanksgiving when they left, and told Pilar to keep her posted. She wanted a call from her in two weeks to tell her if she got her period or not.

"Don't worry." Pilar smiled. "You'll hear from me either way!" Especially if she got pregnant. And if she didn't, they'd have to come back for artificial insemination again . . . and again . . . and again . . . until it took, or they gave up. Whichever came first, and she hoped it would be the former.

She had wanted to talk to the doctor about GIFT too. It was a procedure she'd read about —gamete intra-Fallopian transfer—a process much like in vitro, but which had better results in women over forty. But Dr. Ward wouldn't even discuss it. "Let's give intrauterine insemination a chance first, shall we?" she said firmly. She said they were way premature in discussing such exhaustive measures. And she was optimistic about artificial insemination. With the chlomiphene, Pilar's progesterone levels were very high, and that would certainly help her get pregnant.

It was a long, peaceful drive home, and they felt even closer to each other after the past few days. And it was a quiet week for them before Thanksgiving. Pilar was trying not to overdo it at the office.

Nancy and Tommy and Adam spent Thanksgiving with them that year, and Todd had gone skiing in Denver with his girlfriend. But he had promised to come home for Christmas this year, so they didn't complain about his not being home for Thanksgiving.

Little Adam was five months old by then, and he was gurgling and cooing, and he had two teeth right in the middle of his lower gum, and it was obvious that Brad was crazy about him. Pilar held him for a long time, too, and as usual, Nancy commented on how good with him she was, which always surprised her, since Pilar had never had children.

"Instinct, I guess," she teased, but neither she nor Brad talked about their plans, or their efforts to have a baby. It was too important to them, too secret, to share with anyone. And Pilar was on pins and needles waiting to see if she was pregnant. She could barely keep her mind on Thanksgiving.

And when the young couple went home that night, Pilar was relieved to be alone again, and talked immediately about how much she hoped the insemination had taken.

"We'll see," Brad said, but he had noticed a funny look in her eyes that rang a chord of memory. It was a sleepy look, but she had no symptoms, no inkling that anything had changed, and he decided that, like Pilar, he was just hoping she had gotten pregnant.

CHAPTER
8

Diana and Andy's Thanksgiving had a nightmarish quality that year. Their life had been a living hell for three months, and sometimes Andy thought he wouldn't get through it. He couldn't talk to her anymore, couldn't stand the bitterness and self-pity and hatred. She hated everyone and everything, and she was angry all the time now. She was angry at life, at the fates which had dealt her such a cruel hand. But there was nothing he could do. They had dealt him the same hand, too, as long as he chose to be with her. But there were days when he wondered if either of them could go on for much longer.

And things had gotten even worse in October, when Bill and Denise had announced that she was pregnant. It had happened literally the night of their wedding. Diana was horrified by the irony of it, and she flatly refused to see them anymore, which made life even lonelier for Andy.

She refused to talk to Eloise most of the time, too, about anything but work at least. And she had stopped mentioning Dr. Johnston to her completely. Eloise no longer mentioned him or her father to her at all; she had long since realized that something devastating must have happened.

Diana wouldn't see any of their friends. And eventually most of them stopped calling. By Thanksgiving, Diana had succeeded in completely isolating them, and Andy thought life had never been more grim than it was at the moment.

And Diana had compounded their miseries by agreeing to spend Thanksgiving with the Goodes in Pasadena. He wanted to force her to cancel it, but much to his chagrin, she wouldn't. They were the only people they'd seen in months, and they were the wrong ones.

"For chrissake," Andy complained, "why did you do that?"

"They're my family! What did you expect me

to do, tell them we don't want to see them anymore just because I'm sterile?"

"That has nothing to do with it. It's just so
difficult for you there. Your sisters ask you questions about getting pregnant all the time, and
Sam is six months pregnant, for heaven's sake.
Do you really need to do that to yourself?" Or
to either of them, for that matter, but he didn't
say that.

"She's still my sister."

He didn't understand her anymore, and he
wasn't sure he ever would again. She seemed to
have a need to punish herself further for what
had happened to her. But the terrible thing was
that she hadn't done anything. She'd chosen the
wrong form of birth control years ago and paid a
hell of a price for it, and there was nothing anyone could do. It was just rotten luck. But it
didn't mean she had to become a rotten person.

"I don't think we should go." He argued with
her right up until they went, and tried to get
her to cancel, but she absolutely wouldn't. And
the moment they got there, she realized her
mistake. Gayle was in a lousy mood, she had a
bad cold, and the kids had driven her nuts all
day. She'd had a fight with their mother when
she suggested Gayle discipline them more, and
she seemed to be annoyed at Jack for not stand-

ing up for her. So she took it out on Diana the moment she arrived, and Andy wished more than ever that they hadn't come. It was going to be a miserable evening.

"Thanks for coming early to help," Gayle spat at her, as she took off her coat. "Were you doing your nails this afternoon, or just napping?"

"Oh, for chrissake, what are you so worked up about?" Diana gave it right back to her, and as Sam came into the room, Andy almost groaned when he saw her. He hadn't seen her since the Fourth of July and she looked like a cartoon of a pregnant woman. And he could see from the frozen look on Diana's face that seeing Sam really shook her.

"Gayle's just pissed off because Mom told her the kids were too wild. And she's right. So are mine. So how are you?" she asked Diana, resting her hands on her enormous stomach.

"I'm fine," Diana said icily. "And I can see how you are."

"Yeah. Fat. Seamus said I look like a Buddha." Diana attempted a smile, and then went off to see their mother in the kitchen. She looked better than ever that year, and she was happy to see her daughter. She was organizing everything and everyone, and loving every moment of it. And she had been so busy in the past couple of months that she hadn't felt her daughter slipping away from her. She just assumed Diana was busy at the magazine, but noticed something she didn't like about her eyes, and she suddenly looked much thinner.

"I'm glad you could come," she said, pleased that all her children and grandchildren were around her. She always enjoyed having them there, even if she had asked Gayle to control them. "Are you all right?" she asked Diana.

"I'm fine," Diana brushed her off. She loved her mother, but she didn't have the heart to tell her about the laparoscopy, or the hell she'd been through. She wondered if she might someday. But for the moment she just wasn't ready. She couldn't bring herself to tell anyone she was sterile. She felt like such a failure.

"You work too hard," her mother chided, hoping it was stress at work she was seeing in her daughter's face as she checked on the turkey. It was a huge golden-brown bird and it smelled delicious.

"Unlike her sisters," her father added, as he walked into the kitchen.

"They work hard with their children." Her mother defended them. She loved all three of her girls, and she knew that their father did too. He just liked making comments like that, and he had always been particularly fond of Diana, and he had also noticed how tired and unhappy she looked, and he was worried.

"How's your magazine?" he asked, as though she owned it, and she smiled at his question.

"Fine. Our circulation is really growing."

"It's a fine-looking publication. I saw a copy of it last month." He had always given her credit for what she did, which made her wonder why she felt so bad sometimes. But now she had good reason to. She had failed at the thing that counted most to all of them. Having babies.

"Thanks, Dad."

And with that her brothers-in-law walked in and asked when dinner would be ready.

"Patience, boys." Their mother-in-law smiled, and shooed everyone into the next room, except Diana. "Are you really all right, dear?" She looked at her seriously. She seemed so tired and pale, and there was something so deeply unhappy in her eyes, almost ravaged, which made her wonder if everything was all right with Andy.

She walked slowly toward her middle child, and remembered what a bright child she had always been, and how conscientious. "Is anything wrong?"

"No, Mom," she lied, turning away so her

mother wouldn't see the tears in her eyes. "I'm fine." And then mercifully, the children burst into the room, and Diana ushered them back outside to their mothers, as Andy watched her. He didn't like the look he'd seen in her eyes since late that afternoon. She was dying inside, and she wanted someone to blame for it. She looked as though she were about to explode with grief, but he knew now only too well that there was no way to help her.

Her father said grace when they sat down, and Diana sat between both her brothers-in-law, while Andy sat across the table from her, between her two sisters. Gayle kept up a constant stream of conversation with him, as she always did, about nothing in particular; the PTA, complaining about how little money doctors made today, and making veiled references to why they never had children. Andy just agreed with her pleasantly, and made an occasional effort to talk to Sam, who talked constantly about her children, and their new baby. Then there was the neighborhood report of who was getting married, who had died, and who was having a baby. And halfway through dinner Diana looked at them in total irritation.

"Don't you people ever talk about anything except pregnancy and childbirth? I'm sick of

hearing about people's deliveries and hemorrhages, and how long their labors took, and how
many babies they already have, and how many
this one makes. Christ, it's a miracle we don't
have to talk about their Pap smears."

Her father looked across the table at her, and
then glanced at his wife with a worried frown.
Something was very wrong with Diana.

"What brought that on?" Sam asked, leaning
back in her chair, holding her back with one
hand, and her stomach with the other. "God
. . . if this baby doesn't stop kicking me . . ."

"For chrissake!" Diana shouted at her, and
pushed her chair away from the table. "I don't
give a damn if your fucking baby kicks your
teeth out. Can't you shut up about it for ten
minutes?" Sam stared at her in shock, and then
started to cry, and then she left the table, but
Diana already had her coat on by then, and she
apologized to her parents over her shoulder.
"I'm sorry, Mom . . . Dad . . . I just can't
take this. I guess I shouldn't have come." But
her oldest sister was already striding across the
dining room and standing in the front hall with
a look of rage on her face Diana hadn't seen
there since she'd set fire to her brand-new electric curlers when they were in high school.

"How dare you behave like that in your parents' house, and talk to any of us like that? Who the hell do you think you are?"

"Gayle, please . . . don't. I'm sorry. Diana is upset. We shouldn't have come." Andy tried to calm the two women down, but it was to no avail. And Seamus had gone to tend to Sam's wounded feelings as she cried in the bathroom. Their parents were distraught to see their children fighting like hooligans, as her mother said, and the children had all started to go wild and leave the table.

But Gayle wasn't going to be easily swayed. She was furious now, and her jealousy of long years was finally finding an outlet. "What the hell does she have to be upset about? Her *job*? Her *career*? Miss High and Mighty, who's too smart and too important to have kids and live like the rest of us. No, she's the big career girl, the Stanford graduate. Well, guess what? I don't give a fuck. So how's that, Miss Career Lady?"

"Good-bye, I'm leaving," Diana called to her parents as she tied the belt on her coat and looked frantically at Andy. She had heard everything her sister had said, and she didn't trust herself to answer. She knew she would lose it completely if she even tried to speak to her, and she didn't want to do that. "Mom, I'm sorry," she called out, and saw her father looking at her. The expression on his face tore at her heart, but she just couldn't help it. He looked as though she had betrayed him.

"You *should* be sorry," Gayle said, as Sam finally came back out of the bathroom and into the hallway. "Look what you did to Thanksgiving for everyone," Gayle said accusingly, and she wasn't wrong, but without knowing it, they had provoked it.

"I shouldn't have come," Diana said softly, with her hand on the door and Andy just behind her.

"Why the hell not? You should have kept your mouth shut," Gayle went on, and then suddenly Diana snapped, and she leapt across the hallway in a single bound, and put her hands around her sister's throat, and squeezed her.

"If you don't shut up now, I'm going to kill you, do you hear me? You don't know anything about me, or about my life, or why I do or don't or may never have children. Do you understand that, you incredibly stupid, insensitive bitch. . . . I don't have babies because I'm sterile, you moron. . . . Is that clear enough for you? Do you get that? I can't have children. My insides turned to shit years ago from an IUD, and I never knew it. Is that clear now, Gayle? Would you like to talk about my job that I no

longer care about? Or my house that's too fucking big for two people who're never going to
have kids, or maybe you'd like to talk about
the Murphy baby again, or the McWilliamses'
twins, or we could just sit here and watch Sam
rub her stomach. Good night, everyone." She
glanced at the shocked faces of everyone, all of
whom were standing by then, and out of the
corner of her eye she could see that both her
younger sister and her mother were crying. But
Gayle only stood there with her mouth open, as
Diana rushed out the front door to their car,
and Andy glanced apologetically at them, and
hurried behind her.

It was quite a scene they left behind, but Diana insisted she didn't care anymore. And secretly, Andy thought the outburst might do her
good. She needed to ventilate, to cry, to scream,
to rail at someone, and if not with her family,
where else? Although he had to admit it had
made for a hell of a Thanksgiving.

He looked over at her with a smile as they
drove home, and she wasn't even crying. "Want
to go for a turkey sandwich somewhere?" He
was only half teasing and she laughed. In spite
of everything, she hadn't completely lost her
sense of humor.

"Do you suppose I'm going insane from all

this stuff?" It had been a nightmarish time for her and maybe it was just as well it was over.

"No, but I think you need to get it out of your system. What about a therapist for both of us? It might help." He'd thought of going to one himself recently, just to have someone to talk to. He couldn't talk to her anymore, and he hated to tell his friends what was happening. He had tried talking to Bill, but with Denise pregnant now, it was too awkward trying to talk to him about Diana being sterile. And his brothers were too young to be helpful. And in his own way, just like Diana, he felt isolated, depressed, and defeated. "I was thinking about a vacation too."

"I don't need a vacation," she said instantly, and he laughed.

"Sure. Okay. How about if I drive you back to Pasadena right now so we can discuss it? Or maybe you'd like to wait for Christmas and try for a second round? I'm sure your sisters will be happy to oblige you. I don't know about you," he said seriously, "but I am not spending Christmas this year in Pasadena." And she had to admit, she didn't want to go either.

"I'm not sure I could get the time off from work to go anywhere." She had been so distracted for so long, she really felt she owed them something.

"At least ask. Even a week would do us good. I thought we could go to the Mauna Kea, in Hawaii. Half the network will be there, but most of them go to the Mauna Lani. I'm serious, Di." He looked at her as he drove home, and she could see that he was as unhappy as she was. "I don't think we've got a lot of mileage left in us, unless we do something major about our batteries, or our engines, or something. I don't know how to deal with it anymore, or with you, and what you feel. I just know that we're in trouble." She knew it, too, but she had been too upset even to try to reach him. She was lost in her own agonies and could do nothing to help him. She wasn't even sure about taking a vacation with him, but she thought that the suggestion that they each see a therapist was a good one.

"Okay, I'll try to get some time," she said half-heartedly. He was right though, and she knew it. And then, as they drove up to their house, she turned to him with a sad expression. "Andy, if you want out . . . I'll understand. You have a right to a lot more than I can ever give you."

"No," he said, as tears filled his eyes. "I have

a right to what you promised me . . . for better or worse, in sickness or in health . . . until
death do us part. It never said anything about
the deal being off if you can't have babies.
Okay, so that's terrible. I admit it, it hurts me
too. But I married *you* . . . and I love *you.*
And if we can't have kids, then that's the way it
is. Maybe we'll adopt one some day, maybe
we'll figure out something else, maybe they'll
come up with some fantastic new laser that will
change things for you, or maybe not, but I don't
care about all that, Di. . . ." There were tears
on his cheeks as he held her hands. "I just want
my wife back."

"I love you," she said softly. It had been a
terrible time for both of them, the worst of her
life, and she knew that it still wasn't over. She'd
have to mourn for a long time, and maybe she'd
never be the same again. She just didn't know
yet. "I'm just not sure who I am anymore . . .
what this means . . . what this makes
me. . . ." She still felt like such a failure.

"For right now, it makes you a woman who
can't have kids, a woman with a husband who
loves her very much, a woman who had a terrible thing happen to her and she never knew it
. . . that's who you are. You're the same person
you always were. None of that has changed. The

only thing that's changed is a tiny piece of our future."

"How can you call that tiny?" She looked angry at him again, but he squeezed her hands harder to bring her back to reality.

"Stop it, Di. It *is* tiny. What if we had a child and it died? It would be terrible, but you and I wouldn't end there. We'd go on, we'd have to."

"What if we couldn't?" she asked sadly.

"What choice do we have? To ruin two lives, to destroy a good marriage? What kind of sense does that make? Di, I don't want to lose you. We've lost enough as it is . . . please . . . please . . . help me save our marriage. . . ."

"Okay . . . I'll try . . ." she said sadly, but she wasn't even sure where to start anymore, how to be what she once had been, and he could see that. She wasn't even doing a good job at the magazine, and she knew it.

"All you have to do, Di, is try. Day by day, step by step, inch by inch . . . and maybe one of these days we'll get there." He leaned over and kissed her gently on the lips as he said it, but he didn't even hope for more. They hadn't made love to each other since before Labor Day, and he didn't dare approach her anymore. She had told him there was no point to their lovemaking now. Nothing mattered. Her life was over. But tonight he could see a glimmer of hope, a tiny shadow of what she had been before Dr. Johnston had told her she couldn't have babies.

He kissed her again, and then helped her out of the car, and they went inside arm in arm. It was the closest they had been in months, and he wanted to cry, he was so relieved. Maybe there was hope for them . . . maybe they would make it. He had almost lost hope. And now, maybe it hadn't been such a rotten Thanksgiving after all. He smiled at her as she took off her coat, and she laughed as she remembered Gayle's face, and she admitted to Andy that she'd been really awful, but a tiny part of her had enjoyed it.

"It probably did her good." He grinned, and led her into the kitchen. "Come on, why don't you call your mom and tell her you're okay, and I'll make you a bologna sandwich. Something really festive."

"I love you," she said softly, and he kissed her again, and then she slowly dialed her parents. Her father answered the phone, and she could hear the children raising hell in the background.

"Dad, it's me . . . I'm sorry. . . ."

"I'm very worried about you," he said honestly. "I feel terrible that I didn't know what kind of pain you were in." He knew her well enough to know that her outburst had been the culmination of her distress, and just seeing it had made him ache for her, and feel as though he had failed her as a father.

"I think I'm okay now. Maybe tonight did me good. But I'm really sorry if I ruined Thanksgiving."

"Not at all." He smiled across the hall at his wife, coming to see who it was. He tried to let her know it was Diana. "It gave everyone something new to talk about. It was actually very refreshing," he teased, and Diana's mother looked at him sadly. At least she had called them. She had known something was wrong, but she'd had no idea what, and Diana had never told them. "I want you to call me if you need me . . . or your mother, from now on. Is that a promise?"

"I promise," she said, feeling like a child again, as she looked across her own kitchen at her husband. He had his jacket off and his sleeves rolled up, and he was very busy. And for the first time in a long time, he looked happy.

"We're here for you, Diana, whenever you

need us." Diana's eyes filled with tears, as did her mother's as she listened.

"I know that, Daddy. Thank you. And tell Mom and the girls I'm sorry, too, will you please, Dad?"

"Of course I will. Now take care of yourself." His eyes were damp. He loved her so dearly and he hated to think of her in pain.

"I will, Daddy. You too . . . I love you. . . ." As she hung up, she was suddenly reminded of her wedding day. She and her father had always been so close, and they still were, even though she hadn't told him about this. But she knew that if she had wanted to, she could have. And what he had said was true. They were there for her, and she knew it.

"Ready for salami, pastrami, and bologna on rye?" Andy asked ceremoniously with a kitchen towel over one arm, and a huge plate of sandwiches for her. It suddenly felt as though they had something to celebrate, which was strange. But in a way they did. They had found each other again, and that was no small thing. It had almost been too late, and they had just climbed back up over the cliff. Happy Thanksgiving.

* * *

Charlie cooked a perfect turkey for Barbie. And she was there with him this time. She didn't go anywhere, or come home late. She still felt guilty about their anniversary. But Charlie was also aware, as they sat down to dinner together that night, that something was missing between them. He had felt it for a while, possibly since she'd spent the Labor Day weekend in Las Vegas, or maybe even before that. She had come back itching for excitement again, talking about the shows they'd seen, and the friends they met up with, and wanting Charlie to go out dancing with her. But he was usually too tired to do it. And he wasn't a great dancer anyway. But he noticed, too, that suddenly she was complaining constantly about what he didn't do for her, and how square he was, even the way he dressed, which really wasn't fair, since he never bought new clothes for himself, only for Barbie. Maybe Mark had been right, Charlie mused to himself, and he shouldn't have let her go to Las Vegas.

Ever since she got back, she stayed out with her girlfriends all the time, she went to the movies and dinner with them, and once in a while she even called him and said she was too tired to come home and she had decided to stay overnight at Judi's. He never complained, but he didn't like it either. He had mentioned it to Mark, who had reminded him again that he'd better keep her on a short leash or he'd be very sorry.

And Charlie kept telling himself that if they had a child, everything would change. She'd be different, she'd settle down. She wouldn't want the glamour or the flash, or maybe even to be an actress. He hadn't brought up the subject of a family again since June, but he had continued to be cagey about following her cycles, and nothing had happened. He still came home with champagne a couple of times a month, and he always made sure that he made love to her on one of those times, at just the right time. And if she was drunk enough, she never reminded him about precautions. But despite his best efforts, sometimes as often as twice in a night, just to be sure, she still hadn't gotten pregnant. He had even asked her once if she was on the pill, since Mark had made him think of that, and she was surprised and asked him if he wanted her to take it. But he just told her that he'd read an article about how dangerous it was for women who smoked, and since she did, he was concerned. But she assured him she wasn't on it. And still, she hadn't gotten pregnant.

Mark had given him the name of his brother-in-law's specialist by then, and Charlie had an appointment to see him the Monday after Thanksgiving. He was seriously worried. The comment she'd made about never getting pregnant by him, no matter how careless she was, had weighed heavily on him, and he wanted to check it out now.

"The turkey's great," she said, and he was pleased. He had made stuffing, and cranberry sauce, and sweet peas with pearl onions, and sweet potatoes with marshmallows on them. And he had bought mince and apple pie for dessert. And he served it warm with vanilla ice cream.

"You should run a restaurant," she complimented him, and he beamed as he poured their coffee and she lit a cigarette, but she looked as though her mind were a thousand miles away as she smoked it.

"What were you thinking about just then?" he asked sadly. She looked so beautiful at times, but lately she seemed so distant and so distracted. It was as though she were drifting away from him and he could feel it, and didn't know how to stop it.

"Nothing much . . . what a good dinner it was. . . ." She smiled at him through a haze of smoke. "You're always so good to me, Charlie." But that didn't seem to be enough, he could sense it.

"I try to be. You mean everything to me, Barb." But she hated it when he said things like that. It put such a burden on her. She didn't want to be everything to him, or to anyone else. It was too much weight to put on anyone, and she wasn't up to it, and more than ever now she knew it. "I just want you to be happy." But she wondered if she would ever live up to his expectations.

"I am happy," she said quietly.

"Are you? Sometimes I'm not sure. I'm a pretty dull guy."

"No, you're not." She blushed. "Sometimes I want too much"—she smiled wistfully—"and I even drive myself crazy. Don't pay any attention to me."

"What do you want, Barb?" He knew how badly she wanted to be a success as an actress, and she didn't want kids. But other than that, she never talked about her dreams, or what she wanted for them. She just seemed content drifting along from day to day, and satisfying her immediate needs. She never seemed to give much thought to the future.

"I'm not sure what I want sometimes.

Maybe that's the trouble," she admitted. "I want my acting career. . . . I want friends. . . . I want freedom. . . . I want excitement. . . ."

"What about me?" he asked sadly. She hadn't mentioned that, and she blushed when he said it.

"Of course I want you. We're married, aren't we?"

"Are we?" he asked pointedly, and she didn't say anything, but she nodded.

"Of course we are. Don't be silly."

"What does marriage mean to you, Barb? It doesn't really fit with any of the things you just mentioned."

"Why not?" But she knew it too. She just wasn't ready to confront it yet, and she didn't really think he was either.

"I don't know, I just don't think of freedom and excitement as synonymous with marriage, although I guess they could be, if you worked at it. I guess you can do anything you want to, as long as you're willing to make it work." He watched her as she put her cigarette out and lit another, and he wanted to ask her if she was happy with him, but he didn't dare to. He was afraid of her answer. And as he looked at her, he

kept thinking that if they had a child, everything might be different. A baby would be just
the cement they needed to keep them together
forever.

CHAPTER
══9══

M ark gave Charlie the day off, and he drove to L.A. the Monday after Thanksgiving. He didn't say anything to Barb, and she had an audition for a bathing suit ad that day, so she didn't even notice when he left, or the fact that he was wearing his best suit, and looked extremely nervous. She was doing her hair and her nails, and she had the radio on full blast in the bathroom. He called out to her when he left, but she didn't answer.

And as he drove to L.A., he thought about how worried he was that he was losing her. She hadn't said anything, but her mind just seemed to be in a different place now. She was even more self-involved than usual. It wasn't done with malice, he knew, but it also wasn't easy to live with. She forgot the dates they made, left her makeup everywhere, and their bedroom looked like a battleground of brassieres and pantyhose, and she let crumpled clothes fall wherever and whenever it suited. She was a great girl, and he was crazy about her, but as Mark said, he also knew he had spoiled her. He didn't expect her to do anything for him, he never asked her for the money she made for the modelling work she did, and she usually spent it on clothes when she went out with Judi. And the one thing he really wanted from her, he knew she was reluctant to give him. And his plan to trick her hadn't worked so far. Now he had to find out why, and fix whatever might be broken. And once it was, he grinned to himself as he parked on Wilshire Boulevard, watch out, Barbie!

Dr. Peter Pattengill's office surprised him by how cheerful it was. It was filled with bright prints, and flowering plants, and bright colors. It looked like a happy place, and not the kind of office where you had to whisper. Charlie was relieved as he gave the nurse his name. They hadn't told him anything before he came in, and he had no idea what they were going to do to him, or if they were going to give him the famous ice shorts. He smiled as he thought of it, and pretended to flip through magazines, but he couldn't concentrate on anything, and then finally they called his name, and he was ushered into Dr. Pattengill's office.

He was sitting at his desk, and he stood up with a broad smile as Charlie walked in. He was of fair height, with broad shoulders and dark hair, and dark brown eyes that looked both kind and wise for a man his age. He looked to be in his early forties. He was wearing a bright tie and a tweed jacket, and before the doctor said a word, Charlie knew he liked him.

"I'm Peter Pattengill, Mr. Winwood." After he introduced himself, Charlie asked him to call him by his first name, and Pattengill suggested he sit down, and asked him if he'd like a cup of coffee. But Charlie was much too nervous to drink anything, and he declined it. He looked terrified and young, almost too young to be one of Pattengill's patients. He was a urologist, with a specialization in reproductive disorders. "What can I do for you today?"

"I'm not sure." Charlie smiled hesitantly, and the doctor looked at him warmly. "I'm not exactly sure what you do . . . except that I've heard about the Jockey shorts with ice. . . ." He blushed furiously as Peter Pattengill smiled at him.

"They serve a useful purpose. But I must admit, at first they sound a little silly to our patients. They bring the testicular temperature down, which enhances fertility." He opened a chart on his desk as he said it, and picked up a pen as he looked at Charlie. "Why don't we start your history, Mr. Winwood? . . . Charlie."

He asked him about any severe or chronic illnesses he might have had, VD, mumps as a child, and Charlie shook his head negatively to all his questions.

"Are you and your wife currently trying to get pregnant?" he asked, to clarify why Charlie had come to see him. The young man was so shy, he hadn't even explained that much to the doctor.

"Yes . . . well, I am."

Peter smiled broadly as he sat back in his chair and looked at Charlie. "Maybe we need some serious talking here," he teased him gently. "This is an activity that has to be engaged in by *two* people. We are not talking about a solo sport here." Charlie laughed and went on to explain the situation.

"She doesn't really want to get pregnant. I do."

"I see. And has she been using birth control?" By then, momentarily, Peter Pattengill had stopped writing.

"Not if I get her drunk enough." Charlie realized it was a terrible confession. But he could be honest here. He knew he had to be with the doctor.

"That's quite a project."

"Yes, it is. And I know it sounds pretty bad, but . . . I know she'd really love a baby if we had one."

"Maybe you should talk to her. Maybe if she cooperated, things might go a little more smoothly."

"Well, they've gone smoothly enough . . . except that, so far, nothing's happened."

"Do you get drunk too?" The doctor eyed him suspiciously, there was always the possibility that the boy was a little crazy, but Charlie shook his head solemnly, and looked like an errant schoolboy.

"No, I don't. And I know it's a rotten thing to do to her. But I really think she'll be glad one day, if she gets pregnant. But right now, nothing's happening, and I just wanted to be sure I was okay . . . you know . . . like maybe just check my sperm count." Charlie wasn't even entirely sure how they did that.

The doctor smiled at his naïveté. There were

a few more steps than that, but he was beginning to get the picture. "How long have you been married?"

"Seventeen months. But I haven't been really paying attention to things, I mean her cycle . . . until about five months ago, but even that hasn't made a difference."

"I see." The doctor made a note on the chart, and then looked up at Charlie again, to reassure him. "That's not a very long time. It frequently takes a year, or even two, to achieve pregnancy. You may be worrying unnecessarily. And also, pregnancy isn't always easy with an unwilling partner. In fact, it's unusual for me to see only one half of the couple. It only gives me half the information I need. The problem may well rest with your wife, if there is one."

"I thought that maybe if you checked me out and everything was okay, maybe in a few months, I could talk to her, and she might come in to see you." He still had no idea how he would get her to come in, but this was a first step, and he thought it might ease his worries. "She thought it was kind of unusual that even when we're careless about birth control, she never gets pregnant. She said that one day, and it's kind of worried me ever since."

"Has your wife ever been pregnant before, Mr. Winwood?"

"No, I don't think so," he said with certainty.

"Well, let's get things started." The doctor stood up and Charlie followed suit, not knowing what to expect, and a nurse appeared and led him to an examining room with bright abstract prints on the wall, and a skylight. She handed him a small vial, and pointed to a stack of magazines, among them *Hustler* and *Playboy,* and several others Charlie had never ever heard of.

"We'll need some semen from you, Mr. Winwood," she said gently. "Just take your time, and press the buzzer when you're ready for us to collect it." Charlie stared at her in amazement as the door closed, not sure what to do next. He knew, but couldn't quite believe it. They were so matter-of-fact about everything. Here's the bottle, now go to it. But on the other hand, he had come here for the answers to his questions.

He sat down with a sigh, undid his pants, and reached for one of the magazines, feeling more than a little foolish. And it was a while before he rang the bell for the nurse to return. He waited a lot longer than he had to. But he wanted time to cool down, and by the time she returned, he

tried to look nonchalant, and she removed the
vial discreetly without comment.

Dr. Pattengill came in shortly after that to
check him for varicoceles—varicose veins in the
testicles—which frequently caused sterility.
And then a technician came in to do some blood
work. They were going to check his hormone
levels with the blood, and do an analysis and
culture with the semen, and in a few days
they'd have some information for him. But in
the meantime, the doctor was very reassuring.
He assured him that he saw nothing of concern
and he was hoping that Charlie was worried
over nothing. He suspected that he was just
anxious and impatient.

To Pattengill, Charlie seemed healthy
enough, and he hoped for his sake that there
would be no problems. He asked Charlie to
make another appointment for the following
week, asked him to bring a vial of fresh semen
with him this time, and then left him.

And as Charlie got to the fresh air outside, he
found he was immensely relieved to be there.
He had liked Pattengill, but just talking to him,
and worrying about it all, had made him very
nervous. He hadn't enjoyed producing the sample for him, and was relieved that he could take
care of it at home next time. They had given

him a small vial to take home for collection. But just the implications of being there, and the prospect of what they might do to him, was very unpleasant.

He called Mark afterward, when he got home, and thanked him again for the referral.

"How was it? Are you okay?"

"So far so good, and he's really a nice guy."

"Did he give you a clean bill of health?" Mark asked worriedly. Charlie looked fine to him, but who knew with things like that? His brother-in-law had looked fine too.

"Not yet. I have to wait for my test results next week."

"Did he give you the ice pants yet?" Mark teased, and Charlie laughed good-naturedly as he lay down on the couch and kicked off his shoes. He was utterly exhausted.

"Maybe he'll give me those next week."

"I hope not. You're gonna be fine, kid. Take it from me. I know. See you tomorrow," he said cheerfully, hoping he was right.

"Thanks, Mark . . . for everything."

"No problem."

And as Mark went back to work, he hoped that everything would come out all right for Charlie. He was a great kid, and Mark thought he deserved to get whatever he wanted.

* * *

"Okay, what does it say?" Brad asked anxiously as she did the test. It was just like the test she did to check her hormone surge every month at the time of ovulation.

"I don't know yet. It hasn't been long enough." She was timing it with her watch, and Brad was standing just outside the bathroom. "Go away. You're making me nervous."

"I'm not going anywhere." He smiled at her. "I want to know if the turkey baster worked."

"You're disgusting." But she was dying to know too. She could hardly stand it . . . another sixty seconds . . . fifty-five . . . forty . . . the test was almost over and nothing had changed, and then she saw it . . . the bright blue that meant her hopes had come true . . . the miracle had happened to her. . . . She looked up at him with tears in her eyes, and he had seen it too. She was pregnant. "Oh, my God," she said quietly, looking at him, and then suddenly worried. "What if it's a false positive? I think that happens sometimes."

"It's not." He was still smiling as he moved closer to her and took her in his arms. He had never thought their life would change to this extent. And he had never expected to be so much in love with a woman . . . and a baby. "I love you, Pilar . . . so very much," he said as he closed his eyes and held her, and there were tears on her cheeks when she looked up at him.

"I just can't believe it. I never really thought it would work. All those pills, and the ultrasounds . . . and that ridiculous room with the videotapes and dirty magazines. . . . Wow!"

"I don't think you need to tell the baby all that when he or she grows up. I think maybe we can skip that part, and just tell him it was a moonlit night and we were very much in love. I think you can drop the part about the turkey baster."

"Yeah, maybe you're right." She grinned as they walked back to their bedroom. And suddenly he had an overwhelming desire for her, as though to make this baby even more his than it was now.

He pulled her slowly down on the bed next to him, and kissed her long and hard, feeling her breasts, which were just the least bit fuller. He had wondered about that a few days before, and suspected that she might be pregnant.

They lay together for a long time, and Pilar wanted him desperately. And then afterward, she was remorseful. "You think that's bad for the baby?" she asked, feeling guilty but well sated.

"No, I don't." His voice was deep and sensuous, as she ran a hand over his chest, and then down to the part of him that gave her such pleasure. "Being pregnant is perfectly normal."

"Ha!" She laughed at him. "If it's so normal, how come it's not so easy?"

"Sometimes good things aren't. It wasn't easy catching you either." He kissed her again, and they got up and went to make breakfast. They sat on their terrace afterward in shorts and T-shirts. It was a beautiful December day, and their baby was due in August.

"Wait till Nancy hears." Pilar grinned as she helped herself to another helping of scrambled eggs. Suddenly, she was starving. "Do you think she'll be stunned?" Pilar laughed happily as she thought of it, and her husband grinned. They had never been happier in their lives.

"I think it's safe to say so. You're the one who's told everyone over the years that you'd never want to have children. You're going to have a lot of explaining to do, my dear." Not to mention what her mother was going to say. But Pilar was used to that. The one she really wanted to tell was Marina. She knew how happy she'd be for her and how supportive.

"Let's tell the kids on Christmas," Pilar said with a luminous smile.

He smiled at her, wondering if they should wait, just to make sure everything was all right, but he didn't want to scare her. And when she saw the doctor the next day, she said everything was fine. She could work, she could play tennis, she could make love, nothing to excess, and lots of rest and a healthy diet. But she led a healthy life anyway, and she talked about working right up until the last minute. And then she was going to take a few months off, and eventually go back to the office. She couldn't imagine giving up work, or staying home for more than a short time in the beginning.

She had everything worked out. She was going to take care of the baby herself until she went back to work, and then she was going to find a nice au pair girl who would be loving to the baby. She was going to have an amniocentesis in late March or early April to determine if the child was genetically healthy. It was a test that checked for problems like spina bifida and Down syndrome. And it would also tell her the sex of the child, if she wished to know it, which she did. And whenever she did her Christmas shopping, she kept buying little odds and ends for the baby. She even ordered an English pram she liked when she went to Saks. It had a navy-blue hood, and a white enamel basket.

"You're certainly getting ready, aren't you?" Brad teased. She was so excited, she couldn't imagine how she was going to wait until August. She told her secretary and her partners at their Christmas lunch, and they almost fell out of their seats. And she laughed happily at the look on their faces.

"Surprised ya, didn't I?"

"You're kidding, right?" Her partners couldn't believe it. She had always been the champion of the feminist cause, one of the early supporters of legalized abortion in California. What had happened to her? Was it change of life? Middle age? Mid-life crisis?

"No, I think it's marriage," she confessed. "I don't know . . . I just started thinking how sad it would be if we never had a baby."

"You're lucky it wasn't too late," her secretary said quietly. Her husband had died when she was forty-one, and when she married "the man of her life" two years later, they had been desperate to have a baby. Neither of them had ever had children before, and they had tried everything to conceive and nothing had worked. And her husband was dead set against adoption.

Alice and Bruce were particularly pleased for

her, and Marina had been jubilant when Pilar told her.

"I feel so lucky," Pilar said softly. "I really didn't think it would happen, even once we made up our minds. It's such a miracle when it happens. When you're young, you think it's no big deal, you screw, you get knocked up. And if you're fifteen in the back of a pickup truck, you can count on it. After that, nothing is quite so certain. You take every test, you do it on the right date, and at best you have an eight-to-ten-percent chance of getting pregnant. It's a wonder anyone ever does." She grinned. But she had. And she was thrilled. She told everyone her plans to work right up until the end, and everyone was excited for her when they heard. Pilar Coleman had everything she wanted.

Unlike Charlie Winwood, who sat in Dr. Pattengill's office, staring at him in disbelief. He had just told him that his sperm count was just under four million. Charlie thought that was great news for about five seconds, until the doctor explained it.

"Forty million is minimal for the normal range, Charlie." He looked at him seriously, anxious to be supportive. "Four million is way too far below that." And the concentration of sperm had been less than one million per milliliter, which was five percent of what it should be. And less than two percent had been moving, again shockingly low, when fifty percent would have been normal.

"Is there anything we can do to bring it up, so to speak." He smiled, and the doctor did too.

"Possibly hormones. But you may just be too far below the normal range. I'm not sure we can bring your sperm levels up far enough, but I'd like to check you again before we do anything." He had brought the other vial in. "We'll do another check now, and one more next week. And while we're waiting for those results, I'd like to do a few more tests. One of them is a sugar test to check for fructose. With your low volume of sperm, we could be dealing with a blocked duct and that could give us an important clue."

"And if it is blocked?" Charlie asked, his face white beneath the freckles. He hadn't expected this . . . but Barb had been right. There was a reason why she wasn't getting pregnant. He had a low sperm count.

"If there's a blockage, there are several possibilities; we can do a testicular biopsy, or a vasogram. But that's a long way off, and I doubt that you'll need that. I'd like to do an orange dye test on you, to see why the sperm don't move well. And the hamster test." He smiled. "You've probably heard of that. Everyone who's ever had a friend with a fertility problem seems to know about that one."

"No, I'm afraid I don't." What were they going to do to him now?

"We use a hamster egg and impregnate it with your sperm. It's actually a sperm penetration assay. But if the hamster egg is impregnated, the fertilizing capability of your sperm may be sound, and if not, it can be indicative of a serious problem."

"I never even had one as a kid," Charlie said unhappily, and the doctor smiled gently.

"We'll know a lot more next week."

But the week before Christmas was the worst in Charlie's life. He went back to Dr. Pattengill, and got what to him was a death sentence to his marriage. The second sperm count was far worse than the first, and the third even more depressing. In one of them he had almost a zero sperm count, the motility of his sperm was poor, and there was no blockage to account for the low semen volume. And even the hamster test had been disastrous. The hamster had not gotten pregnant, but Pattengill didn't find the results of the hamster test surprising, given the numbers. And there was absolutely nothing they could do. If his hormone levels were higher, it might have been worthwhile trying chlomiphene, but he was too far below the normal range to try that, and with no blockage to account for it, there was no appropriate surgery either. "You have to think of alternative plans for your family," the doctor said softly. "With these sperm counts, it's just about impossible for you to impregnate anyone. I'm really sorry."

"There's absolutely no chance?" Charlie's voice was a squeak in the suddenly airless room, and for the first time in years, he felt his asthma.

"Virtually none." It was a death sentence to him, and he was sorry he had ever come. But maybe it was better knowing than hoping.

"Nothing I can do, Doc? No medicine, no treatment?"

"I wish there were, Charlie. You're very close to what we call essentially a zero sperm count. You just can't make a baby. But you can adopt. If your wife is willing, you might want to consider donor sperm, and have her artificially inseminated. Then you could go through the birth process together. That works very well for some people. Or you may even want to consider not having children. Some couples are very happy 'child-free,' as they call it. It allows you more

time, greater closeness, less stress in some
ways, than the addition of children to a marriage. Even biologically related children can
add enormous pressure to a marriage. You and
your wife should talk about all your options. We
can provide counseling to help you find what's
right for both of you," he said gently.

Great. Charlie sat staring dumbly out the
window. *Hi, Barb, well, I found out today I'm
sterile, you don't have to worry about having
kids anymore. . . . What's for dinner?* He
knew that she would never agree to adopt, let
alone to artificial insemination. The idea of even
suggesting it to her almost made him laugh
. . . except that he wanted to cry so badly.

"I don't know what to say," he said as he
looked at the doctor.

"You don't have to say anything. It's a lot to
absorb all at once. And I know how painful it is
for you. It's terrible news. It feels like a death
sentence, but it isn't."

"How do you know?" Charlie said tersely, his
eyes filled with tears. "It looks a lot different
from that side of the desk."

"That's true, and I don't usually tell my patients this, Charlie. But I have the same thing
you have. In fact, mine is more severe, not that
that makes much difference. Classic azoo-

spermia, in my case. Zero sperm count. My wife and I have four children, and all of them are adopted. I know how you feel. But there are other solutions. You won't get your wife pregnant this month, or any other month, but that doesn't mean you can't have a family, if you want one. But as I said, the right answer for you may even be not to have children. Whatever's right for you. You have to find those answers."

Charlie nodded, and eventually he stood up, and shook the doctor's hand and left. Peter Pattengill hadn't been quite the miracle worker Mark's brother-in-law had promised. There were no miracles for Charlie. There was nothing. There never had been. No parents, no family when he was growing up, and now no kids of his own, and sometimes he wondered if there was even Barbie. She was so separate from him, so distant and independent. Lately he hardly saw her anymore, she was always at auditions, or out with friends, and he was always working. And now what was he going to tell her? That he was sterile? Great . . . and how would you like to have artificial insemination with donor sperm, sweetheart? That would be a big hit with her. He could hardly believe it.

He sat in his car for half an hour before he started it, and as he drove home, the Christmas

decorations he saw looked like an insult. It reminded him of when he'd been in the state
home as a boy, and he used to look out and see
homes across the street with Christmas trees,
and lit-up reindeer on the lawn, and mothers
and fathers and children. He had always wanted
to be one of them, and he couldn't even have
that now. It was like a cruel joke. And all his
life, that was all he had ever wanted.

When he got home, Barb was out, but this
time she had left him a note, and said she was
going to an acting workshop and wouldn't be
home till after midnight. It was just as well, he
couldn't have faced her anyway and not told
her. He poured himself a stiff glass of Scotch
and went to bed, and by the time she got home,
he was so drunk he was unconscious.

CHAPTER
═══ 10 ═══

Pilar called her mother on Christmas Day, and the temptation to tell her about the baby was great, but somehow she managed to resist it. And she also knew that half of her desire to tell her was to prove her wrong, and let her know that she was not too old to have children. But Pilar was smarter than that, and she said nothing about it as she wished her a Merry Christmas.

She called Marina, too, who was in Toronto, celebrating the holidays with one of her many sisters.

And later in the day, Brad and Pilar opened their presents with Todd and Nancy and Tommy and little Adam. Pilar had spoiled everyone, especially the baby. There was a huge teddy bear, and a little swing, and some adorable clothes she had found in a boutique in L.A., and a beautiful German rocking horse she had ordered from New York. And she had lovely gifts for everyone else. She was thrilled to see Todd, looking handsome and well and full of tales of his job and girlfriend in Chicago. And she felt closer to Nancy than she had in years. They had so much in common now, although her stepdaughter did not yet know it.

They had a wonderful meal, and as they drank champagne and ate Yule cake afterward, Brad smiled at her, and she nodded.

"I have something to tell you all, which I know will come as something of a surprise. But life is full of wonderful surprises." She smiled at Adam gurgling in his high chair as she said it. He was wearing a little red velvet suit she had bought him and given Nancy before Christmas.

"You're becoming a judge too!" Todd guessed, pleased for both of them. "What an impressive family!" Todd saluted.

"You're buying a new house!" Nancy offered, hoping that her father would let her live in this one if they decided not to sell it.

"Better than that." Pilar grinned. "And much more important—and no, I'm not becoming a judge. One is enough in this family, I'll leave those important matters to your dad." She smiled tenderly at him while everyone waited, and then she took their breath away, as she spoke softly but proudly. "We're having a baby."

There was total silence in the room, and then Nancy laughed nervously. She didn't believe it. "You're not."

"I am."

"But you're so old," she said rudely, as her father watched her. She reminded him suddenly of the spoiled little girl she had been when she objected to his going out with Pilar when he first met her.

"You told me you had friends older than I who were having first babies," Pilar said quietly. "You told me I should think about it before it was too late." She was forcing her to remember her own words, and Nancy didn't like it.

"But I never thought . . . I just . . . don't you and Daddy think you're too old for a child now?" she said bluntly, while her husband and brother watched her in silence.

"No, we don't," her father said calmly, "and apparently Mother Nature doesn't think so either." He was happy about the baby, and for Pilar, and he wasn't going to let Nancy spoil it. She had her own life, her husband, her child, and she had no right to cast a shadow over theirs, or spoil Pilar's pleasure by being jealous. "I'm sure it's a surprise for all of you, but we're very happy, and we hope you will be too. And I think it's wonderful that Master Adam will have a new uncle." He laughed, and Todd raised his glass to them.

"Well, Dad, you two are always full of surprises. But I'm happy for you both, if it's what you want," he said fairly. "I think you're both good sports. I can't even imagine having kids, especially if they turn out like us"—he looked pointedly at his sister—"but good luck to you both!" He toasted and then drank, and Tommy added his good wishes. Only Nancy looked annoyed, and she never recovered before they left. She snapped at Tommy when he picked the baby up, kissed her father good-bye with tears in her eyes, and never even thanked Pilar for their presents.

"I guess she hasn't grown up as much as I thought," Pilar said softly after they left. "She's furious with me."

"She's a spoiled brat, and our life and what we do with it is none of her business." He refused to let his children run his life, just as he refused to run theirs. They were grown-ups, and so were he and Pilar. And he wasn't going to be affected by what his children thought. He wanted Pilar to have this baby. He knew how much it meant to her, and she had a right to have children, and if it was late in her life, then that was her business and no one else's.

"Maybe she thinks I'm competing with her," Pilar mused as they cleared the table and stacked the dishes in the sink, to leave them for their cleaning woman the next morning.

"Maybe. But it's time she learned the world doesn't turn around her. Tommy will set her straight, and so will Todd." He was staying with them for a few days during his vacation.

"I thought Todd was wonderful and it must have been a shock to him too."

"Probably, but at least he's mature enough to know it's not going to change anything in his life. Nancy will figure that out eventually, too, that it doesn't diminish my affection for them. But she'll make your life miserable in the meantime, if you let her." And then he looked sternly at Pilar. "I don't want her upsetting you right now. Is that clear?" He sounded very firm, and she smiled at him as they went back to their bedroom.

"Yes, Your Honor."

"Good. And I don't want to hear from the little beast until she remembers her manners."

"She'll be okay, Brad. It was a big surprise for her."

"Well, she'd better shape up, or she'll be in big trouble with her father. She gave you enough trouble fifteen years ago to last for several lifetimes. She has no tickets left for this one, and if need be I'll remind her of that. But I hope I won't have to."

"I'll call her next week and invite her to lunch and see if I can unruffle her feathers."

"She should be calling you," he growled, but she surprised them both by calling to apologize later that night. Her brother and husband had forced her to admit that she had no right to disapprove of what they did, and she had behaved very badly. She cried when she talked to Pilar and told her how sorry she was for being rotten to her, and Pilar cried too.

"It's all your fault, you know," she said emotionally into the phone, "if Adam weren't so cute, I might never have done it." But there was a lot more to it than that and she and Brad knew it.

"I'm sorry . . . and you were so sweet to me when I told you about Adam."

"Don't worry about it." Pilar smiled through her tears. "You owe me a cheesecake." It was her only craving for the moment.

And the next morning when they got up, there was a cheesecake in a pink box on the front step, with a pink rose on it. And Pilar cried all over again when she showed it to Brad. But he was glad that Nancy had come to her senses so quickly.

"Now all you have to do is relax, and have the baby." It seemed like an endless eight months to wait till August.

Diana and Andy spent a quiet Christmas in Hawaii, and it was just what they needed, as they lay in the sun and baked day after day at the Mauna Kea. It was the first time they'd been alone and away since the agonies of what they'd been through, except for their disastrous weekend in La Jolla in early September. And both of them were startled to realize how close they had come to destroying their marriage. They seemed to have nothing in common anymore, nothing to say, nothing to share, nothing to look forward to. They had been treading water for almost four months, and in truth they'd actually been drowning, until Thanksgiving, when for a moment there was a glimmer of hope.

It took two days of lying on the beach before they spoke to each other about anything other than food and weather. But it was the perfect place for them. There was no television in the rooms, nowhere to go, nothing to see, they just lay on the beach, and slowly began to recover.

On Christmas Day they shared a quiet dinner in the main dining room, and then went for a long walk on the beach, holding hands at sunset.

"I feel like we've been to the moon and back this year," Diana said quietly. After a year and a half of marriage, she was no longer sure what she wanted or where they were going.

"I felt that way too," he admitted to her, as they sat on the white sand and watched the surf roll in. And in a little while, when it was dark, the giant manta rays would come in to shore to feed, and the hotel guests would watch them. "But the thing is, Di . . . we made it . . . we didn't go under. . . . we're still here, talking to each other, holding hands. . . . That means a lot. . . . We survived it."

"But at what price," she said sadly. She had given up all her dreams. And what was there to look forward to now? All she had ever wanted were children . . . but she had also wanted Andy. And he was still there. The only thing lost were her babies. It was hard to live like that, but on the other hand, he was right. Losing their dreams hadn't killed them either.

"Maybe it'll make us stronger in the long run," he said thoughtfully. He still loved her. He just didn't know who she was anymore, or where to find her. She had been hiding from him emotionally for months, and from herself. She had been in her shell, going to work earlier and earlier every day, coming home later and later, and getting right into bed when she got home, and falling asleep the moment she got there. She didn't want to talk to him or anyone, she scarcely called her parents, and never her sisters, or her friends. They had suddenly all become strangers. And she'd taken every trip she could get her hands on in the office. He'd offered to meet her a couple of times, thinking they could take a few days of pleasure at the end of the trip, but she didn't want to have a good time, and she didn't want to be with him. And she always said she was too busy.

"The big question," he said hesitantly, wondering if it was too soon to broach the subject, "is where do we go from here? Do you want to be married to me anymore? Has there been too much pain for us to get back to the good stuff again? I just don't know what you want anymore," he said, thinking how tragic it was that he was asking her if she wanted a divorce, sitting beneath this gorgeous sunset in Hawaii. She was wearing a white cotton dress and she already had a deep suntan after two days, and her dark hair was blowing in the breeze tantalizingly. But no matter how beautiful he still thought she was, he also knew she didn't want him.

"What do *you* want?" She answered his question with one of her own. "I keep thinking that I have no right to hang on to you. You deserve so much more than I can give you." She was ready to give him up, for his sake, if not for her own. And she would live alone, and pursue her career. She knew she would never marry again if he left her, or at least she thought so. She was twenty-eight years old and ready to give it all up, if that was what he wanted, but it wasn't.

"That's bullshit, and you know it."

"I don't know anything anymore. All I know is what isn't. I don't know what is, or what's right, or what I should do, or even what I want." She'd even thought of quitting her job and moving back to Europe.

"Do you love me?" he asked softly, moving closer to her, looking into the eyes that were always so sad now, so empty, so broken, everything inside her had been scorched and burned and torn from her soul, and there were times when he thought there was nothing left but ashes.

"Yes, I do," she whispered. "I love you very much . . . I always will . . . but that doesn't mean I have the right to keep you. . . . I can't give you anything, Andy . . . except myself, and there's not much left now."

"Yes, there is. You've just buried yourself, in work, and pain and grief. . . . I can help you climb out of all that, if you'll let me." He had started seeing a therapist a few weeks before, and he was feeling stronger.

"And then what?" she asked. To her it seemed so fruitless.

"Then we have each other, which is more than a lot of people can say. We're two good people who love each other and have a lot to give each other, and the world, and their friends. The whole world doesn't revolve around kids, you know. And even if we had our own, sooner or later they'd grow up and go away, or maybe they'd hate us, or they could be killed in a car accident or a fire. There are no guarantees in life. Even children aren't always forever." The problem for her was that they were everywhere, in the streets, in the super- markets, sometimes even in the elevator at her office, tiny little people with big eyes and open hearts, holding their mothers' hands, or crying and being held and comforted in a way Diana would never be able to do now. There were women with huge pregnant bellies everywhere she looked, filled with hope and promise in a way Diana would never know, never share, never feel in her heart or her body. It wasn't easy to give all that up, and it didn't seem fair to her that Andy had to.

"I think it's unfair of you to live a childless life, because I have to. Why should you do that?"

"Because I love you. And it also doesn't have to be childless. It can be, if we want it to be. But if not, there are other options."

"I'm not sure I'm ready for that."

"Neither am I. And we don't have to make any decisions about that now. All we have to do is think about us, and do something before it's too late and we blow it. Baby . . . I don't want to lose you. . . ."

"I don't want to lose you either," she said, as tears sprang to her eyes, and she turned away then. Over his shoulder, far down the beach, she could see children playing, and she couldn't bear it.

"I want you back . . . in my dreams . . .

in my life . . . in my days . . . in my heart . . . in my arms . . . in my bed . . . in my future. God, I've missed you," he said, and he pulled her closer, feeling the warmth of her body next to his, and he ached for her. "Baby . . . I need you. . . ."

"I need you too," she said as she started to cry. She needed him so badly. She couldn't do it without him, couldn't give up all those dreams, and yet somehow in the midst of the horror, she had lost him.

"Let's try . . . please let's try. . . ." He looked at her and she smiled and nodded. "It won't always be easy, and maybe sometimes I won't understand, and I won't always be there . . . but I'll try to be. And if I'm not, tell me." All he wanted was to get her back now.

They walked slowly back up to their room, hand in hand, and for the first time in months he made love to her, and it was much, much better than either of them had remembered.

Charlie and Barbara's Christmas was strange. Afterward, that was the only word he could think of to describe it. Peculiar. Odd. Perhaps even amazing. He cooked Christmas dinner, as usual, and she went to Judi's in the morning, she said, to give her her present. And for once, Charlie was just as happy to be alone. He had a terrible hangover again, he had been drinking much too heavily, and he knew it. But he had been trying to absorb what Dr. Pattengill had told him, and he couldn't. He would never get his wife pregnant. Never. A near-zero sperm count. He remembered, too, what the doctor had said about himself, but that didn't help much. He didn't care how many children the Pattengills had adopted. He wanted a baby, his own, with Barb. Now. And he knew he couldn't. Or at least his mind knew, but his heart kept refusing to believe it.

She was back by four o'clock, and full of bounce and excitement. She'd obviously had a few drinks, and she got playful with him while he was basting the turkey, but he just didn't want to play. He had bought her a little fox jacket that she loved, and she went into the bedroom and took off all her clothes, except her black lace panties, and then she came back out in the fur jacket and the panties and high-heel shoes, and all he could do was laugh. She looked so funny and so cute, and it was all so pointless.

"You're a silly broad, you know that?" He

smiled and pulled her down next to him on the couch and kissed her. "And I love you."

"I love you too," she said, looking mysterious, and a little tiddly. He poured her favorite champagne with dinner. The turkey was perfect, and he felt better by the end of dinner. He knew he had to make his peace with it somehow, and then she came and sat on his lap. She was wearing a pink satin dressing gown he had bought her for her birthday, and the view was very inviting.

"Merry Christmas, Barb." He kissed her neck gently, and felt her back arch beneath his hands, and then she pulled away from him and looked at him tenderly. He saw something in her eyes, but he wasn't sure what it was, and then she kissed him.

"I have something to tell you," she whispered.

"Me too . . ." he said hoarsely. "Let's go in the bedroom and I'll tell you—"

"Me first," she said, pulling away from him again. "I think you're gonna like this." She looked mischievous and he looked amused as he sat back in his chair and waited.

"This better be good. If it isn't, I'm tearing your robe off right here, and to hell with the bedroom." Just being with her raised his spirits.

There was an endless pause as she smiled hesitantly, and then she told him. "I'm pregnant."

He stared at her in utter amazement, unable to speak at first, and then slowly he went pale. "Do you mean it?"

"Of course I do. Would I kid you about a thing like that?" Given what Dr. Pattengill had said, maybe.

"Are you sure?" Could he have been wrong? Could they have been counting someone else's sperm that were too few and too sluggish? "What makes you think so?"

"For chrissake," she said, looking annoyed as she got off his lap and lit a cigarette from the candles on the table. "Here, I thought you'd be so happy. What is this? The Spanish Inquisition? Yeah, I'm sure. I went to the doctor two days ago."

"Oh, baby." He closed his eyes, so she wouldn't see the tears there as he held her. "I'm sorry. . . . I just . . . I can't explain it. . . ." He just held her and cried, and she had no idea why, but he didn't know whether to get down on his knees and thank God, or damn her. Had she been playing around? Was it someone else's child? But without telling her what he knew, he couldn't ask her.

He was strangely quiet for the rest of the day, and she made a few phone calls while he washed up the dishes from dinner. But it was obvious she hadn't gotten the reaction she expected from him, and she didn't understand it. And then at last they went to bed that night, and he held her, praying that Pattengill had been wrong. But before he could open his heart up to her, and the baby she said was his, he knew he had to ask him.

It was an endless wait for three days before he could get back in to see the doctor. And he scarcely saw Barbie. She was out with friends, going shopping, and she even said she had an audition the day after Christmas. He didn't question her this time. He didn't say anything. He had to see Pattengill first. That was all he wanted. But when he finally sat across the desk from him again, the physician shook his head firmly.

"Charlie, I don't think it can be. I'd like to tell you it is, and I've seen crazier things than that. But it's highly unlikely you fathered that baby. I've had infertility patients surprise me before, but Charlie, believe me . . . I just don't think so. I wish I could tell you something different." Somehow, he had known. He had suspected it all along. All the nights she never came home until he was asleep, all the "girl-friends," the "girls' nights out," the visits to "Judi," the mysterious "auditions," and the "workshops" that never led anywhere. She hadn't had an acting job in months. And he just knew that, no matter how much he wanted it to be, she wasn't carrying his baby.

When he left Pattengill's office, he drove home slowly, and he was almost sorry when he found her there. She was talking to someone when he came in, and she hung up as soon as she saw him.

"Who was that?" he asked noncommittally, as though she were really going to tell him.

"It was Judi. I was telling her about the baby."

"Oh." He turned away so she wouldn't see his face, wishing that he didn't have to tell her, but he knew he had to. And slowly, slowly, wishing the world would come to an end first, he turned to face her. "We have to talk," he said quietly, and sat down in a chair across from where she sat, looking incredibly sexy.

"Something wrong?" She looked nervously at him and uncrossed her legs, and then she lit another cigarette and waited.

"Yeah."

"Did you lose your job?" She looked genuinely frightened and then relieved when he shook his head. What else could be wrong? He didn't play around, she was sure of that. He was too nice a guy to do that.

"No, it's nothing as simple as that." He went on, "A while back, I went to see a doctor. Right after Thanksgiving."

"What kind of doctor?" she asked, looking nervous.

"A reproductive endocrinologist," he said importantly, "a fertility specialist. You said something a long time ago, about being surprised you never got pregnant when we fooled around and weren't careful. And I guess you got me worried. So I decided to check things out. And I did. . . ."

"And?" She tried to look unimpressed, but she already sensed his answer, and her heart was pounding.

"I'm sterile."

"He doesn't know what he's talking about," she said, and she got up and paced the room. "Maybe he'd like to examine me, to be sure I'm pregnant."

"Are you?" he asked pointedly. There was always the chance she was lying about that, and now he desperately hoped so.

"Of course I am. I can do a test for you, if

you'd like to prove it. I'm two months pregnant." It made him wonder what she'd been
doing in late October. "The guy's crazy."

"No," Charlie said pointedly. "But I guess I
am. What's going on, Barb? Whose baby is
it?"

"Yours," she said, and then turned away, her
head bowed. She started to cry, and then slowly
she turned to face him. "Okay, it doesn't matter
whose it is . . . it's a rotten thing to do to you,
Charlie. I'm sorry." But if he hadn't known, if
he hadn't said anything, she would have kept
lying, and he knew it.

"I thought you didn't want kids anyway. Why
this one?"

"Because . . . I don't know. . . ." And then
she decided it was too late for lies. He knew the
truth anyway. He might as well know the rest of
her story. "Maybe because I've had too many
abortions, maybe because I knew how badly
you wanted a baby. . . . Maybe I'm getting old
. . . or soft . . . or stupid or something. . . .
I just thought—"

"Whose is it?" He was heartbroken to ask her
these questions, and they were pointless, except
as instruments of torture.

"Just a guy. Someone I met in Vegas. I used
to know him a long time ago, and he moved

here in October. He said he could get me a job. He had great connections in Vegas. So we got together a few times. I just thought . . ." But she couldn't go on, she was crying.

"Do you love him, or did you do it for a job, or just the fun of it? What does this guy mean to you?"

"Nothing," she said, but she couldn't look Charlie in the eye. And he suspected that the other man had all the flash he didn't. Thinking that made him wonder if she had ever loved him at all. Maybe it had all been a bad joke from the beginning. And all he'd wanted was a wife and kids, a family, the real thing. But maybe he had no right to it. How could he give a kid a good home if he'd never had one himself? What did he know?

"Why did you do it?" he asked her miserably, crying like a schoolboy.

She looked at him honestly then. "Because you scare me. You want everything—you want everything I ran away from. Every time I get close to you I get scared. You want kids, and family, and all that bullshit that doesn't mean shit to me. I don't want to be tied to anyone. I just can't do that."

He listened to her with tears rolling down his

cheeks, she was shattering all his dreams, and she knew it.

"You want to know why I feel that way, Charlie? Maybe you should. I had a family, brothers and sisters, and a mother and father . . . and you know what? My brother screwed me for seven years. He started when I was seven, and you know what, my mom let him do it. He was such a 'difficult' kid, she was afraid he'd get in trouble with the cops if he didn't let off 'steam,' so that's what I was, his escape valve. I had my first abortion, thanks to him, when I was thirteen, and two more a year later. And then my father tried to get a piece of the action. . . . Nice family, huh, Charlie? Doesn't that just make you want to run out and have kids? Yeah, me too. So I left. I went to Vegas, and turned tricks for a year, and then I got a job as a showgirl, and I had a couple more abortions there too. And then one more here when I got knocked up by an agent. And no, I don't want this baby, Charlie, but I figured you did." He did. But not someone else's. But he sat staring at her, aching at what she had just told him.

"I don't know what to say, Barb. I'm sorry for everything, the past, us. I guess we both got a rotten break."

"Yeah." She blew her nose and lit another cigarette. "I never should have married you. You wanted all that stupid Howdy Doody stuff. I should've told you it's all crap, but I wanted to believe I could do it. But you know what? I can't. I just can't be who you wanted me to be, that sweet little wifey stuff. It's just not me. I thought I'd go nuts sitting here in this apartment, talking about having kids, and watching you vacuum and cook dinner. Fuck dinner, Charlie, I want to party!"

He closed his eyes as he listened to her. He couldn't believe what she was saying. But it was all true, and he knew it.

He opened his eyes and looked at her and wondered if he ever knew her. "So what do you want to do now?"

"I don't know. I think I'm going to move in with Judi."

"What about the baby?"

"No big deal. I know what to do." She shrugged as though it didn't matter, and he forced himself not to think of how sweet she had looked when she first told him.

"What about the guy? Doesn't he want his kid?"

"I never told him. He's got a wife and three

kids in Vegas anyway, I'm sure he'd be real excited about this one."

"I don't know what to say." Charlie felt as though his whole life had been turned inside out, and it had. He could barely think, let alone make important decisions. "Why don't you give me a few days."

"For what?" She looked puzzled.

"To work this out in my head. I don't know what I think or feel or want anymore. I don't know what to tell you."

"You don't have to tell me anything," she said softly, sorry for the first time in her life. "I understand."

He was crying then, and he felt incredibly stupid. She was so worldly wise, so hardened, so used, and he was crying the way he had when people he'd been living with for a year said they couldn't take on a child with asthma. "I'm sorry. . . ." He couldn't stop crying as she took him in her arms and held him, and then she went into their bedroom, and packed up a few things. And a little while later she called a cab and went to Judi's.

But Charlie just sat in a chair and cried all day. He couldn't believe what had happened. He didn't even have the guts to call Mark, because he knew what he would say, that she was trouble, and he was better off without her. But if that was true, why didn't he feel any better? He had never felt worse in his life. He was sterile, and the wife he loved had left him.

CHAPTER
11

Brad and Pilar spent the evening with friends on New Year's Eve, and everyone was amazed when Pilar told them about the baby. She had certainly come full circle in the past year. From inveterate single woman to wife, and now mother. It was a far cry from the way she'd felt about life two decades before, but now her evolution suited her to perfection.

After dinner, the entire group danced to old show tunes, and at midnight they kissed and drank champagne, and Brad and Pilar went home about one-thirty. She was more tired than usual, she liked late nights, but it was also draining explaining their new circumstances to everyone. And ever since she'd been pregnant, she'd noticed she was sleepy.

"People are so funny, aren't they?" Pilar grinned. "I love watching their faces when I tell them I'm pregnant. First, they think I'm kidding, and they don't know what to say, and then they go wild. I love it."

"You're a funny girl." Brad smiled, but he noticed that she winced when he helped her out of the car, and he wasn't sure why. "Are you okay?"

"Yeah . . . I just had a weird cramp, that's all."

"Where?"

"I don't know, in my stomach somewhere," she said vaguely. She'd had cramps a few days before, too, but when she'd called Dr. Ward, she'd said that that was normal, they were probably stretching pains as her uterus started growing. And she assumed that was what was happening again when she felt another cramp as she hung up her clothes, but this one was stronger. And then there was another one . . . and another . . . and she felt something warm run down her leg . . . and as she looked down, she saw that she was bleeding. "Oh, my God . . ." she whispered, and then she called hoarsely for Brad, and she just stood there, bleeding on the carpet. She was too frightened to move, or do anything about it. She didn't know what it meant, but she knew it wasn't good, and the moment Brad saw it, he rushed her into the bathroom. He lay her down on towels on the rug, and tried to elevate her hips to stop the bleeding, but she was bleeding heavily by then, and she was terrified as she watched him.

"Am I losing the baby?"

"I don't know. Don't move, sweetheart. I'm going to call the doctor." He rushed to the bedroom to use the phone, and came back to her a few minutes later. It was too far to go to L.A. for Dr. Ward. He had called Pilar's old gynecologist instead and he had said to get her to the hospital as fast as they could. He promised to meet them there in ten minutes. And he'd been kind enough to reassure Brad that he had seen some women bleed very badly and still keep their babies. Dr. Parker was an old-fashioned kind of man, in his early seventies, and Brad had always liked him.

Brad told her that as he wrapped her in towels and put a jacket around her shoulders, but they left a trail as they left the house, and he lay her on the backseat wrapped in a blanket and several towels. And then he drove as fast as he dared down the hill to the hospital. By the time they got there, she was pale, and she was crying from the pain and fear that she was losing her baby. She said it was the worst thing she'd ever felt, and when the doctor tried to examine her she screamed. And he looked at Brad and shook his head, and explained to him that she was not just bleeding, she was losing tissue.

Dr. Parker tried to explain gently to Pilar what was happening and she looked from him to Brad in terror. "The baby? Is it dying?"

"It's probably not viable anymore," he explained as he held one hand, and Brad gently held the other. "Sometimes these things just can't be helped." Helen Ward had already warned her weeks before that older mothers were more likely to miscarry.

But she was sobbing as she lay bleeding and in pain, and she couldn't believe that the baby they had wanted so much was gone. It wasn't fair. Why did it have to happen?

"We're going to take you upstairs in a little while and do a D&C, it will get everything cleaned out, and that should stop the bleeding. I want to wait a little while though, because Brad says you had quite a lot to eat. I think in another hour or two you should be okay, and I'll give you something for the pain in the meantime." But the "something" the nurse offered her didn't come close to touching the pain, and for the next two hours she lay in bed and gritted her teeth and tried not to scream at the contractions. She couldn't believe that anything could be so painful. She was completely overwrought and hysterical when they took her away, and she kept asking Brad what if the baby wasn't really dead, what if they did a D&C and the baby would have been okay, then it would be like having an abortion. He tried to reassure her, as the doctor had, that the baby was gone, and they had to clear her uterus of the dead tissue.

"It's not dead tissue," she had screamed at him uncontrollably. "It's our baby!"

"I know, sweetheart, I know." He took her right to the doors of the operating room as they took her in on a gurney, and the doctor let him wait in the recovery room for her. But as soon as she came to, she started crying. She said not a single word. She just lay there and sobbed all night, as Brad stood by helplessly and watched her.

"It's going to be hard for her," the doctor said to Brad before he left. "Miscarriage is one of the great underrated miseries of our day. It's a death, there's no way around it. We used to think it was 'just one of those things' and expect women to bounce back in a few days. They

don't. It takes months . . . sometimes years
. . . sometimes never . . . and at Pilar's age,
she can't be sure of another baby."

"We'll keep trying," Brad said more to himself than to the doctor. "We'll try. We managed
this one."

"Tell her that. She's going to be miserable for
a while. Some of it is real, and some of it is
hormones." But Brad realized that what he was
feeling was real, too, and when he went back to
her room, he cried for her, for the baby they
had lost, and the grief they were both feeling.

He drove her home that afternoon, and put
her to bed. He wanted her to stay there for a
few days, and that night Nancy called to tell her
about a fabulous new crib she'd seen for their
baby.

"I—I can't talk to you right now. . . ." Pilar
was engulfed in tears as she handed the phone
to Brad, who didn't do much better. He went
into the other room and explained, and Nancy
hung up, shocked, and sorry for them, thinking
that maybe Pilar was just too old even to try it.

They spent a long and lonely New Year's
Day, thinking of the child they'd lost, the
dreams they'd shared, and sat quietly together,
in silent mourning.

* * *

On New Year's Day, Charlie woke up at six-fifteen. He'd been awake half the night, and finally fell asleep around four. But he just couldn't sleep these days, and he had finally decided what he wanted to do about Barbie. He didn't like what she'd done, and she'd have to promise him it wouldn't happen again, but he couldn't leave her now. She needed him, and he loved her. How could he let her down now? And maybe this baby was just what they needed to save them.

It was too early to call, so he got up and showered and shaved, read the newspaper, paced the room, and finally at nine o'clock he drove over to Judi's. He hadn't talked to Barb in three days, and he hadn't known what to say to her when she left. He was just too shocked by the news that she was pregnant. In a strange way, too, he was sorry he had ever gone to see Dr. Pattengill. If he hadn't, he wouldn't have known he was sterile, and he would have believed the baby was his when she told him. But things weren't that simple anymore. Or were they?

He rang the bell, and they buzzed him up a minute later. Judi opened the front door to him, and then looked surprised to see him. She started to say something and then thought better of it. There was a guy with her she'd been seeing off and on since June, and the new roommate who had taken Barbie's place when she and Charlie got married. Judi looked awkward suddenly, and so did Charlie. They both knew what was happening, and Charlie also knew by then that Judi must have covered for her whenever Barbie saw the guy from Las Vegas. She had betrayed Charlie, but her only real loyalty was to Barbie. And now she was sorry things had turned out the way they had. Barbie had told her as soon as she had found out she was pregnant. Judi had told her to just get rid of it and not say anything, the baby's father was married to someone else anyway. And Barbie said she would at first, but then she got all caught up in how much Charlie wanted a baby. In a crazy way, she thought she might be able to convince him it was his, and then she wouldn't have to have another abortion.

"Hi, Charlie," Judi said softly. "I'll go get Barbie." But she was already standing in the hall by then. She looked tired and pale and unhappy.

"Hi," he said to her, feeling like a kid on a first date as Judi and the others disappeared in the direction of the kitchen. "I'm sorry I haven't called. I needed time to think."

"So did I." There were tears in her eyes, and she was choking on a sob. Seeing him made it all so much harder. She realized now what she'd done to him, and how wrong it had been to lie to him about the baby.

"Can we sit down somewhere?" Charlie suddenly looked older, and more mature. He had been through a lot in the past few days. In fact, he felt as though he had aged ever since he'd been told he was sterile.

She had been sleeping on the couch in the living room, and she didn't want the others to hear them in the kitchen, so they went into Judi's bedroom. Barbie sat down on the unmade bed, and Charlie perched uncomfortably on the edge of the room's only chair, looking at the girl he had married. They had come a long way in less than two years, and most of the trip hadn't been unpleasant. It just didn't feel like much of a marriage, but Charlie felt sure that would change now. And with a child, they would have so much more to hold them together.

"I want the baby, Barb. I've thought about it a lot, and I think we could make it work. Hell, if anyone had adopted me, I wouldn't have been related to either of them. And this baby never

has to know that I'm not his father. His birth
certificate will say I am, that's enough for me."
He smiled gently at her. He was willing to forgive her for everything, and she cried miserably
when he told her. And for a while all she could
do was shake her head at him. It was a difficult
time for both of them, and he reached out and
took her hand, but she only let him hold it for
an instant. He tried to tell her that everything
would be all right. But she just didn't want to
hear it.

"I had an abortion yesterday." She finally
managed to get the words out, and he felt as
though he had been struck a blow. He had
never realized she would do something like that
so quickly.

"Are you kidding?" But who would kid about
a thing like that? He just didn't know what else
to say, as they sat staring at each other in the
deafening silence. "Why?" Everything she said
sounded crazy and stupid. But he was in completely over his head emotionally and he knew
it.

"Charlie, I couldn't have that kid. It wouldn't
have been fair to you, or me, or the baby. All his
life you'd have known that I cheated on you. He
would have reminded you of it every day, every
time you'd have seen him. And I . . ." She

looked up at him, with eyes filled with pain. "The truth is, no matter how guilty I felt about what I did, or how sorry I was, or how much I hated to have another abortion . . . I just don't want a baby. Yours or someone else's."

"Why? A baby would be the best thing that could happen to us. And now we'll have to adopt one," he said unhappily. That baby might have been the perfect solution, and now even that was no longer an option. A part of him felt relieved, and another part of him was devastated.

"Charlie"—her voice was soft and barely audible in the small room—"I'm not coming back to you." She hung her head, unable to look at him after she said it.

"What?" His face went white beneath the freckles. "What do you mean?"

She forced herself to look at him again. "Charlie, I love you . . . you're everything a woman would want in a husband. But I—I just don't want to be married. I never knew that about myself before. I felt like I was dead sitting home with you every night. I thought I could do it, but I just couldn't. That's why this happened, I guess. At first, when we got married, I was so relieved to have someone decent take care of me." The tears rolled relentlessly down her cheeks as she said it. "I thought it was all like a dream. But eventually, for me, the dream turned into a nightmare. I don't want to answer to anyone. I don't want to be stuck home all the time. I don't want to live with one guy, and one thing I know for sure is that I don't want to have a baby, yours or anyone else's, and I sure as hell don't want to adopt one. I talked to the doctor yesterday, and I'm going to get fixed in a few weeks. I just don't want to have any more abortions."

"Why did you do that without at least talking to me?" he asked, fixating on the child again. As though dealing with that would make every-thing else she had said not have happened. She had said she wasn't coming back to him, but she couldn't mean it. She was upset, she didn't know what she was saying.

"Charlie, it wasn't your baby. And I didn't want it."

"That wasn't fair," he said, crying too. Nothing was. Nothing that had happened was fair, but nothing ever had been, not since the very beginning of his life when his parents walked out on him. And now she was walking out too. She was just like all those people in the foster homes who kept him for a while, and then de-cided he was nice, but they just didn't love him.

What was it with him, he asked himself as tears streamed down his cheeks and he cried like a child, why was it that no one ever loved him? "I'm sorry . . ." He tried to apologize for everything he felt, and for the tears, but Barbie just shook her head. He only made her feel worse, but she was absolutely sure now of what she was doing. She realized that she should have done it months before, before she had the affair with the guy in Vegas. "Why don't you come home for a while, and we can try again? We can have an open marriage, or something, you can come and go as you like. No questions asked, no explanations." But even hearing himself say the words, he wondered how he could have said it. He knew it would have driven him crazy. And she knew it even better.

She had made up her mind, and nothing he said was going to change it. "I can't do that, Charlie. It wouldn't be fair to either of us."

"What are you going to do?" He was worried about her too. She needed someone to take care of her, she wasn't as tough as she pretended.

"Judi's going to quit her job, and we're going back to Vegas."

"To what? Another five years on the chorus line, and then what? What'll you do when you're too old to model bathing suits and show your boobs off?"

"I'll have 'em fixed, and show 'em off some more, I guess. I don't know, Charlie. But I know I can't be what you want, and what you deserve. I'd rather die in Vegas as a showgirl."

"I can't believe this." He stood up and walked across the room, to stare out the only window. The view of the street was bleak, like everything in his life now. "You're really not coming home with me?" He turned to look at her again, and she shook her head firmly. They had both stopped crying by then, but he felt as though a giant had put a fist through his solar plexus.

"You deserve better than I could ever give you," she said sadly. "Some nice girl who'll appreciate everything you have to give, who wants to stay home and cook for you; you can adopt a couple of kids and be very happy."

"Thank you for working it all out for me," he said miserably. He knew as he stood there that he would never try again. He couldn't force her to come back to him, but he knew he would never remarry.

"Charlie, I'm sorry . . ." she said again as they left the room, and she watched him walk down the stairs as he left Judi's apartment. He didn't turn and look back at her. He couldn't. It would have reminded him too much of all those terrible times the foster parents had taken him back to the institution.

CHAPTER
=== 12 ===

For the rest of January, Charlie felt as though he were walking under water. He went to work, he packed her things, he dropped them off, he moved to a studio apartment in Palms, and he sat up all night thinking. He wanted to understand why things had gone wrong, but he was never sure. Had he wanted too much, was it his desire to have kids? Was it that that had pushed her over the edge? It was impossible to admit that she just didn't want to be married. She had already filed for divorce by the end of the month, and a few days later she called to tell him she was leaving for Vegas. She said she'd let him know where she was, so they could get the rest of the paperwork filed. She sounded businesslike and in control by then, which Charlie wasn't. He had cried for an hour after he hung up the phone, and even Mark wasn't able to console him. He kept telling him that there were other fish in the sea, that she wasn't the only one around, and that he'd be better off with a girl who was a little more like him. He didn't want to remind him that he had been wary of her from the start. What was the point now?

And he kept reminding Charlie that he had been through the same thing, when his wife had left him for another man and moved to California.

"And I had kids!" he said, to underline how much worse it had been for him, but that only reminded Charlie further of how bleak his life was, and how empty his future. He refused to go out with anyone else, and all of Mark's efforts to get him out and introduce him to friends were fruitless. He even refused to go bowling. It was just too soon for him, and he wanted to rethink his life now.

He was even beginning to think that he was better off without kids, that it was a blessing that he was sterile. What did he know about kids anyway? He'd never had a normal childhood. How could he expect to be a decent parent? He said as much to Mark, who told him he was crazy. His friend was heartbroken to see him so devastated, and even suggested he go to a psychiatrist he knew in the Valley, but Charlie didn't want to do that either.

"Look, kid," Mark tried to explain one night, as they were leaving work, "you're not thinking straight. You'd probably be the best father in the world, because you understand what a kid needs, because you never had it. You picked the wrong girl, that's all, it's as simple as that. She was a nice kid, but she wanted the bright lights and the big time. You want to cook and stay home and raise a family. So . . . you find the right girl eventually, you settle down, and you all live happily ever after. Stop thinking your life is over, Charlie, because it isn't. Just give it some time. The wounds are still fresh, you're still bleeding." He was, and what Mark said was true, but Charlie didn't want to hear it.

"I don't want to find someone else. And I don't want to get married. Hell, I'm not even divorced yet."

"Oh . . . so that's why you won't go bowling anymore . . . why we can't go out for a beer and a pizza. What do you think, I'm asking for a date? Listen, you're cute, but you're just not my type, and little Gina might get pretty upset, you know. . . ." Charlie started to laugh then, and

Mark gave him a friendly shove. "Just take it easy on yourself, will ya?"

"Yeah, yeah, I'll try . . ." he said, smiling for the first time in ages.

He went out for dinner with Mark a few days after that, and the following weekend, he even went bowling. It was a long, slow process, but he had finally begun to heal. It still hurt terribly when he thought of her, and he still couldn't believe what she'd done to end their marriage, but little by little he came out of his shell again. And he started playing baseball on weekends with a bunch of twelve-year-old orphans.

Pilar spent the month after her miscarriage in a crushing depression. She took time off from work, refused to talk to anyone, and stayed home, in her nightgown, brooding. Brad tried to urge her to see friends, but it even took Marina several attempts to see her.

She came with an armful of books, about grief, about the loss of pregnancy, about mourning. She always thought information was the best tool, but Pilar didn't want to hear it.

"I don't want to know how miserable I am, or how miserable I should be," she said, glaring at her friend, rejecting her and the books she'd brought her.

"But maybe you'd like to know how to make yourself feel better, and when you can expect your life to get back to normal," Marina said gently.

"How normal will it ever be? I'm a middle-aged woman who made a lot of stupid decisions in her life, and as a result will never have children."

"My, my, aren't we feeling sorry for ourselves." She chided with a smile.

"I have a right to."

"Yes, you do, but not as a lifestyle. Think of Brad, think of how hard this is for him." It was Brad who had begged Marina to come by and see her. Pilar wouldn't even answer the phone, or take her calls when he did.

"He has children of his own. He doesn't know anything about it."

"No, but other people do. There are groups for things like this. Other women lose pregnancies too. You're not alone, Pilar, even though you think you are. It may feel like it now, but you're not. Other women lose babies, have still-births, lose children they've known and loved for several years. It must be the worst blow there is," she said sadly, feeling for her friend, as Pilar started to cry again.

"It is," she admitted, with tears streaming down her face, "and I feel so stupid. I know this must seem ridiculous to everyone, but I feel as though I lost a baby I knew . . . a little person I already loved . . . and now he's dead and I'll never know him."

"No, but you may have another child. It won't change this, but it might help."

"I think that's the only thing that would," Pilar said honestly. "I just want to be pregnant again." She blew her nose in a mass of tissues as she said it, and Marina smiled sympathetically.

"Maybe you will." She never liked to offer false hope, and there was no way of knowing if Pilar would get pregnant.

"Yeah, and maybe I won't. And then what?"

"Then you go on again. You have to. Your life was fine before, it will be again. Babies are not everything, you know." But as she said that, she remembered an incident years before, and she shared it with Pilar. "You know, I'd almost forgotten, until just now. My mother lost her ninth child, I think she must have been about two months pregnant. Maybe a little more. And with eight children, you'd think it was no big deal, but you would have thought her oldest child had died. She completely fell apart, and went into serious mourning. My father didn't know what to do with her. She stayed in bed and cried, and the other seven kids went wild, except when I was around to keep them in line, but my poor mother was a mess. She was depressed for months, and then, of course, she got pregnant. She had two more kids after the one she lost, but you know, she talked about it right up until she died, about how terrible it had been, how sad, how much she had missed that baby. She had friends who had actually lost a child, but I think this was actually just as bad for her, and she always talked about the baby who died as though she knew him."

"That's how I feel," Pilar said, finally feeling as though someone understood her. She felt a sudden bond with Marina's mother and what she had felt for her lost baby.

"It must be one of those mysteries of life that no one really understands, unless you go through it."

"Maybe," Pilar said, looking gloomy again. "It's the worst thing that's ever happened to me," she said, and meant it. She felt as though her heart were going to break each time she thought of it, and there was not a moment of the day when she didn't.

"Well, just think of my mother. She had two more kids after that, as I said. I think she was about forty-seven when she lost that baby."

"You give me hope." Marina was the first person who had, a godsend as usual, unlike Pilar's mother, whom she never called. She had never told her about the baby in the first place. And she would have just reminded Pilar that she had warned her that she was too old. And now she certainly felt it.

She stayed in deep mourning for several weeks after that, much to Brad's despair. Alice and Bruce were handling her cases at work, court dates had to be changed, and her clients were being told that she was ill, and everyone was seriously worried.

Nancy even came by to try to cheer her up, but when she came, she brought the baby, and that only made things worse. Pilar was almost in hysterics by the time Brad came home, and she told him she never wanted to see another baby, and she didn't want Adam in the house again, until he was older.

"Pilar, you have to stop," he said, feeling agonized and helpless. "You can't do this to yourself."

"Why not?" She didn't eat, she didn't sleep.

She had lost ten pounds, and looked five years older.

"It's not healthy. And next month we want to try again. Come on, sweetheart. You have to try to pull yourself together." But the truth was, she just couldn't. From the time she woke up until the time she went to bed, she felt as though she were carrying a crushing weight on her heart. There were times when she didn't even want to go on living. "Please . . . sweetheart, please." Finally, hoping to cheer her up, he took her to San Francisco for a weekend, but as luck would have it, it was the week she got her period. All he could do to cheer her was remind her that in two weeks they'd be back at Dr. Ward's with the turkey baster and the dirty movies.

"Oh, God." She made a face, and in spite of herself, she laughed. "Don't remind me."

"Then you'd better enjoy it now." He teased her for the rest of the trip that he was going to take her to Broadway to buy "marital aids" to add to the doctor's collection.

"You're a pervert, Bradford Coleman. If anyone suspected what a filthy mind you have, while sitting on the bench, they'd disbar you." She smiled, looking like herself again for the first time in weeks.

"Good. Then I could stay home and make love to you all day." But even that didn't hold much appeal these days. She had tried explaining it to her therapist and to Brad. She felt that the miscarriage was her ultimate failure as a woman. "I *lost* the baby. . . . It's like leaving it on a bus somewhere, or forgetting it in the park . . . or eating it. . . . I *lost* the baby," she had said with tears running down her face, which made her the ultimate failure as a mother.

It was difficult reasoning with her. What she felt didn't come from her mind. It came from her heart. Her mind knew she might have another chance, and Brad had told her again and again that they'd continue trying. But her heart knew nothing except what it had lost. The baby she had wanted so badly. And each time she let herself think of that, the sorrow she felt made her chest ache.

Diana was cautious when she and Andy returned from their holiday. She didn't want to push her luck. Things had been wonderful for them in Hawaii, and they had come home renewed, not like the people they had once been, but in some ways maybe better. But knowing how rocky the road had been, she didn't want to add any pressure. She had decided not to see her family for a while, and not to address any of their questions. It was almost two months since she'd seen or talked to Sam, but she just couldn't deal with the impending reality of her baby. For Diana, it was just too painful.

The name of the game for them these days was to avoid pain. And Diana would have gone to any lengths to do that. She was invited to two baby showers at work, and declined both. And she and Andy had agreed that for a while at least they were not going to discuss alternate solutions to having a baby. They were both in therapy, separately, and it seemed to be helping.

Her job was going well, and she was enjoying it again. She enjoyed chatting with Eloise from time to time, but their friendship seemed to have cooled. Eloise was thinking of moving on, and Diana was still all wrapped up in saving her life and her marriage. For the first week after their trip, Diana enjoyed coming home every night more than anything. She was anxious to see Andy and spend time with him. And he had taken to calling her three or four times a day from his office, just to say hello and see how she was doing. She felt closer to him than to anyone else, and their life was still pretty quiet. Diana didn't feel ready to see friends again, and Andy didn't press it. And neither did their friends. Bill and Denise hadn't called in months. Andy had finally explained to Bill that seeing them was too difficult for Diana, because Denise was pregnant. He seemed to understand, and the two men still played tennis when they could, which wasn't often. They both had other responsibilities now, and other pressures.

Diana rarely even bothered to check the phone machine when she got home anymore. No one called them anymore, except her mother from time to time, or Andy's brothers.

But in mid-January, when she got home early one night, she flicked it on, and listened to the messages while she turned on the oven and started dinner. Predictably, her mother had called, which made her smile, and some woman selling magazines, and there were three messages for Andy, one from Bill about a tennis tournament at the club, one from his brother, Nick, and the third from a woman. She had a sensuous voice, and all she said was that the message was for Andy, and he would know why she'd called him. And then, in a deep, smoky voice, ". . . just have him call me." She left her number and her name, Wanda Williams. Diana raised an eyebrow and laughed. Even in their worst moments in the past year, she hadn't suspected him of cheating. She knew that some men did, in the face of those kinds of tensions, but she didn't think he had. And she also didn't think he was dumb enough to have his girl-friends leave him messages at home. She wasn't worried about it, but more amused, and she teased him about it that night at dinner. She figured it was an actress from one of the shows he handled at the network.

"So, who's the woman with the sexy voice who called you today?"

"What?" He frowned and reached for another piece of bread, looking distracted.

"You heard me. Who is she?" Diana was smiling. She loved teasing him, and usually he was a good sport, but this time he clearly didn't like it.

"What's that supposed to mean? She's one of my brother's friends, I think she's out here for a while, and she wanted me to help her buy a car, or something."

"A car?" Diana laughed openly at him. "That's the worst crock I've ever heard. Come on, Andrew . . . who is she? Who is Wanda Williams?" She imitated her voice when she asked, but Andy did not find her amusing.

"I don't know who she is. Okay? She's just a name. I've never met her."

"She sounds like Dial-a-Date," Diana said, imitating the husky voice on the phone again. "Call me. . . ."

"Okay, okay, I get it." By then he had eaten three pieces of bread, and he was actually looking nervous, which startled Diana.

"So are you going to call her? . . . about the car, I mean." She was riding him, and he was starting to look really angry.

"Maybe. I'll see."

"You're not." She was starting to look upset, there was something about his story that didn't jell, and she didn't like it. "Andy, what is this?"

"Look, it's something I'm doing on my own, okay? Am I entitled to a little privacy?"

"Yes." Diana looked at him hesitantly. "Maybe. But not with women."

"I'm not screwing around. Okay? I swear."

"Then what are you doing?" she asked softly. She couldn't understand why he was so secretive about this girl. What in God's name was he hiding?

"She's a friend of a friend of mine. She knows one of the lawyers I work with, and he wants me to talk to her about a project." He didn't want to tell her that she was one of Bill Bennington's old girlfriends, and he had suggested Andy call her.

"Then why did you lie to me and tell me she was a friend of your brother's?"

"Look, Diana, don't. Okay? Just don't push me."

"Why, for chrissake?" She jumped up from the table then, suspicious of him. Maybe he was screwing around and she didn't know it. "What are you doing?"

"Look, dammit . . ." He had done every-thing he could not to tell her, but now he saw he had to. "I didn't want to talk about this now. I just wanted to talk to her first, and see what I thought of her when I met her."

"Great . . . what is this? Are you dating?"

"She had a child for someone last year. She's a surrogate. And she'd like to do it again. I thought I'd check it out and talk to her, and then I was going to ask you what you thought about it." He said it very quietly, trying to brace himself for his wife's explosion.

"What? You're going to Miss Rent-a-Womb to check her out, and you weren't even going to tell me? What are you going to do, sleep with her to see if it takes? For God's sake, Andy, how could you do this?"

"I was just going to talk to her, for God's

sake. It would be done by artificial insemination if we went ahead with it, and you know that."

"Why? Why are you doing this? I thought we agreed to not even discuss it for the next few months."

"I know. But this thing came up last week, and people like that aren't easy to find. And by the time you're ready to talk, she might be having someone else's baby."

"Who is she?"

"She's an actress of sorts. She doesn't believe in abortion, and she says she gets pregnant very easily, and she thinks she's doing something nice for people by offering this service."

"How kind of her. And how much does she charge?"

"Twenty-five thousand."

"And what if she keeps the baby?"

"She can't. You get an ironclad contract. And she didn't make any trouble for the guy last year. I talked to him myself. And they're thrilled. They have a little girl, and they're crazy about her. Baby, please . . . at least let me talk to her."

"No. What if she uses drugs, what if she has a disease? What if she doesn't give up the child? What if . . . oh, God . . . don't ask me to do this. . . ." She lay her head down on the table and sobbed. She wanted to scream at him. Why was he putting her through this again? They had just barely made a first step back into their marriage, and she wasn't ready for this now.

"Baby, you're the one who said you wanted '*my*' baby, that it wasn't fair for me not to have '*my*' child. I thought this would be better than adoption, at least the baby would be half ours. You didn't want to hear about a donor egg transplant when the doctor suggested it, and this seems like a viable alternative solution."

"What is this? A scientific experiment, for God's sake?" She looked at him then, her eyes filled with hatred. "I hate you, Andrew Douglas. How dare you put me through this?"

"I have a right to a child too. We both do. And I know how badly you want one."

"Not like this. Do you know the stress we'd be under until it would be all over? And I don't want your sperm in some other woman. What if she falls in love with you and the baby?"

"Di, she's married."

"Oh, for heaven's sake. You're all crazy, you, her, and her husband."

"And you're the only sane one among us?" he said angrily.

"Maybe."

"Well, kid, you sure don't look it." She looked

deranged and anguished to the point of breaking. "Look, I'm going to go talk to her sometime
this week. That's all. I just want to know what
the terms are, what she's like, what would happen. I want to know what our options are, if we
want to do this now, or anytime. And Diana, I'd
like you to come with me."

"I don't want anything to do with this. I can't.
It'll push me right over the edge." And she had
just barely gotten back on her feet again. She
didn't want to risk it.

"I think you're stronger than that," he said
calmly. He wanted to do this. He had thought
about it a lot in the last few months. And he
wanted a baby. He wanted Diana, but he
wanted a family, too, and if he could have a
child of his own conception, all the better.

"I think you're a sonofabitch," she spat at
him, and then locked herself in the bathroom.
And when she came out again, Andy had already called Wanda Williams and they had an
appointment for the next afternoon at The Ivy.
It seemed an odd place to choose, but it was
what Wanda wanted.

"Are you coming?" he asked that morning,
and she shook her head. And before he left for
work, he pressed her again, and she said nothing. Bill asked him at work that morning how it

went, and Andy told him tensely that Diana had gone crazy. He had no idea if she would even come to meet the surrogate, and Bill wished him luck as he hurried off to an important meeting.

Diana sat in her office at noon that day, thinking of them, and wondering what the girl looked like. And then finally, she couldn't stand it. She called for a cab, and went downstairs. She got to the restaurant half an hour late, but they were sitting comfortably at a back table, with the woman's husband. Andy looked startled as she walked in, and he introduced her to the Williamses, John and Wanda. They looked reasonable and sane, decently dressed, and not drugged out or stupid. Wanda was a pretty girl who talked a lot about it being important to her to do something "meaningful" for someone in her life, and John seemed not to care one way or another. As he put it, "money is money." They were to pay for her medical care, a small amount of clothing, and loss of salary for two months, since she really couldn't do much work then. And her "fee," as she put it, was $25,000. She would sign a contract agreeing not to use alcohol or drugs or take undue risks, and in the hospital when the baby was born, she would turn it over to them with no problem.

"What if you decide to keep it?" Diana said bluntly. All she had ordered was a cup of coffee.

"I won't," she said clearly, and said something about not violating her karma. Her husband explained then that she was very involved in Eastern religions.

"She's not that crazy about kids," her husband added after that. "She never wanted to keep the last one."

"And what about you?" Diana asked him. "How do you feel about your wife being pregnant with my husband's sperm?"

"I figure he wouldn't be doing this if he didn't have to," he looked pointedly at her and Diana felt the arrow to her heart instantly, but she never wavered. "I don't know, I figure this is her thing. It's what she wants to do." Diana had an underlying feeling that they were both crazy, but there was certainly nothing visibly "wrong" with them. It's just that the whole project seemed so awful.

They left it all hanging after lunch, and Andy said he'd call them in the next few days after he and Diana discussed it further. "I do have another candidate to interview," Wanda explained. "I'm seeing him tomorrow."

"She only does this for people she really likes," her husband offered, looking accusingly at Diana. Clearly, she hadn't been "nice" enough, and could well have put the whole project in danger. It made Diana feel hysterical to think she was being "interviewed" by these fruitcakes.

They left before the Douglases did, and Diana sat staring angrily at her husband. "How could you do this to us?"

"Why were you so rude to him, asking how he felt about my sperm? For chrissake, Diana, they may reject us."

"Oh." She leaned back in her chair and rolled her eyes in anger. "I don't believe this. She's sitting here telling you about her karma, and you want her to have your baby. I think the whole thing is sleazy. And so was her husband."

"I'm going to call Dr. Johnston and see how we'd do this."

"I don't want any part of what you're doing. I just want you to know that," she said clearly.

"That's up to you. I'm not asking you to put a dime into this." She knew he'd have to borrow the money from his parents, and she wondered how he was going to explain it.

"I think you're sick. And I think it's pathetic, the lengths people like us will go to have a baby." But there was one much simpler solution, and as she sat there she knew she should have done it much sooner. She stood up and looked at him and shook her head and walked out of the restaurant. There was a cab waiting outside and she got into it, and gave him her home address. And by the time Andy got out of the restaurant, after paying the tab, she was gone. And so were all her things when he got home from work that night. She was gone. For good. She had left him a note on the kitchen table.

"Dear Andy . . . I should have done this months ago. I'm sorry. This is all so stupid now. You don't need a surrogate. You need a wife . . . a real one . . . who can have a baby. Good luck. I love you. I'll have my lawyer call you. Love, Diana." He stood staring at the piece of blue paper in his hand, and he felt terrified and numb. He couldn't believe she'd done it.

He called her parents that night, casually, to see if she'd gone home, but his general inquiries told him she hadn't. Her mother suspected instantly that something was wrong, but she didn't want to ask. They hadn't seen Diana since her outburst at Thanksgiving, even though they spoke to her regularly on the phone, and her father had had a long talk with her only that weekend.

In the end, Diana had gone to a hotel. And

that weekend, she rented a place to live. There was no point kidding herself anymore. It was insane. The lunch at The Ivy had told her everything she needed to know, how desperate they were, how irrational, how foolish. It was ridiculous for Andy to be thinking of impregnating that girl. What in hell was he doing?

Andy called Diana every day at work, and she wouldn't take his calls. And when he showed up, she refused to see him. The dream had come to an end, and the nightmare along with it. For Diana and Andy, it was over.

CHAPTER
=== 13 ===

"Okay," Pilar said with a hesitant smile, "here we go again." She flicked on the video, and two women began licking each other's genitals, as Brad looked at her with a sheepish grin, feeling incredibly foolish.

"I'm not so sure about your choice of movies."

"Oh, shut up." She laughed. She was trying hard to be a good sport again, but Dr. Ward had reassured them that it could take as many as ten or twelve tries to get pregnant again, and even then she might lose it. They were going to try progesterone suppositories this time, for three months, if she did get pregnant. But there were no guarantees, she told them. And every minute of every day, Pilar was not getting any younger.

Slowly, she peeled away Brad's clothes, as he watched the film, and stripped off her own, gently rubbing his erection, and in a very short time, they had the desired semen. The nurse took it away and Pilar couldn't help teasing him.

"We'll have to buy that one to watch at home. I think you liked it."

This was not an easy road they had chosen. The artificial insemination went smoothly again this time, and Dr. Ward warned them again that it was highly unlikely it would take on the first try. Pilar was back on chlomiphene again, which made her extremely nervous and seemed to depress her further. It was a hard time for her, and she wondered if she would ever recover from the miscarriage. She thought about it all the time, and even when the pain seemed to ebb, something would inadvertently start it off again, seeing someone carrying a child in their arms, or a pregnant woman, or seeing baby clothes in a window, or if they hadn't heard about the miscarriage, friends congratulating her for being pregnant. She knew now only too well how foolish it had been to tell people so early that she was pregnant. It would take months to tell everyone now that she wasn't. And each time she had to explain, they told her how sorry they were, or asked incredibly unfeeling questions, like whether or not she'd been able to see if it was a boy or a girl, or how big it was when she lost it.

Brad took her shopping that day to cheer her up, and they stayed at the Beverly Wilshire Hotel. It was nice being away with him, and he tried to turn it into a festive occasion. The next day was Valentine's Day, and when they got to the hotel, he had sent her two dozen red roses.

To my love, always, Brad, the card said, and she cried when she read it. She had begun wondering lately if she was foolish to want more than this, maybe it was wrong, and just too greedy. Maybe she had been right all along. Maybe having a baby just wasn't all that important. It was hard to give up the dream of it now, but she was really beginning to think that she was misguided to pursue this. Maybe it just wasn't meant to be, and she had to let go of the idea of having children. She said as much to Brad that night, that she was exploring her own thoughts on the subject.

"Why don't we see what happens for a while? And if it makes you too unhappy, we'll stop. It's up to you."

"You are too good to me," she said and clung to him, still hurting, but grateful for his presence.

They rented an erotic movie and watched it on the video, and they both laughed, and ate the chocolates provided by the hotel. "You know,

these could become a habit," Brad said, grinning at her.

"The chocolates?" she asked, feigning innocence, and he laughed.

"No, the movies!"

They made love when the movie was over,
and then drifted off to sleep in each other's
arms, still not sure of the answers.

On Valentine's Day, Charlie went to buy flowers for the woman at work who helped do his
reports for him. She was an enormous woman,
with a big heart. He bought her pink and red
carnations with baby's breath, and she threw
her arms around him and cried, she was so
touched when he gave them to her. He was
such a nice boy, and poor kid, she knew he was
getting divorced, and sometimes he looked
pretty lonely.

At lunch, he went and bought himself a sandwich and took himself to Palms Park near Westwood Village, where he could watch old people
stroll, and lovers kiss, and children playing. He
liked going there sometimes, just to watch the
kids.

He noticed one little girl with long blond
braids, big blue eyes, and a cute smile, and he

laughed as he watched her playing with her mother. She played tag and hopscotch and jump rope and jacks, and her mother was almost as pretty as she was. She was a tiny little blond, with long straight hair and big blue eyes, and a childlike figure.

Eventually they played catch, and neither of them could throw or catch the ball. Charlie was still watching them and smiling long after he had finished his sandwich. And suddenly, he was startled when one of their wild throws hit him. He took the ball back to them and they thanked him. And as she did, the little girl looked up at him and grinned. All her front teeth were missing.

"My goodness, who knocked out your teeth?" Charlie asked her.

"The tooth fairy did. And then she paid me a dollar for each one. I got eight dollars," she said, still grinning.

"That's a lot of money." Charlie looked vastly impressed, and the little girl's mother smiled at him. She looked just like the child, except for the missing teeth, which Charlie mentioned. And the young woman laughed.

"Yeah, I guess I'm lucky the tooth fairy didn't kick mine out too. Mine might have been a little more expensive." In point of fact, she was grate-

ful that her husband hadn't knocked them out
before he left her. But she didn't mention that
to Charlie.

"I'm gonna buy my mom a present with the
money," the little girl announced and then
asked him if he'd like to join them. He hesitated, but only for a moment, not wanting to
annoy her mother.

"Okay. But I'm not a great ball thrower either. By the way, my name is Charlie."

"I'm Annabelle," the little girl announced,
"but everyone calls me Annie."

"I'm Beth," her mother said quietly, looking
Charlie over carefully. She seemed cautious,
but friendly.

They had a good game of catch, and then
hopscotch again before Charlie had to go back
to work, reluctantly, to sell textiles.

"See you again sometime," he said as he left
them, knowing that he probably wouldn't. He
hadn't asked for their number or their names.
He liked them both, but he had no interest in
pursuing an unknown woman and her child. He
hadn't had a date since Barbie left and he didn't
want one, and he figured she was probably married anyway. But she sure was cute.

"Bye, Charlie!" Annie waved as he left the
park. "Happy Valentine's Day!"

"Thanks," he called back, and left them, feeling good. There was something about them that brightened up his whole day, even long after he left them.

It took Andy almost a month to find out where she lived. And at first, once he got the address, he wasn't sure what to do with the information. Her attorney had told him, in no uncertain terms, that Mrs. Douglas was through with the marriage. It had been eighteen months and a lot of tears, and she didn't even want to see Andy again. She wished him well, but she had made it very clear that it was over.

He had continued to call her at work several times after that, and she still wouldn't take his calls. And all he could think of was that stupid lunch with the surrogate and her husband. That was where it had ended. What a pathetic way to end a marriage. They were ridiculous, both of them . . . the "sperm seekers" . . . looking desperately for babies. He didn't care anymore if he never had a kid. All he wanted in his life was Diana.

And then, inadvertently, when he ran into Seamus and Sam, they told him where she was living. She had rented an old cottage in Malibu, and she was living on the beach. It was one of the first places they had looked before they were married. And he knew how much she loved the ocean.

He got the address from them by telling them he needed to drop off some of her things. And they said how sorry they were about what had happened.

"It was a lot of stupidity and bad luck," Andy explained sadly. "She got the bad luck, and I was the moron."

"Maybe she'll get over it," Sam said softly. She looked as though she were about to have her baby any minute, and in fact she and Seamus were on their way to the doctor for a checkup. For an instant, Andy felt jealous of them, and then he reminded himself that that was still not an option.

For two days, he mulled over what to do with the information they'd given him. If he just dropped by, she wouldn't let him in, or maybe he could hang out on the beach waiting for her to go out and get some air, but what if she didn't? And then on Valentine's Day, he decided the hell with it, he bought her a dozen roses and drove to Malibu, praying that she'd be there, but she wasn't. He lay the roses down carefully on the front steps, with a note. It didn't say much, just "I love you, Andy," and then got back in his car, and just as he did, she drove up. But she didn't get out of her car when she saw him.

He got out of his, and went over to talk to her, and reluctantly, she rolled down her window.

"You shouldn't have come here," she said firmly, trying not to look at him. She looked thinner and more beautiful than he remembered her. She was wearing a black dress and she looked sexy and elegant as she got out of the car, and stood near it, as though she needed it for protection. "Why did you come?" She had noticed the flowers on the doorstep and didn't know if they were from him. But if they were, she didn't want them. She was through torturing herself and she wanted him to be too. They had to let go now.

"I wanted to see you," he said sadly, looking like the boy she had married, only better. He was handsome and young and blond and thirty-four years old, and he still loved her.

"Didn't my lawyer tell you what I said?"

"Yeah. But I never listen to attorneys." He grinned, and she smiled in spite of herself. "In fact, I never listen to anyone. Maybe you know that."

"Maybe you should. It might do you a lot of good. You could save yourself a lot of head-aches."

"Really? How?" He feigned innocence, he was just so happy to see her. He wanted to keep her there talking, so he could be near her. And even in the sea breeze, he could smell her per-fume. She wore Calèche, by Hermès, and he had always loved it.

"You could stop banging your head into walls, for one thing," she said gently, telling herself she wasn't affected by him. This was the test, being near him and not giving in to him.

"I love banging my head into walls," he said softly.

"Well, don't. There's no point anymore, Andy."

"I brought you some flowers," he said, not sure what else to say. And he didn't want to leave her.

"You shouldn't have done that either," she said sadly. "You've really got to stop now. In five months you'll be free, and you can have a whole new life without me."

"I don't want that."

"We both do," she said firmly.

"Don't tell me what I want," he snapped at her. "I want you, dammit. That's what I want. I don't want some stupid fucking surrogate, I can't believe how dumb all that was. . . . I don't even want a baby. I never want to hear the word again. All I want is you . . . Di. . . . Please give us another chance . . . please . . . I love you so much. . . ." He wanted to tell her that he couldn't live without her, but the tears in his throat stopped him.

"I don't want a baby either." She was lying, and they both knew it. If someone could have waved a magic wand over her at that exact moment and made her pregnant, she would have grabbed the opportunity in a second. But she could no longer allow herself to think that. "I don't want to be married. I have no right to be," she said, trying to sound convincing. She had almost come to believe it.

"Why? Because you can't get pregnant? So what? Don't be so stupid. You think only fertile people are allowed to get married anymore? That's the dumbest thing I ever heard of."

"They should marry people like themselves, so no one gets hurt."

"What a great idea! Why didn't I think of that? Oh, for chrissake, Di, grow up. We got a rotten break, but it's not the end of the world. We can still make it."

"*We* didn't get a rotten break," she corrected him, "*I* did."

"Yeah, and I ran around like a lunatic interviewing Buddhist starlets as surrogate mothers. Okay, so we both went a little insane. So what? It was tough. It was brutal, in fact. It was the worst thing I hope I ever live through. But that part of it is over. Now we have the rest of our lives to live. You can't just give up on us because we got a little crazy."

"I don't want craziness anymore," she said, and she meant it. "There's a lot of things I won't do to myself anymore, things I used to think I 'had to.' I don't go to baby showers, or christenings, or hospitals when babies are born. Sam had her baby yesterday and I called and told her I'm not going. And you know what? It's okay. It's what I have to do to survive these days, and maybe one day I'll be able to handle it, and if I can't, then that's tough, but that's the way it is. I'm not going to make myself uncomfortable anymore or miserable, or be married to someone who should be having kids and isn't because I'm his wife and I'm sterile. And I'm not going to drive myself buggy with surrogates, or donor eggs. Fuck all that shit, Andy. I'm not doing that to myself anymore. I'm just going to live my life, and get on with it. I've got my work. There are other things in life than children and marriage."

He looked at her, thinking about what she'd said. Some of it made sense and some of it didn't. And work was not an adequate substitute for children and a husband.

"You don't deserve to be alone for the rest of your life. You don't need to be punished, Di. You didn't 'do' anything. It happened to you. That's bad enough. Don't make it worse by being lonely." His eyes filled with tears as he said it.

"What makes you think I'm lonely," she said, irritated with him for his assumptions.

"Because you've been biting your nails. You never do that when you're happy.

"Oh, go fuck yourself." She smiled in spite of herself. "I've had a lot going on at work." And then she looked at him, they'd been talking for an hour, and they were still standing next to her car in the driveway. There couldn't be any harm in letting him in for a little while. They'd been married for eighteen months, and together for a long time before that, surely she could let him into her living room for a few minutes.

She invited him in, and he seemed surprised, and she put the roses in a vase and thanked him.

"Do you want something to drink?"

"No, thanks. Do you know what I'd really like?"

She was almost afraid to ask him. "What?"

"To walk on the beach with you. Would that be all right?" She nodded, and changed her shoes, and put a warmer jacket on, and he let her lend him one of his old sweaters that she'd taken with her.

"I wondered where this thing had gone." He smiled as he put it on. It was an old friend and he liked it.

"You gave it to me when we were dating."

"I was a lot smarter then than I am now."

"Maybe we both were," she conceded. They walked down the steps of the balcony off her living room, and onto the beach they both loved. He wondered why they hadn't looked harder for a house here. The beach was so beautiful and they both loved it, and there was something soothing about it now. It was so simple and so close to nature.

They walked in silence for a long time, looking at the ocean and feeling the wind on their faces. And then, without saying anything, he took her hand in his, and they walked some more. And after a while she looked up at him, as though trying to remember who he was. But it was too easy now to remember as she walked beside him. He was the man she had loved so much . . . who had made her so happy . . . before everything went sour.

"It's been tough, hasn't it?" he said as they sat down against a dune, far down from the house she had rented.

"Yeah, it has. And you were right . . . I am lonely . . . but I'm learning things about myself, things I never knew before. I was always so obsessed about having kids that I never stopped and thought about who I was and what I wanted."

"And what do you want, Di?"

"I want a whole life, a real marriage with a whole person that doesn't depend on having kids to hold it together. I still wish I could have them, but I'm not so sure I couldn't survive now without them. Maybe that's what I needed to learn from all this. I don't know. I haven't figured it all out yet." But she had come a long way since she had left him. "I've always been confused about who my sisters were, and who my mother is, and who I am. And whether or not I'm different or the same. They always say I'm so different from them, but I'm not really sure I am. I've always been driven by the same things, family, kids. But I'm driven by other things, too, that's where I'm different. I've always worked harder than any of them did, I needed to achieve, to be 'the best.' Maybe that's part of why this hurts so much. I failed this time. I didn't win. I didn't get what I wanted." It was an honest appraisal, and Andy admired her candor.

"You're someone very special," he said softly, as he looked at her. "You didn't fail. You did your best, that's what matters." She nodded, trying to believe he was right. And he had to fight himself to keep his hands off her. And despite all his promises to himself to behave when he saw her, he leaned over and kissed her, but she didn't move away, and her eyes were damp when the kiss ended.

"I still love you, you know," she whispered in the wind, as she sat close to him. "That's never going to change. I just didn't think it was good for us to be together anymore." Then suddenly she laughed, thinking of Wanda. "Wanda was the worst, wasn't she? But my sense of humor was all shot to hell by then. It was only a couple of days ago that I started thinking how funny and awful it was. It made me want to call you."

"I wish you had." He'd been desperate for her since she left, and he would have been thrilled if she'd called him. "You blew it for me,

of course. Wanda chose the other guy. Her husband said Wanda just wasn't comfortable with
your karma."

"I love it. I hope she has quadruplets. Why
do people do things like that to themselves?"
she asked, looking out at the ocean. There was a
gray haze on the horizon, and the sun was setting slowly.

"You mean look for surrogates? Because they
get so desperate, just like we did. And in
Wanda's case, I guess she sees herself as
Mother Teresa."

"I think the money plays a big part in it. It's
kind of a sick thing, because the buyers are so
desperate and the sellers know it."

"That's the story of life, I guess. I'm glad your
karma was so lousy at lunch. That would have
been a disaster."

"I think I was half out of my mind by then, or
possibly even more than half." But she seemed
very sane now, and very calm, and he had never
loved her more than he did at this moment.

They walked slowly back to her house, and
they talked for hours, about other things finally
than infertility and babies. There had to be
something else in their lives, and maybe now
there could be. But when they'd been going
through it, it had been all-consuming. It had

been like that for the entire time they were married.

They didn't even bother to eat dinner that night, and when he finally got up to leave, they were both surprised that it was midnight.

"Would you like to go out tomorrow night?" he asked, terrified she would get angry at him and refuse, but slowly she nodded.

"I'd like that."

"How about Chianti?" It was a simple Italian restaurant on Melrose with great food, and they both loved it. "And maybe a movie."

"That sounds nice." He kissed her again then, and they both felt like kids when he left. She watched him go, and she waved. And then she walked out on her terrace and stood for a long time, staring at the ocean.

CHAPTER
=== 14 ===

Charlie went back to Palms Park several times, hoping he would find Annabelle and Beth, and he did. They chatted and played ball, but he never dared to ask for Beth's number. He couldn't figure out if she was married anyway, she didn't wear a ring, but she never said anything about being divorced either. Charlie loved watching them, and Annie was adorable with her missing teeth, and her excitement about everything. And her mother was always pleasant to talk to. It was nice just watching them be a family and enjoy each other. He felt as though they were old friends by the third time they met in early March, and it was then that Beth started opening up with him. She talked about Annabelle being in kindergarten,

and said that she worked at UCLA Medical
Center nearby, as a nurse's aide. She had
wanted to be an R.N., but hadn't been able to
finish her training. They had only known each
other for a few weeks, but he felt surprisingly
comfortable with her, as they sat on a bench and
watched Annabelle play hopscotch. He had
brought her a lollipop, just in case they were
there. He was eating lunch at the park almost
every day, just so he could see them.

"I've got a cold," Annie announced to him
when she came back to where they were sitting,
but she seemed to be in good spirits. And a
moment later, she went back to the swing,
which gave him a chance to talk to her mother.

"She's wonderful," he said warmly.

"I know. She's a great kid." And then she
turned to him with a shy smile. "Thank you for
being so nice to her . . . the candy, the gum,
the lollipops. You must like kids."

"I do," he nodded.

"Do you have any of your own?"

"I . . . no . . . not yet . . ." And then he
realized what he'd said, and forced himself to
change it. "No, I don't. And I probably never
will," he said cryptically, "but that's a long
story." She wondered if his wife couldn't have
any, or if he even had a wife, but she was too

shy to ask, and he didn't explain it. "I'd like to adopt some kids someday. I was an orphan, and I know what it means to need a family and not have one." He didn't tell her how many foster homes he'd been in, or how many people had turned him away because of his allergies and his asthma. The nicest family he'd ever known had had a cat and he couldn't live there. And they said it would have just broken their heart to give their cat up. So they gave up Charlie. "That's tough on a kid. . . . I'd like to change that for someone, before it's all over." He smiled. He'd thought about that a lot recently. He was even thinking of adopting a child as a single parent. He knew people were doing that, and when he had some more money saved up, he was going to check it out. And in the meantime he had his Little League kids, whom he played with every weekend.

"That's a nice thing to do." Beth smiled. "I was an orphan too. My parents died when I was twelve. I grew up with my aunt, and I ran away when I was sixteen and got married. It was a stupid thing to do, but I got mine in spades. I wound up with a man who drank and cheated and lied and beat me up every chance he got. I don't know why I stayed with him, except by the time I wanted to leave, I was pregnant. I had Annie when I was eighteen." That made her twenty-four now, which seemed amazing, she seemed a lot more mature than most girls her age, and it was obvious that she was a good mother.

"What happened? How'd you get away from him?" Charlie was horrified at the idea of anyone slapping a woman around, particularly a girl as nice as she was.

"He walked out on me, and I never heard from him again. He had someone else, I guess, and six months later he died in a bar fight. Annie was a year old and I came back here, and that's been it ever since. I work in a hospital at night so I can be with Annie all day, and my neighbor listens for her, so I don't have to pay a sitter."

"Sounds like a pretty good arrangement."

"It works for us. I'd like to go back to school eventually, to get my R.N. Maybe someday." Listening to her, Charlie wanted to do anything he could to help her.

"Where do you live?" He was suddenly curious to know more about her.

"Just a few blocks from here, on Montana." She told him the address and he nodded. It was a poorer part of Santa Monica, but respectable, and they were probably safe there.

"Would you like to have dinner sometime?" he asked, after they watched Annie on the swing for a few more minutes. "You could bring Annabelle. Does she like pizza?"

"She loves it."

"How about tomorrow night?"

"That sounds great. I don't have to be at the hospital till eleven. I leave the house around ten o'clock, and I come home at seven-thirty in the morning, in time to get her ready for school and make breakfast. And then I sleep for a few hours before I pick her up. It works out pretty well." They had worked out their own system, and it worked for them. But he felt sorry for Beth, having so much responsibility on her shoulders, and no one to help her.

"It doesn't sound like you get much sleep," he said gently.

"I don't need much, I'm used to it. I get about three hours in the morning, while Annie's at school, and I have a nap when she goes to bed at night, before I leave for work."

"That doesn't leave much time for fun," he commented sympathetically as Annie bounded over to him. She seemed to be feeling better. And Beth told her about the invitation to pizza.

"With Charlie?" She looked surprised and pleased and her mother nodded, looking happy too. She was pretty and young, and she hadn't had room for a man in her life for a long time. But seeing Charlie suddenly made her feel different. "Wow! Can we go out for ice cream too?" Annie asked him and he laughed.

"Sure." It made him feel good just being with them, and he watched the little girl as she went back to the swings. Seeing her half made him want a child of his own again, and half made him realize that he didn't have to have one. There were other children in the world who would cross his path, and warm his heart, just as she did. And lately he had begun to feel that there was also something very pleasant about having his freedom. Mark had tried to tell him that, but he was finding it out for himself now. He glanced at Annabelle, and then he and Beth exchanged a warm smile as they both wondered about the future.

This time Pilar didn't have the heart to do the pregnancy test the minute she was late. She was afraid it would be negative anyway, her body was probably still too upset after the miscarriage. The doctor had told them their chances of success the first time they did artificial insemination again were slight. So she waited. And waited. And after a week, Brad threatened to do the test himself if she didn't do it.

"I don't want to know," she said miserably.

"Well, I do."

"I'm sure I'm not pregnant." But he wasn't as sure, she was tired all the time, and her breasts were larger and tender. And there was something about her that made him suspect it.

"Do the test!" he argued. But she said she couldn't face it again, and she wanted to give up the clomiphene. She hadn't taken it since her last period anyway, but she didn't want to start it again if she found she wasn't pregnant. She was beginning to think that the stress it caused her was just too disruptive.

Brad called her local gynecologist, Dr. Parker, finally, and they agreed that she was scared. He told Brad to bring her in to the office and he'd check her there, and as soon as he did, he suspected that she was pregnant. They did a urine test and it was positive. Pilar was definitely pregnant.

She looked weak with delight, and Brad was thrilled. After all she'd been through by now, he really wanted her to have this baby. They prescribed progesterone suppositories for her, to keep her progesterone levels up and help support the pregnancy, and the rest was up to

Mother Nature. The doctor warned her that she could miscarry again, and it was possible that she'd never carry a pregnancy to term. Nobody could tell her what was going to happen.

"I'm going to stay in bed for the next three months," she said with a terrified look in her eyes, but Dr. Parker insisted she didn't have to. And then they called Dr. Ward to tell her that the insemination had been a success, and on the way home Brad insisted that it was that movie.

"You're hopeless." She grinned, feeling scared, and excited, and happy. But she was so afraid she would lose it again, and this time they agreed not to tell anyone until after she was twelve weeks pregnant, and out of danger of a miscarriage. But there were still a million other things that could go wrong, she reminded Brad later that night. She could have a late miscarriage, or even a stillbirth. The baby could die in utero, strangled by the cord, or for a multiple of ghastly reasons. Or it could suffer from Down syndrome, as a result of her age, there was a high risk of that, or spina bifida. Her head swam as she counted off the possible disasters, and Brad shook his head as he listened.

"Just shut up and take it easy. What about flat feet or a low IQ, or Alzheimer's when the kid gets old enough to get it? Why don't you just relax, sweetheart, or you're going to be hysterical by the time you have this baby."

But when she had a sonogram at nine weeks, they were both hysterical, and so was Dr. Parker. She was having twins, there was absolutely no doubt, and they were fraternal. There were two amniotic sacs and Pilar cried with joy, as they watched their tiny hearts beat.

"Oh, my God, what now!" she said in amazement. "We have to get two of everything," she said, still totally overwhelmed by the realization that she was having two babies.

"What we have to do now," the doctor said firmly, "is have one mom take it very easy for the next eight months. I hope that's okay with both of you, because otherwise we're in for trouble. We don't want to lose these guys."

"God, no," Pilar said, closing her eyes, knowing only too well she couldn't bear it.

CHAPTER
═══ 15 ═══

In March, Andy started spending more and
more time at the beach with his wife. Diana
finally let him spend the night with her a
month after he'd found her.

"I don't want to go back to the house," she'd
said quietly, and he understood that. Not yet at
least. She still needed time, and they were
happy in Malibu together, in her little cottage.

He came there straight from work every day,
and he brought her little gifts and flowers. She
cooked dinner for him sometimes, and more
often than not they went out to their favorite
places. It was a special time of recovery for
them, and rediscovery of who they were, and
how much they meant to each other.

It was early April before she went back to

their house again, and she was surprised to realize how much she had missed it.

"It's a nice old house, isn't it?" she said, looking around, and feeling like a stranger. It had
been three months since she'd been in it.

"I guess we thought so when we bought it,"
he said cautiously, and they spent the weekend
there. But the following weekend they both
found they missed Malibu, so they went back to
the house she had rented. They were having a
good time feeling young and unfettered. It was
a perfect life, and Diana amazed him one night
in mid-April when she said to him that she actually liked not having children.

"Do you mean that?" he asked. They had
spent every night together for the past month,
and he was happier than he'd ever been, and
she looked relaxed and pleased, and like a
whole new person.

"Yes . . . I think I do mean it," she said
slowly. "We're so free. We can do whatever we
want, go wherever we want, whenever we want
to. We don't have to think about anyone but
ourselves, and each other. I can get my hair
done without worrying about rushing home to
baby-sitters, we can eat dinner at ten o'clock,
we can leave for the weekend at the drop of a
hat. I don't know, maybe for a whole lifetime it

would be pretty selfish, but for right now, I think I like it."

"Hallelujah!" he said, and then the phone rang. And when he hung up, he looked at Diana strangely.

"Who was that?"

"An old friend." But he looked pale and she was worried.

"Is something wrong?"

"I don't know," he said honestly, and she wondered at his expression.

"For a minute, I almost thought it was the lovely Wanda." She smiled and he looked sheepish.

"You're not far off," he said, walking around the room with an odd look, and she watched him, suddenly worried.

"What's that supposed to mean?" She looked frightened now. "Another surrogate? Oh, Andy, no . . . we can't go through that all over again. I thought we agreed that that part of our life was over, at least for now, and maybe for always." They hadn't made any permanent decisions yet, but there were times when she really felt she might well be comfortable never having children.

"I think this is different." Andy sat down and

looked at her. "Last September, when we found out . . . when Dr. Johnston—"

"Said I was sterile," she cut him off matter-of-factly.

"I spoke to an old friend of mine from law school. He handles private adoptions in San Francisco. I told him I didn't want any fly-by-night stuff, but if he ever got a good one, from a nice wholesome mother, we'd be interested. That was him. I'd forgotten all about it." Andy was looking at her intensely. He didn't want to force her into anything, but they had to make up their minds quickly. There were several other people waiting for a child, and Andy's friend was offering it to them first, as long as they let him know by the morning. It was Friday night, and the baby was due any minute. The girl had just decided to give the baby up for adoption.

"What did he say?" Diana was still as she sat very straight and listened. The mother was a twenty-two-year-old girl, it was her first child, and she had just waited too long to have an abortion. She was a senior at Stanford and her parents didn't know about the child, the father was a med student at UCSF, and neither of them felt they could afford a baby. They were both willing to give it up, but only to the right people. And Eric Jones, Andy's friend from school, knew that Andy and Diana were perfect.

They had gone back and forth about whether or not to put it up for adoption, and they had finally decided for sure only that morning.

"What if they change their minds?" Diana asked with a look of terror.

"They have the right to do that until they sign the final papers," Andy told her honestly, and she looked worried.

"And how long is that?"

"Usually about six months, but they can sign them sooner if they want to."

Diana nodded as she listened to him. "I couldn't go through that. Imagine what it would be like if they took it away. . . . Andy, I can't. . . ." Her eyes filled with tears, and he nodded. He understood perfectly, and he wasn't pushing her.

"It's okay, baby. I just wanted to tell you. It wouldn't be fair if I didn't."

"I know. Will you hate me, though, if we don't take it? I really don't think I can. The risks are just too enormous."

"I could never hate you. I think if we wanted to do an adoption, this is an ideal opportunity, but nothing says we have to do it. Now, or later. It's your call completely."

"I feel like I've only just gotten back on my feet . . . and we've just gotten our marriage back together. I don't want to jeopardize that, or risk a terrible disappointment."

"I understand," he said, and he did. They spent a peaceful night in each other's arms, and when he woke up the next morning Diana was gone. He got up and went to look for her, and found her sitting in the kitchen, looking awful.

"Are you okay?"

She looked desperately pale and he suddenly wondered how long she'd been up, or if she'd gone to bed at all. "No, I'm not," she answered.

"Are you sick?" he said, looking worried, and then she smiled bleakly and shook her head, which relieved him.

"I'm not sure yet. I think I'm just scared to death." And then he knew, and he smiled as he looked at her. "Andy, I want to do it."

"The baby?" He held his breath as he waited, he wanted it, too, but he hadn't wanted to sway her. Now that she had let go a little bit, and found her way again, he knew the baby would be a wonderful addition to their marriage.

"Yes. Call them." She could barely speak, she was so nervous as he dialed Eric Jones in San Francisco. He answered on the second ring, sounding groggy. It was eight o'clock in the morning.

"We want the baby," Andy said tersely, hoping they were doing the right thing, and that the baby was healthy, and praying that the birth parents wouldn't have a change of heart in the next six months, or before that. He knew that would destroy Diana, and possibly their marriage.

"You'd better get here quick," Eric said happily. "She went into labor about an hour ago. Can you get on a plane now?"

"Sure," Andy said, trying to sound calm, but feeling like a lunatic as he put the phone down and kissed Diana. "She's in labor, we've got to fly to San Francisco."

"Now?" She looked stunned as he called the airline.

"Now!" He waved her out of the kitchen and told her to pack for both of them, and five minutes later he was upstairs, throwing things to wear out of his closet with one hand, and using his razor with the other.

"What are we doing?" She started to laugh as she looked at him. "Last night I was telling you how happy I was that we didn't have children, and now we're running around like two nuts, running to San Francisco to catch a baby." And then suddenly she looked frightened again.

"What if we hate them? . . . What if they hate us? Then what?"

"Then we come home again and I'll remind you of what you said last night, about how nice it is not having children."

"Christ, why do we put ourselves through this?" She groaned as she pulled on a pair of gray slacks and black loafers. Her life had become a roller coaster ride again and she wasn't at all sure that she liked it. And yet she knew that she wanted it. And she could feel the doors of her heart slowly opening again, and it was both terrifying and painful. There was no way to protect yourself from getting hurt. If she was going to love this child, she had to allow herself to be completely open.

"Look at it this way," he said as he threw his razor into his suitcase and kissed her. "It beats the shit out of having lunch with Wanda."

"I love you, do you know that?" She smiled at him as he locked their suitcase.

"Good, then zip up your fly and put your shirt on."

"Don't push me around, I'm about to have a baby." She put on a silk shirt, and grabbed an old, dark-blue blazer.

It was a sweet moment in their lives, and neither of them wanted to forget it. They drove to the airport in record time, just made their plane and were in San Francisco at eleven-thirty in the morning.

Eric had told them how to get to the hospital. She was at Children's Hospital on California Street, and Eric was waiting for them in the lobby, just as he'd promised.

"Everything's going fine," he reassured them, and he escorted them upstairs to the waiting room for the delivery area, and then he left them. Andy was pacing, and Diana just sat, staring at the door, not sure what she was expecting, and a few minutes later Eric came back with a young man, and introduced him simply as Edward, the baby's father. He was a nice-looking young man, and it was funny, he looked a lot like Andy.

Edward was blond and athletic, with good features, and he was pleasant and intelligent when he started talking to them. He told them that Eric had told him all about them, and he and Jane were very excited about the idea of their taking the baby.

"You're sure you don't want to keep it?" Diana asked him pointedly. "I don't want to go through this and have my heart dragged through a wringer," she said, and they all knew she meant it.

"We won't do that, Mrs. Douglas . . . Diana . . . I swear it. Jane knows she can't keep this child. She wanted to for a while, but she just can't. She wants to get her masters, I'm in med school. Our families are supporting us, and they just wouldn't support that decision. And I wouldn't even let her ask them. The truth is, we don't want a child. We have nothing to give it right now, emotionally or otherwise. It's not the right time for us, and we'll have plenty of other children later." It seemed kind of a cavalier thing to say, as far as Diana was concerned, and she was always impressed by how confident people were about the future. How did he know that everything would be all right later? How could they give away a baby on the assumption that they could always make another one later? Look what had happened to Diana. "We're sure," he promised again. And he sounded to the Douglases as though he meant it.

"I hope so," Andy said soberly. They asked him a few questions then about their health, their drug habits, their families. And Edward asked them questions about their lifestyles, their beliefs, their home life, their attitudes about children. And as far as they could see,

Eric had been right. It was a perfect cross-match.

And then Edward surprised them. "I think Jane would really like to meet you."

"We'd like that very much," Andy said. He had expected to meet her after the birth, but Edward seemed to be beckoning them beyond the door that said LABOR AND DELIVERY, DO NOT ENTER.

"You mean now?" Diana asked, horrified. It would have been like having a stranger at some of her tests, although admittedly it was a happier occasion, but it was nonetheless private, and they were total strangers.

"I don't think she'd mind." She'd been in labor for six hours by then, but things had slowed down, Edward said, and they were thinking of giving her Pitocin to speed up her labor.

He had the confidence of a medical student as he led them down the hall, and then took them into the labor room where he had left Jane, leaving only Eric in the hallway.

Jane was a pretty girl with dark hair, propped up against the pillows in a hospital bed, panting furiously with a nurse, and then she stopped and stared at them as the contraction ended. She knew who they were. Edward had told her they were there, and she had told him that she wanted to meet them.

"Hi," she said shyly, but she didn't seem to mind their being with her. Edward introduced them to her, and he seemed very protective of her. She looked younger than she was, and there was a gentle, childlike quality about her. She had exactly Diana's coloring, and there was a similarity about their eyes which even startled Andy.

And then, as they spoke, the contractions started again, and Diana thought they should leave the room, but Jane signaled them to stay with her. Andy looked faintly uncomfortable, but the young couple seemed so at ease with them that in a moment, neither he nor Diana really felt too awkward.

"That was a bad one," Jane said, looking at Edward, and he checked the fetal monitor and nodded his approval.

"They're picking up, maybe they won't have to give you the Pitocin."

"I hope not," she said, and smiled at Diana. And as though a bond had already formed between them, she reached for Diana's fingers when the next pain came. It went on like that until about four o'clock, and Diana and Andy stayed, and by then, Jane was starting to look tired. The pain was really getting her down, but it seemed to be leading nowhere.

"It's taking forever," she complained, and Diana felt like her mother as she gently stroked her forehead and offered her ice chips, and she didn't even have time to think how extraordinary it was that only the night before she didn't even know about this girl, and now Jane was giving her their baby. Edward had had a private conversation with Jane, and afterward told Eric that he and Jane definitely wanted the Douglases to adopt the baby. As far as they were concerned, it was a done deal, and when Eric asked Andy and Diana, they had agreed it was all in order. Now all they needed was the baby.

At five o'clock, the doctor came in to check Jane again, and Andy went out in the hall to chat with Edward, but Jane had asked Diana to stay with her. And Diana felt so motherly toward this girl suddenly, and so protective.

"Hold on," Diana said gently, "just hold on, Jane . . . it'll all be over soon." She wondered why they didn't give her anything for the pain, but the nurse explained that the contractions hadn't been effective enough yet, she was only five centimeters dilated after ten hours of labor.

"You'll take good care of my baby, won't you?" she suddenly asked nervously, as another pain came when the doctor left. He had said they were a long way off yet.

"I promise. I'll love it as my own." She wanted to tell her she could come and see it whenever she wanted, it seemed so cruel to be taking her baby away after all this, but she knew that she and Andy wouldn't want her to come back to visit. "I love you, Jane," she whispered when the next pain came, and she really meant it, "and I love your baby." Jane nodded when she heard the words, and then she started to cry. The pains were brutal.

They broke her waters at six o'clock and after that the pains really began raging. Jane had all but lost control by then, and Diana wasn't even sure she knew who was with her. It had been an exhausting afternoon, but when she tried to leave for a little while, Jane clutched frantically at her, it was almost as though she needed Diana to be there.

"Don't go . . . don't go . . ." was all she could pant between pains as Edward stood on one side of her, and Diana on the other. And then finally, finally, the nurse said she could start pushing, and the doctor appeared, and suddenly they threw green pajamas at Edward, Andy, and Diana.

"What are these for?" Andy whispered to the
nurse.

"Jane wants you both at the delivery," Edward explained. They each dressed in the tiny
bathroom, and then they followed Jane down
the hall at a dead run, while she was pushed on
the gurney to the delivery room. They put her
quickly on the table, draped her, and put her
legs in stirrups, and then covered her legs in
blue paper. And suddenly everything around
them seemed frantic. She was screaming and
doctors and nurses were coming in and Diana
was suddenly terrified that something was
wrong, but everyone seemed calm, just busy.
And she had her hands full, talking to Jane as
Edward held her shoulders, and told her when
to push at the doctor's signals. She was pushing
with all her might, and then suddenly Diana
saw a bassinet enter the room, and she realized
this was for real. And when she looked up at the
clock after they'd been there for a while, she
was surprised to see that it was almost midnight.

"We're almost there, Jane," the doctor said.
"Come on, keep at it, just a couple more big
pushes . . ." And with that, he signalled to Diana. He knew why they were there, and he was

happy for her. He beckoned to her to come and look between Jane's legs, and when she did, she could see the baby crowning. A tiny head with dark hair, slowly pushing its way through . . . pushing . . . pushing . . . as Jane worked, and then suddenly there was a cry, and she was out of her mother and into the world, looking up at Diana with amazement, as Diana let out a little cry, and Andy stood beside her crying.

The doctor wrapped the baby carefully in a drape and handed her to Diana, still attached to Jane by the cord, and Diana felt rivers of tears run down her cheeks until she could barely see, and when she looked up, all she could see was Andy.

They stood side by side, looking at the miracle of her, and then Diana gently handed her to Jane as soon as the cord was cut. She had worked so hard to give birth to her, she had a right to hold her. But Jane only held her for the briefest moment. She put her to her breast, and then kissed her, and handed her to Edward. She was crying, too, by then, and she looked absolutely exhausted. Edward looked at his daughter long and hard, seemingly without emotion, and then handed her to the nurse. The baby was weighed and checked, and all her birth scores were perfect. She weighed seven pounds fourteen ounces, and was twenty-one inches long, and finally, after almost two years of agony, Diana had her baby. She stood looking at her in the bassinet. She had big, wide eyes, and a look of astonishment as she seemed to stare at her brand-new parents. And they stared at her, and held hands, in awe of the miracle of life, and unspeakably grateful to Jane and Edward.

CHAPTER
=== 16 ===

A ndy and Diana ran around like lunatics the
next day, buying diapers and tiny T-shirts
and nightgowns, and little socks and booties, warm hats and blankets, and the endless
list of things they were told they'd need when
they picked the baby up on Monday morning.
And that afternoon they met with Edward and
Jane again, and signed the preliminary papers.

Jane looked better than she had at midnight
the night before, but she looked somewhat
shaken by the ordeal, and she got very emotional when she saw Diana. She tried to thank
her for everything she'd done, and for loving
her little girl, but in the end, all she could do
was cry as Edward held her.

"I'm so sorry." Diana cried, too, as she

watched them, she felt as though she were stealing the baby from them, and for an instant her own resolve almost melted. "I promise you, we'll take such good care of her . . . and she'll be so happy."

Diana hugged Jane again, and when Andy finally led her from the room everyone was crying. And then when they stopped at the nursery to look at her, they knew they had done the right thing. She was so beautiful and so tiny as she lay sleeping. They spoke to the pediatrician before they left, and he told them what kind of formula she'd be on, and what kind of schedule to expect her to keep, how to care for her umbilical cord, and he suggested they take her to their pediatrician the following week, and Diana looked at Andy blankly, and then she thought of her sisters.

"I'll call Sam." She smiled suddenly. She hadn't talked to her sister in weeks. They hardly spoke anymore. Mostly because she didn't want to hear about her baby. "Boy, is she going to be surprised!" She laughed as they got in the elevator at the hospital, and they walked to Sacramento Street for something to eat. It had been an exhausting but wonderful two days, and they were going to pick the baby up in the morning. Jane would be checking out then, too, but she had decided not to see the baby again. It was just going to make it too difficult for her.

"You don't think she's going to change her mind, do you?" Diana asked Andy nervously that night, and he thought about it for a minute before he answered.

"No, I don't. But I think it's a possibility we have to face in the next months until they sign the final papers. They could change their minds in the end, but they seem pretty sure to me. Edward is, certainly. And I think she is, too, it's just a very emotional time for her, this must be just brutal."

Diana couldn't imagine what it would be like, giving a baby up, and she was glad she had never had to face that kind of decision, but she knew instinctively that she wouldn't have been able to do it. And then Andy and Diana talked of other things, like what they were going to name the baby. They still hadn't decided definitely, although Hilary seemed to be their favorite.

They both called their offices that morning and said they wouldn't be in due to "illness." Andy wanted to stay home for at least another day, and Diana knew that she wanted to take a long time off, or even quit, but she hadn't figured all that out yet.

Eric Jones met them at the hospital, and he had more papers for them to sign. He had already seen Edward and Jane, and he told the Douglases they had just left, which was a relief to them. They wanted that part of the adoption behind them. Now all they wanted was their baby.

Diana looked anxious as they rode up in the elevator, carrying a wicker basket covered in white eyelet lace, and they had brought a car seat to put in the limousine they hired to take them to the airport. This was a big event for them. They were finally bringing home their baby. And she even had a name. They had decided that morning on Hilary Diana Douglas.

She was sound asleep when the nurse picked her up, and they let Andy and Diana go into the nursery wearing gowns over their street clothes. The nurse showed Diana how to dress her and how to change her, and told her when to give her formula and when to give her glucose and water instead. The hospital provided them with a dozen bottles of each. And the nursery nurse explained that if Hilary had been her natural child, her own milk wouldn't be in yet, so they didn't want to overdo it with the formula until another day at least. She was less than two days old, and a very young baby.

And as they handled her, she opened her mouth and yawned, and then she looked sleepily at Diana and Andy. And then she closed her eyes again as Diana dressed her. And as she did, Diana felt something she had never felt for anyone before, not even Andy. It was a welling up of love and joy that almost overwhelmed her. There were tears sliding down her cheeks as she dressed the little girl in a pink dress, and a warm pink sacque, and little pink knit booties. She had a matching hat with little pink roses on it, and she looked adorable when Diana picked her up and held her. And Andy thought Diana had never looked more beautiful as he watched her.

"Come on, Mom," he said softly, and Diana held her on her shoulder as they went out in the hall to meet Eric. The baby was already signed out by the hospital. She was theirs now.

They hugged him and thanked him, and he went downstairs to see them into the waiting limousine, and Diana nervously adjusted the seat belt. There were three suitcases of baby clothes in the trunk and a huge teddy bear Andy had bought.

"Thank you for everything," she called back to Eric as the limousine pulled away, and he

waved at them with a smile. It had been wonderful to watch them.

And then Diana settled back in her seat, next
to the baby, and looked at Andy. It was difficult
to believe how much had happened to them in
less than forty-eight hours.

"Do you believe this?" she asked with a grin,
still afraid to believe it had really happened. But
the tiny fingers curled around her own told her
it was real. And looking at little Hilary, everything seemed so perfect.

"I still can't believe it," Andy admitted in a
whisper, he was afraid he might wake the baby.
And as they drove to the airport he looked at
Diana and grinned. "What are you going to do
about your job?" She had just gotten serious
about her career again, and now suddenly, everything was topsy-turvy.

"I guess I'll take maternity leave. I haven't
figured that out yet."

"They'll love that," Andy teased. But he was
planning to take at least a week off, too, to help
Diana and get to know their daughter . . .
their daughter . . . their baby. . . . The
words still seemed so foreign to them when
they said them. And whenever Diana let herself
think of it, she still ached over Jane's loss, and
their gain. It seemed a hard way to get a baby,

to cause someone else so much pain and take the baby from her. But it was what Jane had wanted, and they had all agreed to.

Hilary woke up just before they boarded the plane, and Diana changed her and fed her some of the glucose. And then she went right back to sleep as Diana laid her down in the little basket. She held her in her arms on the flight home, and she felt the cozy warmth of her on her chest as the baby lay there, sleeping soundly. It was a feeling she'd never had before, the overwhelming sensation of love and peace and warmth that comes from holding a sleepy baby.

"I don't know who looks happier, you or Miss Hilary," Andy said as he smiled at them, and indulged in a drink on the plane. He really felt he deserved it.

By dinnertime they were home, and Diana looked around, feeling as though she had been gone for a lifetime. So much had happened to them, so much had changed since that fateful phone call on Friday night. Was it only three days? Neither of them could believe it.

"What room should I put her in?" Andy whispered to Diana as he carried the basket.

"Ours, I think. I don't want her too far away from us. And I have to get up with her at night anyway to feed her."

"Yeah, yeah, yeah, I know," he teased, "you just don't want to be away from her for a minute." But he couldn't blame her. He wanted her close to them too. And he was already wondering, as he gently set her down in the basket next to their bed, if it would be difficult to adopt another.

Diana called her sister, Sam, that night, and asked for the name of the pediatrician, for a "friend," and Sam couldn't see the grin on her older sister's face when she did it. Sam gave her his name, and then Diana asked her how the baby was, and if she'd like to drop by the next day for a visit.

But Sam had finally understood how sensitive Diana was, and she was very cautious when she answered.

"I don't have anyone to leave the baby with, Di. Seamus is working on a new painting. I could come when the other two are at nursery school, but I'd have to bring him." And she knew Diana wouldn't want that. She had only seen him once since he'd been born, and from a very considerable distance.

"That's all right. I don't mind," she said easily, and Sam frowned at her end, suspicious.

"Are you sure?"

"I'm positive." She actually sounded as though she meant it.

"Are you feeling better about things?" Sam asked cautiously. She had been shocked by her sister's outburst over Thanksgiving. But in the months since, she had come to understand how great the pain was and she felt stupid about how insensitive they'd all been, and how unaware of her problems.

"I'm much better, Sam," Diana said. "We'll talk about it tomorrow."

And then she called her mother. Her father was out of town, which was disappointing. But she invited her mother over for coffee at the same time Sam was coming. And then she called Gayle. They were all free, and she didn't tell any of them why they were invited. But when she hung up after inviting Gayle, she was grinning from ear to ear. She was one of them at last. She had finally made it. She was a member of the secret society. She had a baby.

"I'm glad you're happy, sweetheart," Andy whispered to her that night. He had never seen her like this, and now he realized more than ever how much she had wanted a baby. It surprised him to realize that it didn't bother him at all that the baby wasn't biologically related to him. He couldn't have cared less. He thought she was gorgeous. And when she woke up for the first time that night, they both jumped up and grabbed a bottle. After that, they took turns, and in the morning, Andy looked at Diana, tired but happy.

"You forgot to call someone last night," he said sleepily as he went back to bed. He had just called his office to tell them that he wouldn't be in again that day and probably not the next one either. He told them he was still sick, and he would have to explain the rest later.

"Who did I forget to call?" Diana looked confused as she thought about it. She'd called both her sisters and her mother. She'd have her father over as soon as he got back from his trip. "I can't think of who." Maybe Eloise, but they really weren't all that close now.

"No, I meant Wanda . . . you know . . . Wanda Williams."

"Oh, you jerk." Diana laughed as the baby started to cry. She fed Hilary then, and bathed her, and had her all dressed in one of her new outfits before her family arrived to meet her. But suddenly, as Diana looked at her, before they all came, she realized that what was important was not her family, or how they reacted to her, or what they thought of Diana now that she had a child—what was important was the baby, the little person she was, the woman she would grow to be, and all that she would come to mean, and already meant, to Andy and Diana. She was someone they had waited what seemed like a lifetime for. They had prayed for her, and fought over her, and almost destroyed each other and themselves when they thought they wouldn't find her. She meant more to them than they could ever tell her, and what other people thought of her actually meant nothing. Diana hoped that her family would love Hilary, and she was sure they would, how could they not? But if they didn't . . . it just didn't matter. Diana realized that she hadn't failed at trying to have a child. She had simply done things differently. She had met an insurmountable problem, met the devil in her soul, and survived it. Problem solved. Life continues. There was no victory or defeat here. There was life with all its riches, all its joy and despair, and its infinitely precious gifts. Hilary was one of them, perhaps the greatest Diana would ever receive. But she knew now that Hilary's arrival in her life was not a victory for her, it was a blessing.

And as she smiled down at the sleeping child, the doorbell rang, and it was her mother.

"How are you, sweetheart?" her mother

asked worriedly, and Diana could see in her eyes that she was frightened.

"I'm fine."

"Why aren't you at work?" She sat down on the couch, her knees pressed tightly together in her navy Adolfo suit, her hair freshly done, and both her hands clutching her handbag.

"Don't look so worried, Mom. Everything's okay. I'm on vacation."

"You are? You didn't tell me you were taking a vacation now. Are you and Andy going away?" She knew they'd been separated for a while, but Diana had told her as soon as they got back together. She was good about things like that as a rule, never causing them worry unduly. Only the heartbreak of her infertility had remained a painful secret. But her mother never discussed that with her. She didn't want to pry, or ask embarrassing questions, but Sam had told her that there was no hope Diana could ever have a baby, and her son-in-law, Jack, had confirmed it.

She was about to tell her mother that she and Andy weren't going away, they were staying in town, when the doorbell rang again, and it was Sam with her baby. He was two months old, and looked adorable sound asleep in his car seat. Diana realized as she looked at him, that only days before it would have made her heart ache to see him. Now he was just a sweet-looking, cuddly baby.

"Something wrong?" Sam asked as soon as she came in the door. Diana laughed as she helped her set the baby down, and Sam watched her in consternation. Something had happened to her, she seemed so much less skittish than before, so sure of herself, so undisturbed by the baby. Sam almost wondered if she was pregnant, but she would never have dared to ask her.

"Nothing's wrong. Mom asked me the same thing. She thought I got fired because I'm home." Sam saw her mother in the living room then, and was even more surprised, as she followed Diana. "I'm on vacation this week and I thought it would be fun to get together. It's nice to see you, Sam." Diana smiled at her, and the two sisters exchanged a look that warmed their mother's heart, she was happy to see it.

Gayle arrived ten minutes after them, complaining about traffic on the freeway, her car, and the lack of parking.

"So what's the occasion?" She looked around the room suspiciously when she saw her sister and her mother. "This looks like a family pow-wow."

"Well, it's not." Diana smiled easily. "There's someone I want you to meet," she said calmly. "I'll bring her right in. Sit down, Gayle." Sam was already sitting next to her mother on the couch, nursing her baby.

Diana disappeared for a few minutes then, and without waking the baby up, she picked Hilary carefully out of her basket and put her on her shoulder. She hung there all warm and cozy as Diana clung to her, giving her little kisses on her head as she walked back to the living room, and then she stood there, and they stared at her. Sam just sat there and smiled, and her mother started to cry, and Gayle looked at her in amazement.

"Oh, my God . . . you've got a baby."

"We sure do. Hilary," Diana said as she sat down next to Sam, putting the baby in her lap so they could see her. She was a beautiful little girl, she had perfect skin and lovely features, and tiny little hands with long, graceful fingers.

"She's so beautiful," her mother cried, and then she leaned over to kiss her daughter. "Darling, I'm so happy for you."

"So am I, Mom," Diana said as she kissed her, and then Sam gave her a warm hug, and the two sisters laughed as they cried, and Gayle bent down for a closer look at the baby.

"She's gorgeous," she pronounced. And then she looked at Diana. "You're lucky, you took the easy way out, no labor, no thirty pounds to lose, no saggy boobs, just a gorgeous kid and your skinny body. If I weren't so happy for you, I'd hate you. Maybe now we can be friends again. This hasn't been easy for us either, you know." She spoke for all of them, but as always, the tension had been greatest between her and Diana. Sam was always exempt from their fights, she always had been. She was the baby.

"I'm sorry," Diana said, as she looked down at her little girl. "It's been an awful time, but now it's over."

"Where did she come from?" Sam asked curiously, fascinated by the delicate features.

"San Francisco. She was born at twelve-thirty A.M. on Sunday morning."

"She's terrific," her brand-new grandmother announced, and she could hardly wait to tell her husband, and go out and buy the baby a present. She couldn't even imagine what Diana's father would think, but she knew he'd be pleased and relieved after all Diana had been through.

The ladies stayed for almost two hours, and then finally they all left, regretfully, after kissing Diana and the baby repeatedly. Andy came home from his errands just as Sam left. He had gone to the office to pick up some papers and explain that he needed the rest of the week off. They had been surprised by his good news, but good sports about giving him the time off, and they told him to take the next week off, too, if he felt he was needed. He had stopped by to see Bill Bennington, too, and told him the news about the baby.

"Does this mean we can go out to play again?" Bill teased. He understood about Diana having a hard time dealing with Denise's pregnancy. She had been confined to her bed lately anyway, things hadn't been easy. They were afraid the baby would be premature, or she might even lose it. But they were in the home stretch now. Her due date was only eight weeks away, and in another month they were going to let her get up, and it would be all right if she had the baby. "When can we see her?" Bill asked excitedly. He knew they were having a girl, too, and he liked the idea of him and Andy going out with their daughters.

"Maybe we can play doubles in a few years," he suggested and Andy laughed, and then promised they'd drop in on Denise whenever she felt up to a visit.

"We'll call," Andy promised, and then went back to Diana and the baby. She had given him a long shopping list, and he needed a few things of his own. But he could see when he got home that she had had a great time with her mother and sisters.

"Successful mission?" he asked cryptically and she grinned. "How did the princess behave?" She was sound asleep back in her basket.

"Impeccably. And they loved her."

"Who wouldn't?" He looked down at her, fascinated by every move she made, every inch of her. He adored her. And then he remembered something else. "Did you call your office?"

"I tried, but none of the right people were there. I thought maybe I should go in and explain it." She had a lot to say to them, and she owed them an explanation as to why this had happened with no warning.

And when she went in late that afternoon, she was impressed by how understanding they were. They offered her full maternity leave, which was five months, beginning at that moment. And as soon as it was over, she had her job back. She was fairly sure she still wanted it, although she had always wondered what she would do if she had a baby. Early on, she had thought she would give up work, and later she had thought about going back to work, or trying

to work part time. She could never have kept
her job as a senior editor if she worked part
time, but she could have done a lot of interesting things for them. And she just wasn't sure
now. She had five months to spend with Hilary
and figure it out, and by then she'd know what
she wanted.

She thanked the editor in chief for her generosity, and went to pack up her office. They
would need it for someone else while she was
gone, and it only took her an hour to box it all
up and send it downstairs to her car with their
porter. And on her way out, she stopped in to
see Eloise. She was just taking a soufflé out of
the oven.

"God, that looks good." The air was heavy
with the perfume of her cooking, and when
Eloise saw her she smiled.

"So do you. I haven't seen you in ages. Got
time for a cup of coffee?"

"Just a quick one."

"You got it."

Diana sat down at the counter, and a moment
later Eloise handed her a steaming cup and a
small dish with some of the soufflé on it.

"I'm not sure about this recipe, try it and see
what you think."

Diana took one bite and closed her eyes in ecstasy. "This is sinful."

"Good." Eloise was pleased. "So what's new with you?" She knew what a tough time Diana had had in the past year, they had met occasionally and Diana had filled her in. But she had looked grim through most of it, and she had also withdrawn from everyone she knew. She and Eloise had drifted apart then, but Diana still liked her. "You're looking good," Eloise complimented her. Diana had been looking good ever since she got back with Andy. She seemed to put her life back together then, and her happiness no longer seemed to depend on whether or not she had a baby. But she seemed more serious than she had been. Inevitably, there were scars from what she'd been through.

"Thanks." Diana looked mischievous as she sipped her coffee. "We had a baby this weekend." She grinned as Eloise's jaw dropped.

"You *what*? Did I hear you correctly?"

"You did." Diana beamed. "A little girl named Hilary. She was born on Sunday, and we're going to adopt her."

"Well, good for you!" Eloise looked thrilled for her. It was the ultimate gift, and she knew how much they would love that baby.

"They just gave me five months' maternity

leave. But I'll be back. You can come and visit, and I'll be back by the end of the year. Just don't give up cooking."

"I won't." Eloise looked at her ruefully. "But I won't be cooking here. I just accepted a job in New York. I gave notice this morning. I'm leaving in two weeks. I was going to tell you as soon as I saw you."

"I'm going to miss you," Diana said quietly. She had a lot of respect for Eloise, and she was sorry she hadn't gotten to know her even better, but so much had been happening in her own life for the past year. There hadn't been much room for friendships, and Eloise understood that.

"I'll miss you too. You'll have to come visit me in New York. But I want to see the baby before I go. I'll call you this week."

"Terrific." Diana finished her coffee and gave her a hug, and Eloise promised to come by that weekend, and on the drive home, Diana thought of her and how much she'd miss the magazine while she was gone. But by the time she got home, her thoughts were filled with her baby, and the magazine that had once consumed every moment of her time might as well have been on another planet.

* * *

In May, Charlie and Beth had known each other for three months, and he felt as though he had known her for a lifetime. They could talk about anything, and he spent a lot of time telling her about his childhood, and how it had affected him, and as a result, how strongly he felt about families and having a home. He told her about his disappointment with Barbara, and how hurt he was that she had left him. But he understood it better now. He'd thought about it a lot, and he was starting to realize that it had been a mismatch.

But there was still one thing he hadn't told her, and he wasn't sure he ever could. All he knew was that he had no right to marry again, but as long as it never got to that point, he didn't have to tell her. She didn't need to know that he was sterile.

He liked her too much to tell her the truth. He was afraid he'd lose her. He had lost too much in his life, too many people he cared about, to risk losing Beth and Annie.

They spent Mother's Day together, and he took them to brunch in Marina Del Rey. He had taken Annie out to buy Beth flowers first, and Annie had made her a beautiful card at school. That afternoon they went to the beach, and they laughed and played and talked. He was wonderful with the little girl, and when Annie was off playing with some other children on the beach, Beth looked at him and casually asked the million-dollar question.

"How come you never had kids, Charlie?" she asked casually, as she lay with her head on his chest, on the sand, and she felt him stiffen when she asked the question.

"I don't know. No time, no money." It didn't sound like him, and he had already told her that one of his disagreements with his wife was that she didn't want children. He had also explained that she'd gotten pregnant by someone else, and that had ended their marriage. He hadn't gone into the details, that he'd been willing to accept the child, and she'd already had an abortion when he told her. "I don't think I'll ever marry again," he said slowly. "In fact, I know I won't," he said, and she turned to look at him with a shy smile. She hadn't been fishing for a proposal. She was merely curious about his past, and interested in everything about him.

"That wasn't what I asked you. Don't be so uptight. I wasn't proposing to you. I asked why you never had kids." She looked perfectly relaxed, but she could see then that he didn't. She wondered if she had said something wrong, and then slowly he sat up, and she sat up and watched him. There was no point kidding her. He liked her too much. And it would have been wrong to lead her on, and then disappear one day, which he'd thought of doing. He decided he might as well tell her now. She had a right to know who she was wasting her time with.

"I can't have kids, Beth. I found out six months ago, just before Christmas. They did a bunch of tests, and to make a long story short, it turns out I'm sterile. It was quite a shock," he said, still looking devastated by what he told her. And he was terrified of what she'd do now. Probably leave him, like everyone else had. But telling her was the right thing to do, and he knew it.

"Oh, Charlie . . ." she said sympathetically, sorry she'd asked him. She reached out a hand to touch his, but this time he didn't take her hand in his own, and he suddenly looked oddly distant.

"Maybe I should have told you sooner, but it's not exactly the sort of thing you want to tell someone on a first date." Or ever.

"No." And then she smiled gently, and teased him a little. "You could have said something, though, and saved us both a lot of trouble with precautions." They had been using condoms, which they both knew was a good idea these days in a new relationship, but she had also used a diaphragm, and he had never told her not to, which seemed funny to her now, but not to Charlie. "Never mind," she said softly and then she frowned. "So what's this bit about never getting married again? What's that all about?"

"I don't think I have the right to get married, Beth. Look at you, you have a beautiful little girl, you should have more children."

"Who says I'd even want them? Or even can have them." She looked at him wisely.

"Wouldn't you? Can't you?" He was surprised, she loved Annie so much that it was hard to imagine her not wanting more children.

"Yes, I can have more children," she said honestly. "I guess it would depend on who I married, if I did. But to tell you the truth, I'm not sure I want more. Annie is enough for me. I never really thought of having more than Annie. But I'd be perfectly happy having just Annie. I was an only child, it didn't do me any harm. And in some ways, it's a lot simpler. I couldn't afford another one right now anyway. Sometimes I barely have enough to feed me and Annie." He knew that, and he had been doing what he could to bring her little gifts, and groceries, and take them out whenever they could make it.

"But if you married again, you'd want more children. So would anyone . . . so would I . . ." he said sadly. "One day I'd like to adopt some. I've been saving some money this year so I could adopt a little boy. They allow single-parent adoptions now, and I want to find a kid just like I was, stuck in some miserable institution with no one to love him. I want to change his life for him, and maybe for some more kids, if I can afford it."

"How many were you thinking of adopting?" she asked nervously.

"Two . . . three . . . I don't know. It's a dream of mine. I used to think of that even when I thought I could have my own children."

"Are you sure you can't have your own?" she asked solemnly.

"Positive. I went to an important guy in Beverly Hills, and he says there's no chance. I think he's probably right too. I've taken a lot of chances in my life, especially when I was young, and nothing's ever happened."

"It's no big deal, you know," she said quietly. She was sorry for him, but she didn't think it was the end of the world, and she hoped he didn't either. And it certainly didn't change her opinion of his manhood, which was most impressive.

"It shook the hell out of me for a while," he explained. "I always wanted kids of my own, and I was trying so hard to get Barb pregnant to save our marriage." And then suddenly he laughed at the irony. "In the end, someone else beat me to it." It didn't bother him as much anymore though. He was sad it hadn't worked out with Barb, but in the past few months he had become philosophical about all that, especially since he'd met Beth and Annie. The only thing that bothered him now was that the love he felt for Beth could go nowhere. He still believed, no matter what she said, that he had no right to marry her and deprive her of more children. She was young now, but she might well want more later.

"I don't think you should let it bother you," she said honestly. "I think any woman who really loves you would understand and wouldn't give a damn if you could have kids or not."

"You think so?" He looked surprised and they lay down in the sand again, with her head on his shoulder. "I'm not sure you're right," he said quietly, after thinking about it for a moment.

"Yes, I am. I wouldn't give a damn."

"You should," he said, sounding fatherly. "Don't limit your future, you're too young to do that," he said firmly, and she sat up again and looked down at him sternly.

"Don't tell me what to do, Charlie Winwood. I can do anything I damn well want, and I can tell you right now, I wouldn't give a damn if you were sterile." She said it loudly and firmly and he winced, and looked around, but no one seemed to be paying any attention to them, and Annie was nowhere near them.

"Why don't we put it on billboards?"

"Sorry." She looked mollified and lay down next to him again. "But I mean that."

He rolled over on his stomach then on the sand, and cupped his face in his hands, as he watched her lying near him. "Do you really mean that, Beth?"

"I do."

That changed a lot of things for him, and it made him think seriously about their future, but it seemed wrong to marry a young girl like her, and not be able to give her babies. He knew there were sperm donors, of course, Pattengill had suggested that for him and Barb, but Charlie also knew he'd never do that. But if she meant what she said, maybe Annie was enough

. . . or they could adopt some kids. He lay on the sand smiling at her, and then without saying another word, he rolled over and kissed her.

CHAPTER
═17═

On their anniversary that year, their second one, Andy and Diana stayed home, because there was no one she trusted the baby with, and she was just as happy going nowhere.

"You're sure?" Andy felt a little guilty not taking her out, but he had to admit he didn't mind staying home with his wife and baby.

Diana was enjoying her time off from work, she was spending all her time with Hilary, and she was trying to figure out what to do when her leave was over. She liked being at home, but she was starting to think that she might like to go back to work eventually, maybe part time. She was even thinking about getting another job, one with more flexible hours. But she still had three months to make her mind up.

Andy was busier than ever at the office now, with new series, new stars, new contracts.

And Bill Pennington had taken a long leave. Denise had had the baby early, at the end of May, and there had been complications, but the baby was home now, and they were ecstatic.

Diana had visited her, and tried to help her out. She felt like an old hand now, after two months. She got a lot of advice from Gayle and Sam, and she got a lot of help from an excellent pediatrician. And the rest of the time, she followed her instincts. Most of child rearing seemed to be common sense. Her father had said that to her the first time he came to see the baby. And when he first saw her, he cried. It meant so much to him to know that his own child was at peace now. He held Diana for a long time in his arms, as tears rolled down his cheeks, and then he smiled at the baby.

"You did a good job," he said, and Diana suddenly wondered if he'd forgotten she hadn't given birth to her, and that worried her. It would have been the first sign that he was failing. And so far he wasn't.

"Daddy, I didn't have her," she reminded him cautiously, and he chuckled.

"I know that, silly girl. But you found her and brought her home. She's a blessing for all of us, not just for you and Andy." He had stood and looked at her for a long time, and then he had stooped to kiss her. A little while later he left, after assuring Hilary's parents that she was the prettiest baby he'd ever seen. And he sounded as though he meant it.

They had christened the baby at the beginning of June, and celebrated at Diana's parents' house in Pasadena. These days, everything seemed to revolve around the baby. So much so that Andy thought Diana was looking exhausted. It was partially lack of sleep, every night she got up three or four times, and for the first month, Hilary had had a lot of colic. But now she was fine, the one who wasn't was Diana. And the night of their anniversary, when they stayed home, Andy noticed that Diana didn't even bother to put on makeup. Seeing her looking so beat almost made him sorry they'd given up the beach house Diana had rented during their separation. They loved it, but now, with Hilary, they couldn't afford it.

"You feeling okay?" He looked worried about her, but at least she seemed happy.

"I'm fine. Just tired. Hilary got up every two hours last night."

"Maybe you should get someone in to help you, you know, a nice au pair."

"Never mind that." She pretended to glower at him. She wasn't letting anyone take care of their baby. She had waited too long for this, and paid too dearly with her soul to let another woman even touch her. The only one she allowed to help her was her husband.

"I'll do bottle duty tonight. You get some sleep. You need it."

He cooked dinner for her that night, while she put the baby down. And they talked for a long time afterward about how their life had changed, and how far they had come in two years. It was hard even to remember a time when Hilary hadn't been with them.

They went to bed early that night, and Andy wanted to make love, but Diana was asleep before he came out of the bathroom. He stood for a moment and smiled at her, and then he gently put the baby's basket next to his side of the bed, so he'd hear her when she woke up for her next feeding.

But the next morning, after a good night's sleep, Diana looked worse. And she looked absolutely green when he poured her a cup of coffee.

"I think I've got the flu," she complained,

and then worried about giving it to the baby. "Maybe I should wear a mask," she said, and he laughed.

"Listen, she's more durable than that. And if you have the flu, she's already been exposed anyway." It was Saturday and he volunteered to take care of the baby all day. Diana slept all afternoon, and she looked groggy that night when she cooked him dinner, and he noticed that she didn't eat anything. She just wasn't hungry.

By Monday, nothing had changed. She had no temperature but she looked like hell. And he told her when he left for work to call the doctor.

"Don't count on it," she said, looking exhausted again, and he hadn't really seen her eat all weekend. "I never want to see another doctor for the rest of my life."

"I didn't say call a gynecologist, I said call a doctor." But she absolutely refused to. And some days she looked okay, others she looked worse; sometimes it depended on how much sleep she got, sometimes it didn't. But worrying about her was driving him up the wall, and she absolutely refused to listen.

"Look, stupid," he finally said to her in July, just before their family picnic on the fourth in Pasadena, "Hilary and I need you. You've been feeling lousy for a month, now go do something about it. You're probably anemic from being up all night and never eating."

"How do normal mothers do it? They seem to do fine. Sam doesn't go around dragging ass." It depressed her to feel as lousy as she did, but she had to admit that a lot of the time now she really felt rotten. And at their family picnic the next day, Andy spoke to his brother-in-law, Jack, and told him to push Diana into seeing a doctor.

Jack managed to catch a few minutes alone with her, after lunch, when she was feeding the baby. "Andy's worried about you," he said bluntly.

"He shouldn't be. I'm fine." She tried to brush him off, but he wasn't that easy to get rid of, and Andy had warned him, and urged him to be persistent.

"You don't look that great, considering that you're young and beautiful and have a gorgeous baby," he teased. He was happy for them, and he had been immensely relieved when Gayle told him they'd adopted a baby. He had seen what distress she'd been in, and he had been deeply sorry for them.

"Why don't you go get a blood test?" He

tried again, because he'd promised Andy, but it was obvious to him that Diana was stubborn.

"What's that going to tell me, Jack? That I'm tired? I already know that. I've had enough tests to last me a lifetime."

"This isn't the same thing, Diana, and you know that. I'm talking about a checkup. That's nothing."

"It may be nothing to you, but it's something to me."

"Then why don't you come see me? I can do a simple blood test, make sure you don't have some kind of a low-grade infection that's wearing you down, see if you're anemic, give you some vitamins. No big deal."

"Maybe," she said hesitantly, but before they left that afternoon, he pressed her again.

"I want to see you in my office tomorrow."

It seemed dumb to her, but she felt so rotten the next morning when Andy left for work, that she ended up throwing up for an hour, and lying half passed out on the bathroom floor while the baby cried lustily in the bedroom. "Okay," she whispered as she lay there, feeling like she was going to die, "I'll go . . . I'll go . . ." And an hour later, she and Hilary were in Jack's office.

Reluctantly, she admitted to him what had

happened that morning, and it had happened before. She had a vague suspicion that, after all the agonies of the year before, she might have wound up with an ulcer.

He glanced at her as she explained, and then asked her a few questions, about the color of the vomitus, did it look like coffee grounds, had she ever thrown up blood, to all of which she said no, and he nodded.

"What's all that about?" she asked anxiously, while Hilary slept peacefully in her basket.

"I just want to check your ulcer theory out, and make sure you've not vomiting either old or fresh blood." He was a gynecologist, but he wasn't totally unfamiliar with these kinds of questions. "If we suspect an ulcer, you should have an upper GI series. But let's not worry about that yet." He drew some blood and made some notes, listened to her chest, and then palpated her stomach and lower abdomen. And then he looked at her, over his glasses. "What's this?" he asked, feeling a small mass low down in her belly. "Was that there before?"

"I don't know," she looked frightened and reached down to touch it. It had been there for a while, she knew, but she couldn't remember how long, weeks, months, days. She was so tired she just couldn't think of when she first felt it.

"Not long. Maybe since we had the baby." He frowned at her again, felt some more, and then sat down across from her in a chair with an odd expression.

"When was your last period?" he asked, and she tried to think. It had been a while, not that it made a difference.

"I don't know," she tried to think. "Maybe not since Hilary came, a couple of months maybe. Why, is something really wrong?" Maybe now, in addition to all the other things wrong with her reproductive tract, she had a tumor. "Do you think it's a growth of some kind?" Oh, Christ, that was all she needed. Maybe she had cancer. What would she ever say to Andy? *Sweetheart . . . I'm really sorry . . . but I'm going to die and leave you with this baby.* Her eyes filled with tears as she thought of it, and her brother-in-law patted her hand.

"I think it could be that, but I think it might be something else. What do you think the chances are that you might be pregnant?"

"Oh, come on." She laughed at him and sat up. "Don't play that game with me, Jack. Bullshit. What did the doctor say? I had a one in ten thousand chance of getting pregnant, or was it one in ten million? I can't remember."

"I think it's a possibility. And if you weren't

my sister-in-law, I'd do an exam. How about if I bring in one of my partners to check you, and we could do a quick urine test, and at least that would be ruled out. I don't mean to upset you by suggesting it, but it could explain all your symptoms."

"Yeah"—she glowered at him angrily—"So would cancer."

"There's a happy thought." He patted her leg and left the room, while she fumed. She was furious with him for even raising that specter. She'd had enough of that torment in her life to want never to think about it again. Pregnant . . . bullshit! She raged to herself, and then Jack came back in the room with an attractive young woman. He introduced her to Diana, who barely managed to be civil.

"We just want to rule out pregnancy," he explained. "She's had some serious infertility issues that have been laid to rest, and allegedly pregnancy is not a possibility, or if it is, a very slight one. But I find some symptoms that I'm finding confusing."

"Have you done a pregnancy test yet?" she asked him and he shook his head, and asked Diana to lie down again. He showed her what he felt, and when he squeezed it, Diana felt an odd cramping sensation.

"Does that hurt?" he asked.

"Yeah," she said, staring at the wall. They had no right to do this to her. It was like raising the dead, and it wasn't fair. She didn't want to hear it.

"Check it out, will you, Louise?"

"Sure." He thanked her and left the room, and Louise helped settle Diana into stirrups. Just being there made her start to shake, and Louise pretended not to notice as she put on gloves and began the examination.

"Who did you see about the infertility?" she inquired conversationally as she felt Diana's insides, all the way to her tonsils.

"Alexander Johnston."

"He's the best. And what did he say?"

"Essentially, that I'm sterile."

"Did he say why?"

"From an IUD I had when I was in college, or that was what he thought. I never had any symptoms, but my tubes are blocked, and both ovaries have severe adhesions."

The examination continued and Diana wondered how long it would go on. "I guess that ruled out in vitro fertilization," Louise said pleasantly, and Diana nodded. "Did he suggest a donor egg?" she asked, but Diana winced and shook her head, both from the question and what she was doing. None of it brought back happy memories for Diana.

"Yes, he did. And I wasn't interested. We adopted a little girl in April." And with that, Louise looked down at Hilary and smiled.

"So I see. She's a real beauty." And with that the examination ended. She smiled at Diana, and before she could say anything Jack was back in the room, his eyes full of questions.

"Well?"

Louise looked at her ruefully, and at her partner. "I don't like contradicting my colleagues," she said cautiously, while Diana waited for a verdict of cancer, "but I'd say Dr. Johnston was mistaken. That feels like a ten-week uterus to me. If you hadn't told me there were problems here, I'd never have questioned it for a minute. Could even be more. When was her LMP?" Last menstrual period. Diana knew all the terms and hated hearing them again, as she closed her eyes, feeling dizzy.

"End of March, early April. She can't remember."

"That makes her roughly three months pregnant."

"What?" Diana stared at them in amazement. "Are you kidding? Jack, don't do this to me."

"I'm not. Diana, I swear. I really mean it."

Louise excused herself and left them then, and
Jack asked Diana to go to the bathroom and pee
in a cup so he could do a pregnancy test, and
when he did, it confirmed his diagnosis. Diana
was definitely pregnant.

"I'm not . . . I can't be . . ." she kept saying over and over again, but she was, and when
she left his office, she looked dazed, and made
him promise not to tell anyone until she did.

She drove straight to the network then to see
her husband. He was in a conference, and she
was in jeans, and she was carrying Hilary sound
asleep in her car seat.

"I have to see him," she explained to his secretary, *"now!"* And something in her face told
the woman Diana meant it. She hurried in behind closed doors, and two minutes later Andy
came out running.

"What's wrong? Is the baby okay?" He
looked frightened to see her, and she looked
deathly pale and very sober.

"She's fine. I need to talk to you. Alone."

"Come into my office." He took the baby
from her, and she followed him to a glass-and-
wood-panelled room with a dazzling view. And
then he turned to look at her with worried eyes.
"What's wrong, Di?" Something terrible had
obviously happened. He didn't dare guess what.

But she didn't mince words with him, she just looked at him in total confusion. "I'm pregnant."

"Are you serious?" He stared at her and then he grinned. "Are you kidding me?" He couldn't stop grinning, and she shook her head, still looking shell-shocked.

"Three months, do you believe that?"

"No, but baby, I'm so happy for you . . . and for me . . . and for Hillie . . . my God, three months, it must have happened right when we brought her home from San Francisco. How amazing." But he had heard of that before, people who conceived instantly when they adopted, after years of unsuccessful trying.

Diana sat down, looking happy but sheepish. "I was so tired, I can't even remember making love to you then."

"Well, I hope it was me," he teased. "Who knows? It could be an immaculate conception."

"Not likely."

"My God, I can't believe it. When's it due?"

"I don't know. January something. I was too stunned to hear what Jack said. January tenth or something."

"I can't believe this. We ought to call Johnston and tell him."

"To hell with Johnston," she said grumpily,

and stood up to kiss her husband. And then he swept her off her feet and whirled her around the room in his excitement.

"Hurray for us . . . hurray for you! We're pregnant." And then suddenly, he grew more serious. "How do you feel? Christ, no wonder you've been feeling so lousy."

"Yeah, and the funny thing is, Jack says the worst is already over. He said I should be feeling better in the next week or two."

"Good, let's go out to dinner tonight to celebrate. L'Orangerie. We'll put the baby in the cloakroom if we have to." He kissed her again, and went back to his meeting, and Diana stood for a long time, looking at the view, and thinking of what had happened, with amazement.

Pilar was taking it easy that summer. She had her amniocentesis in June, and it had scared her to death, but it went smoothly. They'd had to take fluid out of both sacs, with two huge separate needles. But they already had their results, and now they knew that they were a girl and a boy, and both were healthy.

And once she had the results, Pilar knew she had to call her mother. She had called her on a Saturday afternoon, almost hoping that she was away for the weekend. But instead she was on call, and picked up the phone on the first ring. She was keeping an eye on two very sick children that weekend.

"Oh, it's you," she said, sounding surprised. "I thought it was the hospital. How are you?" Pilar suddenly remembered how she had felt as a child, always an intrusion among far more important matters in her mother's life. But now she had something important to tell her, too, and she wondered how her mother would take it.

"I'm fine, Mother. And you?"

"Very well, keeping busy. And Brad?"

"He's fine," Pilar went on nervously. "Mother, I've got something to tell you."

"Are you ill?" She sounded concerned, and Pilar was touched to hear it.

"No, I'm fine . . . I . . . Mother, I'm pregnant." She said softly, with a happy smile, suddenly convinced that her mother would think it as wonderful as she did.

There was a long silence at the other end, and then Elizabeth Graham was at her coolest. "How foolish. I said as much to you when you married Brad. You're both far too old to even think about having children."

"That's not what our doctors said. We discussed it with them before we got pregnant."

"This was planned?" She sounded shocked.

"Yes, it was."

"How incredibly stupid." She was sixty-nine years old by then, and some of her ideas were not the most modern.

Pilar felt as though she had been slapped by her mother's reaction, and yet talking to her was no different than it had ever been. But it was always the same old game, with Pilar ridiculously expecting her to be someone she wasn't, never had been, and never would be.

"There's more." Shocking her mother was beginning to amuse her. "They're twins."

"Oh, my God. Did you take fertility drugs?"

"Yes, I did," Pilar said with a wicked grin. Brad walked into the room, listened to the conversation for a moment, and wagged his finger. She was torturing her mother now and loving every minute of it, like a naughty child who is savoring its misdeeds to the fullest.

"For heaven's sake, Pilar, who is the fool who advised you to do this?"

"Mother, this is what we wanted. But we went to a specialist in L.A. She is supposed to be at the top of her field, and she came highly recommended."

"What's her name? Not that I'm familiar with that field, but I can ask around."

"Helen Ward. But you don't need to ask anyone. We did, and we heard nothing but good things about her."

"She can't be very bright if she's encouraging forty-four-year-old women to get pregnant. I do everything I can to deter them. I see the results of those mistakes, and believe me, they're disasters."

"Not all your patients have mothers over forty, do they? Some of them must have had young mothers."

"That's true. But you can't force nature's hand, Pilar. You pay a terrible price when you do that."

"Well, so far, everything's fine. The amniocentesis came out normal, and both babies are fine, genetically anyway."

"Did they warn you that there's a risk of infection from the test, or you could simply lose them?" The voice of doom, all the way from New York. Not a single word of congratulations. But by now, Pilar expected nothing from her. She had given her mother the news. And how she dealt with it was up to her now.

"They warned us of all that, but the danger is past now. Everything went very smoothly."

"I'm glad to hear it." There was a long silence between them then, and Elizabeth Graham sighed and finally broke it. "I really don't know what to say, Pilar. I wish you hadn't done this. I suppose it's too late now, but you were really ill-advised. What you've done is risky and un-wise. Imagine how you'd feel if you lost those babies. Why put yourself through that?"

Pilar closed her eyes, still thinking about her miscarriage. Getting pregnant again had filled her heart, but there was also a place there that would never forget the loss, and she knew that.

"Please don't say that," Pilar said quietly. "We're going to be fine."

"I hope you're right." And then she added the coup de grace. "Brad must be getting se-nile." But this time Pilar could only laugh, and after she hung up, she reported her mother's diagnosis to her husband. And he was as amused as she was.

"I was hoping you wouldn't notice."

"Well, my mother's onto you, sir! You can't fool the Good Doctor Graham!"

"Listen, you gave her a pretty hard time. You must have shocked the hell out of her, and you were enjoying every minute of it. The poor woman thought she was free and clear, and sud-denly you surprise her with not one grandchild, but two. That's pretty heavy stuff for someone like her."

"Oh, for heaven's sake, don't make excuses for her. The woman is inhuman."

"No, she's not," he defended her, "and I'm sure she's a damn good doctor. She just isn't your idea, or mine, of a great mother. It's not her thing. But there are other areas of her life that might even make her a worthwhile human being."

"You sound like my shrink," Pilar said in disgust, and then she kissed him. But at least she had told her mother the news. Now she could concentrate on Brad, and her babies.

They celebrated Adam's first birthday in July. Pilar was five months pregnant and looked eight, but so far everything was fine. But most of the time she was condemned to bed rest. With twins they didn't want to take any chances and have her deliver early.

"How do you feel?" Marina asked when she came to visit her one day, and Pilar laughed as she struggled to sit up in bed. It was like wrestling with a rhino.

"Like Yankee Stadium, and then some. Most of the time it feels like World War III in there. I'm not sure these guys are going to be such great buddies. They spend most of their time kicking each other in the shins, and knocking the wind out of me." Even crossing the room was getting a little dicey. She felt so huge, and she was amazed by the enormity of her belly.

"You sure don't go halfway when you do things," Brad commented with a smile, watching her get into the tub one day. She really looked inhumanly enormous. And most of the time, just watching her, you could see knees and arms and elbows, and little feet just kicking and moving. Pilar thought it was wonderful for a while, but it was getting very uncomfortable by the middle of summer.

And by September, she was feeling absolutely miserable. She had heartburn all the time, and her belly felt as though it were about to explode, her skin was taut and cracking, her back was killing her, her ankles were twice their normal size, and if she did much more than walk out to her terrace, she got contractions. She couldn't go anywhere, and she didn't dare leave the house. She wasn't even supposed to leave her bedroom for fear that her uterus would get "irritable" and she'd go into preterm labor. Her partners sent work home to her, but she didn't feel very useful just lying there. And by the end of the month, she wondered how much longer she could stand it.

Her due date was still six weeks away, and it seemed like the longest six weeks of her life, but in every part of her, even when she complained, she knew it was worth it.

"See if I watch dirty movies with you again," she grumbled at him one night, when she was particularly uncomfortable, and Brad laughed as he massaged her swollen ankles.

"That's what you get for playing with the big guys."

"Stop bragging."

"I'm not." He smiled, and leaned over to gently rub her tummy. His hand was instantly met by a sound kick, and then he could see a flurry of action. "Boy, they just don't quit, do they?"

"Not if they can help it. The only time they sleep is if I'm moving, and God knows I don't do that much." He laughed as he watched them again, and he was as excited as she was. But sometimes he was sorry for her too. She looked so miserably uncomfortable, and there was precious little he could do to help her.

And he was concerned about the birth, too, although he hadn't said much to Pilar. But he had had several serious conversations with Dr.

Parker. For the moment, he saw no need for a cesarean, but he had every intention of doing one if either of the twins switched from their head down position, or if either of them was in distress during the delivery.

She had scheduled a Lamaze instructor to come to the house in October, and as Brad looked at her, he couldn't help wondering if she'd make it. She was already thirty-four weeks pregnant, and Dr. Parker was hoping for at least thirty-six before she went into labor.

CHAPTER
═══ 18 ═══

October was a hellish month for Andy and Diana. She was almost six months pregnant by then, and the final adoption papers for Hilary had to be signed by Jane and Edward. Eric had spoken to them recently and assured Diana that there was no problem. They were going to sign them.

Until he called early one Tuesday morning, and asked to speak to Andy. Andy was silent as he listened on the phone, and he never lifted his eyes once to look at her, and Diana knew instantly that something terrible had happened. She held the gurgling five month old closer to her, and as she did, the baby sensed her tension and started to cry, as though she knew that something was wrong. And when Andy hung up the phone, Diana knew it, too, before he told her.

"What's wrong? They didn't sign the papers, did they?"

With tears in his eyes, Andy looked at her and shook his head. "No, they didn't. They want to think it over for a few more days. And they may want to come down and see the baby."

He hated to tell her that, hated to upset her now, but she had to know, especially if there was going to be a problem. Jane just wasn't sure anymore. She didn't know if she wanted to go to school, she wasn't sure she had done the right thing, giving her baby away, all of which were reasonable concerns, except to Diana and Andy. "Edward still wants to sign, but Jane wants a few more days. And she told Eric she might want to see her."

"She can't," Diana said, jumping to her feet nervously. "They gave her up . . . they can't have her back now." Diana started to cry as soon as she said it.

"Baby"—he tried to reason with her as gently as he could—"they can do anything they want to, until they sign the papers."

"You can't let them do that to us." She was crying as she held the child, and he gently took Hilary from her and put her over his shoulder.

"Just try to stay calm." He didn't want her losing their baby over this one, even though he loved Hilary deeply. "We just have to wait and see what happens."

"How can you say that?" she screamed at him. She loved Hilary as her own child, and she knew that no matter how loved their baby was, it would never be more loved than this one. This was her first child, first love, and she wasn't going to give her back to anyone. "I don't want Jane to see her."

But when Eric called again, he said that Jane and Edward were coming down. He said Jane seemed distraught when they spoke on the phone, and he thought it would be best if Andy and Diana tried to stay calm and let her see the baby.

"I understand," Andy said to his friend, "but Diana doesn't. She's hysterical over this whole thing." And he had also explained to Eric that Diana was pregnant. And that was a problem for Jane too. She was afraid that now, if they had their own child, they might be partial to it and not Jane's baby.

"Oh, God," Andy said as he listened to him. "Why is life never simple?"

"Because it wouldn't be any fun that way, would it?" Eric replied, and Andy sighed. This

entire episode was not going to be easy on Diana.

In the end, Edward and Jane stayed in L.A.
for two days. They stayed at a motel nearby, just
off the freeway, and came to the house repeatedly. Jane wanted to see them, and she insisted
on holding the baby, which almost drove Diana
to distraction. She was afraid Jane would run
out of the house with her, but she didn't. Most
of the time, she just sat there and cried, and
Edward said nothing. Their relationship
seemed a lot more tense than it had been when
Hilary was born, and Jane seemed a lot more
nervous. And then, on the second day, Diana
knew why, when Jane admitted to her that she
had just had an abortion. She hadn't wanted to
go through a delivery again, but it had altered
her thinking about the adoption. She suddenly
wondered if she had done the right thing giving
up Hilary five and a half months before. And
she was convinced that the only reason she got
pregnant again was out of guilt, and because she
wanted to have a baby.

"So now you want mine," Diana finally exploded. "She's *our* baby now. We've stayed up
with her when she was sick, we get up with her
four times a night, we carry her and hold her,
and love her."

"But I carried her for nine months," Jane said, horrified, as the two men watched them, feeling inept and helpless.

"I know you did," Diana said, trying to regain her composure. "And I'll always be grateful to you for giving her to us. But you can't just take her away from us again. You can't just say 'here, love her forever,' and then 'no, gee, sorry, I changed my mind because I had an abortion.' What about her? What about her life? What are you offering her? What's changed in the last five months? What makes you think you would be better for her than we would?"

"Maybe just because I'm her mother," Jane said softly. She felt guilty doing this to them, but she had to know if she wanted this baby. "I don't want to regret this for the rest of my life," Jane said honestly, but Diana was honest with her, too, and she was older.

"You will. Jane, you always will. You'll always think of what could have been, and how life could have been different. We all do. And giving up a baby is about the biggest thing a woman can do. But five months ago, you thought you wanted to do that."

"We both did," Edward added calmly. "And I still do. But Jane is having second thoughts." He thought she should have had an abortion in the first place, but since she didn't, it was still no reason to keep the baby. He had told her as much, but she was panicking now about giving up the baby.

"I just don't know," Jane said when she left them again, and Diana wanted to scream and beg her not to torture them anymore. She just couldn't take it. And she'd had contractions all day, which worried Andy.

And Edward terrified them that night, when he called from the hotel at midnight and asked if they could come by. Jane had something important to tell them.

"Now?" Andy looked horrified, and Diana looked sick when he told her.

"She's taking the baby away, isn't she? She is . . . is that what he told you?"

"Diana, stop it. He didn't tell me anything. He just said that Jane has something to tell us."

"Why is she doing this to us?"

"Because it's a big decision for her too." And they both knew it had to be awful. They couldn't imagine giving Hilary up, yet they expected Jane to do it forever. It didn't seem fair somehow, yet they all knew life wasn't fair. And they prayed she'd live by her earlier decision.

The wait for them to come seemed interminable, and finally at twelve-thirty, they rang the doorbell. Jane looked upset and pale, and it was obvious that she had been crying. And Edward looked annoyed with her. His patience had just about run out in the past two days, and he was anxious to go back to San Francisco.

Diana invited them to come in, but Jane just stood there and shook her head, and then she started crying. "I'm sorry," she whispered, and then looked at them as Diana braced herself for the worst, and unconsciously held her pregnant belly, as though to at least save that baby from being taken. "I'm sorry," Jane tried again. "I know this has been hard for you too"—she choked on the words—"but I had to be sure. I know I couldn't . . . I can't . . . I guess I always knew I couldn't keep her." Diana thought she was going to faint as she clutched Andy's arm, and he put his arm around her to make sure she wouldn't. "We're going back to San Francisco now." And then she handed Diana an envelope. "I signed the papers." Diana started to cry, but Jane seemed in better control suddenly than she had been in days, and then she looked from Diana to Andy.

"Could I see her one more time? I promise I'll never try to see her again after this. She's yours now." She looked so pathetic as she stood there that Diana couldn't say no to her, and she led her quietly upstairs to see her baby. Hilary was sound asleep in her new crib, in the corner of their bedroom. She had her own room upstairs, filled with stuffed animals, and the gifts people had given her, but they liked having her close to them. And Andy and Diana didn't have the heart to move her out of their bedroom.

But now, Jane stood looking down at her, her heart full, her eyes overflowing, and she put gentle fingers on the baby's cheek, like a blessing. "Sleep well, sweetheart," she whispered to the sleeping child as both women cried. "I'll always love you." She stood for another minute then, watching her, and then she bent and kissed her, as Diana felt a lump in her throat slowly choke her. Jane lingered for a last moment as Diana watched, and then she went quietly downstairs, without a word, or her baby. She squeezed Diana's hand as she left, and she walked out to the car, followed by Edward. And Diana couldn't stop crying when the door closed behind them. She felt guilty and sad, and sorry for Jane, and so relieved that Hilary was theirs now. It was an avalanche of feelings she had no idea how to deal with as she clung to Andy.

"Come on," he walked her slowly upstairs, holding her up as her emotions overwhelmed her. It was almost two o'clock in the morning by then. They were both drained by the emotions of the past few days, and Andy thought it was a miracle she didn't go into labor.

He made her stay in bed the next day, and he took care of the baby. And Eric Jones flew down personally to get the papers. Everything had been signed. Everything was done. Hilary Diana Douglas was safe and theirs forever.

"I can't believe it's over," Diana said softly, when Eric left. No one could take her away from them now, no one could come back and change their minds. No one could take her from them.

CHAPTER
═══ 19 ═══

Pilar and Brad's babies were due in early November, and for the last month she absolutely couldn't set foot out of bed, except to use the bathroom. Her cervix had begun to shorten weeks before, and she had already begun to dilate. And every time she did get up, even for a minute, she had contractions. She was bored just lying there, and nervous that something might go wrong, that one of them might strangle on the cord, or somehow hurt each other.

She practiced her Lamaze breathing with Brad, and by Halloween the babies had almost stopped moving. They had so little room to move by then, and she looked like a cartoon of a woman who had swallowed a building. She

stood and looked at herself in the mirror sometimes, and she could only laugh at the incredible distortion. She looked as though she were
carrying baby on top of baby on top of baby.

"That's quite an accomplishment," Brad
teased her one night as he helped her out of the
bath. She couldn't do anything alone anymore.
She couldn't bathe without his helping her,
couldn't put on her shoes, or even her slippers,
and in the first week of November, she couldn't
even get off the toilet unless someone helped
her. Marina came by whenever she could, and
Nancy came to keep her company frequently
while Brad was at work. And she always congratulated Pilar for being such a good sport, and
said she wouldn't have traded places with her
for love or money. As she told her husband
when she went home, other people were going
on with their lives, going out to dinner and having fun, and poor Pilar was blown up like a
blimp, about to explode with babies.

Her mother called frequently, and she
seemed to have adjusted to the idea of Pilar
being pregnant. And she offered to fly out several times, but Pilar didn't want her.

Pilar complained that she hadn't even been to
the hairdresser for six months, but whenever
she got too depressed, Brad reminded her that

it was worth it. And she knew it anyway. It was just incredibly wearing lying there and waiting to go into labor.

Both of the twins appeared to be in good shape, and on one of his visits to the house, the doctor had told her that one of them was slightly larger, probably the boy, he suspected. That was usually the case, but not always. And he also told her that they were bringing in a team of doctors for her delivery. Because of her age, and the fact that it was a multiple birth, he wanted another obstetrician working with him, and two pediatricians for the babies.

"It sounds like a party," Brad said, lightening the moment. He had noticed that Pilar looked concerned when he started talking about "a team," and what would happen if she needed a cesarean section. They still saw no reason for it, but they wanted to be prepared for everything. But Brad noticed in the last two weeks, as she approached her due date, that Pilar was very nervous.

Dr. Parker had also told her that he wouldn't let her go past her due date. There was too much at stake, particularly with two babies. But one week before her scheduled due date, Pilar started having contractions early one morning. The doctor said she could get up and walk around the house for a while to get the labor going. She was amazed by how weak she was, after lying down for so long, and how shaky her legs were. And she was disappointed to find that she couldn't do much walking. She just didn't have the strength, and her belly was too heavy.

By late that afternoon, the pains were coming regularly, and Brad made her a cup of tea, and then everything stopped again. The nearness of it seemed tantalizing as they waited.

"God, I just want to get this over with," she said to Brad. But absolutely nothing more happened that afternoon, until her water broke just after dinner. And still the contractions didn't come, but the doctor asked her to come in to the hospital anyway. He wanted to get her settled and watch her.

"What is there to watch?" she complained, as Brad drove her to Cottage Hospital. "Nothing's happening. Why are we going to the hospital? This is stupid." But as she said it, she looked so huge that Brad could only laugh at her, and he was relieved to be bringing her to the doctors. He had no desire to have his first lesson as a midwife delivering twins at home. It was enough, as far as he was concerned, that he had agreed to be at the delivery. He was faintly squeamish at the thought of it, but he knew Pilar needed him, so he'd agreed to be there when she asked him.

Dr. Parker checked her when she got in, and after he did, she had a few mild contractions. And he was pleased to find that whatever contractions she'd had that morning had continued to dilate her cervix. It was obvious to him that it wouldn't be long till Pilar had her babies.

"Something will get started soon," he promised, and then went home. But he said he'd be back again as soon as they called him. She and Brad watched TV for a while, and she dozed for a little bit, and then suddenly she awoke with a strange sensation. It was an enormous feeling of pressure.

She called for Brad, and she looked faintly panicky, so he called the nurse and let Pilar explain it.

"I think you might be in labor, Mrs. Coleman." She smiled, and went to call the doctor, and a little while later a member of the house staff came to check her. Pilar made some objection to it, and just as she was discussing it with him she had a huge contraction. Her whole enormous belly seemed to be caught in a huge vise and squeezed until it forced the air out of her and she almost couldn't bear it. She squeezed Brad's hand and tried to remember to breathe, and someone she couldn't see cranked her bed up.

"Oh, God . . . that was awful," she said softly when it was over. Her hair was damp, and her mouth felt dry, just from one contraction. But her body knew she had a lot of work to do, and before the attending physician could discuss examining her again, she had another. And the nurse hurried out of the room to call her doctor and tell him that Pilar Coleman was in active labor.

The second obstetrician came in to see her and to examine her and when he did, the contractions got instantly worse, and she tried to struggle against him. Suddenly things were getting out of control for her, two more doctors came into the small labor room, while two nurses worked on the IV in her hand. Another nurse strapped a monitor to her belly to check the fetal heartbeats, and the size of her contractions. But the pressure of the belt from the monitor made the contractions seem worse.

It was horrible, she felt like an animal, strapped and trussed and being pulled at from all directions. Too much was happening, and she seemed to have no control over it whatsoever.

"Brad . . . I can't . . . I can't . . ." She

was trying to get away from all of them, but her enormous girth, and the ferocious pains, made it impossible for her to move at all. "Brad, make them stop!" She wanted all of them to leave her alone, to take off the belt and the IV, to stop hurting her. But they couldn't leave her alone, her babies' well-being was at stake, and Brad felt helpless as he watched her.

He tried to say something to the head nurse, and finally to her doctor when he returned.

"Isn't there something we can do to make it easier for her?" he said hopefully. "The monitor is so uncomfortable, and I think the exams make the contractions worse."

"I know they do, Brad," he said sympathetically, "but she's got a lot of baby in there, and if we're not going to do a cesarean, we need to know what's going on. And if we do, all the more so. We can't fool around." And then the doctor turned his attention to the patient.

"How're we doing here?" he asked Pilar with a cheerful smile.

"Like shit," she said, and suddenly she wanted to throw up. She retched with each pain, and all the other miseries were still going on, and with each contraction, she felt more pressure, and an ever greater urge to push down. Maybe she was getting to the pushing stage, she thought hopefully, maybe that was what she felt, maybe this was the worst of it and it was almost over by now, but when she asked the nurse, she said that pushing was still a long way off. This was only the beginning.

"Drugs," she croaked when the doctor came closer to her head again. She could hardly even speak now, she was in such anguish. "I want drugs."

"We'll talk about that in a while." He put her off, and she started crying again as she grabbed at the doctor's sleeve.

"I want them now," she said, struggling to sit up, but the monitor held her down, and so did the next pain, which left her clutching Brad's hand. "Oh, God . . . listen to me . . . somebody listen to me. . . ."

"I'm listening, sweetheart," Brad said. But she could hardly see him. There were so many people in the room, and there was so much going on. How had all of it gotten so out of hand, and why weren't they listening to her? All she could do was lie there and sob between contractions, when she wasn't screaming.

"Make them do something . . . please . . . make it stop. . . ."

"I know, baby . . . I know . . ." But he didn't know. And he was beginning to regret the whole thing. All the hormones and the drugs, and the trips to Dr. Ward's, and this was what it had brought her. It agonized him to see her in such pain, and he couldn't do anything to help her. He had never felt so useless.

"I want her in the delivery room," the second obstetrician said to Dr. Parker. "If we need to section her, I want to be ready to go."

"That makes sense," Pilar's doctor agreed, and suddenly there was even more action in the room, more people, more machines, and for Pilar more exams, and more contractions.

They rolled her gurney down the hall, though she begged them to stop and move her while she was between pains, but they wanted to get her set up as quickly as possible. According to what the doctor told Brad, things were moving very fast now, and they wanted to be ready. They had to think of the babies' safety, and not their mother's comfort. It was one o'clock in the morning by then, and Brad felt as though they had been there forever.

In the delivery room, they switched her from the gurney to the delivery table, put her legs in stirrups, covered them in drapes, tied down her arms, and switched the IV to her arm, and she complained bitterly about her position between contractions. She said her back and neck were

breaking, but no one was listening to her for a
moment. They were far more engaged in other
things. There were three pediatricians in the
room by then, several residents, a fleet of
nurses, and both her doctors.

"God," she said hoarsely to Brad between
pains, "what are we doing? Selling tickets?"
The monitor was still on, and someone seemed
to be checking her cervix each time she
breathed. According to the nurse, she was at
ten, which meant she was ten centimeters dilated and could push now.

"Okay," everyone cheered, but Pilar didn't
care, and it was obvious to her they weren't going to give her drugs now.

"Why can't I have anything?" she whined.

"Because it's not good for your babies," one
of the nurses said firmly.

But a minute later Pilar couldn't ask for anything, because she was in so much pain, and she
had started pushing.

It looked nightmarish to Brad as he watched,
they shouted, she pushed, then screamed, and
almost the moment the pain ended, it began
again, and they began shouting, and she was
screaming. He couldn't understand why they
didn't give her anything for the pain, except that

the doctor kept insisting it would depress the babies.

It seemed hours that she pushed and nothing came. And when Brad looked at the clock, he couldn't believe that it was almost four o'clock in the morning. He wondered how much more she could take before she became completely incoherent from what they were doing. And then suddenly there was fresh excitement. Two isolettes appeared, and the circle of masked faces drew closer. Pilar seemed to scream endlessly, it was a long endless wail that had no end and no beginning, and then suddenly everyone was shouting, urging, encouraging, and he saw the head of the first baby, pushing its way into the world, his long, slow wail matching his mother's.

"It's a boy!" the doctor said, and Brad was instantly worried by his bluish color, but the nurse said not to worry, and a minute later, he looked better. They held him out to Pilar for a moment to see, but she was too exhausted to pay much attention. Her pains were continuing as before, and the doctor had to use forceps to move the next baby into a better position. Brad couldn't look at what they did to her, he only prayed as he held her hands in a death grip that she'd survive it.

"Hang in, sweetheart . . . it'll all be over soon. . . ." He hoped that he wasn't lying to her, but he had no idea, and she just cried as he held her.

"Oh, Brad . . . it's so awful. . . ."

"I know . . . I know . . . it's almost over. . . ." But this baby was even more stubborn than the first, and at five o'clock he saw the two doctors conferring.

"We may have to do a cesarean if the girl doesn't come out quickly," they explained to Brad a few minutes later.

"Would that be easier for her?" he asked quietly, hoping she couldn't hear him. But she was in such pain, and pushing so hard, that she wasn't listening to what anyone was saying.

"It might be. She'd have general anesthesia, of course, we couldn't possibly get an epidural into her now, but it would also be a double whammy for her, a vaginal birth with an episiotomy, and a section. Not an easy recovery. It all depends on what the baby does in the next few minutes." The first one had already been checked, and was in an isolette, wailing loudly.

"I don't care what you do," Brad said distractedly. "Just do what's best, and easiest for her."

"I want to try to get the baby out vaginally

first," the doctor said, and went at her again with forceps. He worked and pushed and squeezed, and just when they were about to give up, the baby moved, and slowly began moving down between her mother's legs. It was six o'clock by then, and Pilar was barely conscious, and then suddenly she was there, a sweet little face, she was a tiny little baby. This baby was half her brother's size, and she looked around worriedly, as though searching for her mother. And almost as though she sensed it, Pilar raised her head and saw her.

"Oh, she's so beautiful," she said, and then dropped her head back again, smiling at Brad through her tears. It had been excruciating, but it was worth it. She had two beautiful babies, and as she lay and looked at him, two nurses took the baby away the moment the cord was cut, and they lay her in the second isolette for the pediatrician to check her further. But this time, they heard no further cry, and suddenly the room was very quiet.

"Is she okay?" Pilar asked anyone who'd listen to her, but suddenly everyone was very busy. Brad could see his son in his isolette in a corner of the delivery room, with two nurses watching him kick his legs and flail miserably, looking for some comfort. But he couldn't see his daughter, and he took a step away from where Pilar lay so as to see her better. And then he saw them, suctioning her desperately, and trying to breathe for her. A doctor was giving artificial respiration, and then compressing her tiny chest, but the baby lay still now. She was gone, and nothing they did revived her. Brad looked in shocked horror at the doctor's face, and Pilar lay on the gurney just behind him asking questions. He almost felt his heart stop. What in God's name could he tell her?

"Are they okay? Brad? . . . I can't hear the babies. . . ."

"They're fine," he said numbly, as someone gave Pilar a shot. It seemed a little after the fact, but she was instantly woozy and half asleep, and Brad looked at the doctor standing before him.

"What happened?" he asked numbly. It had been a grim experience, and even his son's birth was barely consolation.

"It's hard to say. She was very small. We think she lost a lot of blood to her brother. They call it twin to twin transfusion. It weakened her, and then she just couldn't breathe on her own. Undeveloped lungs, I suspect, and too small to survive so much trauma. Maybe I should have sectioned her," he said miserably, and Brad turned to look at his wife peacefully sleeping in the delivery room, drugged at last, oblivious to what had just happened, and he couldn't begin to imagine what he was going to tell her. So much joy had turned to agony so quickly.

But the pediatricians all agreed with the obstetrician, there was clearly something wrong with the baby's lungs, which no one had known, or suspected. Her heartbeat had been steady during the delivery, but having lost blood to her twin, she was simply unable to survive out of the womb, without her mother. They had done everything they possibly could to revive her.

Brad knew all the facts. But it was still impossible to understand why it had happened. And as Pilar was wheeled away to the recovery room, Brad stood looking at his little girl, as tears crept down his cheeks. She looked so sweet and so perfect. She was as beautiful as she had been when she was born, and now she looked as though she were sleeping.

Her brother was crying unhappily, as though sensing that something had gone wrong. He was so used to being close to her, to kicking her, to being with her, and suddenly she was gone, as was their mother.

Without thinking, Brad reached a hand into the isolette and felt her. She was still warm, and he stood staring at her, wanting to hold her.

What would he tell Pilar? What could he say? How could he tell her one of them had died? She would wake expecting to find two miracles, and instead she would find she'd been stricken with a tragedy in a single moment. It was a cruel joke to have played on them, and he stood for a long time, looking at what seemed to be their sleeping baby.

"Mr. Coleman," a nurse said gently. They wanted to take the dead baby away. And someone was about to tell him that arrangements had to be made. They would have to make burial arrangements for their baby. "Your wife is awake, if you'd like to see her."

"Thank you," he said, looking gray. He touched the tiny hand again, and then left her, somehow feeling that he shouldn't, that she still needed him, but of course, she didn't. "How is my wife?" he asked the nurse, as he finally followed her to the recovery room, looking bleak.

"Feeling better than she was a little while ago." The nurse smiled. But not for long, Brad thought, as he tried to sort out his feelings.

"Where are they?" she said weakly, when she saw him. She had lost a lot of blood, and been through so much pain, and now she would have to be stronger than she ever had before. He

almost couldn't bear it. And there were tears in
his eyes when he looked at her.

"I love you so much, and you were so brave,"
he said, trying to fight back tears unsuccessfully,
wishing things were different and not wanting
to scare her.

"Where are the babies?" she asked again.

"They're still in the delivery room," he said,
lying to her for the first time in their life together, but he knew he had to. She didn't have
to know yet, it was too cruel to have seen that
tiny angel's face and then learn that she was
gone so swiftly. Her brother looked so much
sturdier, so much better prepared for life than
his sister. "They'll be out soon." Brad lied again,
and she drifted off to sleep.

But there was no hiding the truth from her
the next morning. The doctor came in to tell her
with Brad, and for a moment, Brad thought the
shock was going to kill her. She grew deathly
pale and closed her eyes, and for a moment she
swooned as she sat in her bed, and Brad
reached out and caught her.

"No . . . tell me that's not true!" She
screamed at him, "You're lying!" She screamed
at her husband and the doctor. The doctor had
actually said the words, and he had told her
very simply. Her baby girl had died shortly af-

ter birth, from blood loss to her twin in twin to twin transfusion, complicated by undeveloped lungs. She simply could not have survived, he told her.

"That's not true!" She screamed hysterically. "You killed her! I saw her! She was alive . . . she looked at me. . . ."

"Yes, she did look at you, Mrs. Coleman," he said sadly. "But she never began adequately breathing. She never took a full breath. She never cried, and we did everything we could to save her."

"I want to see her," Pilar said, sobbing, and she tried to climb out of bed, but she found she was so weak, she couldn't. "I want to see her now. Where is she?" The two men exchanged glances, but the doctor was not against showing Pilar the child. They had done that many times before, sometimes it helped a family to see the child, and say good-bye. The baby was downstairs in the morgue, waiting for burial, but there was no reason why her mother couldn't see her. "I want you to take me to her."

"We'll bring her to a room in a little while," he said very gently, as Pilar leaned against her husband, sobbing and trying to absorb what had just happened. She had been so happy the night before, even for a moment, even as hideous as it had been, and now she was gone. She hadn't even gotten to hold her. "Would you like to see your son now?"

She started to shake her head, but then she looked at Brad and nodded. He looked so devastated, he was so overwhelmed by what happened to them, she knew she had no right to make it worse, but all she wanted to do was die, and join her baby.

"We'll bring him in," the doctor said, and returned a moment later with her strapping son. He weighed nine pounds, which was enormous for a twin. But his tiny sister had weighed less than four. He had gotten everything he needed to survive, at her expense, and she hadn't gotten enough. It had been a classic case of survival of the fittest.

"He's beautiful, isn't he?" she said sadly, almost as though he weren't there, and she didn't reach out her arms to hold him. She just sat staring at him, wondering why he had lived and his twin sister hadn't. Brad held him as they both looked at him, and then he placed him gently in his mother's arms, and she cried copiously as she kissed him.

And when at last the nurse took him away, she asked again to see her daughter.

They took her in a wheelchair to a room

downstairs, it was an empty room, and it was very cool, and everything about it was bleak and sterile. And a moment later they brought her in, still in her isolette, tightly wrapped in her blanket, her tiny face so sweet, so pure, she still looked to Brad as though she were sleeping.

"I want to hold her," she said to him, and he reached in carefully and placed her in her mother's arms, where she had never yet been, and Pilar sat quietly as she held her. She touched her eyes, her mouth, her cheeks, the tiny hands with her lips, and kissed each tiny finger, as though she hoped to breathe life into her. As though she could change what had happened the night before, because she couldn't accept it.

"I love you," she whispered softly to her, "I always will. I loved you before you were born, and I love you now, sweet baby."

She looked up at Brad then, and saw that he was crying uncontrollably, he just stood and shook with grief as he watched Pilar hold the baby. "I'm so sorry . . ." he said to her. "I'm so sorry. . . ."

"I want to name her Grace," Pilar said quietly, and gently touched his hand. "Grace Elizabeth Coleman." *Elizabeth* for her mother. Somehow that seemed right now. And all Brad could do was nod. He couldn't bear the thought that in the midst of so much joy, now they had to bury this baby.

Pilar sat for a long time, just holding her, and looking at her face, as though she needed to be sure she would always remember her . . . perhaps when they met again one day in Heaven. . . . And then at last the nurse came for her again, and they had to leave the baby, so she could go to the funeral home Brad had called early that morning.

"Good-bye, sweet angel," Pilar said, and kissed her again, and as they left the room, she felt her heart torn from her soul with a pain she would never know again. It was a piece of her rent from deep within, and gone to be buried with her baby.

When they went back upstairs, their baby boy was sound asleep in his bed in her room, and another nurse was waiting. She was somber-faced, knowing where they'd been, and she gently helped Pilar back into bed, and handed her her sleeping son.

"I don't want him now." Pilar shook her head and tried to send him away, but the nurse would not be dismissed and she put the child in the mother's arms and looked into her eyes firmly.

"He needs you, Mrs. Coleman . . . and you need him. . . ." And then she left the room, and left the little boy with his parents. They had fought long and hard for him, and he had come and brought with him both tragedy and blessing. But it wasn't his fault his sister had died. And as Pilar held him, she felt her heart soften. He was so sweet and round, so different than little Grace had been. He looked all boy . . . and she had looked like a tiny angel, a mere whisper of a child . . . a whisper gone back to God forever.

It was an odd day for them, a day of joy and grief, of anger and elation mixed with sorrow and disappointment, a rainbow of emotions none of them understood, but at least they were together. Nancy came and sobbed in Pilar's arms, unable even to tell her what she felt, but her tears said enough. And Tommy cried, too, and told them he was so sorry. Todd called, not having heard about Grace, and Brad cried terribly when he told him. And in a moment alone, Pilar called her mother and told her. And for the first time in her life, her mother truly surprised her. She wasn't the Good Doctor Graham, but the grandmother of a child who had died, the mother of a woman suffering terrible grief, and for almost an hour, they talked and

cried together. And she took Pilar's breath away
when she told Pilar of the son they'd had, who
had died of crib death before she was even
born.

"He was five months old. And in some ways I
don't think I was ever the same again. I always
blamed myself because I had been so busy after
he was born, I never spent enough time with
him. And then I got pregnant with you, and I
never dared get close to you. I was so afraid you
would die, too. I never wanted to care that
much about any human being again. Pilar . . .
darling . . . I'm so sorry. . . ." Her mother
sobbed, and Pilar cried uncontrollably. "I hope
you know how much I've always loved
you. . . ." She could barely speak through her
own tears, and Pilar choked on her emotions of
more than forty years as she listened.

"Oh, Mommy . . . I love you. . . . Why
didn't you ever tell me?"

"Your father and I never talked about it.
Things were different in those days. You weren't
supposed to talk about painful things. It was
embarrassing. We were all so stupid then. It
was the worst thing I ever went through, and I
had no one to talk to about it, and eventually I
just learned to live with the pain. It helped
when you were born, and I was glad you were a

girl. At least you were different. . . . His name was Andrew," she said softly. "We called him Andy. . . ." And as she said it, she sounded so sad and young, and Pilar's heart went out to her. She had lived with her grief for almost fifty years, and Pilar had never known. It explained a lot of things, and it was too late now for the little girl she had been, but it meant a lot to her now to hear what had happened.

"It won't go away easily," her mother said gently. "It'll take a long time . . . longer than you think you can bear. And it will never go away completely. You'll live with it every day, Pilar, or maybe you'll forget for a day or two, and then something will happen to remind you. But you just have to go on, day after day, moment after moment . . . for Brad's sake, for your own . . . for your little boy. . . . You have to go on, and the pain will fade eventually. But the scar will stay on your heart forever." They cried together again after that, and eventually, reluctantly this time, Pilar hung up the phone. But for the first time in her life, she felt as though she knew her mother. She had offered to come out for the funeral, but Pilar had asked her not to. She knew now how painful it would be for her, and she didn't want to put her through it. And for once, Elizabeth Graham didn't argue.

"But if you need me, I'll be there in six hours. You just remember that. I'm no further away than a phone call. I love you," she'd said again before she hung up, and Pilar felt as though she'd gotten a gift from her. It was just a shame it had to be provoked by so much tragedy.

And through it all, their son woke and slept, and cried for his mother, and whenever she or Brad held him, he was happy and quiet. It was as though he already knew them.

"What'll we call him?" Brad asked her that night. They had named Grace, but they hadn't named her brother.

"I like the name Christian Andrew. What do you think?" she said sadly. The middle name was for the brother she hadn't known about until that day, and she had told Brad after her mother had told her.

"I like it." He smiled through his tears. It felt as though they had been crying all day, and they had. The day they had waited for for so long had turned into a day of mourning.

"Life is a mixed blessing, isn't it?" she said quietly as Brad sat beside her that night. He didn't want to leave her, but she thought he should go home. He looked worse than exhausted. But he insisted he didn't want to leave her, and a nurse had wheeled a cot into the room in case he decided to stay. She thought they needed to be together.

"It's all so strange, you expect one thing and you get another, you pay a price for everything in life, I guess . . . the good, the bad, the dreams, the nightmares . . . it all comes rolled up together. Sometimes it's hard to tell them apart, that's the hard part." Christian was to be their joy, and Grace their sorrow, and yet they had come to them together. She had wanted children so badly finally, and now she had lost one before she even started. It seemed to taint everything, and yet when she looked at Christian sleeping quietly beside her, life seemed infinitely worth living. And as Brad looked at her, he wondered how she'd gotten through it. It had been the worst agony he'd ever seen, and then at the end of it all, they'd lost a baby.

"Life is full of surprises," Brad said philosophically. "I thought I'd never recover from it when Natalie died." She had been Nancy and Todd's mother. "And then suddenly there you were, five years later . . . and I've been so happy with you. Life has a way of blessing us once it's punished us. I imagine Christian will be that way too. We've been hit hard . . . but perhaps he will be the greatest joy we share for the rest of our lives."

"I hope so," she said softly, looking down at him, and trying to forget the little face she would never see again . . . the baby she would always remember.

CHAPTER
=== 20 ===

Christian cried lustily the day they left the hospital and took him home. Pilar dressed him before they left, in a little blue knit suit she had bought. She wrapped him carefully in a blue blanket and held him close to her, as a nurse rolled them downstairs in a wheelchair. A nurse's aide followed with a rolling table full of flowers. And all most people knew was that she had had the babies. No one knew that one of them died. And double everything had come in, in pink and blue, with little dolls and teddy bears and Raggedy Ann and Andy.

Brad drove them home, and they gently put Christian down in the bassinet in his room. Brad had already taken the second one out and put it in the garage. He didn't want Pilar to see it. But she knew it had been there, and when she opened the drawers to put the baby's night-gown on, she found the little pink ones, too, and she felt as though her heart were being squeezed as she closed the drawers. She almost couldn't bear it. So much sadness and so much joy all at once. It was impossible to forget that there had been two babies, and now there was only one. How would she ever forget her?

Christian was a good baby and easy to feed. Her milk had come in copiously, as though even her body wasn't aware that there were no longer two babies. And she held him as she nursed and sat in the rocking chair in his room and Brad watched her.

"Are you going to be okay?" he asked quietly. He was worried about her. She hadn't been the same since the babies had been born and Grace had died. And he was almost sorry they'd had them. It was just so painful.

"I don't know," she answered honestly, as she held the sleeping baby. And then she looked down at him, he was so perfect and so small, and yet so round and healthy. He was every-thing Grace hadn't been, with her tiny features and miniature face. She had looked perfect, too, but infinitely smaller. "I keep trying to under-stand why it happened. Was it my fault? Was it something I did? Did I eat wrong, did I lie on one side all the time. . . . Why?" Her eyes filled with tears again as she looked at her husband, and he stood next to her as they looked down at Christian.

"We have to be careful not to blame him," Brad said, "not to make him feel later on that he somehow wasn't enough, and we wanted more. I suppose this is just what was meant to be," he said, and bent down to kiss her, and then Christian. He was a beautiful child and he had a right to a life of joy, not to the burden of having come into the world as a mixed blessing.

"I don't blame him," Pilar said sadly, crying openly. "I just wish she were here too." But perhaps she would be, in some way, a sweet presence, a loving spirit. It was so little to hold on to.

Pilar slept fitfully, and in the morning, she woke up feeling as though someone had dropped a ten-thousand-pound weight on her chest. She remembered what they were doing that day.

She showered, and fed the baby as soon as he woke up. Her breasts felt huge, and she had so much milk that she sprayed his face at first when he tried to eat, and he made such funny faces at her that she laughed in spite of the way she felt, and Brad heard her.

"What's going on in here?" he asked, as he came into the nursery wearing a dark suit. It was the first time she had laughed in days and it was a relief to hear her.

She showed him and he laughed too. "He looks like one of those little old actors in vaudeville getting it in the face from a seltzer bottle, doesn't he? . . . kind of like Harpo Marx."

"Actually," Brad said, smiling, "I think he looks a little like Zeppo." He was surprised by how much he felt for him, how much he already loved him, and how sorry he was that he had come into the world without his sister. He seemed so innocent and so dependent on them —Brad couldn't remember his other children being quite so small, or so needy, or perhaps even the baby felt that something terrible had happened. Where was she? He had lived with his sister for nine months, and now she was gone. It had to be traumatic for him too. Even he wasn't exempt from the pain they were feeling.

"Will you be dressed soon?" Brad asked gently. She nodded as she set down the sleeping baby after he'd eaten. It would have been so perfect if there had only been him, it would have been such undiluted ecstasy, and now it was so different. It was half happy and half sad, half agony and half beauty, everything was so bittersweet and so tender to the touch. She couldn't bear feeling anymore, and she stood looking at him for a long time, thinking how much she already loved him. But she had loved Gracie too . . . that was the amazing thing. She had known her little face the moment she arrived and it was carved in her heart for eternity, just as her name was.

She wore a simple black wool dress, which hung from her shoulders with no waist, that she had worn to the office when she was first pregnant. Black stockings, black shoes, and she found a black coat that fit, and then she stood mournfully and looked at her husband.

"It seems wrong somehow, doesn't it? We should be celebrating and instead we're mourning." And there were so many people to tell, everyone they knew had known they were having twins, and now they would have to be told they didn't.

Brad put the baby in the car, and he never woke when they put him in his car seat. And they drove to All Saints by the Sea Episcopal Church in Montecito in total silence. There was nothing Pilar could say to him, nothing that would take away the pain, or make it any different. He patted her hand when he parked the car, and Nancy and Tommy were waiting on the sidewalk with Marina. Tommy was wearing a dark suit, like Brad, and Nancy looked devastated as she held her baby. She hadn't been able to find a baby-sitter, so in the end she just brought Adam. And he screamed with glee the moment he saw Pilar and Brad. For an instant, it lightened the moment.

The minister was also waiting for them, and he had led them inside, but Pilar was in no way prepared for what she saw there, the tiny white casket surrounded by lily of the valley, waiting at the altar. It was a travesty, a lie, a cruel joke that Nature had played on her, first promising her so much, and then taking away half of it, and a sob caught in her throat the moment she saw it.

"I can't bear it," she whispered to Brad as she dropped her face into her hands, and Nancy began to cry softly, while Tommy took the baby, and Christian lay sleeping peacefully in his car seat. They were the ways of God, the minister reminded them, to give and to take, to laugh and to cry, to mingle joy with sorrow, but the pain of it was almost too great to bear as he blessed the little girl who had been theirs for only a moment.

Afterward, Pilar felt as though she were in a dream, a nightmare, as she followed Brad outside, and they followed the hearse to the cemetery. At the gravesite they stood silent and miserable in the rain, as Pilar began to panic.

"I can't leave her here. . . ." She choked on the words as she clung to Brad, and Brad's son-in-law stood near them, with Marina close to them, but at a discreet distance. Nancy had stayed in the car with both little boys, she just couldn't stand it anymore, she had told her husband. It was too awful, too sad, that tiny box, and their ravaged faces. It was a terrible time for all of them, particularly Pilar and Brad. He looked a thousand years old, and she looked as though she were going to collapse as the minister gave little Grace a final blessing.

Pilar put a small bouquet of tiny pink roses on her casket and stood staring at it for a long time, sobbing softly, and then Brad led her away and back to the car, but she almost didn't seem to know where she was going. And then she sat staring straight ahead as they drove home, and she said nothing. Brad and Marina held her hands, but she had nothing to say to them, or anyone.

Brad didn't know what to say to her, he didn't know how to comfort her or what to do. Even though Brad felt the loss when Grace was born, she had been a stranger to him. But Pilar had carried them for nine months, and she knew them intimately in a way no one else did.

"I want you to lie down," he said as they got home after they'd dropped everyone else off. And the baby began to stir when he put him in his basket.

She nodded and went to their bedroom, and she lay there in her black dress, saying nothing and staring at the ceiling, wondering why she couldn't have died, and they have lived. Why wasn't one given different choices? Who would she have chosen? What would she have done? She knew in an instant that she would have gladly sacrificed herself to save them. She tried explaining that to Brad and he looked horrified. As much as he mourned their lost child, he would never have wanted to lose his wife, and he was furious at the suggestion.

"Don't you realize how much we need you?"

"No, you don't," she said bleakly.

"What about him?" He motioned to the next

room. "Don't you think he has the right to a mother?" She shrugged, unable to answer. "Don't talk like that," he said. But she was depressed all day, she wouldn't eat, she wouldn't drink, it affected her milk eventually, and it made the baby fussy. It was as though they all wanted to cry and object to what had happened to them, and none of them knew how, least of all Pilar, who wanted to scream until she couldn't breathe anymore, but instead, she just sat and stared at Christian.

"He needs you, and so do I," Brad reminded her again. "You have to pull yourself together."

"Why?" She sat and looked out the window, and then finally he got her to drink some tea, and then a cup of soup, and at least she had enough milk to feed the baby.

She got up with him several times that night, as Brad slept. It had been an exhausting day for him, too, and he was desperately worried about Pilar. And as the sun came up, she sat in the rocking chair, holding Christian, and thinking about both her babies. They had been separate entities, separate people, separate lives, each with their own destiny and future. Christian had had his own fate to fulfill, and Gracie's mission had been accomplished early. Perhaps it was as simple as that, perhaps she was destined to be with them only for a moment. But suddenly Pilar realized that she had to let her go, that she had to touch her memory now and then, but she could not take her with her. And Brad was right, Christian needed her. Hopefully, he would have a long life with them, and she wanted to be there beside him. For the first time in five days, she felt at peace as she sat holding him. The blessing was theirs, not as they had expected it, or thought it would be, but as it was meant to be, and as it was, and she had to accept it.

"You up?" Brad stood sleepily in the doorway. He had looked for her in their bed, and he hadn't found her. "Everything okay?"

She nodded and smiled at him, looking very wise, and very sad, and also very lovely. "I love you," she said quietly, and he sensed that something had changed in her, something deep inside had broken and torn, and almost ripped her apart, and now slowly it had begun healing.

"I love you too." He wanted to tell her how sorry he was, but he didn't know how to tell her anymore. There were no words, just very deep feelings.

And then suddenly Christian stirred. He

yawned and then opened his eyes and looked at them very intently.

"He's quite a guy," Brad said proudly.

"So are you," Pilar said as they kissed in the morning sunlight.

CHAPTER
21

Todd came home to them for Thanksgiving that year. He wanted to see the baby, who was two and a half weeks old, and he also knew what an ordeal they'd been through and he wanted to be there with them.

Pilar already looked a little better by then, although she still had a lot of weight to lose, and she wasn't going out yet. She was still weak, and drained by the ordeal, and she didn't feel ready to face her friends and start explaining. It was still too painful.

Todd didn't know what to say to her about it at first, and then eventually he told her he was sorry they had lost the baby.

"What a miserable thing to go through." His dad had seemed very shaken up when he'd called to tell him of Christian's birth, and Gracie dying, but Pilar was taking it much harder.

"It was awful," she admitted quietly, though the wounds were healing slowly. She still felt a terrible ache when she thought of her, but she was beginning to allow herself to enjoy Christian. She was talking to her mother more frequently, and some of what she'd told her of her own experience had helped Pilar. It helped talking to someone who'd been through it, but she still didn't want her to come out. She didn't feel up to seeing anyone, not even her mother.

"Nothing's ever as simple as it looks," Pilar said quietly to Todd, thinking of what agony it had been to get pregnant, and then her miscarriage . . . and now Gracie. "You think it's all going to be so easy, and just the way you plan, but sometimes it isn't. It's taken me forty-four years to figure that one out, and believe me, it hasn't been easy." Childbearing had not been the easiest thing she'd done so far. Her career had been a great deal simpler, and even marrying Brad. But somehow, she knew in her heart of hearts that all of this was worth it. She wouldn't have given up Christian for anything. And even at the price she'd paid, she knew he was worth it, at twice the price, although even thinking that amazed her. "What are you two doing? Solving the problems of life?" Brad teased as he sat down next to them.

"I was about to tell him how much I love him." Pilar smiled at her stepson and then her husband. "He's a very special person."

"That's a nice change after being a pretty rotten kid." He grinned. He was a handsome boy, and he looked a lot like Brad.

"You were okay," Brad conceded half-heartedly, but with a teasing smile. "And you're not bad now. How's Chicago?"

"Okay. But I've been thinking of coming back to the West Coast. Maybe getting a job in L.A. or San Francisco."

"Boy, would that be rotten luck!" his father teased again and Pilar smiled broadly.

"We'd love to have you back out here."

"I could baby-sit on weekends."

"Don't hold your breath," his sister advised Pilar as she joined them. "Every time he stays with us, he sleeps right through Adam's screams, lets him play with the phone, and feeds him beer to 'keep him mellow.'"

"Yeah, and he loves it, right? Who's his favorite uncle?"

"He doesn't have a lot of choice there, does he?" his sister razzed him.

A little while later Christian woke up and

shouted loudly for his mother. She went to feed
him, and when she came back, the young people were ready to leave, and Todd kissed her
and held her in a warm hug.

"You look great, and my brother is gorgeous."

"So are you. I'm glad you came home." He
looked down at her and nodded, and he was
glad too. They looked like they'd been through
a lot, especially his dad, who seemed to have
aged, and was obviously still desperately worried about her, but they seemed to be doing
okay. And Pilar was sad, but she seemed to be
coping.

"Do you think they'll do it again?" Todd
asked his sister after they left, and were driving
back to her place in the car.

"I doubt it," Nancy said, and then added con-
fidentially. "A friend of mine went to a fertility
specialist in L.A. and she said she saw them
there. They never said anything to me, but I
don't think Pilar had such an easy time getting
pregnant. They kind of acted like it was a big
surprise, but I don't think it was. I think it was
hard work. And now they've had such a hard
time with the baby dying."

Todd nodded. He was sorry for Pilar, he had
always liked her.

"I don't know," he said after a while, "I guess

they must think it's worth it." And as he said it, he glanced over at his chubby little nephew fast asleep in his car seat in the backseat beside him. "Maybe it is . . . who knows?"

And then, as Nancy glanced into the backseat at her sleeping son, she nodded.

In Santa Monica, Beth had cooked an enormous turkey, and she was basting it for the last time when Charlie arrived with a huge chocolate turkey for Annie, and flowers for her to use as a centerpiece for their Thanksgiving table.

"Wow! What's all this?" she exclaimed, looking surprised and touched. He was always so thoughtful. They had been seeing each other for nine months, and she had never known anyone like him. He cooked, he brought presents, he bought groceries for them, he took them out, he sat for hours reading to Annie. He was just the kind of person Beth had always dreamed of and never found. He was a dream come true, and Annie absolutely loved him.

"Happy Thanksgiving, you two." He smiled as he set the flowers down, and Annie immediately began to take the brightly colored foil off the chocolate turkey.

"Can I eat it now?" she asked excitedly, and

her mother told her she could have one bite, and then she had to save the rest till after dinner. She made the most of the one bite, and took off the gobbler's head, while Charlie kissed her mother.

"Can I help?" he offered, but she said everything was done. She wanted to cook for him this time, and it was the most elaborate meal she had cooked in years. Usually she and Annie went out and either ate at a restaurant, or at friends', it depressed her too much to cook for just the two of them on Thanksgiving. But this year there was so much to be grateful for. Everything had been so happy for them ever since Charlie had come into their lives. He seemed to chase the bad times away, and make everything right with them again. He made her feel as though someone cared, and she wasn't alone anymore. She didn't feel the weight of the world on her shoulders.

When Annie was sick, he came and helped take care of her, and when she had trouble with her landlord, she talked to him, and during a strike at the hospital, he had even lent her money. She had paid every penny of it back as soon as she went back to work, she didn't like taking advantage of him, but he was just an incredibly kind person.

And that fall he had gotten involved with one of the orphans' homes and he was still playing ball with a bunch of kids every Saturday morning. And afterward, he would talk about what they meant to him, and how he'd still like to adopt a little boy, when he felt he'd saved up enough money.

She had never been as much in love with anyone in her life, and he was so good to her, but he never even hinted at the possibility of a future. He still felt he had no right to marry anyone, since he couldn't have children. But she always told him she didn't care, and even if he didn't marry her, she thought he had a right to know that there were women who would think themselves lucky to have him, with or without babies.

"What's the big deal about that?" she had asked the last time they'd discussed it, one night after Annie was in bed, and they had made love. Their sex life was extraordinary, and it was always hard to believe he couldn't have children. But she also knew that one did not guarantee the other. "I don't know why you make such a big deal about it," she chided him, "lots of people can't have kids. So what? What if it were me? Would you feel different about me?"

For the first time, he thought about it, and he had to admit he wouldn't. "I'd be sorry, because you're so good with them, you should have kids . . . but I'd still love you," he said gently, and then they'd gone on to other things. There always seemed to be so much to talk about when they were together.

On Thanksgiving, the three of them chatted constantly all through dinner. The turkey was great, and so were the mashed potatoes and the peas and the stuffing. She had gone all-out for him, just as he always did for her, and she sheepishly admitted that she thought his cooking was better.

"Not on your life," he said, smiling, "this was fantastic." And the best part of it was that they were together.

Afterward, the three of them went for a long walk, and Annie scampered ahead of them and then ran back to them, and by the time they got home again, she was pleasantly exhausted.

They put her to bed at eight o'clock, and then watched TV, and Charlie made popcorn and it was delicious. And halfway through the first show, he began feeling amorous, and they lay on the couch and made out, like two kids, until they completely forgot whatever it was that they'd been watching. Annie was sound asleep by then, and they tiptoed into Beth's room, and quietly locked the door, and a moment later they lay naked in each other's arms, overwhelmed with passion.

"God, Charlie . . ." Beth tried to catch her breath afterward. "How do you do that to me?" It had never been that way before, with anyone. And it was wonderful for him, too, because he loved her so much, and wanted her, and this time he knew his trust was well placed and she wouldn't hurt him. He had been dazzled by Barbie three years before, but she had been the wrong girl for him and now he knew that. He knew a lot of things now, and he saw things differently than he had even six months before. Beth had changed his life, and even his views about having children. She had made him realize how he would feel about her if it were she who couldn't have children. And suddenly he had realized that it really wouldn't matter to him at all, that he would love her anyway, and that she had a right to a full life, whether or not they had children. It didn't seem to matter so much anymore, and he stopped feeling guilty about what he couldn't do and couldn't have and couldn't offer her. There was so much he could offer her, and now he wanted to, more than ever.

"I want to ask you something," he said that night as he lay holding her, and she turned her face up to his, and he smiled, thinking how much she looked like Annie. "I want to tell you how much I love you, first," and as he said it, she trembled. She knew that he felt he could never marry her, or anyone, and she wondered if he was about to tell her that he was moving on, that it had been nice, but it was over. She felt her body shake as tears filled her eyes, and she knew she didn't want to hear what he was saying.

"You don't have to say anything," she said, hoping to discourage him. "You know I love you." She lay there praying he wouldn't tell her what she feared, but he looked so sober as he lay turned toward her on her bed.

"There's something I want to ask you."

"Why?" Her big blue eyes looked enormous.

"Because you're important to me, and I don't have a right just to tie up your life, as though I owned it."

"Don't be silly . . . I . . . we have a good time together. I'd rather be with you than any-where . . . Charlie, don't—"

"Don't what?" He looked startled.

"Don't go." She wrapped her arms around his

neck and started to cry like a little girl, and he looked at her in amazement.

"Do I look like I'm going anywhere? This wasn't about going, it was about staying." He smiled, touched by her reaction.

"You're staying?" She looked stunned, as she pulled away from him, her face covered with tears and her eyes filled with emotion.

"I'd like to. I'd like you to stay too. I was going to ask you"—He hesitated for a beat, and then went on—"Will you marry me, Beth?"

She grinned from ear to ear, and kissed him so hard it made the bed shake. "Yes, I will," she said breathlessly when they came up for air, and he rolled over in the bed with her, laughing with excitement.

"Oh, wow! I love you! When? . . ." And then, he looked worried. "Are you sure? Even though we can't have kids?" He wanted to be sure, just one last time, she had a right to refuse him.

"I thought we were going to adopt," she said calmly.

"We were? When did we say that?"

"You said you wanted to adopt a little boy, maybe even two."

"But that was if I stayed single. Now I have

you and Annie. Would you be willing to adopt, Beth?"

"I think I'd like that." She nodded pensively, and then looked at him. "It would give a home to someone who really needs one, instead of just adding another baby to the world. . . . Yes, I really would like that. . . ."

"Talk to me about getting married first. When?"

"I don't know." She grinned. "Tomorrow. Next week. I have a week's vacation coming before Christmas."

"Christmas," he beamed, "and never mind the vacation. I want you to quit that job, I don't want you working nights after we're married. You can work part time somewhere while Annie's in school, or get that R.N. degree you want." It would only take her a year in school, and he could manage the rest, he was doing really well on commissions. "Christmas it is." He smiled as he looked at her, and pulled her closer to him again, and in a moment their bodies confirmed it.

CHAPTER
══ 22 ══

Charlie and Beth were married on Christmas Day at United Methodist Church in Westwood, and Annie was their only attendant. They had a tiny reception at a local restaurant with a few friends. Mark was there, of course, with his newest girlfriend, and it was exactly what they had wanted. No showy event at the Bel Air, no jazzy guests. He had no one to show off to. He had a real woman and a real life, and a little girl who was his now. They had already talked about Charlie adopting her, and she said she wanted to be Annie Winwood.

The three of them went to San Diego on their honeymoon. They went to the zoo, and visited the naval base, and stayed at a pretty little hotel Charlie knew, and they went for long walks on the beach. It was exactly what he had always dreamed, and never found before. Until Beth changed everything for him.

She had quit her job, and gotten a job in the office at Annie's school. Everything had worked out perfectly. And she wanted to go back to school for her nursing degree in September.

"Are you as happy as I am?" Charlie asked her as they walked on the beach in their bare feet the day after Christmas. It was a glorious day, and the sand was cool, but it was warm enough for Annie to go barefoot. And she was having a great time running ahead of them and running back, like a puppy.

"I think I'm happier." Beth smiled. "I've never had anything like this. My life was such a mess the last time I got married. I was stupid and young, and he was such a bastard. I never got anything decent out of that whole mess."

"Yes, you did"—he smiled, reminding her—"you got Annie."

"That's true. I guess there's a blessing in everything. But sometimes it takes a long time to see it." He still wasn't sure about the blessing he had gotten out of his marriage to Barbie. That had been so disappointing. But at least it was over, and now he had a real life to look forward to with Beth. It was a life that offered him everything he wanted, companionship, tenderness, honesty, love.

"I just hope I can make you as happy as you've made me," he said as he put an arm around her shoulders, and she smiled, she felt so safe when he was beside her.

"You already have," she said softly, as Annie waved them on.

"Come on!" she shouted in the breeze. "Wait till you see the sea shells!" They smiled and ran after her, chasing each other down the beach and laughing, as the sun rose in the winter sky and seemed to smile down on them with a blessing.

Christmas at the Goodes was chaotic, as usual, only this year slightly more so. Gayle and Sam and their husbands and broods were there, and Andy and Diana had come back to the fold to spend Christmas with them, with Hilary, of course, and Diana was eight and a half months pregnant. She lumbered around, trying to chase Hilary as she pulled herself to a standing position everywhere and endangered her life with whatever she found on the coffee table.

"She's a handful, isn't she?" her mother commented admiringly. She was a beautiful baby and a happy little girl, and the source of endless joy to Andy and Diana. Everyone remembered the fact that they hadn't been there the year before, their marriage had almost been on the rocks, and they had gone to Hawaii to try to repair it. It was after that, Diana had reminded him just the other day with a wry look, that Wanda the surrogate had wandered into their lives and out again just as quickly. But the separation that had resulted had done them both good. And then suddenly there was Hilary in their lives, and now their own baby. It made their heads swim, but Diana had never been happier in her life. The pregnancy had gone well, and she was feeling terrific.

She had extended her maternity leave, of course, and the magazine was giving her until June to return now.

"How's it going?" Jack asked amiably as he watched her and his wife set the table, while Sam tried to settle a violent dispute between her two older children.

"Fine." Diana smiled, she still remembered the day he had told her she was pregnant and she thought he was crazy.

"Any day, I'd say."

"I'm not due for almost three weeks," she said knowingly, and he shook his head and frowned, pondering her stomach, and then gently felt it like a large melon.

"I'd say you're a lot closer than you think, Di. It's practically between your knees. How long's it been since you've seen your doctor?"

"Oh, for chrissake, Jack," his wife growled at him, "stop playing Dr. Kildare, it's Christmas."

"I'm just telling her she's closer than she thinks, the baby's dropped, and I'll bet you anything the head's engaged."

"Yeah, that's what you told me, and I was two and a half weeks late."

"All right." He shrugged, throwing his hands in the air. "So I'm human." And then he turned to Diana seriously again. "I'm serious. You ought to go in, in the next few days, to get checked, I really think it's dropped. I've never seen a baby so low on a woman who wasn't in labor."

"Maybe I am and I don't know it." She laughed at him, and then she reassured him that she was seeing her doctor on Monday.

"Stranger things have happened." He laughed, and then went to share a drink with his father-in-law. He was off call and could let his hair down.

The girls helped their mother as usual, and when the bird was cooked, the men carved it,

and huge platters of food went out to the dining
room. Everyone was in a good mood this year,
the children were lively but well behaved, there
were no family feuds, and everyone had long
since forgiven Diana for her Thanksgiving outburst the year before. Once they realized what
had been happening to her, they all understood
it. Even Gayle seemed to soften toward her sister.

"You're not eating anything," her older sister
said, as she glanced at Diana across the table.

"No room." She smiled, and then glanced at
Andy. He was having a good time, talking to
Seamus. Their Irish brother-in-law always had
wild stories to tell about someone. They were
usually not true, but they were always funny.

And when their mother went to put seconds
on the trays, Diana went out to the kitchen to
help her. She said her back ached and she
needed to get up. And as she went into the
kitchen, Andy noticed that she looked distracted. And then he saw Jack watching her and
wondered. She was rubbing her back again
when she came back, and made several trips
back to the kitchen to help her mother, and Sam
whispered softly to Jack, "She's awfully rest-
less." He nodded and went back to his dinner,
chatting with everyone at the table. And a few

minutes later, Diana was back in her chair and she seemed fine. She was laughing and talking, and then suddenly she stopped, and glanced at her husband. But he didn't see her watching him. She excused herself then and went upstairs, and a few minutes later she came back, and said nothing.

It was after dessert that she said to Sam that she wasn't feeling so great and she was going upstairs to lie down, but not to tell anyone. It was just indigestion.

And it was another hour later when Andy looked around for his wife and couldn't find her. "Has anyone seen Di?"

"She's upstairs throwing up," her oldest niece supplied, and Andy hurried upstairs to find her.

"Do you think you should go up too?" Gayle asked her husband, and he teased her.

"I thought you told me to mind my own business."

"Maybe I was wrong."

"She probably ate too much. They'll call me if they need me. And even if she is going into labor, this is her first baby. She could walk to the hospital from here, and still have plenty of time."

"Very funny. You know how I am." She had barely made it to the hospital for her first two, and he had delivered her last one in their kitchen.

"Everyone's different," he reminded her, and Diana had certainly proved that by seeming to be sterile, and taking two years to get pregnant.

But Andy came downstairs a few minutes later, looking worried. "She says she's sick to her stomach," he said to Jack quietly. "She threw up a few times, and now she says she has terrible cramps. I thought I should take her home, but she doesn't want to move. She said she hurt her back helping Mom with dinner." Jack listened, and took the stairs in twos on his way up to Diana as Andy followed.

"Hi, there," Jack said cheerfully to her, "I hear you've been attacked by a wild turkey."

"I feel awful," she admitted, and as she said it, she winced and held her huge belly.

"What kind of awful?" he asked calmly, but he already knew, and he was stunned when he felt her stomach. It was as hard as rock and she was having a huge contraction.

"I feel sick, and I've got awful cramps . . . and my back . . ." She rolled away then, and clutched the bed as she had another pain. "I think I have food poisoning . . . but don't tell Mom. . . ." She looked pale as she turned to face him again and he smiled.

"I don't think so. I think you're in labor."

"Now?" She looked stunned and a little frightened. "But it's not time."

"Looks to me like it is." And as he said it, she had another contraction. He timed this one and it was long and hard, and he wondered how fast they were coming. But in another two minutes he had his answer. He frowned as he glanced from her to Andy. "How long have you been having these?"

"I don't know," Diana said vaguely, "I've sort of had cramps all day. I just thought it was something I ate. . . ." She looked embarrassed now, realizing that she hadn't known she was in labor.

"No sign of your waters breaking?" She was much further along than he thought, and he wished he could examine her, but he wasn't sure she'd let him.

"No," she said firmly in answer to his question. "Just this little trickle of something since yesterday morning, but no real gush of water," she said, anxious to prove him wrong. She still remembered what Jane had gone through when Hilary was born, and she was scared now.

Jack looked at Andy, and then at Di and smiled. "Sweet girl, that *was* your water. It doesn't have to be a gush. I think we'd better get you to the hospital right now."

But as he said it she grabbed his arm, and almost shouted, "No! . . . no! This is nothing. . . ." But she was in such pain she couldn't talk through the contraction this time, and she didn't seem to hear them. She was panting and out of breath when it ended, and the next one came less than a minute later, and she cried as she tried to struggle. "Oh, God . . . what is this . . . Andy . . . Jack . . ." Jack hurried into the bathroom to wash his hands, and came back with a stack of towels which he quickly put beneath her, and then he gently checked her and she didn't even seem to notice as she grabbed Andy's arm and cried. She was fighting each pain and she couldn't get control of what she was feeling. And then suddenly, there was a terrible burning sensation, and an unbearable pushing like an express train trying to push through her. "Oh, God . . . it's coming . . . it's coming. . . ." She looked panicky as she looked from her husband to her brother-in-law, and Jack nodded and glanced at Andy.

"Yes, it is, Di . . ." She was clearly about to have the baby. And he spoke very calmly to her husband. "Andy, dial 911. Call an ambulance, tell them there's a woman giving birth here, and that there's a physician present. She's fine, everything's going smoothly. She was probably in mild labor since yesterday and didn't know it."

"Don't leave me," she cried as Andy started to go, but Jack nodded firmly and urged him to make the phone call. And as soon as Andy left the room, she had yet another powerful pain and the express train seemed to run through her again. Jack had pushed her legs wide apart by then, and he could already see the baby crowning.

"Push, Di . . . come on . . . push that baby out . . ."

"I can't . . . it hurts too much . . . oh, God . . . it won't stop . . . it won't stop . . ." She wanted it to stop but it wouldn't, and then Andy was with her again, and he told Jack that the ambulance was coming. And no one downstairs knew yet what was going on. There hadn't been time to tell them.

"Push, Di," Jack told her when the contraction started again. They were a minute apart now, and then suddenly as she groaned horribly and Jack held her legs and Andy her shoulders, the baby almost flew out of her, and into Jack's hands. He was a huge baby boy, with a shock of blond hair, and he looked amazingly like his baby sister. Diana looked down at him in amazement and he looked at her, and his father laughed. He was the most beautiful sight he'd ever seen.

Diana let her head fall back onto the bed, as she smiled up at her husband and told him how much she loved him. "He's so beautiful . . . and he looks like you." And then she looked at Jack with a shaky grin. "I guess maybe you were right . . ." All three of them laughed and the baby let out a wail as his uncle held him. And just as he did, they could hear the sirens outside.

"You'd better go explain," Jack said to Andy, who was still in shock from what had just happened. They had come for Christmas dinner, and they were going home with a baby. Nothing ever happened exactly as they planned it.

Andy hurried downstairs and told everyone they had a son, just as his father-in-law opened the front door to the paramedics.

"She's up here," Andy called, and everyone looked at him in amazement.

"Is she all right?" her father asked as her mother and sisters hurried up the stairs, and Seamus slapped Andy on the back.

"You don't do things by halves, lad, do you?"

"I guess not."

Jack had cleaned her up by then, and he cut the cord with the instruments the paramedics had brought, and a moment later she and the baby were well wrapped up on a stretcher and on their way out the door to the ambulance, with everyone running beside them and wishing them well. Andy thanked Jack, and Diana waved. It had been worse than she thought, and in some ways better. At least it had been quick, but it had been so intense that it had surprised her.

And then they were in the ambulance, and Sam had promised to take Hilary home with her until Diana got back from the hospital with the baby.

"You people certainly keep things lively around here," their father murmured as he closed the door after they'd left, and he broke out the champagne, and poured for everyone, even a little to the children.

"To Andrew and Diana, and their children," he toasted solemnly, and his wife had tears in her eyes, knowing how hard it had been for them. But now they had two beautiful children.

"He's the cutest thing I've ever seen," Diana whispered to Andy in the ambulance as she held the baby to her chest, wrapped in blankets.

He was looking around with huge eyes filled with curiosity and interest. He was very alert, and he seemed very peaceful.

"Wait till Hilary sees him," Andy said and they exchanged a smile. They had had two babies in nine months, from destitution to abundance almost in a single moment.

She and the baby only stayed in the hospital overnight, and the next day they were home again, with Hilary. And they named the baby William, after her father.

"Billy and Hillie," Diana teased as she watched him sleeping in a crib in the corner of their bedroom. Suddenly they were surrounded by the little people they had wanted for so long, it seemed a plethora of blessings.

"You're terrific," Andy whispered as he kissed her.

"So are you." She kissed him back, the agony forgotten, the emptiness, the sorrow. And yet she knew that all of it had made this moment infinitely more precious.

CHAPTER
23

ndy and Diana spent their third anniversary in Hawaii, on the beach at Waikiki
with their children.

Hilary was fourteen months old by then and
toddling everywhere, and discovering everything. She loved the sand and the ocean and her
parents, and her baby brother William. He was
a fat, healthy five and a half month old by then,
cooing and gurgling and laughing. And the two
of them were a handful. They were keeping Diana busy night and day and she was due to go
back to her job at *Today's Home* in two weeks,
but only part time. She still wasn't sure she
wanted to leave her children at all, but she also
wanted to give Andy a hand. With two children
to support suddenly, they could use the money.

And even working part time would mean sacrificing some of the luxuries they liked, but Diana just didn't want to give up her time with the kids to go back to work full time, and Andy agreed with her completely. They had waited too long for this for her to miss it. She was already dreading the hours she'd be away from them, and she had just hired someone to come in and take care of them the days she'd be working. She was a nice German girl, who had been an au pair before, looked clean and neat, and spoke decent English. And she was only going to work for them while Diana was working. The rest of the time, Diana wanted to take care of her children herself, and Andy wanted to help her.

He had gotten a promotion at the network that year, and he had his hands as full at the office, but he loved coming home to them, and seeing the look of contentment on her face, knowing that their dreams had come true, even on the days that the washing machine broke down and there were diapers everywhere, and Hilary had made new murals in their bedroom with Diana's lipstick. Life would be full of that for a few years, but they both had a sense of how precious it was, and how fleeting.

"What beautiful children you have," a woman

from Ohio said to them on the beach in Hawaii
one afternoon. "How old are they?"

"Five and fourteen months," Diana smiled
and the woman looked at her in amazement.
They were even closer than her own, who had
been thirteen months apart, and they had kept
her plenty busy.

"You don't know how lucky you are to have
children so easily," she told them seriously.
"You have a wonderful family. God bless you."

"Thank you," Diana said with a long, slow
smile at her husband.

In June, Charlie took Beth and Annie to Rose-
mead one afternoon, and they drove down a
quiet street toward an ominous-looking brick
building. He had waited for this day for a long
time, and he said nothing as he parked the car.
But Beth touched his hand, she knew, and Annie sensed that this was an important moment.
She knew what was happening, and why they
had come, but Beth wasn't totally sure that she
understood it.

They were ushered inside and asked to sit
down. The paperwork had been started six
months before, and everything appeared to be
in order.

Charlie and Beth had already come here several times for counselling, and meetings. The institution was run by nuns, and they still wore the old habit. And just being here brought back painful memories for Charlie. He had been in too many institutions just like this one. He still remembered the sound of their beads as they walked, and the cold dark nights in a narrow bed, the terrible nightmares he had, and the constant fear that he would be suffocated by asthma. Just being here made it hard for him to breathe, and instinctively he reached out for Beth's and Annie's hands as they waited.

"Have you ever been here before?" Annie asked in a loud whisper, and he nodded. "I don't like it."

"No one does, sweetheart. That's why we're here." They were going to save one soul from this lonely prison.

They had met the child before, and Charlie's heart had gone out to him the moment they saw him. He was four years old, and very small, the nuns had said. He had respiratory problems when he was born, and they were sorry to tell Mr. Winwood that he had asthma. If that didn't suit him, of course, there was a little girl . . . but the nuns had been startled to hear that it suited the Winwoods to perfection.

The social workers had checked Beth and Charlie out, and they'd even spoken to Annie, and they were satisfied that the boy would have a good home. He wasn't a baby, of course, and this could be difficult, they would have to expect a period of adjustment.

"We know all that," Charlie had said gently. He knew all of it, how desperately he had tried, how he had cooked and cleaned for them, and begged them to love him. And how they had always taken him back, eventually, and how it felt to be back in the iron bed on the lumpy mattress in the cold drafty dormitories he was so afraid of.

A door opened and two nuns stepped out, Charlie could hear their beads, but when he looked up they had gentle faces, and as their Dominican robes swung, he saw the small child just behind them. He was a thin, pale little boy in corduroy pants, an old navy blue sweater and faded sneakers. He had bright red hair, and he looked at each of them with quiet terror. All morning he had hidden in his room, terrified they wouldn't come. He already knew that people never did what they promised. The nuns had told him that the Winwoods were coming that day, but he didn't believe them. And he knew they were taking him somewhere, but he wasn't sure where, or for how long he was staying.

"The Winwoods are here for you," the taller of the two nuns said quietly, as Bernie nodded. They had actually come for him. He still couldn't believe it.

He looked questioningly at all three of them, as though he didn't quite believe his eyes, as Charlie walked slowly toward him.

"Hi, Bernie," Annie said softly, and he wheezed. He had been having asthma attacks for days before and he was scared to death they would change their minds if they knew it.

Charlie watched him with tears in his eyes, and then he held out his arms, and the boy came slowly to him. "We're taking you home with us . . . to stay forever and ever. I want to be your dad . . . and this is your mom now . . . and Annie is your sister."

"Like a real family? *Forever?*" The child looked at him with wide eyes filled with suspicion. They had told him as much, but at four, he hadn't totally understood it, nor did he believe them. He was just hoping they'd come and take him out again. That was all he wanted.

"That's right," Charlie said calmly, feeling his heart flutter within him. He remembered so well what it was like, except that they had never said that to him. They had just told him he was coming to stay for a while, and then they would bring him back. They never made any commitment.

"I don't have a family. I'm an orphan."

"Not anymore, Bernie." They were ready to make a total commitment to him, and the nuns all said he was a wonderful boy, very bright and good-natured and loving. He had been given up at birth, and placed in several foster homes, but no one had adopted him because of his asthma. It was just too much of a headache to cope with.

"Could I bring my bear?" Bernie asked cautiously, glancing at Annie again. She was looking at him and smiling.

"Sure. You could bring all your things," Charlie said softly.

"We have good toys at our house," Annie vouched for them, and the little red-headed boy inched slowly toward Charlie. It was as though he was drawn to him, as though he sensed that they had a lot in common and he would be safe here.

"I'd like to go with you," he said, looking up at the man who so wanted to be his father.

"Thank you," Charlie said, as he took him gently in his arms, wanting to tell him that he loved him, but he just held him there as Bernie clung to him, and then in the softest voice of all, Bernie whispered the one word Charlie had always longed for.

"Daddy," he said, his face buried in Charlie's chest, as Charlie closed his eyes and smiled through his tears, and Beth and Annie watched them.

Pilar and Brad spent their anniversary quietly that year. They knew they had a lot to be thankful for, and a lot to think about. Christian was a gorgeous baby. He was seven months old by then, and a total joy to them. They adored him.

Pilar had hired a baby-sitter and gone back to work after four months, but she was still only working mornings, and she loved showing up with Christian in a stroller at the courthouse. Brad showed him off to everyone, and people had finally stopped asking where the other twin was.

It had been a long, hard haul and it had taken a lot out of them. Brad always said he was glad they'd done it, but he wouldn't do it again. And Pilar teased him that she missed Dr. Ward's dirty movies. They had sent her a note when the twins were born, and told her that their baby had died, and she had written them a very nice letter. Pilar always remembered what she'd said to them, that there were no guarantees to anything, and that sometimes fertility as well as infertility could be a mixed blessing. It had been for them, but in the past few months, the scale had been heavily weighted on the good side. Christian was a source of constant joy to them, and Pilar was grateful every moment that she had decided to have a family before she no longer had the choice to do that.

Her mother had been out to see the baby by then, and she was crazy about him too. It had been the first good visit she and her mother ever had, and they both enjoyed it.

Nancy was pregnant again, and hoping for a little girl this time. Eventually, Pilar had told her about her infertility treatments, and she couldn't believe what they'd gone through. It had taken so much strength and courage and perseverance.

"And a little craziness. It becomes a kind of obsession, like staying at the roulette table until you lose everything or win a fortune."

"Looks to me like you won," Nancy had said to her, but they both knew what it had cost her, and her grief over losing Grace. She had never really been able to enjoy Christian at first without thinking of her. It was only now, with the gift of time, that she could truly enjoy him.

"Sometimes I feel like I missed his first few months," she had told Brad more than once. "I was in such a haze of misery I don't remember anything." She had packed up the other baby's things, and taken the little girl toys out of the room. She'd put everything away in a big box marked "Grace," and Brad had put it in the attic, because she didn't want to give it away, didn't want to forget, wasn't ready to let go when she did it.

But by the time their anniversary came, she felt like herself again, and she looked it.

"Well, life certainly hasn't been dull this year." She smiled. Last year they had known they were having twins, and she'd been pregnant.

"At least you're not pregnant this year," he said, but she still hadn't wanted to go out. She liked staying home with him, and she'd been exhausted for the past few weeks after a difficult case she'd been preparing. He accused her of getting soft when she admitted how tired she was. "Used to be you'd tear me apart in court and then want to go dancing."

"What can I tell you?" She shrugged with a grin. "I'm two thousand years old."

"What would that make me?" he mused and she laughed. She was forty-five, and he was sixty-four, but he still didn't look it, and he was busier than ever. She felt as though she had aged a lifetime in that year, but he insisted she didn't look it. It was only lately that she was dragging, but she put it down to the fact that she was still nursing Christian, and working. She had waited so long to have this child that she wanted to savor every moment with him.

Two weeks after their anniversary though, she was still tired, and she had taken on three new cases. One was a difficult adoption case, which interested her, the others involved a lawsuit at a restaurant, and a major squabble over some expensive real estate in Montecito. All three cases were interesting and varied, and the people were extremely demanding.

She talked to Brad about all three of them late one night, and he was concerned about her. She looked wrung out, and in the middle of their conversation she went to nurse the baby.

"Don't you think you're wearing yourself out?" he asked as he came into the nursery and sat down. "Maybe you should stop nursing him, or cut back at work or something." It was rare for Pilar to look so tired.

"I'm using the nursing as birth control." She smiled, since it wasn't entirely true. She loved nursing him, and he was thriving. "I'd rather give up work than this," she said honestly as he watched her. There was a wonderful bond between mother and son that always touched him.

"Maybe you should give up work again, until he's a little older."

But she shook her head. "I can't do that, Brad. It wouldn't be fair to my partners. I've been sitting on my behind for over a year, and now I'm only working mornings." But she was taking files home, and doing work on a number of other cases.

"Well, you look like you're working overtime. Maybe you should go see the doctor."

And finally, in July she did, and told him her symptoms. She reminded him of how old Christian was, and that she was still nursing. There was no question of a pregnancy, unfortunately, since she and Brad had agreed not to do any more heroics, and Dr. Ward had told her that after forty-five it was almost impossible that she'd get pregnant. She'd never had a period again since his birth anyway, which they said was because she was nursing. She wondered sometimes if she'd just slip right from this into menopause, which seemed a little odd, but stranger things happened.

The doctor ran a few simple tests on her, and called her at the office to tell her that she was anemic, probably still from her delivery. He prescribed some iron pills for her, which made Christian complain about her milk, so she stopped taking them and forgot it. He had found nothing more serious, and she felt better in another week, until they went to watch the regatta, and standing beside Brad, she looked up at him with an odd expression, and then fainted.

He was horrified, and she went back to the doctor again, they did more tests, and this time when she got the results, she was shocked into silence. She had never thought it possible, never even dared to dream of having another child, but she was pregnant. The doctor had called her with the news just before she left her office at lunchtime to go home and feed Christian, and he told her that now she would have to stop nursing. He also warned her of the risk of miscarriage at her age, and all the other dangers and pitfalls she knew only too well; Down syndrome, chromosomal defects, a stillbirth, the veritable minefield she had to run at her age in order to produce a healthy baby. And in the end, it was all the luck of the draw . . . fate . . . and whether or not you were destined to have this baby.

She stood in the courtroom watching him, as he rapped his gavel to recess for lunch. He was hearing a criminal case and the defendant was led away by the bailiff. Brad was surprised to see her when he looked up, she was standing at the far end of his courtroom.

"You may approach the bench," he said resoundingly as the courtroom cleared, and she walked slowly toward him. It reminded her of their days together in court so long ago. She had met him nineteen years before, and they had come so far together, and shared so much, tragedies and ecstasies, and precious moments.

"What do you have to say for yourself?" he said sternly, as he looked down at her, and she smiled at him, feeling suddenly young again, and that life was very funny.

"You look cute in your robe," she said, looking very undignified, and he smiled in answer.

"Want to come visit me in my chambers?" he said, looking very wicked as she laughed.

"I might. But I've got something to tell you first." He just wasn't going to believe it.

"What is this? A confession? Or a statement?"

"Possibly both . . . and sort of a joke . . . and maybe a shock . . . and in the end a blessing. . . ."

"Oh, God. You cracked up the car, and you're trying to tell me it was an old wreck anyway and we needed a new one."

"No, but that's very creative. I'll remember that the next time I need it."

She was suddenly beaming as he watched her, never suspecting for a moment what she would tell him.

"What have you done?" he asked firmly, suddenly wanting to reach down and kiss her. Everyone else was gone, and they were all alone in his courtroom.

"I'm not exactly sure it's what *I've* done . . . I think you helped."

He frowned as he looked at her, confused by what she'd said.

"I think you've been watching dirty movies

again and you didn't tell me." She wagged a finger at him.

He laughed out loud as he looked down at her. "What does that mean?"

"It means, Your Honor . . . that without heroics, or hormones, or anyone's help but yours . . . I'm pregnant."

"You're *what*?" He looked stunned as he stared at her.

"You heard me."

He came down off the bench and walked down to her, looking at her with a smile, not even sure what he felt or why, or whether or not he wanted to go through it again, and yet in an odd way he was happy.

"I thought we weren't going to do this again," he said, looking tenderly at her.

"So did I. Looks like someone else figured it differently."

"Is that what you want?" he asked gently, he didn't want her to go through it again if she didn't want to.

She looked at him long and hard, she had thought about it a lot on the way to meet him in his courtroom. "I guess like everything else in life, as Dr. Ward said . . . it's kind of a mixed blessing . . . but yes . . . I want to. . . ." She closed her eyes and he kissed her then, and he held her for a long time, thinking that he had always wanted to do that to her, in his courtroom. It had taken nineteen years, but he had finally done it.